THE LISTENER

Steve Copling

PublishAmerica
Baltimore

First printing

ISBN: 1-4137-0908-7
PUBLISHED BY PUBLISHAMERICA, LLLP
www.publishamerica.com
Baltimore

Printed in the United States of America

For Sonora, without whom my life would be empty

ACKNOWLEDGMENTS

There are many people I want to thank for making this book a reality. First and foremost is my wife, Sonora, whose patience with me while I pursued this dream has been gracious and understanding. My writers' group, *The Every Other Tuesday Night Group*, Deborah Crombie, Dale Denton, Jim Evans, John Hardie, Viqui Litman, and Gigi Norwood. Special thanks to Stan Beeman on the cover art, and my son, Justin, for the web site, www.stevecopling.com.

Lorri,

Good luck keeping Chris in line. I feel your pain.

Hope you enjoy the book.

Steve Copling

AUTHOR'S NOTE: While Plano, Texas is a real city, I took literary license with several locations to fit them into the story. A few places I mentioned within the city don't exist at all. As far as the characters within the Plano Police Department, all are fictional. Actions by these characters that violate departmental policy and state laws are to benefit the story and in no way reflect the current practices of anyone inside the department.

ONE

From across the crowded food court, Leigh couldn't see the woman's ears, only the gaudy, diamond-studded loops that dangled from them. But she could see Enoch at the next table, staring, his eyes fixed upon the woman like a hawk's targeting a field mouse.

The woman was on a cell phone talking a whirlwind, free hand flying, guffawing so loudly that patrons at other tables aimed disgusted looks her way. She was a large woman with big hair. Her rosy cheeks shook when she laughed and the skin hanging from her chin reminded Leigh of a rooster's beard. The woman oozed money. And she had Enoch's attention, which meant she'd be dead by midnight.

Leigh stepped behind a group of teenagers and closed her eyes, beads of sweat trickling between her breasts. Kneading one of the lumps in her shoulder bag, she considered pulling out her camera and risking a picture. But if Enoch saw her...

Leigh trembled and looked back at the woman, who had moved the phone from her left ear to her right, allowing a clear view of what *else* had attracted Enoch's attention. Large, round, and flat, her ears stuck to the side of her head like oversized sand dollars.

Just like the others.

Leigh imagined them preserved by a food dehydrator, mounted on a board with a blue felt background, and proudly positioned in the center of Enoch's growing collection.

Suddenly weak-kneed, Leigh grasped the nearest chair and sat down, losing the back of Enoch's head in the crowd. She closed her eyes, swallowed, and pushed the memory away. She would survive this. *Had* to survive this. She climbed from the chair and carefully maneuvered alongside a group of shoppers.

The mall on this Friday wasn't as busy as Leigh had expected only three-and-a-half weeks before Christmas. But since she hadn't been in the Dallas area long, she didn't really know what to expect. Because of the dinner crowd she was able to watch Enoch from much closer than her comfort zone. She hadn't been this close to him in ten months and his proximity raised the hair on the back of her neck. But Leigh needed to know about this woman, whether or not she was a worthy target, whether or not Enoch would probably kill her later.

Through a gap in the crowd she saw him writing, now with his back to the fat woman, his head cocked to one side, listening … taking notes.

Leigh dug into her shoulder bag and removed a hand-held scanner, resting it in her lap to shield it from passersby. She then placed a pair of headphones on her ears and activated the scanner.

She could see the fat woman's lips, decipher a few of her words, hear an occasional burst of laughter. With her scanner programmed to search the 800-megahertz range, Leigh located the woman's cellular call in under a minute. She was talking to another woman, something about her Lexus needing the tires rotated. Leigh matched the words with the woman's lip movement and locked the frequency, turned up the volume, and slid the scanner back into her bag.

The crowd between Enoch and Leigh thinned again. He was still scribbling, still leaning back, his head cocked to one side. Standing, Leigh wrestled the strap of the bag over her shoulder and slipped into a passing group of teenagers.

She needed a photograph of Enoch near the fat woman as evidence. From the bags surrounding the woman's table it was clear she'd been shopping, something the police would learn later from the receipts.

If Leigh eventually sent it to them, her picture would tell the cops that Enoch had red hair, that he was left-handed and powerfully built, and that his posture clearly showed him eavesdropping. And it would show them that a murderer could look just like little Opie Taylor from the *Andy Griffith Show*.

As Leigh flanked Enoch, she heard over the scanner the woman mention that Bill was out of town until Tuesday.

Enoch smiled.

Bill must be the woman's husband.

"Dear, Jesus," Leigh prayed quietly, "please save this woman."

Taking a camera from her bag, she checked all the buttons. She hadn't quite mastered all the functions of this model, but she'd only stolen it the day before yesterday and she'd been busy.

The fat woman announced into the phone that she'd gone to the bank earlier to withdraw one thousand dollars for an antique dresser. Leigh exhaled and steadied herself. If Enoch hadn't had a reason to kill her before, that tidbit of information had just given him one.

A group of Santas paused near Leigh's column and she took the opportunity to raise her camera and peer out. Enoch hadn't moved, nor had the woman. She snapped two photos and ducked back behind cover. She smiled weakly at one of the Santas and stuffed the camera back into her bag.

The woman ended her call. Leigh's earphones fell silent. She looked out around the column and saw the woman gathering her bags. Enoch was folding a napkin, his makeshift notepad, and slipping it into a pocket. He stood and slowly collected his dinner trash, snatching quick glances at the fat woman as she waddled off.

This is where it gets tricky, Leigh thought. She had parked her Oldsmobile five rows from Enoch's Land Cruiser, but knew Enoch would have to follow the woman to her car in order to know which one to follow away from the mall. Once he knew that, he would sprint to his car and drive like crazy to catch her.

Leigh couldn't follow him that closely. So she'd just go to her car and wait. As soon as she saw him sprinting for his, she'd pull out and follow him from there. Still risky, but she'd done it before.

It took twelve minutes after Leigh had settled in her driver's seat. Enoch raced around the lower level of Sears and hit the remote to unlock his doors on the run, barely breathing from the effort. He had the Land Cruiser started and rolling before Leigh had time to drop her car into gear.

Enoch gunned it and turned west around Sears, shooting across the outer edge of the parking lot. Then he hit his brakes, ducked down a row of cars, and stopped. Up ahead, seventy yards away, Leigh saw a gold Lexus turn north on Alma Drive. Enoch sped up, turned north, and dropped in behind the Lexus just as it reached the traffic light at 15th Street.

Leigh hung back, two lanes over, and stopped in Enoch's blind spot over his right shoulder. She glanced inside the Lexus and recognized the woman, who was on the phone again.

Headphones back into position, Leigh punched the scan button and found the woman's familiar voice. Her phone was transmitting on cellular frequency 833.175. Leigh added forty-five megahertz and picked up both sides of the conversation.

"...Yeah," the woman said. "I could do that."

"Si, Miss Jane. You want me to wait for you to come?"

A moment of scratchy silence. "Well ... I'm just leaving the mall."

"I... have to get home. Maybe..." The Hispanic female sounded young, unsure, servant-like.

"Tell you what," Jane said. "Leave the key under the flower pot in the backyard, next to the pool house. You remember the alarm code?"

The light turned green. Leigh glanced at Enoch, who had a pen poised against one of those small note pads stuck to the windshield above the dash. She knew he was scanning the call, too. She punched her car north, on Enoch's tail.

On Leigh's headphones the young voice paused. Then, "The alarm code? Uh... yes... I think... yes, here it is, in my address book."

"Okay," Jane said, "just don't forget to lock up. Did you clean the oven? I overfilled a pie yesterday."

"Si, Miss Jane. Clean as new."

"I'm on my way home," Jane said. "Have a nice weekend. See you next Friday."

The transmission went dead.

A chill swept over Leigh when the call ended. Enoch hadn't heard the alarm code; maybe Jane would live through the night. If she could only get inside her house and lock herself in before Enoch figured out a way to get her thousand dollars.

Ten minutes later, as the sun dipped below the horizon, Jane pulled into the driveway of a house on Tanner Drive. Leigh couldn't read the numbers.

Enoch drove four houses down and pulled into the driveway of a house posting a 'For Sale' sign. One of Jane's neighbors, a man who obviously didn't keep up with the weather, was in his yard planting a colorful stand of late fall flowers. Leigh pulled to the curb five houses before Jane's and cut the engine. Sliding over to the passenger seat, she slumped down and waited. Nine houses separated her from Enoch. She wished it were nine states.

Wondering how quickly her ragged Oldsmobile would be noticed in this neighborhood, Leigh switched her scanner to search for household cordless phones. Twenty-five minutes later she'd learned that Jane didn't like cats, but was forced to live with one because of her husband; she enjoyed her new big-screen TV and stereo system, both recently acquired as a result of Bill's monthly bonus; and that she missed her twin girls, now in college, missed the noise in the empty house. She rattled pots and pans, talked above the noise.

Leigh listened with increasing anxiety. She knew Enoch was scanning and would patiently sift through all the unimportant details and gossip, extracting only the profitable information. Jane would be an easy, unexpected

Christmas bonus for him.

It was nearly nine PM when the phone finally fell silent. Leigh had been there for almost three hours; the darkness fully shadowed her inside her car and Enoch inside his. She could feel the early signs of the much-heralded cold front, due to blast the Dallas area at midnight. According to the weatherman, this was the last mild evening for the next several weeks. By tomorrow temperatures would be in the mid-teens during the day and single digits at night.

When another car passed, Leigh turned her face away from the headlights. Despite her ragged Oldsmobile, no one seemed to notice her.

A scent of scorched BBQ sauce drifted into her partially opened window and Leigh realized how hungry she was. Then she saw movement from Enoch's car, saw a shadow creep toward Jane's house, and scale the fence leading into her back yard. At that moment Leigh gave thanks she hadn't eaten anything.

By the time Leigh saw Enoch exit Jane's front door, it took all of her concentration to raise her camera. Through the magnification of the camera lens she recognized Enoch's familiar strut, his slight limp, his thick legs and broad shoulders. The gloom of the night hid his face from her, hid the scar that ran across his forehead, his square jaw, his piercing green eyes. But she knew his features as well as she knew her own.

Enoch turned to the left, back toward his car. He carried something in his right hand, but the darkness hid it. He carried Jane's cat in his left.

As he moved away from her, fading into the darkness, the vise of fear slowly released her. And she shook uncontrollably.

During the hours she'd been waiting for Enoch to come out of the house, the temperature had dropped at least twenty-five degrees. Her warm breath had long ago fogged the windows and only when she couldn't see a thing had she risked starting her car to use the defroster.

Enoch backed out of the driveway, headed toward her. She hid her face and crouched in the seat. She waited until the sound of his engine faded before peeking behind her and catching a glimpse of Enoch's fading taillights.

The wind howled and rocked her car as she considered her next move. Finally, she swallowed her fear, grabbed the camera, and stepped from the car. The cold air slapped her as it screamed from the north. The short walk to Jane's house proved the longest of her life.

Her throat tightened as tears gathered in her eyes. Wrapping herself tightly in her jacket, she leaned into the cold and prayed for strength.

At the front door she hesitated, collected her courage, and knocked. The sound died as soon as her knuckles slapped against the hard, cold door. She knocked harder, afraid to use the doorbell glowing in the darkness to her right. She glanced at the street as she waited, hoping not to be seen by some insomniac. Or Enoch, who might decide to come back and retrieve some item of value he had seen but forgotten to take.

No one answered. After a full minute she knocked again. She wore no gloves and the sharp rapping stung her cold hands. She blew on them for warmth as she watched the street.

Still no answer. She pulled her jacket sleeve down over her right hand and tried the knob. Unlocked. Despite the cold, sweat moistened her hairline. She drew a breath and pushed the door open with her foot.

Enoch had destroyed the place. A single, shadeless lamp stood in the middle of the den and cast shadows into the corners of the room. Around this solitary lamp, furniture was slashed and overturned, pictures destroyed, broken glass lay everywhere. Stepping through the doorway, she gave the door a bump with her hip. It swung soundlessly on its hinges but didn't catch in its lock. She clicked it shut with her elbow.

From where she stood, she could see that Enoch had opened all of the windows and the back door that led to the patio. Already the inside of the house was as cold as outdoors. Touching nothing, she stepped through the wreckage and walked from room-to-room, looking for the woman. Not on the first floor. Leigh climbed the stairs. Searched the rooms to the right. Nothing. To the left, at the end of the hallway, a door stood open.

She smelled the sour odor from the hallway. Death. Or human terror. Before meeting Enoch, Leigh had never believed you could smell someone's fear.

She approached the door and peeked in. The master bedroom hadn't been destroyed as the others, but it was the room that held the nightmare. She stood outside the door, hesitating, as the wind howled through the open windows. The cold cut her to the bone.

She stepped into the room. The bed sat to the left, crimson. A trail of blood led from there, across the floor, and into the bathroom.

Her empty stomach churned, bile pushed into her throat. Covering her mouth, she followed the blood trail. It disappeared under the closed bathroom door.

Intent on what lay beyond the door, she jumped and screamed when she caught her reflection in the vanity mirror. The image staring back was horror-stricken, almost unrecognizable. Her hair hung straight and limp, her thin, gaunt face reflected the months of stress.

She let her eyes slip from her reflection and refocused on the bathroom door, sliding her jacket sleeve over her hand. She edged the door open, and then nearly choked on the bile that rose in her throat.

TWO

Detective Greg Rush rubbed his forehead as he took a careful step into the bathroom. The marble bathtub brimmed with ice, a lighter shade of black cherry than that covering the bed. Bloody water had spilled onto the marble floor and frozen into a pink skating rink stretching almost to the door. Jane McElroy sat in the middle of the tub propped up by two golf clubs, one under each armpit. The ice encased her mid-stomach, her head leaned back against the long, gold-plated faucet, and her left arm hung out over the edge of the tub. Pink icicles connected her fingertips to the floor. An electrical cord, looped around her neck, ran to her right wrist, holding her arm so that she appeared to be talking on the cellular phone duct taped around her hand.

Her left ear was gone.

A large woman, Jane weighed two-fifty plus. Her black hair looked twisted and teased, puffed up like a fully expanded package of Jiffy Pop popcorn. She was clothed, but her blouse was unbuttoned, her bra cut away, exposing breasts and a long surgical cut running south from her breastbone and disappearing into the ice.

Pulling his stocking cap lower onto his head, Rush closed his eyes and leaned his head back. The frigid cold had long penetrated his suit pants and long underwear, and now seemed to radiate from within his bones.

He could hear Chinbroski behind him, breathing into his gloved hands as though his foggy breath might actually make a difference.

Rush opened his eyes, glanced at the body again, and confirmed that he hadn't missed anything. He hadn't. The scene still looked like a Hollywood set where some special-effects guy had gone totally overboard. Jane's skin looked waxen, plastic almost, white as a plucked turkey. The ice, black in some places, had small chunks of tissue sticking through like miniature icebergs. Human sludge, Rush thought, pulling out his handkerchief and wiping his nose. He turned toward his partner and shook his head.

Rick Chinbroski, the only human Rush knew with a neck wider than his head, swung his thick arms back and forth and cleared his throat. "Did I tell you?" he said, his words thick and slurred. He'd been there since five-thirty

AM. It was now six-fifteen.

The entire house was frozen, exposed for three days to the worst cold front to hit the Dallas area in a hundred years. No heat, every window open, ceiling fans on high, the suspect had used the cold to his advantage, killing Jane before the freeze, then flooding the bathroom and leaving the house open to the elements.

Rush stepped around his partner and carefully slid out of the bathroom. Once again he scanned the twenty-by-twenty master bedroom, decorated in middle-aged going on old-fart. Bunches of ugly knickknacks, too many pictures of family, a much-too-bright patchwork comforter. Artwork that looked like an afterthought hung undisturbed above the bed and over the low dresser just to the left of the closet.

The blood on the bed showed dark red, almost black. The black cherry. Gallons of it, or so it seemed. And it shimmered, having crystallized from the cold. Wide and jagged, the blood cut a trail across the room, from the king-sized bed on the left, to the bathroom door on the right.

"Check out the message," Chinbroski said, moving past him, across the room. He nodded toward a dresser.

Rush stepped over the blood trail. The note was written on a piece of paper the size of a three-by-five card. Lipstick pencil. He'd missed it on his first visual survey of the room. The writing slanted left, jagged letters barely readable.

"Hey high-heel," he read aloud, *"this chuckish huger bloocheed on the teleef and yabbelowed about how higgy she was. Beark was dehigged so he had to string her. The greeley's gonna tidrick quick, so otto catch him. P.S. PIKE TO HIGHROLLERS."*

He read it again to himself before looking over at Chinbroski.

Chinbroski laughed out loud, stress, Rush knew, and the sound echoed off the frozen walls.

"Written by someone other than the suspect?" Rush wiped his nose and looked at Chinbroski. "That the way you take it? Third person?"

"What it looks like. So we talking a team job? Maybe trying to throw us off?"

"Throw us off? We were thrown off before we started." Rush slowly walked back to look at the frozen pond in the bathroom, silent several moments as he absorbed the scene one more time. "What do you know so far?" he asked finally.

Chinbroski pulled out a small pad and sniffed against the heel of his hand.

"The dead lady's husband, Bill McElroy, is due back late tonight from somewhere out of the country, Japan, I think, getting back here as fast as he can. Haven't talked to him yet. Have seven messages showing on the answering machine. Five from Bill, with the last one at five this morning asking Jane to pick up, wondering why she's not home. The woman who found her, Rhonda Niebrook, next-door neighbor, spoke with Jane four days ago. That was Friday. They was supposed to have lunch on Saturday, but Jane didn't show. Said Bill called her this morning and asked her to check the house. He was scared cause he'd called so many times without an answer."

Rush moved his numb toes around, but couldn't feel them. "Where's the Niebrook lady now?"

"Home. Told her I'd send somebody over later. She's shook up cause she had to tell Bill about his wife." Chinbroski paused. "At least we ain't gotta deliver *that* news."

Only a small victory, Rush thought, looking at his partner's clothes, and noticing for the first time that he wasn't wearing his crime scene coveralls. Randy McBride, Plano PD's lead evidence tech, insisted on having fiber and shoe tread comparisons of everyone who'd been in the scene prior to his arrival. "You tell her we're gonna need her clothes and shoes?"

"Not yet," Chinbroski said. "Shouldn't be a problem."

"McBride's gonna throw a fit you dressing like that."

"Hey, when I got the call they didn't even tell me the broad was murdered. Least I'm wearing my rubber bands."

With the frost so thick throughout the house, he and Chinbroski's footprints were clearly distinguishable with the rubber bands. They'd been careful to avoid stepping on those left by the neighbor and responding patrol officers.

Rush walked to one of the two windows in the bedroom. It looked out over the front yard. From outside the house the screams would have been muffled, a kind of strangled, smothered sound like someone holding a pillow against the mouth. From inside the screams would have been revolting, a gurgling, wet-lung type where no words were discernible. The image made his face heat with anger.

From outside, the house didn't look like a crime scene at all: white columns, arched entry, and a circle driveway. Three large oak trees stood naked in front, their bushels of dead leaves deposited across the front lawn, the sharp wind whipping their branches as though punishing them for making such a mess. The first signs of daybreak were beginning to overtake the dim, hopeful glow of Christmas lights strung along rooflines of nearby houses. Frost on manicured lawns reflected the multicolored lights, giving the neighborhood a holiday feel. *Some holiday*, Rush thought. *A murder three weeks before Christmas.*

He sighed and turned back into the room. Chinbroski was at the door leading into the hall. "I'm going down to wait for McBride," he said. "You staying up here?"

Rush shook his head. "I gotta call the lieutenant, get him briefed. I'll do that from downstairs." He stepped over to the door and looked back. "Let's give Jane her last few minutes of privacy."

Fifteen minutes later Randy McBride stood just outside the master bathroom door inspecting the scene, eyes recording every detail. His appearance reminded Rush of Ichabod Crane. Nearly six-five, lanky, with basketball player arms, not much of a chin, and unruly salt and pepper hair, his half-glasses sat permanently on the very tip of his hawk-like nose, defying gravity every second they failed to fall off.

An outstanding criminalist, McBride refused to allow anyone to help him process a scene. He was a retired FBI lab tech, the best crime scene guy Rush had ever seen. "Guess we're gonna have to break the ice with her," McBride said.

Chinbroski glanced at Rush, then spoke to McBride. "You ain't been in the room thirty seconds and you're joking about the dead lady."

Chinbroski had disliked McBride ever since the day, two years before, when McBride called him a Neanderthal. And meant it.

"I won't mention that you aren't dressed properly, Chinbroski," McBride said, turning, looking him up and down. "And as much as I'll hate to touch them, I'll need your clothes by the end of the day. Maybe you can dig in a Dumpster somewhere to replace them."

"Listen, you son of a…"

"I'm not playing referee, guys," Rush said, cutting him off.

McBride turned away from Chinbroski and slid over to the bathtub. After a moment he glanced at Rush. "See the brown substance in front of her belly, just under the surface of the ice?"

Rush skated over. The ice in the tub was so dark from the blood, had so many other dark spots, he hadn't noticed anything in front of her belly. Looking closer, he saw what McBride saw. "What about it?"

"Her last bowel movement. Her sphincter muscles released everything in the water. Means she gave up the ghost in the tub, not on the bed."

"Gave up the ghost," Chinbroski said. "You can't just say dead?"

"Got some greenish-red skin around her eyes," McBride told Rush, ignoring Chinbroski. "On her neck, too." He stepped back. "Hard to say how long she's been dead. This ice throws a wrench in things. But I'd say several hours before she froze."

Rush walked out of the bathroom and over to the note. "Tuesday now. Cold front hit late Friday, midnight or so. So we're talking between late Friday and midday Saturday." He turned to Chinbroski, who had wandered over to the hallway door. "Gives us a time frame when we canvass the neighbors."

Chinbroski nodded.

As McBride's camera started clicking inside the bathroom, Rush focused on the last line of the note: *PIKE TO HIGHROLLERS*. What's *PIKE*? Does it mean travel? climb? look? And what's *HIGHROLLERS*? A rich guy? Physical location? Group of people?

The note, on top of the dresser and against the center of the mirror, looked deliberately positioned for the detectives to find.

Rush tightened the scarf around his neck, pulled his collar up. He stepped over the dragging blood trail to the hallway door. "Let's do our canvass."

Chinbroski's cell phone rang. It wasn't his phone exactly, it was assigned to them as a team. Except Rush never got to enjoy it because Chinbroski always hogged it. In the six months they'd had it, Rush might have taken it home twice.

Chinbroski punched up the call. It only took a moment for his face to tighten with anger.

"Didn't I tell you not to call this number? Didn't I? I can't talk to you about that."

Rush started toward the door, but Chinbroski grabbed his arm.

"Something funny?" Chinbroski said into the phone. "Hey, go to hell... I can't talk to you about that... Yeah, I'll be there... Well, talk to the D.A. Hold on." He held the phone out to Rush. "Your kid."

"Daniel?"

"Tell that pencil necked geek to stop calling me," Chinbroski said.

Rush took the phone. "Danny, stop calling him."

"Hey, Dad. He still hasn't found his sense of humor?"

"Forever lost. You ask him about the Garcia case?"

"I did. He should've had an interpreter. Roberto didn't understand Chinbroski's version of Miranda. I'll get it kicked."

Rush followed Chinbroski out of the bedroom. "That's what lawyers do. You should be talking to the D.A."

"That's not any fun. Just reminding Chin about the suppression hearing in a couple of weeks."

"Only I can call him Chin. And he has a subpoena. You're abusing the friendship you used to have with him by calling his cell phone." Rush started down the stairs behind his partner.

"Even though I've succumbed to the dark side of the force, I know he still loves me. Why are you two together so early? Violating someone else's rights?"

"I'm sure you'll be right there to catch our mistake if we do."

At the bottom of the stairs Rush found several detectives waiting to help with the canvass.

"Hold on, Danny." Rush pushed the phone against his chest. "Chin, pick your team. I'll take what's left." Back into the phone, "Sorry. Where was I?"

"That I'll catch your mistake. And I will. Victory's on the horizon and it'll be public. I'm gaining ground."

Rush laughed, "Gaining ground? The score's 4-0, me."

"But I'm throwing a shutout to your partner."

"Great. Listen, Danny, I'm kind of busy here."

"What are you out on? What team is Chin picking?"

"You're about one question away from being nosy."

"Lawyers are nosy."

"You have anything for me? Or was the goal of the morning to bust Chin's ass?"

"That's all. I'll call for you next time." The call clicked in Rush's ear. He was about to slip the phone into a pocket when Chinbroski walked over and took it from him.

"What's his problem?" Chinbroski asked.

"Just bringing some sunshine into your morning."

"You abuse him when he was little?" Chinbroski shook his head as he tied the scarf around his neck. "Raising a kid who gets his rocks off trying to beat his old man in open court. Got such a hard-on, he works 'em pro bono. But when he can't beat you he starts ripping *my* cases to shreds. A real friend would put a stop to that."

"At least Danny charges to defend the people you arrest. He must know easy money when he sees it."

"Go to hell, Rush."

Rush waved his team toward the front door. "The canvass, Chin. You want east or west?"

Much happened during the next six hours. McBride melted the ice in the tub, the ME removed the body, and the media relations officer gave a few details to the press. Chinbroski shut off the water to the house in case pipes had frozen and split, and McBride sectioned off the bedroom and used his special vacuum to pick up hair, fiber, and dirt evidence. Senior police department brass wandered in for a peek, staying only long enough for an eye full, but not long enough to get their names listed in any of the investigative reports.

At a few minutes before one PM, McBride was ready to share his findings. He instructed Rush and Chinbroski to gather around the stripped, blood-soaked bed.

"The guy's left-handed," McBride said. "About six feet, give or take an inch. White, strawberry colored hair." He leaned forward and indicated several drops of blood splattered on the wall just to the left of the bed. "These confirm the height and his left handedness."

Chinbroski leaned in and looked closely at the bloodstains. "I went through a bloodstain investigation school once. Never could make sense of it."

Rush knew that despite Chinbroski's personal dislike for McBride, he had tremendous respect for the man's talent.

"Let me show you." McBride positioned himself in front of Chinbroski. "These drops here," he pointed to several rows on the wall, "are elliptical rather than circular. On this flat vertical surface the stain becomes elongated, almost a teardrop shape. We know the killer was standing here when he cut her open. If he were right-handed, these splatters wouldn't be on this wall at all."

Chinbroski said nothing.

"And his height is easy to establish by the spots on the wall by the head of the bed," McBride went on. The glasses on the tip of his nose quivered when he spoke.

"Also, I found his hair almost everywhere right at this spot. Of course, when I was vacuuming I found it in a whole lot of other places. Got some fiber transfer off the suspect's body. And some dirt off his shoes. I'll collect dirt samples from outside later."

Chinbroski nodded again as though this information would answer all of their questions. "A left-handed redhead. That'll help. What else? What kind of fiber?"

"Some interesting blue strands. Automobile carpeting, I suspect, so maybe he has a blue car, assuming the fibers aren't from the owner's cars. Also some red fibers, cotton. Found some of those stuck to the victim's collar. And feathers. Goose down all over the bedspread, maybe from a slit in a vest or coat. Also, he was wearing a pair of Nike Air Jordan's. Size eleven, as close as I can figure. That fits my height theory."

Rush moved away from the bed and stood in the bathroom doorway. The small room looked almost sterile with the body gone and the water cleaned up. "No prints?"

"Nothing. Not surprising with frost covering everything. Found some smears that tells me he probably wore gloves. I might pick up some fibers from those, but I doubt it. I'll print the note at the office. Maybe something there."

Chinbroski rubbed the back of his neck. "So let me get this straight. He didn't kill her on the bed, right? He dragged her to the bathroom while she was still alive."

"Right," McBride said. "Then lifted her into the tub."

"Don't see how she lived that long. All the blood on the bed and floor." Chinbroski shook his head. "Should've bled to death before she got to the tub."

"Not the way he cut her," McBride said. "He just opened her up. Almost a surgical cut. No apparent injuries to internal organs. I'll bet the cause of death will be blood loss. He probably let her bleed out on the bed until she got so weak she couldn't resist. He tied her up while she was still alive, I know that. Saw the marks on her wrists and ankles. Didn't find anything he might have used, though. Must have taken his rope with him."

"So he's reasonably strong," Rush said. "To be able to lift her into the tub. Anything else?"

"A team killing is what I think."

Rush snapped a look at Chinbroski then back to McBride. "Say again."

"Team killing. There was a woman in here. Medium height, judging from her size nine Puma running shoes. Dark brown hair. She got sick and threw up in the sink."

Chinbroski, with a scowl on his face, crowded McBride. "We've been here for over six hours and you're just telling us this?"

"Don't know for sure if it was the brown-haired woman who threw up in the sink, but somebody did. I found one of the brown hairs mixed in with the vomit. DNA will tell us."

"You found evidence of a damn woman?" Chinbroski said again. "And you didn't tell us until now? We'll have to do our canvass again."

McBride leaned over, spoke around Chinbroski, looked at Rush. "A second hair was inside the sink, lying right there in plain view. Didn't know whose it was at first."

"So it could be anybody's," Rush said, snapping a look at his partner again. "Husband's, daughter's … Maybe the neighbor who found her. Chin, Ms. Neibrook have brown hair?"

"Silver to the roots."

"But it could be family's," Rush said.

"Both daughters are blonde," McBride said. "The husband's bald. All according to the family picture over on the dresser. Anyway, if the hair and vomit match, I think she was here during the murder because the partial footprint is in front of the sink. Didn't notice it at first, what with all the other blood, but it's there. And then there's the third hair, another single, brown strand, inside the bathroom on the floor next to the tub. On top of the blood. And a fourth hair in front of the dresser that held the note."

"How can we match the hairs and the vomit?" Rush asked. "You got roots?"

"Yep. And that's the funny part. Three of those four hairs have a bulb attached. All but the one mixed with the vomit." He paused and looked at Rush with raised eyebrows.

"So what?" Chinbroski said. "People lose hair all the time."

"True. But three of the four still have a small sliver of skin. I saw thousands of them in the lab with the Bureau. We *can* match the vomit with the hair."

Chinbroski looked at Rush and shrugged.

"Neither of you get it, do you?" McBride said.

And suddenly Rush did. "She pulled three hairs and left them for us to find."

THREE

Conducting surveillance on cops was a first for Leigh. She'd cased banks, driven getaway cars, and stolen baskets of mail after shadowing unsuspecting route carriers. But those escapades always involved steering away from cops, not covertly devising schemes to draw them to her.

But that was before. Before Enoch turned her life inside out.

The four-day wait for Jane's neighbor to come snooping around was the longest of Leigh's life. She'd contemplated placing an anonymous phone call, so badly did she crave getting a detective on her trail. But she waited, knowing that the note and carefully placed hairs would pique their curiosity enough for her purposes.

What she needed now was the lead detective's face, his name, his home and work e-mail addresses, his home phone, cell, and beeper numbers. Feeding him information, directing him from afar, would be safe, as long as she used variety in her delivery.

She had watched for the past three days from a vacant house across the street and down the block from the dead woman's. The magnificent structure had sweeping staircases and plush wool carpeting, and though a fine shelter, it didn't help much when dealing with the two-hour sleeping shifts while waiting for someone to find poor Jane.

With a duffle bag of necessities to last a full week, Leigh had sneaked into the house on the heels of a careless realtor, disabled the alarm system with a couple of snips from a pair of wire cutters, and squatted in an upstairs bedroom overlooking Jane's house without being detected, despite two more realtor showings.

Now, using a camcorder perched atop a tripod, she filmed the comings and goings at Jane's house down the street. It appeared she had a choice of two homicide detectives. The first, who arrived at 5:30 AM, was late thirties and built like a solid block of granite. But the other, an early-fifties bespectacled, narrow-shouldered, blond, seemed the leader. Leigh had watched them canvass the neighborhood and the blond did all of the talking and pointing, while the block of granite jotted notes.

The scene was strangely quiet for such a brutal murder. Three or four black & whites, a crime scene van, the detective's cars, and three or four other cars that had dropped in but not stayed. Leigh had expected more. News vans, helicopters, crowds of neighbors pushed against yellow tape. But there was none of that, just a few cops, almost as if the death of the fat lady didn't rate anyone's attention.

Leigh zoomed the camera and focused on the front door as the medical examiner wheeled a gurney into the house. Later, she focused clearly on the blond detective's face as the gurney, burdened with the oversized body bag, was lifted into the M.E.'s van.

The blond was attractive. Not in a Hollywood way, more rugged, commanding, authoritative. Real. Certainly real enough to lock her ass up for not stopping this murder, she knew.

Leigh filmed the license plates of both detectives' cars, ran a few more seconds on each detective's face, and packed up her bag. After wiping down everything she'd touched, she waited until both detectives had gone back into the house before slipping out the back and hiking the ten blocks to the shopping center where her car sat waiting.

Things were coming together. Now she'd pray for timing, which she had no control over. But the timing would mean the difference between life and death.

* * *

Rush hadn't yet digested the news of a strange woman leaving hairs behind on purpose when the front doorbell rang. With Chinbroski on his heels, he went downstairs.

At the front door was Jerry Holken, the patrol officer who'd responded to the scene and was now guarding the house outside. As the responding officer, he'd drawn the job of record officer, of keeping a log of everyone who entered the house.

"Hey, Jerry," Rush said, the frigid air biting his face. "What's up?"

Holken looked over Rush's shoulder and nodded at Chinbroski. "I would come in out of this cold, only I'd have to put myself off the list again." He glanced at the clipboard clutched to his chest and shook his head. "I'll just stay here."

Rush waited for him to get to the point.

"Well, anyway, got a wit outside." He flicked his head toward the street.

"Out in the car parked across from mine."

Rush almost laughed at Holken's use of the term wit, short for witness. "A wit, huh? A wit to what?"

Holken shrugged. "Not sure. Wants to see a detective."

"Tell him I'll be out in a minute."

The patrol cop waved acknowledgment as he walked away. Then he stopped. "By the way. I get off in an hour. Got the evening sergeant sending somebody out to relieve me. You want me to give the new guy my list or have him start his own?"

"Give him yours."

Holken nodded and turned away again.

"Hey, Jerry. Seen Hanisch?" Rush had made the obligatory phone call to his lieutenant at 6:45 AM. He hadn't shown all day. Rush wasn't complaining. But he was curious.

Holken stopped again and turned. "Sarge told me Hanisch is home sick. Maybe it's just too cold for him out here. Freeze his hair." He wiped a glove across his nose and grinned.

"Thanks, Jerry," Rush said, pushing the door closed against the wind. Hanisch sick. Thank God.

Chinbroski had already pulled on his stocking cap. His heavy coat hung on a doorknob near the front door, as did his scarf. Like most of his wardrobe selections, Chinbroski's horizontally striped sweater didn't match his seventies-style, vertically striped pants. The sweater stretched across his back and looked ready to come apart at the seams.

"You know, Chin," Rush said, pulling on his cap. "I haven't commented on your *Brady Bunch* outfit today. And what's with those pants?"

"Big pockets, Rush. For my Mustang." Chinbroski patted the .380 in his back pocket. "I just bought this stuff."

"Let me guess. Bought it with your eyes closed."

"Old joke."

"From a thrift store."

Silence.

"A garage sale. A homeless guy."

"You ain't baiting me, Rush. You know I'm saving my money."

Chinbroski had earned his reputation as the worst dresser in the department. On his first day as a detective ten years earlier, Rush had thought his new partner joking, wearing orange polyester pants, a brown silk shirt, and an *I Love Lucy* tie. He'd been sent home to change. And had several times since.

"So," Chinbroski asked. "You wanna bring the witness in here?"

Rush considered the idea a moment. Never a good idea to bring a witness into a crime scene, although not unheard of. But since any witness, including this one, might be the guy who did it, Rush didn't want him in there. That way, if the evidence placed him inside the house, at least they could say it wasn't them who allowed him in. "How about we go outside, see if he has anything, then take him to the station."

Chinbroski nodded, "Sounds like a plan."

A white Cadillac sat idling across the street from Holken's patrol car. As Rush approached he saw a white male in the driver's seat. The man, talking on the phone, was alone.

They approached the car and the witness held up a finger like he'd be off the phone in just a sec. It was more like 120 secs.

Chinbroski cursed under his breath and finally pounded on the glass. "Come on, man. Hurry the hell up!"

A real second later the man ended his call and rolled down his window. "Hey, guys, sorry about that."

He was mid-forties, dressed in a suit, and wore an expensive overcoat. He spoke with a faint Boston accent, wore a Rolex, and had hair sprayed into a tight part high on the side of his head.

"Want to climb in my car?" he asked. "Get out of the cold?"

It was inviting, but the same rule applied. If this guy was the murderer, Rush wasn't about to contaminate the inside of his car. "It's a hard offer to turn down," he said. "But how about we just stand out here. I'm Detective Rush. This is Chinbroski."

He stuck his hand out the window. "Fred Billups. I'm a realtor. I have a showing four doors down in twenty minutes. How about we go down there?" He pointed to a house on the same side of the street as the crime scene. "That's where I saw what I saw," he added. "Might as well get out of the cold. The house is vacant."

Rush peered through watery eyes at a large two-story with a Ebby Halliday sign in the front yard. Glancing at Chinbroski, then back at Fred Billups, he shrugged. "Okay. But is what you saw outside the house or inside? We don't want to contaminate anything."

"No, no, no," Billups said. "Just saw a couple cars, that's all. Nothing in the house." He looked from Rush's face to Chinbroski's. "I mean, I don't think anybody's been in there. You're free to look."

"Fine," Rush told Billups. "We'll meet you over there." He rubbed his tingling hands together and strode off toward the house.

"Guy's got dark brown hair," Chinbroski pointed out as they walked.

"Yeah, I noticed. Maybe he's got teeny-weenie little feet and he's the one McBride thinks is a woman."

Chinbroski stopped in the middle of the street and looked at him. Rush went on for a couple of steps before stopping and looking back. "What?"

"You being funny like that fool McBride?" Chinbroski looked stiff, standing there bundled from head to toe with only his face exposed to the cold.

"I'm not being funny. When we get in the house, I'll interview him while you measure his feet. See if they'll fit into a woman's size nine Puma." He turned and left his partner standing alone.

Chinbroski cursed under his breath as he hurried to catch up. "You're just a regular comic, Rush. You and McBride, you two oughta go on tour. Call yourselves the Cute Clichés."

Fred Billups had the front door of the house open by the time they arrived. Inside, the warmth swallowed them. Rush loosened his scarf as Billups led them into the kitchen. Custom woodwork, plush carpeting, glossy wood floors; High ceilings, expensive light fixtures, leaded windows. Not Rush's style. Never would be. Unless he got rich, then it might.

Chinbroski asked the first question. "So, what's a place like this go for?"

Just what I would've asked our only witness to a brutal slaying, Rush thought.

"Four hundred and seventy-nine thousand," Billups announced, waving his arms around like one of the detectives might actually buy it. He handed each detective a business card. "Got a pool out back."

"You take a check?" Rush quipped.

Billups grinned.

"So what is it you saw?" Rush asked. "You said a car?"

"Yeah. Four nights ago, Friday about eleven, I cruised by on my way home. This is one of my listings and I try to go by all of mine at least once a day if I can. Especially the vacant ones." Billups leaned against the dishwasher. He looked confident, relaxed. "Anyway, about eleven, I drove by and saw a Land Cruiser parked in the driveway, right about where my Caddy's sitting now. I'm thinking, hmm, maybe somebody's walking around the place in the dark, you know? So I parked in the street in front of the driveway."

Chinbroski hunched over a counter and wrote it down.

"I never saw anybody here so I left." Billups paused a moment before going on. "Saw a woman, though, on my way out."

Chinbroski jerked his head up, then cut his eyes at Rush.

Billups noticed the reaction. "Is that important?"

"The woman," Rush asked, "you saw her near the Land Cruiser?"

"Down that way," Billups said, pointing toward the McElroy house. "Sitting in an old car, slumped down. Like she was trying to hide or something."

"She driving?" Chinbroski asked.

Billups shook his head. "She was in the passenger's seat. I remember because I thought she might be waiting for somebody."

The two detectives looked at each other. Turning away from Billups, Rush walked across the kitchen and looked out into the back yard. The uncovered swimming pool appeared frozen solid.

"So you didn't see the woman until after you inspected the Land Cruiser?" Rush asked, turning.

"Right. But I really didn't inspect the Land Cruiser. All I did was check the house. Made sure all the doors were locked, no windows were broken, that sort of thing."

"No plate number?" Chinbroski asked.

"No," he shrugged.

"Not even if it was a Texas tag?"

Billups scratched his head and looked at the floor. "It was pretty dark. I really didn't notice. Once I saw the house was okay, I just figured it belonged to a friend of one of the neighbors."

Rush nodded. The kitchen grew quiet.

"It hadn't been parked there too long, though. The Land Cruiser, I mean," Billups said, interrupting the silence. "I remember feeling a little warmth coming from the grill as I walked past the front." He shrugged. "If that helps any."

"So nothing about the vehicle sticks out?" Chinbroski asked. "No bumper stickers, no dents, no odd paint job?"

Billups shrugged again. "It was dark." His forehead creased in thought. "Maybe had dark tinted windows. But I don't know. Just a Land Cruiser."

"What about the color?"

"Dark. Blue maybe. Green. Could have been black, though."

"The woman," Rush said. "Let's talk about her. In the passenger's seat, slumped down. Drunk maybe? Asleep?"

"Drunk, I don't know. But asleep, no. When I drove by she turned her face away, like the light hurt her eyes or something."

"What kind of car?" Rush asked. He moved over and stood behind Chinbroski. If McBride's time frame theory was correct, that Jane McElroy had been killed late on Friday, this woman Billups saw could be important.

"Old," Billups said. "Big, like a sedan. Maybe an Oldsmobile or Buick."

"You talking eighties old? Seventies? What?" Chinbroski asked.

"Late seventies, probably. Decent condition. But odd for this neighborhood, which is why I noticed it in the first place."

Rush asked, "So it was parked where?"

"From here? Down the block a way. Maybe three or four houses past the house you came out of. Where the murder happened."

"How'd you hear about the murder?"

Billups looked at Rush and shrugged. "Friends with Rhonda Neibrook's husband. Golf-playing buddies, workout partner. Saw him at the gym during lunch today. Said Rhonda found the body."

"So the broad was hiding down in her seat?" Chinbroski confirmed. "She bundled up?"

Interesting question, Rush thought, one that might trip the guy if he was making up this entire story.

"Not that night," Billups said, not tripping. "This was right before the cold front blew in. The night of. In fact, if my memory serves, the front was blowing in that very moment. Wind going crazy."

"And this was about eleven PM?" Rush confirmed.

"Right about."

"How you so sure?" Chinbroski asked.

Billups shrugged. "Thought it was out-of-the-ordinary when I saw the Land Cruiser parked at the vacant house here. I noted the time." He smiled. "Crime nowadays, guy's gotta be careful."

Yet you didn't get a tag. "Describe the woman," Rush said. "Think hard, I know it was dark."

Billups slumped forward slightly, rubbed his chin, closed his eyes. He spoke slowly at first, then gained confidence. "She was young, or seemed to be... early twenties, twenty-five, maybe. Brown hair for sure, below her shoulders. No glasses. Looked to be thin. Or not fat, anyway." He opened his eyes. "That's it. I only saw her shoulders and head."

While Chinbroski scribbled it down, Rush told the realtor to describe the car in more detail.

Again, he closed his eyes. "An Olds or Buick, like I said. Something General Motors. Not sure of the year or color. Didn't see a tag. No body damage that I noticed." Billups looked at Chinbroski then Rush. "That's it. I just didn't know to notice any more. Didn't know it'd be important. Sorry." He lifted his shoulders and then let them drop.

Rush walked over and shook his hand. "Couldn't have done better myself. After your showing, I'll need you to go to the station and give a statement. That a problem?"

"No. Give it to one of you guys?"

"Doesn't matter. Just tell the front desk officer you need a detective. Give the detective my name, tell him I asked you to come in." Rush glanced at Chinbroski and nodded, "Anything?"

Chinbroski stuffed his pad into a pocket. "Can you identify her? I mean if we find her. Pick her out of a line-up?"

He shrugged. "Maybe."

"You willing to be hypnotized? See if we can get more out of you?"

Billups shrugged again. "If you think it'll help."

"It's helped in the past." Chinbroski turned to his partner. "Rush?"

"Wouldn't hurt," he said. "How about we talk about it later, Mr. Billups?" He reached out and shook his hand again. "Thanks for the information. We'll see our way out."

They started through the house, bundling up as they went. Billups walked with them until they got to the door. The cold slapped at them as they stepped outside. It actually felt refreshing. For a few seconds, anyway.

They started down the sidewalk. Rush felt good, like they had something substantial to follow up on.

Then he saw Hanisch's car parked out in front of the McElroy house. *Here we go,* Rush thought.

When Rush was a kid, barely seven years old, his parents were killed in a fiery automobile crash coming home from a rare night alone at the drive-in theater. An uninsured drunk blew a stop sign and T-boned an old gasoline tanker, which ruptured and swallowed his parents in burning fuel.

He lived with his grandmother in a rough part of east Dallas for the next six years, until she died, leaving him without family of any kind. From there it was foster homes until after high school, when he started Army boot camp within two weeks of graduation.

During his years with his grandmother he learned many lessons, most of which came from the receiving end of a bigger boy's fist. There was one boy in particular who tormented him for most of those six years. That boy, the only child of German immigrants, was one of those kids who grew early and demanded that all of the kids in the neighborhood pay homage to him on a daily basis. Rush received more beatings from him than all of the beatings from all of the people in his life combined. In the last year before his grandmother's death, Rush hit a growth spurt. He started honing the finer skills of street boxing with an older boy a couple of blocks over, and when he finally felt ready, he set aside his fear, and in a fit of rage, beat that bully into a three-week hospital stay. Rush had used nothing but his fists and feet and had cherished every brutal blow.

That boy was Gerald Hanisch, Rush's current CID lieutenant. It was soon after that horrific beating that Rush's grandmother died and Rush started his tour of foster homes. With graduation, and the Army and Vietnam, the memory of Gerald Hanisch faded into nothing more than boyhood tales one might tell over a beer. Rush put in his military years doing MP work, then discharged into a life of civilian law enforcement.

Gerald Hanisch had been a cop at Plano PD for three years when Rush joined the department. And though the department was much smaller in those days, Rush hadn't known Hanisch was there until he showed up for briefing and discovered that Hanisch was his first field training officer.

And the old flame was rekindled.

Currently, Hanisch was marvelous to look at, and knew it. Six feet tall, slim, athletic build, enhanced blond hair combed straight back, a slight left hook to his narrow, Roman nose, and sparkling, lively eyes, he hid his fifty-three years remarkably well. GQ cover material.

So unlike Rush, who wouldn't look good on any magazine cover, unless one suddenly got an urge for a medium height, narrow-shouldered, thick legged, wispy haired white guy who wore ten-dollar reading glasses from Wal-Mart.

Rush slowed his pace back to the house, despite the cold wind whipping against him. Rattling off lists in his head, he thought about what information he would hold back.

As if reading his mind, Chinbroski said, "So, how much you gonna tell him?"

Rush held his gloved fingers an inch apart.

"That much?" Chinbroski whistled.

"You take lead and you can tell him whatever you want."

Chinbroski shook his head. "Not a chance. If I took lead the whole thing would officially become my business, and I sure as hell don't want him sticking his nose in my business."

Hanisch had never been a detective. He'd ridden the ranks through patrol, only transferring into CID as part of a departmental career enhancement program. He'd read a couple of books, hung out at a few crime scenes, and dated one of the female investigators. The only good thing he'd accomplished in the last couple of years was to forbid any and all unnecessary cops at crime scenes. Rush figured they were ahead of most departments in that area.

By the time they reached the McElroy house, Rush had decided he was going to tell Hanisch even *less* than an inch worth. Not much risk in that. The police chief was a good friend who understood both the nature of homicide investigations and Rush's history with Hanisch.

After quickly checking Officer Holken's log to confirm Hanisch's name was on the list, Rush pushed through the front door with Chinbroski on his heels.

The heat that now blanketed the house had brought an unwelcome guest: the smell of death. While not as bad as most violent scenes, Rush had always tagged the sickening sweet coppery odor of blood as the smell of terror. And it filled the house, getting stronger as he picked his way through the den and started the climb up the stairs.

Chinbroski was silent; intent on staring at the floor the closer he got to Hanisch.

Rush had known men like Hanisch in the military; loud mouth braggarts who knew the answers to everything. And men like that could usually sense whom they could con and whom they couldn't. From that first day in training Rush had never allowed Hanisch to run a line on him. And in the twenty-five years since, there hadn't been enough kind words spoken by either of them toward the other to compile a complex sentence. And, as hard as it was for Rush to believe, it had gotten worse since Rush's return from an FBI task force a few years earlier.

Rush found him in the middle of the master bedroom, hands stuffed into pockets, staring at the stripped bed. His suit was the usual Italian job, cut to fit his perfect frame, creases as sharp as knives, not a wrinkle to be found. His hair was perfect, as usual, but his face looked beaten. Puffy, watery eyes, red rimmed nose, and flushed cheeks.

Rush noticed that McBride had left. Not unusual. McBride typically sectioned his scene processing in two phases. How convenient that he had missed Hanisch.

The lieutenant turned, looked at Chinbroski and nodded, ignoring Rush. "Tell me what we have here."

Chinbroski shot Rush a look.

"Got a murder, Lieutenant," Rush said, moving over in front of his partner. "We're about finished in here."

Chinbroski, despite his size, was the Plano detective who most feared Hanisch. Though Rush was the only one who knew that.

Hanisch looked away, shifted his body to the right, and turned back to Chinbroski. "Tell me about the victim."

Several beats of silence passed. "You might as well look at me," Rush said, "because I'm lead on this one. We've got a dead lady, frozen, not much evidence, and we're working hard." He turned to Chinbroski. "That about cover it?"

Chinbroski had retreated all the way across the bedroom. He nodded.

Rush looked at Hanisch, who smiled. "Don't try and bait me into snapping at you." His voice sounded rough, congested. "I'm too sick. What's the evidence?"

Rush shrugged and shoved his hands into his pockets. He didn't want to discuss evidence. "Alright, no fights today. I heard you were home sick. Little evidence, no leads, no witnesses." He didn't tell him about the realtor. Semantics, but the realtor wasn't a witness to the actual murder.

Hanisch closed his puffy eyes and cleared his throat. "So, what's next? Canvass the neighborhood?" He strolled over to the bathroom door.

"Done," Rush said. "Nothing."

"I want a team to do it again. There has to be something. Where's the husband?"

"Enroute from overseas. Doing the canvass again is a waste of time."

Hanisch shrugged. "Do it anyway. Enroute from where?"

"Japan. And I'm telling you, Lieutenant, there are no witnesses in the neighborhood."

"Orders, Rush, I give, you follow. What else?"

Rush glanced over to the bedroom door for Chinbroski. The doorway was empty. His partner had skipped.

Rush leaned against a wall near the bed and folded his arms. "We don't have much. I'm going to check with a buddy of mine in the FBI for similar cases reported to VICAP. We found some red hair. McBride thinks he's six foot, left-handed. Probably a strong guy. Not much else."

"You've been out here all day and that's all you've got?"

"We can't fabricate it out of thin air." Then Rush laughed. The truce was about to end.

"What's funny?"

"That you come out here off your death bed to get a few facts so you can impress your girlfriend."

Hanisch's face flashed crimson, knowing Rush spoke the truth. He turned and headed toward the door. "I want a copy of all the crime scene photos on my desk by the end of the day tomorrow."

Rush let him get all the way to the door. "Like hell."

He stopped and turned. "What did you say?"

"I said like hell. I don't have to do that. If you wanna look at the crime scene photos, I'll show them to you. Other than that, forget it."

"You'll have them on my desk, Rush. That's an order."

"That's not an order, that's meddling."

Hanisch's voice was calm, almost amused. "You don't know how much I hope you ignore me. All the photos."

Rush knew there was no written policy requiring him to provide crime scene photos to his chain of command. And Hanisch knew it, too. Rush didn't want him to see the photo of the note on the dresser.

"McBride does the photos," Rush said. "He does two sets. You know that. He'll make me a set and keep one in his files. Come look at mine tomorrow." He'd pull the one with the note.

Hanisch set his jaw, then smiled again, dabbing his runny nose with a handkerchief. "I'll be watching this one. Be expecting updates. Real ones." And with that he strolled from the room.

Rush walked out of the bedroom and watched Hanisch descend the staircase. Just about the time Rush heard Hanisch disappear into the living room below, he heard a quiet whistle from behind him. Chinbroski emerged from his hiding place, a closet just outside the master bedroom. "Rush, you better watch it. One of these days..."

Waving him off, Rush walked over to the top of the stairs to make sure Hanisch had left. "More bark than bite," Rush said. "If I can keep him pissed at me, he'll focus less on the case. Besides, what's life without spice?"

FOUR

The wind whistled through the passenger door, which hadn't closed properly in several weeks, as Leigh struggled with the steering wheel of her old car. Maneuvering around a patch of black ice, she ran over the curb pulling into the Mobil station. The lot was empty, save for a small pickup belonging to the attendant watching a TV behind the counter inside the store.

She cut her headlights and watched the attendant as she drove across the lot. His eyes never strayed from the TV screen.

Leigh thought of her late father, such a lover of Sherlock Holmes' mysteries, and wondered how he might judge her performance as a sleuth thus far. Although he would spin in his grave if he knew of her dark years immediately following his death, she also knew he'd be proud of the turn she'd made, of her commitment to bringing Enoch to justice.

Enoch was cunning, a worthy opponent for the fictional Holmes. Disciplined, focused, a man with a thousand rules for staying out of jail, all of which he'd used successfully so far.

One rule was not establishing patterns. Repeated at least two dozen times during their five-year relationship, he'd preached that as the primary key to avoiding cops.

But she wasn't a cop. She'd found him because of his patterns, tracked him across the country using his rules against him.

Now it was time to nudge the cops in the right direction. For her sanity, just to be able to sleep at night, she had to do something for the families of Enoch's victims.

Leigh parked by the phones at the far edge of the lot. She'd scouted this location before the sun went down to confirm that no surveillance cameras were mounted on the outside of the building.

Bracing herself, she stepped into the frigid wind and quickly dialed the number she'd committed to memory.

A middle-aged female answered on the second ring. "Crimes Against Persons."

"I have a tip about that murder earlier today," Leigh said with a snap to her words. "I want to talk to the lead detective."

After a second of rustling papers, "He's not in. I'd be happy to pass along the information."

Leigh figured the police department had Caller ID. This needed to be a short conversation. "Give me his name and I'll call back. This is sensitive."

"Miss, my whole existence is sensitive. I had someone once who wanted to wait until the next morning to talk to the lead detective and got run over by a bus on the way home. If this is important, please let me help."

The phone felt like an ice cube against Leigh's ear. "What's your name?

"Virginia. What's yours?"

"Anonymous, last name, Whereabouts Unknown. Are you going to give me the lead detective's name or piss away the best lead he'll ever get?"

The silence didn't last long, but it was thick enough to slice with a knife. "Detective Greg Rush."

"Is that the skinny guy or the ugly guy?"

"Since Chinbroski isn't skinny, I assume you think he's ugly."

"That's Rush's partner, Chinbroski? He have a first name?"

"He did this morning. Rick."

"And you're taping this?"

"Why would you think that?"

Leigh hung up the phone, wiped it down, and shivered. The game was officially afoot.

* * *

Rush's neighborhood was about as fancy as Chinbroski's clothes. No special passes were needed to enter, no guards to check visitors, no security patrols. He'd bought the thirty-year-old house on the east side of town five years before, ten years after his first wife had left him for a lesbian lover. He'd purchased the home in celebration of his reconciliation with Daniel, the son to whom he'd never been much of a father.

Only in the last six months, since marrying Mallory, had the house with the cracked driveway and peeling paint begun to look like a home. With Mallory's insistence for an immaculate yard, with her color changes inside, a transformation from ugly duckling to swan was slowly taking place.

His street was dark as he drove slowly toward his driveway. Abe Harrington, his neighbor, hadn't yet scraped a large patch of ice from the street. The ice, from a sprinkler head that had popped just prior to the freeze, had run south and covered most of the entrance to Rush's driveway. Rush knew the old man would never scrape it clear, so he'd thrown some fertilizer on it a couple of days ago. It hadn't helped much.

Slowing his car to a crawl, he tapped his brakes as he made the turn into his driveway. He wondered if his outside water faucets had frozen and split. He also wondered what his heating bill would be at the end of the month. The furnace in the old house hadn't shut off for more than a couple minutes over the last four days. Mallory had all the cabinets open, had a space heater going under the kitchen sink, and had stuffed towels around three drafty windows and under every outside door. The house just wasn't built for cold like this. He wished he could buy Mallory a new one. But money was a problem. She was a full-time student trying to finish her college degree and Rush had taken over paying off her substantial medical bills.

The changes she'd made in the house were those that cost little; paint, cheap curtains and rugs, and artwork purchased from starving artists. She'd saved some of the things from her first marriage, but mostly knick-knacks and personal items. Rush had hauled all of the other stuff to the dump, per her strict orders, and trashed the remnants of her past life.

He wondered how she'd be this evening. It was a coin flip at best. The closer the calendar got to the anniversary of her beating, the more odd she was becoming. He hated thinking of his new wife as strange, but there was no other way to explain her actions over the last couple of months. He'd caught her in the back yard, staring up into the sky and talking to no one. He'd found her in the rocking chair one morning, facing the corner, coloring in a child's coloring book using only the red crayon. She cried often, sudden bursts of tears that left as quickly and unexpectedly as they had arrived. She sometimes stared trance-like at the surgery shows on *The Learning Channel*, muttering to herself, comparing her own surgeries to those occurring on the TV in front of her.

Post Traumatic Stress Syndrome. Rush had seen it in other violent crime victims, and Mallory had fought through it brilliantly in the three years since she'd been left for dead. But she was slipping. Chinbroski knew it, and Daniel, but no one else. She'd last gone to her psychiatrist a few months before they'd married, having been proclaimed ready to face the world. But she was reverting into something Rush simply didn't recognize. He'd put off calling her doctor, in large part because Mallory was so insistent that she was working everything out in her own way. But Rush wasn't convinced. He'd heard of people whose minds had simply cracked, sometimes years after the event, seemingly in the middle of a wonderful recovery. He wouldn't wait much longer. He'd put the doctor's number in his wallet just last week.

Rush parked next to Mallory's Skylark in the garage. He hadn't found his door key by the time the garage door opener light flicked off, so he knocked and yelled for Mallory to open up. Despite his assurances that the overhead garage door would keep intruders out, she refused to budge on keeping any of the doors or windows unlocked. Rush accepted her paranoia with unlocked doors as a positive side effect of post traumatic stress syndrome, even though he'd been locked out several times after simply stepping out of the house to get the mail.

She met him at the door wearing a pair of heavy flannel pajamas and fluffy, bunny rabbit slippers. Her hair was pulled back into a pony tail, and she'd already scrubbed off her Estee Lauder war paint, revealing the thin scars that crossed her forehead, left cheek, and the right side of her neck. A petite five feet two and one hundred and five pounds, Mallory's flannel pajamas hung on her like a burlap sack and hid a body most women would give up gossip for.

"Dressed to go out, are you?" he teased, pecking her on the cheek. Her hair smelled of strawberries, her skin of fresh soap.

"Funny." She twirled around and disappeared toward the kitchen, talking over her shoulder as she went. "Didn't know when you'd be home, so I'll have to throw you a sandwich together. That all right? I've already eaten."

"Fine."

The house was immaculately kept. Three bedrooms, two baths, a small TV room off the kitchen, and a den, all polished and scrubbed by a woman who now demanded order in her life. Earth tones, Berber carpet, decent but shabby furniture, and a 27-inch TV. That was their abode, Middle America average.

By the time he'd flipped through the mail and stripped his coat and tie, Mallory had a sandwich, chips, and beer on a TV tray. She set the tray on the coffee table in front of his recliner. "I need to finish mopping," she said. "How was your day?"

Rush watched as she hurried toward the front door, where a bucket and mop sat waiting. "Didn't you just mop that yesterday?" he asked. And hadn't she mopped it the day before that?

She grabbed the mop and looked back. "Just getting that stain out. Driving me crazy. Won't take long."

Stain? Ceramic tile doesn't stain. Rush grabbed his beer and strolled over.

The entry floor was beige ceramic tile, almost white. He'd never noticed a stain. And since the front door was rarely used, he couldn't imagine how it had gotten dirty since yesterday.

He watched Mallory work the mop, all elbows and grunts. She was hunched over the middle of the entry scrubbing the tile with some kind of ammonia cleaner. It made his beer taste funny.

The floor sparkled like a magazine ad.

"Just won't come out," Mallory said. She stood up and flexed her lower back.

Rush couldn't see a stain and he had no idea what she was seeing. Was she scrubbing out a shadow? Maybe his fifty-something eyes were failing him. "Looks good to me." The entire house looked good to him. He'd never lived in a place so clean. Rush walked back to his recliner and sat down behind his sandwich.

"You got a phone call this evening," Mallory said, having given up on the floor for the moment. She sat down across from him. "Just hung up, in fact."

"Who was it?" He grabbed the ham sandwich and took a bite.

"A guy I've never heard of. I wrote his name down in the kitchen. Willard something. Let me get it." She bounded out of the room like a teenager. For a woman of thirty-eight she possessed endless energy.

"What are you studying?" Rush shouted. It was fascinating how she could care about economic systems, how America's differs from other systems around the world. Economics had to be the most boring major any university had to offer. He'd eat his gun.

"The Solow Growth theory," she shouted back. "Want me to tell you about it?"

"Uh, tomorrow maybe?" He shook his head and drank from his beer.

"Okay, a guy named Willard Jackson," she said, handing him the scrap of paper and flopping down onto the couch opposite him. "A deep voice." She lowered her chin as she mimicked the caller, holding her hand up to her ear. "Hello, is Greg there? I have some serious business with him that I can't tell you, his lowly wife."

"Is that how he sounded?" he asked. "Kind of tall, dark, and handsome? Kind of mysterious?"

"Vague, he sounded very vague. And you know me, I did try and pump him for information." She raised her eyebrows as if that would lead him to tell her of the conspiracy he and Willard Jackson had cooked up. But Rush didn't know.

That was a name he hadn't thought about in months. A former Plano cop, Jackson had quit the department after killing two men with his bare hands. Although the Grand Jury had no-billed him, and the department ruled the killings justifiable, he'd quit anyway, and soon afterwards opened a private investigation firm. He was a friend, but not a close one. They hadn't spoken in the nine months he'd been gone from the PD.

"I wonder what he wanted," Rush said, just before taking another bite of his sandwich.

"He said he might have some information about your new case." Mallory raised her eyebrows again.

Rush sipped his beer, considering that. What new case? He had four cases open: The McElroy murder, a three-week-old robbery case, and two assaults, both a week old.

"Well," Mallory asked, sitting up straight, "what new case?"

"I only have one," he told her, "but I doubt it's the one he's referring to. You sure he said case, singular, not cases?"

"Singular. For sure." She continued to look at Rush with questioning eyes.

And for the next fifteen minutes, through chewing his sandwich, munching his chips, and sipping his beer, he told Mallory about the McElroy case. He left out the gory parts, the condition of the body, and she sat on the edge of her seat, literally, and didn't say a word until he finished. It was her talent, listening, with every ounce of her attention focused on him.

"So I'm going to be busy working some odd hours over the next week or so," he said.

"You wouldn't be seeing much of me anyway," she said. "Finals. Three next week. Two the week after."

He'd forgotten. But he nodded like he hadn't. Mallory took the tray off his lap and headed into the kitchen. She was like that, Ms. Domestic, when she wasn't studying. And despite her quizzing about the Willard Jackson phone call, she rarely asked him about his cases. She'd listen, of course, to anything he had to say. But she very seldom ventured into his world of violence. Having *been* one of his cases was enough.

After Mallory retreated into the bedroom to crack the books, Rush looked at the message she'd written from Willard Jackson. He'd left his office number to B & A Enterprises, his private investigation firm, and his home number. Because of the time, Rush called his house.

After four rings Jackson's answering machine kicked on. At the beep

Rush said, "Willard, Greg Rush returning your call. Listen, it's about eight o'clock, I've been on my feet all day and I'm hitting the sack in about an hour. If you don't get this before then, call me tomorrow or hit me on my beeper." He gave his beeper number and hung up.

Rush's computer was in the den, on a cheap desk, stuck in a corner. Sliding into the chair, he booted up and logged onto the Internet. Unlike Chinbroski, who viewed the Internet as some sort of witchcraft, Rush was of the belief that almost *anything* could be found if one looked in the right places.

But the only thing Rush wanted at the moment, as he pulled up a search engine, was an answer to the odd note left at the crime scene. He pulled out the piece of paper he'd copied the message onto and flattened it out in front of him.

He was about to type one of the words onto the computer when Mallory walked up behind him and slid her arms around his chest. "Whatcha doing, babe." She nibbled his ear.

He reached back and stroked her hair. "A little surfing." He pointed to the paper in front of him. "That's what was left at the crime scene. But if you keep nibbling on my ear I'm going to declare all beaches closed."

She leaned over him and read the note. "Weird."

He typed *dehigged.*

Mallory sat Indian-style on the floor next to his chair. "So what was Chin wearing today?"

Chinbroski's outfit was something she asked about nearly every day. She loved Chinbroski like a brother, but couldn't help laughing at him behind his back. She was convinced that his clothing choices were nothing more than an attempt to draw attention to himself. Rush didn't think so.

"He had horizontally striped pants and a vertically striped sweater."

"No way."

"I asked if it was his *Brady Bunch* outfit."

She laughed.

"And you've seen that raggedy coat he wears, right?"

She shook her head. "I don't think so. What's it look like?"

Rush saw a match for *dehigged* flash up on the screen. "It's black," he said, glancing at her. "Long, almost to his knees. Threadbare, looks almost like one of those old Navy jackets. It is major ugly."

Mallory rolled her eyes. "He spends way too much money on that old Mustang of his."

"True," Rush said. "But what he really needs is a woman."

Mallory said nothing. She never did when Rush mentioned that Chinbroski needed a woman – probably because she didn't think he'd ever find one and she didn't want to seem cruel.

"Boontling," Rush read off the computer screen.

Mallory stood and moved around behind Rush's chair, reading aloud over his shoulder. "'*Boontling, an American English Dialect. Around the turn of the century, Anderson Valley, in Mendocino County, California, was a very isolated farming and logging community. To pass the time, the locals began to use self-developed terms. The language originated with the women and children in the hop fields and eventually spread to become the spoken word for most valley residents. Today, with most fluent 'boonters' in their elder year, the language has dissolved to a few slang terms.*'"

Mallory slapped Rush's shoulder. "That was easy, wasn't it?"

Rush leaned back in his chair.

Mallory looked at him. "You don't look happy."

"Well, we have a note left at a crime scene, and I find out the entire history in under sixty seconds?" But then he thought about the long brown hairs that appeared left on purpose. Maybe discovering Boontling was *supposed* to be easy.

He clicked over to another screen. "Here's a glossary of words." He leaned over and grabbed the paper with the message. Comparing the message to the list of words on the glossary, he scribbled a translation of three words that were on both lists. "'*High Rollers*' is slang for the town of Yorkville, the smallest town in Anderson Valley. Located about ten miles from Boonville. '*Pike*' means to hike or stroll. '*Tidrick*' means meeting or gathering."

Rush scratched out the definition above each translated word. "So now the note would read, '*Hey high-heel, this chuckish huger bloochedon the teleef and yabbelowed about how higgy she was. He was dehigged, so he had to string her. The greeley's gonna meet or gather soon, so otto to catch him. P.S. Hike or stroll to Yorkville.*"

Rush leaned his head back and closed his eyes. Mallory read silently over his shoulder. Then Rush thought of something. "You know Mal, I'll bet 'high-heel' means me, the police or detective. 'Chuckish huger' is obviously the dead woman." Turning, he looked at her.

Remembering Jane McElroy's frozen body, he said, "Because of the telephone duct taped to her ear, I'd also bet that 'bloochedon the teleef' has something to do with talking on the phone." He looked at the note. "What do you think?"

Mallory looked at the note again and nodded slowly. "You may be right."

"May be. I need a more comprehensive glossary. I'm going to surf the net awhile and see if I can come up with a book or something. And if that doesn't work I'll call the Mendocino County Chamber of Commerce out in California. See if they can direct me to a local expert on Boontling."

"That's why you're a detective, dear." She stood and kissed him. "My smart, smart detective."

"Not too smart. I have Chinbroski for a partner, don't I?"

She laughed. "I'm going to study for a while. If I fall asleep would you put my books on the nightstand?"

"Like every other night?"

"Just like."

Rush didn't know how much time had passed when he was jolted awake by Mallory's screaming. The computer screen saver showed rotating boxes, the digital clock showed midnight.

Then another scream pierced the stillness of the house.

He knocked over his chair, bumped into a wall, and almost fell over the couch scrambling toward their bedroom. Mallory was thrashing, arms and legs flailing across the bed.

Rush pulled her to him. Her sweat slicked body, a body patched back together by a team of surgeons, shook just like every other time she relived the nightmare of her beatings. Rush only wished it were a nightmare. But it was worse than that. It was a memory.

FIVE

Rush arrived at the station by six forty-five the next morning. It didn't take him long to find a bunch of nothing.

He checked the computer for any patrol calls of suspicious persons in the McElroy neighborhood over the past month. Nothing. Called the court for traffic tickets written in the area; three women and two sixteen year olds. No help. He checked with Records for traffic accidents: an old man hit a mailbox. He got the names of the mail carrier for that area, the water meter reader, and the gas company employee who services that neighborhood. He'd have Chinbroski interview them later.

He had subpoenas written and signed for Jane McElroy's home phone and cellular phone records by nine thirty. Verizon, the local phone service for most of the homes in Plano, had an office only a few blocks from the police station. Southwestern Bell Cellular had its offices in Dallas. He had both printouts for the last three months in his briefcase by ten forty-five.

He touched base with Chinbroski, who'd interviewed Bill McElroy late last night with nothing important learned, and passed on the names of the mailman and others. Randy McBride had left an envelope of 8 X 10 crime scene photos stuck in his mailbox. Rush studied each one and found himself captivated again at how odd the scene had been. He slipped the one with the note into his briefcase and left the others on his desk in case Hanisch came by to stick his nose into the investigation.

While studying Jane McElroy's cellular phone records, Rush came across something interesting and called Southwestern Bell Cellular to confirm a hunch. Then he called Zeke Bunning, a buddy in the FBI assigned to the Bureau's criminal profiling unit, in Quantico, Virginia.

Zeke was a psychologist from St. Louis who'd grown tired of dealing with bored housewives, troubled teenagers, and eating disorders.

It took Zeke's secretary several minutes to track him down.

"Bunning," he said finally, his voice thick with a Midwestern twang. Deep, but not too, he snapped off each word with a hurried impatience.

"Is this the Zeke Bunning who's never solved a case without the help of local cops?"

There were several seconds of silence before he recognized the voice. "Greg Rush. What in the hell are you doing?"

"Trying to forget all my FBI task force training so I can solve my cases without a cluttered mind."

Zeke laughed. "Probably a wise move."

"I read where you're the lead on those shootings the last three summers. Billy Ray Jackson, isn't that his name?" Over the last three summers, beginning on July 24, a sniper, Jackson, had gunned down a doctor, lawyer, judge, and homicide detective in different states. It was becoming the biggest manhunt in American law enforcement history. And Zeke's face was on magazine covers almost as often as the black man he was hunting. "Anything breaking?"

"Yeah, my ass. Jackson's either a ghost, dead, or invisible."

"Just keep him out of Plano. We don't need that kind of headache."

"As if we have a choice? Hell, the way this guy operates even if I knew he was coming to Plano, we couldn't stop him. It's been a nightmare."

Rush waited a beat. "Sounds like it. Speaking of nightmares, I have a case I wanna tell you about, see what you think. Tell me if you've had anything else like it reported to VICAP."

"Okay."

"What I'd like to do," Rush said, once he'd finished describing the case, "is scan these crime scene photos and e-mail them to you. Then talk again when you've had a few minutes to study them."

Rush heard papers shuffling over the phone. "Fine," Zeke said. "You've caught me in a down time with Christmas coming up." Zeke gave him his e-mail address.

"It'll take me about forty-five minutes." Rush hung up and drove home. There wasn't a computer in the department with a scanner that was also hooked to the Internet. He had everything sent within the hour.

Then Rush made a flurry of phone calls. All of them were to numbers on Jane McElroy's cell phone bill, calls she had made her last day on earth.

Zeke called him thirty minutes after receiving the e-mail. "Pretty damn interesting," he said. "Let's go through the photos one by one." The first photo was that of the living room; ransacked, broken furniture piled in the middle of the room, the single bulb lamp without its shade standing majestically above and directly in the center of the broken furniture. "Every room in the house had a lamp positioned like this?" he asked.

"Except the master bedroom," Rush said. "One thing I found interesting is that only the household belongings were destroyed. Not the house itself. If you were to move everything out of there, change the blood soaked carpet upstairs, you'd never know a crime had been committed."

"You recover any PE out of this room?"

"Not much. The only physical evidence found in that room matching anything found upstairs were a few short red hairs. Human, for sure, probably from the suspect."

"How'd the suspect get in?"

"Don't know. Nothing forced."

"Alarms?"

"Deactivated. And we know she used it religiously." Rush waited during Zeke's silence.

"Okay, let's go on," Zeke said finally.

"Wait, Zeke. What about the lamps? Any thoughts?"

More silence. Then Rush heard a pencil tapping the top of a desk. A Zeke Bunning habit. "Could be some kind of 'I'm brighter than you,' message. Let me study on it awhile."

Pulling out the picture of Jane McElroy propped up in the bathtub, photo five, Rush asked, "Seen anything like it?"

"Is her other ear missing? I can't tell from this photo."

"No. Why?"

"I think I remember a case from California a year or so back where a woman had a phone taped to one of her ears. I thought both ears were missing. Can't remember. Hold on a second."

Rush heard computer keys tapping in the background.

After a considerable pause, Zeke spoke again. "Here it is. Santa Rosa, California, ten months ago, February third. Left ear. Victim's name was Melissa Stanton."

Rush wrote it down and waited for the rest. The California victim was an early twenties white female, murdered at her home while her husband was out of town. Like Jane McElroy, a telephone was duct taped to her hand, which was strung up with an electrical cord and stuck to her right ear. The victim wasn't in a bathtub like Jane, but propped up on the master bathroom toilet. She was also sliced down the middle with her entrails exposed but undamaged. She'd bled to death. "I was mistaken about the second ear," Zeke said. "Just the left taken."

"And the phone was different."

"Right. A household cordless instead of a cellular."

"And no mention of a message?"

"No."

"That's it? No others?"

"Not according to the computer." Zeke paused.

"What else, Zeke? I know those pauses of yours."

"Well, there may be one more. Unconfirmed. I'm looking at some notes I made on my written file."

Rush waited again.

"I remember when the California case, Stanton, was entered in VICAP and sent to my unit, I called the Sheriff's investigator who worked the case. An old guy, Nick Bass. Told me that a month after the Stanton murder he was out fishing with a deputy from a neighboring county, talking about the case. This deputy buddy told him he'd heard about a similar case, but couldn't remember from where."

Rush was confused. "Let me get this. The old guy Bass has a friend who'd heard about a case similar to Stanton, but the friend can't remember from where?"

"Right. The friend's name is Jerry Donald. Worked as a chief in Drake, California at the time I called him. Bass gave me his number. Donald said he'd heard about a case where a lady had an ear sliced off about a year before Stanton. Swears he can't remember where he heard it. He thinks it was while he was sitting in a bar one night with a group of officers from other departments swapping war stories."

"So there's a victim like mine out there somewhere, but it wasn't reported to VICAP. So we're talking three. Two in California, one in Texas. Nothing about a message?"

"The message is new, it seems."

"They recover any PE from Stanton?" Rush asked.

"Some red hair. A few fibers. Didn't have much of a crime scene guy doing the collecting. I do remember that much. About your case," Zeke asked. "What was the message written with?"

"Lipstick pencil."

"Find it?"

"Not sure yet. We collected several from the victim's bathroom, but it'll be a while for the lab reports."

Nothing was said between them for several moments, each lost in his own thoughts. Finally, Rush spoke. "So why the message, Zeke? All of a sudden?"

"Just thinking about that. Don't know for sure. It's odd. No sign of a female at the Stanton scene. And you're sure the female left it?"

"Not absolute, but I'd bet my check. So he picked up a partner who doesn't like what he's doing? Or maybe was at the other scenes but has finally gone over the edge?"

Zeke hesitated before he spoke. "I'm not real comfortable with the partner theory. Killers like this are usually loners, drifters." And then he was quiet again, as if considering the possibility.

"But not unheard of?" Rush asked.

"No. Bonnie Parker and Clyde Barrow, the couple in Nebraska back in the sixties, Charles Starkweather and Caril Ann Fugate, a few other, less notorious man/woman teams. But they're rare."

"What's he telling us with the phones?" Rush had a theory. It was why he had duplicated Jane McElroy's last day of calls just before calling Zeke back, why he'd called Southwestern Bell Cellular to confirm his hunch.

"That's why I was staring off into space just now," Zeke said.

"What about this?" Rush grabbed the cellular readout. "I'm going to fax this list to you. Hang on."

A couple of minutes later Zeke had his copy. "On Jane McElroy's last day she made sixteen phone calls, all but one Dallas area numbers. I had the phone company research which cell sites transmitted the calls. Something interesting. Of the sixteen calls, eleven were made within a one-hour period from the Collin Creek Mall cell site. That's a mall here in Plano. I think she made those calls from inside the mall. We know she was there. Could the killer have overheard some of those calls? Is he telling us how she attracted him?"

"It might explain how he knew she was alone."

"I've called several of the people Jane called that afternoon. She told two ladies her husband was out of town until Tuesday, one about how empty her house was with both girls at college. She told her maid she'd been to a jewelry store and picked up a necklace. And the one long distance call was to her husband, who she told of the eleven hundred in cash she withdrew to buy an antique dresser on Saturday."

"Those items at the house?"

"No cash. We'll be checking for the other things."

"You think the killer overheard Jane at the mall talking on her cellular? And the same killer overheard Stanton on her cordless?" Zeke's tone told

Rush how improbable he thought that was.

So Rush told him his theory. “Scanner. Could’ve scanned the California case, too. Both phones are wireless.”

“Eavesdropping,” Zeke said after a pregnant pause. “Electronically. Since digital technology is still a few years from being the absolute standard, we’re going to have to put up with the security nightmares for a while longer. I wouldn’t be surprised if that’s how he did it.”

“All of this is assuming the killer didn’t know her already or been watching her for months.

“And then we have the message,” Rush continued. “It’s a dialect called Boontling from rural northern California. The wine country. Isn’t Santa Rosa up that way?”

“Yes,” Zeke said. “North of San Francisco.”

“It fits.”

“Seems to. Listen, can I call you to consult on the Jackson shootings? Since you’ve figured this thing out in less than 24 hours, I think I could use your help.”

Rush laughed. “Seriously, if you come across anything like my case, give me a ring, would you?”

“You bet.”

“Thanks for the info.”

Rush hung up and gazed out across his frozen yard. The answer to this case was in the Boontling. He just knew it.

SIX

The library on the east side of town sat in a forty-year-old neighborhood, down the street from the original Plano High School. The building appeared less than ten-years old, and shared a large parking lot with a softball field that presently lay beneath a half-inch of frost.

Inside, the library had everything Leigh needed to conduct her research; microfiche copies of the local paper, Internet access, and enough people for her to be just another face in the crowd.

Rush had a lot of coverage in the *Plano Star Courier*, easily the most celebrated officer on the force. There were eight articles, including a profile that detailed his entire police history. He was a former FBI task force detective who'd been wounded on duty, the only cop on the force to win rookie, officer, and detective of the year awards, had a near perfect solve rate on his homicide investigations, and an attorney son. His law enforcement career consisted of three parts: the twelve years at Plano PD before the five years on the FBI task force, and the eight years since returning.

Computerized records from the county gave Leigh Rush's home address, his current wife's name, his ex-wife's name, and the square footage of his house. The City of Plano web site gave her his salary and a nice color photo of both Rush and Chinbroski. The Internet gave her Rush's son's attorney information, with which she easily found a home address and office phone number.

She tucked all of the information in her purse, wrapped herself tightly into her coat and headed out the door. She'd accomplished so much these last few days she felt a glimmer of hope. Until she realized just how much she had left to do.

* * *

Heading back to the police station, Rush's beeper vibrated against his belt. Pulling it up in front of his face, he recognized the number as one he'd seen last night on the paper Mallory had given him, Willard Jackson's private investigation firm, B & A Enterprises.

He would have dialed the number on his cellular but, like always, Chinbroski had their phone again. Cursing, he whipped into a gas station and used a pay phone, the receiver freezing against his ear. Jackson answered on the second ring.

"Willard, Rush here."

There was a silence for a moment and then the sound of a slamming door. "Sorry," Willard said finally. "Need some privacy around here."

Willard's voice was a mixture Rush had never quite figured out. Rush knew he was from the southern part of Louisiana, so it had a slight Cajun flavor, but only slight. Some of his words reminded Rush of what he'd heard from south Philly, but with no slurring of words. Jackson's English was proper; each word pronounced with a precise, baritone reverberation.

"Listen," Jackson said. "I'm glad you called me back." He lowered his voice. "We need to meet."

Rush let a couple of beats pass before answering. "Do we?"

"It's important. About your— "

A concrete truck rumbled by, drowning out Jackson's words. "Hold on a second," Rush said. "Say that again."

"You on your cellular?" Jackson said quickly. "I don't want to talk if you're on a cellular. Too many ears."

Now that was interesting, Rush thought. Seeing how he'd just spoken to Zeke Bunning about how Jane McElroy may have been scanned on her cellular. But not interesting enough. "I'm on a pay phone freezing my ass off. But look, Willard, I'm tied up with a murder invest..."

"That's what I just said. What I have may relate."

Now that *was* interesting enough. "Okay," Rush said. "When?"

"Now. My office. You know where?"

"I've heard you opened an office on the east side."

"Right." Jackson gave him directions.

The building that housed B&A Enterprises was a run down concrete block structure with a flat, tar roof. Gang graffiti decorated the exterior walls, trash, blown and frozen against the edges of the building, looked like modern art gone awry. With every window boarded up and burglar barred over, the one-story structure looked more like it housed the dead than the living. It was situated at the corner of Tenth and Vine, the center of the worst section of east Plano. Rush suspected that the only reason the long fingers of crime hadn't picked the place clean was because of the people who were B&A Enterprises: Willard Jackson, Jacob Masterson, and Reese Morgan.

After Rush left a message for Jackson the night before, he'd thought about all of the things he'd heard through the department grapevine about B & A Enterprises and the sidekicks Jackson had hired. Jacob Masterson was rumored to be some former secret government agency guy who'd gone over the mental edge and dropped out of society for several years before changing his name and hiring on with B & A. But how would that kind of rumor make it into the halls of Plano PD?

Reese Morgan wasn't quite so mysterious. Like Jackson, Morgan was a former cop. A state trooper who'd spent several years in the narcotics unit as a technical specialist. He'd been in charge of high tech electronics such as body mikes, pinhole lens cameras, night vision gear, and all RF equipment. He also led surveillances and covert operations, and was in charge of targeting some of the worst drug offenders in North Texas. Until he was fired for running an illegal wiretap on the guy he'd discovered was bopping his wife.

As Rush drove through the neighborhood, he marveled that anyone would open a business in the middle of such a desolate section of town.. Maybe they'd done so for some covert or tactical reason, given the type of business they were in. But probably not. Probably desperation, a need to find the cheapest building in town.

The wind howled and pushed against his car door as he opened it to climb out. After wrapping his overcoat tightly around himself he noticed a small group of black, low-pants-wearing, hats-on-sideways, bandanna-colors-displaying gangbangers run from one house on the B & A side of the street, to another. Roaches, he thought. At least the cold would keep them inside.

Before he even closed his car door Willard Jackson, a mountain of a man with shoulders as wide as any he'd ever seen, stepped out the front door to escort him into the building. He was the real reason the neighborhood gangs didn't attempt anything, Rush suspected. His size, his booming voice, and the fact that every gangbanger knew that he'd killed two men with his bare hands while a cop. His icy stare was enough to send chills through the toughest of men, and Willard used that stare ninety-five percent of the time.

As Rush approached he wondered how Jackson had known that he'd arrived. Then he saw surveillance cameras mounted on each of the front corners.

Jackson held the front door open with one hand and stuck his other out for a handshake. "Rush," he said, "been awhile."

Rush winced as Jackson squeezed his right hand. "Nice place."

Jackson snapped a look in both directions before slamming the heavy steel door. "No it's not. But thanks for the compliment."

Leading him into a small conference room at the back of the building, Jackson turned after they entered and waved his arms, showing off his agency. "I know it's not much, but it'll get better."

The room had two desks, three filing cabinets, a refrigerator, a large bulletin board, a map of the Dallas area, shelving holding radios, VCRs, and battery chargers, and a small table with a coffee maker. A bright room, it had stark white walls and a white ceiling. Governmentish. Boring.

Rush glanced at the desk to the left and saw a Jacob Masterson name plate. A steaming cup of coffee sat amid neatly arranged files, videotapes and audiotapes.

The desk to the right must belong to Reese Morgan, The Sloth, as some of the officers at Plano PD referred to him. Although Rush had never met him, Chinbroski always said Reese Morgan was the most disgusting and sloppy man he'd ever met. And Morgan's desk confirmed Chinbroski's claim. Covered with trash, pieces of half-eaten food, used Styrofoam coffee cups, and four *Playboy* magazines left open where he'd been comparing the centerfolds, the desk reminded Rush of a rat's nest. There wasn't a single inch of clean space showing.

Rush shrugged out of his coat and threw it over a chair next to Masterson's desk. Then he sat in that chair.

Willard leaned against the wall in front of him and crossed his arms. "Listen, hate to hurry through this, but I have an appointment."

"Fine," Rush said. "Let's hear it."

"Yesterday I heard about the murder you're working. You know, still have some friends at the PD who tell me things. Then I read about it in this morning's paper. Last night, before I called your house, I got to thinking." He paused and pursed his lips. "I'm pretty sure I had a close encounter with someone who knows your killer."

"Say again."

The big man grabbed a chair and slid it in front of Rush's. "Two weeks ago a woman called me on the phone to talk about hiring me for a job. Identified herself as Leigh. No last name. Said I had to meet her away from my office before she'd discuss why she needed my services. Had to come alone." He grinned. "Like that was going to happen. I met her, but had Reese Morgan, one of my men, wire up my truck and roll tape on the meeting. You want to see the tape or have me run it down to you?"

Rush scratched his head. "Just give me the nutshell portion."

"Okay. She wanted to hire my firm to watch a man until Christmas. Her ex common-law. Wouldn't tell me his name."

"Why did she want him watched?"

"Said it was too risky telling me much until I agreed to help her."

"Did you?"

"Hear me out. Said her ex had fled to Texas. Took her months to track him to the area. She thinks…"

"Whoa, whoa, whoa." Rush held up his hands. "I'm way lost here. Fled from where?

"California."

"No last name on Leigh, no first name on her ex?"

"Right. Got a partial tag on her car, though."

Still too early for that. "Why do you think this is part of my frozen lady?"

"Because of a rambling comment she made during our meet. She said, and I quote, 'You've got to help before somebody else gets gutted. He's loose and looking in Plano.'" Willard raised his eyebrows. "'Loose and looking in Plano,'" he repeated.

And from California, Rush thought. Never one to reveal information if he didn't have to, Rush asked him to continue.

"She said her ex is a bad dude. Real bad. Called him a professional listener, a guy who…"

"Whoa again. A professional what?"

"Listener. The guy scans people. Electronically. Uses the information to commit crimes."

"And?"

"Said she's close to figuring out where he's living. Seen him once, about a month ago, hanging around Collin Creek Mall. She knows he lives north somewhere. McKinney area. Likes rural places, old farm houses, cabins, remote trailer houses, places like that."

It was hard for Rush to catch everything because his mind was drowning trying to compare what Jackson was telling him to the facts of his case.

Shifting in his chair, Rush was about to ask another question when Jacob Masterson, who stepped around and sat at his desk, facing Rush, distracted him. A ninety-eight pound weakling, Masterson's five-foot, herky-jerky frame didn't have a single pound of excess weight.

Jackson made the introduction. "We call him The Prophet."

Rush smiled. "Why's that?"

"A sacrilegious biblical reference, if you ask me," Masterson said.

He looked creepy; nervous tics, rapid eye movements, a sly smile, which he wore as he evaluated Rush.

"Reese Morgan started it because of Jacob's ability to predict people's actions," Jackson said. "And as you come to know him I'm certain you'll understand."

Interesting, Rush thought. *Government training? Maybe the rumors had some merit.*

"He's the true brain of B&A Enterprises," Jackson went on. "Speaks four languages."

"I'm not the brain. And I hate it when they call me the Prophet." Masterson's hair, white and standing on end, swayed back and forth when he moved his head. He leaned back in his chair to put some distance between he and Rush. Then he raised his eyebrows, as though waiting for Rush to comment.

Rush broke eye contact and turned to Jackson. "So what was this Leigh driving?"

From behind Rush, "Hey, dudes." Rush turned to the door.

Reese Morgan ambled into the room as slow as a sloth. His balding head was pink from the cold, his clothes covered his pear shaped body much too tightly, exposing flabby man breasts. His dark, bushy eyebrows almost hid his beady, slanted eyes. "Grabbed some donuts, Prophet. In the bag here."

Jackson made the introductions again. Morgan barely glanced at Rush.

"Thanks," Masterson said. "You get me a lemon filled?" He gently ripped the bag Morgan had placed in front of him, carefully laid out the pastry.

"Out of lemon," Morgan said. "Got you a jelly instead. Strawberry, I think." His eyes finally got around to settling on Rush's, but only for a second.

Rush looked at Jackson again, hoping he'd answer the question about the car. He didn't so he asked again.

"Oh, yeah. An older Oldsmobile. Midnight blue, wasn't it Reese? About an 84 - 85 model? We're talking about Leigh."

Morgan nodded, his mouth stuffed with half of a powdered donut. "California plates." Powdered sugar spewed from his mouth as he spoke. "Got the front half of the tag. Didn't know it'd be so important or..." He waved his hands around, letting the unfinished sentence hang in the air.

Rush looked over to Masterson, whose chin rested on his interlocked fingers. He stared, not eating his donut. Rush felt as though Masterson had stripped away a piece of his scalp and was reading his brain.

"That's about all I have," Jackson said, regaining Rush's attention. "We've got the tape with all the audio." He raised his eyebrows, an invitation to watch.

"Let's see it," Rush said.

Jackson stood and walked to a cabinet in the corner of the room. Swinging the doors open, he grabbed a videotape off the shelf and popped it into a VCR/TV unit. Just before he pushed the play button, Reese Morgan spoke.

"Need to tell him about our theft, Willard."

Jackson turned. The look on the big man's face could have thawed Jane McElroy's frozen pond. "I wasn't going to waste his time with something that has no bearing on the woman."

Morgan crammed another bite of donut in his mouth before responding. "Sure as hell does have a bearing. She needed equipment, she took it. Mine."

Jackson shook his head. "No evidence of that."

Morgan laughed, spewing more powdered sugar, most of it landing on the front of his shirt. "You just don't get it, Willard. You heard her talk about what her ex is into. You don't think…"

"There's no evidence…"

"Wait," Rush interrupted, raising his hands. "What are we talking about here?" He shot a look at Jacob Masterson, who still rested his chin on his hands, staring, saying nothing.

Willard Jackson sighed heavily. "Four days after my meeting with her, last week, Morgan's van was stolen while he was eating lunch at a restaurant across town. Had our tracking system inside, some night vision, 35 mm cameras, pinhole video cameras, circuit board microphones, scanners, some other stuff. Cleaned us out." He looked at Morgan. "But there's no evidence she did it."

"Well, why in the hell do you think she wanted to hire us, Willard? For our looks? Why do you think she wanted to meet? Don't you think she's smart enough to spot our surveillance? I think she knows where her ex is. She's gonna light his ass up with electronics." He chomped another donut and looked at Rush. "You watch the tape," he spewed, "tell us what you think."

Jackson grunted and turned back to the VCR. "You ready, Rush?" he asked over his shoulder.

"Let's see it."

The tape showed the eastern parking lot of Collin Creek Mall, the view was from above; probably from behind the TGI Friday's located to the east, along Highway 75. The camera showed an empty area in the outer reaches of the mall. After a few seconds a brown Ford Explorer pulled into the middle of the vacant area and stopped.

"That's me," Willard said. "My truck is wired with two microphones. My plan is to get her in there. She must have been watching because she pulls up in a minute."

And she did. A mid-eighties, dark blue Oldsmobile slowly drove into the scene and stopped a few feet from the Explorer. The audio on the tape had Willard talking softly into the microphones telling Morgan to zoom in on the woman. The camera zoom made the Oldsmobile grow in size. The woman behind the wheel sat in the car, her head moving back and forth, apparently scanning the parking lot around her.

"I parked up at the Friday's," Morgan said, "because nobody ever looks up. You can see she's suspicious as hell."

She sat in her car for over two minutes. The camera zoomed to the front of the Olds. No front plate. Moving back to the driver, Leigh's face was obscured by the shadow from the roof of the car. She had brown hair that fell just below her shoulders, like the woman seen by the realtor on the night of Jane McElroy's murder.

"This is before the cold front," Rush said. "You say a couple of weeks ago?"

"Right," Jackson answered. "If you look closely you can see her waving for me to come sit in her car. I'm shaking my head because she's the one who wanted the meet. I finally raise my hands in the air like, 'Hey, I'm outta here, Babe.' You can see me start to drive away."

The Explorer crawled forward, around the other side of the Oldsmobile. Just before it moved out of the picture, the Oldsmobile's driver's door shot open. The Explorer stopped, and Rush could see the passenger's door window slide down. Leigh climbed from the old car and shouted for Jackson to stop.

"I guess she wanted to play by my rules," Jackson said.

Rush nodded.

Leigh closed the car door and walked to the Ford. She wore blue jeans, a brown sleeveless tee shirt, and running shoes. She moved with an obvious athletic grace, and even with the distance between her and the surveillance van, the muscle definition in her arms was evident. Early twenties, Rush thought, no older than that.

"*You Willard Jackson*?" Rush heard her ask.

"*That's me.*"

The audio on the tape was clear, no interference. Willard Jackson's voice, even through the hidden microphones, had the same musical quality. "*Climb in*," he told her.

Leigh walked up to the Explorer and grabbed the passenger's door handle. Just before pulling the door open, she looked in all directions and then quickly glanced toward the camera above her.

"There," Morgan shouted, jumping from his chair. "That's when she noticed the van. She didn't look long, but she saw it."

Rush couldn't agree. Her glance was too brief, and it was impossible to see her eyes from that distance. She climbed into the Ford and slammed the door.

"*Sorry I'm so nervous*," she told Jackson. "*Just have to be careful*."

"*Nothing to worry about from us*," Jackson told her.

"*Us*?" Leigh jerked her head around, searching in all directions. "*Who's with you? You were supposed to come alone*."

Jackson paused the videotape and looked at Rush. "That was my bad. But it demonstrates how she picks up on everything. Now remember, as we watch this, that at this point she's told me nothing about why she wants to hire us."

"And what I think she's doing," Reese Morgan chimed in, "is checking out our agency. And just listen to how in the hell she does it. Slick as green snot."

Jackson hit the play button. "*I say us because there's more than just me in my agency.*"

Several seconds of silence passed as Leigh continued searching. Without looking at Jackson, she asked how many investigators he had, asked as though an afterthought, as though filling in dead air space. She propped her right elbow on the door and began combing her hair with her fingers, masking the right side of her face.

"*Two full time*," Jackson said. "*Not counting me. And several more at my disposal*."

Leigh was silent for a moment. "*I'm not sure three is enough*," she said softly. "*Not for this guy*."

"*What guy*?"

"*My ex. Bad dude*."

Leigh's voice had no discernible accent that Rush could detect. She sounded young, like a teenager, but her voice shook, quivered with emotion, and she spoke fast. "*Tracked him from California. Took ten months. Now he's here, in Plano. I've seen him, here at the mall, a month ago. Something like that.*"

"*What's his name*?"

With her right hand, the only hand visible on the video, Leigh pulled at her dark hair, twirling it around a finger. "*I can't share that yet. If we can agree on ... well, if I decide to hire your firm, we'll go over it all.*"

Silence from Jackson.

"*I'm close to finding his house,*" she said. "*Somewhere north of here. North of McKinney, I think. He likes rural places. Old farmhouses, cabins, remote trailers, stuff like that.*" She paused. "*When I find it, can we track him? Electronically*?" More hair tugging.

Rush leaned close to the TV.

Jackson's pause lasted several seconds, seemingly uncertain of how to answer. "*It's expensive,*" he said finally.

She sighed as though relieved. "*Money isn't the issue. Ability is the issue.*"

"*Ability isn't a problem.*"

"*Can we do phones*?" she asked.

"*Phones are expensive.*"

Her hand pulled away from her head, ran along the side of her neck. "*That's a good sign,*" she said after a moment. "*What about video? Covert, inside his house.*"

"Even more money."

She was silent as she looked to her right at a Ford Mustang slowly driving past.

"*What would we be up against*?" Jackson asked her.

She blew out a breath. "*An incredibly intelligent, incredibly ruthless monster.*"

"*Who does what for a living?*"

"Listens."

"Listens?"

"*Professional listener. Acts on what he hears. Blackmail, burglary, robbery, theft, credit cards. You name it.*"

"*Are you saying he listens electronically? Phone taps, scanners, things like that?*"

"Things like that."

Several beats later Leigh continued. "*I'd want to hire you until Christmas. That's what, five weeks? But there's one condition you have to meet before we can go any farther. It's important we agree because I won't negotiate on this point."* She paused.

"*I'm listening."*

"Regardless of what we see him do, once we find him, I mean, regardless of what evidence we gather against him while we're watching, we do nothing."

Jackson didn't respond.

"*No matter what crime*," she repeated. "*Get my drift*?"

"*You're assuming the worst. Or are you expecting the worst?"*

"*No matter what crime."*

"Can you tell me why he's so important? What's driving you to find him, why Christmas?"

"Not unless you agree to my condition."

His response was quick. "*No. Can't do it. Not under those terms."*

"I can pay big."

"*Not big enough*."

"*Your firm's new. I checked. You need the business. There's always a big enough*."

Jackson drummed his dash, the sound echoing on the tape like gunshots. "*I was a cop nine months ago. Still am at heart. For those who enjoy their freedom, there are lines they can't cross. Now you know mine*."

"*So you're solid on that?"*

"As the pavement we're sitting on."

She opened the door, started to climb out, and looked back. "*You should help. Before somebody else gets gutted. He's loose and looking in Plano*." Her voice had a pleading tone, a desperation.

Jackson said nothing for a beat, then repeated himself. "*I'm solid on that point*."

Leigh slid out of the Ford, slammed the door, and spoke through the open window. "*You rent equipment?"*

"I don't think so."

"Well, best of luck with your agency, then." She stepped away and hurried to her car.

Jackson shut off the tape.

"I want to run Randy McBride through your Explorer," Rush said.

Morgan laughed before Jackson could respond.

"What's funny?" Rush asked, turning toward him.

"Well," Jackson said. "I didn't know this would ever be important so I never knew not to run the thing through a car wash."

"Are you talking a full service place where they wipe everything down and vacuum?"

"On three different occasions since that meeting." Jackson shrugged.

Rush nodded. "But I doubt they got what Leigh left for us."

"What do you mean?"

"Her hair sample. She pulled a couple of hairs. I think they're between the door and seat. Didn't you see it?"

Jackson shrugged. "Wasn't looking for it."

"I think she left them for us. And we'll need them."

"Fine. Send McBride over."

Rush glanced at Jacob Masterson. His donut was gone, but he still stared. "What," Rush finally asked him, "do you think of all this?"

He smiled. "Interesting. I noticed your increase in attention at Leigh's old car. You also studied her more closely than I would have deemed necessary. It is obvious to me that she is more important to you than any of us realized. As for the woman," he went on, "I could hear the quite desperation in her voice, the slight change in pitch when she mentioned her ex. The fact that she tracked him all the way from California, if that can be believed, is a testament to her willingness to do whatever it takes to succeed. She is in a frenzy, a gloom of desperation. I think she is quite capable of stealing equipment if she is determined that it will give her an upper hand."

Before Rush could comment, Reese Morgan joined in. "And you saw that ragged ass car she was in. What makes anybody think she could afford to hire us? I'm telling you, she set up that meeting to find just what she found. Equipment. Why else would she demand that Willard come alone and meet her in a public place? She knew we'd have a damn tape running."

Jackson sat backward in his chair again and looked at Rush. "How would she know we have a surveillance van? That means she's done some surveillance on…"

"Your agency," Rush finished for him.

Jackson shook his head. "That would make her one smart young lady. She couldn't have been older than twenty-one or twenty-two. It would also mean she played me like a damn fool."

Rush turned to Morgan. " Did you file a report?"

"The morning it happened."

Rush looked at the three of them. "I guess you know I'll need that tape."

Masterson picked one off his desk and handed it over. "The one we watched was a copy. Here's the original." Then he handed over an audiotape. "I burned the audio onto this. Play it in your car while you drive. Memorize her voice.

It will help you."

Their eyes locked and Rush felt a chill on his arms. Then he stood and grabbed his coat. "Well, listen. You guys may have stumbled onto something. I don't have to say to call if you find her."

"We'll call," Jackson said.

"We'll also be looking," Morgan said. "I want my shit back."

Pulling his coat on, Rush turned toward the door. Then the Prophet spoke. "Detective Rush."

He turned back.

"Her desperation will allow others to die. I don't know what you have, but I suspect that she has allowed that to happen already. Find her and she will lead you. If you allow her to."

Rush nodded, then walked out to his car, so confused by the Prophet that he hardly noticed the cold.

SEVEN

Leigh stared at the phone in front of her, not sure of what to do. She knew that if Rush caught her, he'd throw her *under* the jail. Her explanation wouldn't sway his decision to charge her with everything he could, the boxes of evidence she'd gathered against Enoch over the last ten months would be used against her as proof that she could have saved innocent lives.

It was bad enough that she *had* allowed people to die. Knowing she was guilty and probably should be imprisoned weakened her resolve to protect herself. She battled daily against giving into the fatigue of it all. Then she thought of what drove her, of the sheer force of her love. But despite that love, every passing day she sank deeper into an abyss. Last night was the scene with the Brookfield woman, there was the other body yet to be found, at this moment rotting in his car, the phone taps in Enoch's cabin, the theft of the van, the altering of the crime scene at Jane's house and allowing the poor woman to die. She was up to her eyebrows. And although she didn't think she'd ever be caught, the police occasionally got lucky. If Rush got lucky, she'd never again see the light of day. And that was unacceptable.

She stared at the phone as the wind howled against her apartment window. She needed a lawyer. A good one. But when to make contact? And who?

She stared at the name and phone number in front of her and tried to calculate how a personal relationship would play between lawyer and cop. She didn't know. And she didn't have time to investigate the history between the two.

With a deep breath, she picked up the phone and dialed the number. An energetic man answered crisply on the third ring.

"Daniel Rush. May I help you?"

* * *

Driving away from B & A Enterprises, Rush pondered Jacob Masterson's speculation that the mysterious Leigh had not actually killed anyone, but simply allowed it to happen. Two weeks had passed since her meeting with

Willard Jackson, plenty of time for her to find her ex and install the stolen tracking transmitter on his car. Assuming she *had,* in fact, stolen it.

If she were covertly following her ex, watching his every move, she could have followed him to the murder scene, possibly even gone in after he left. If McBride found hair in Jackson's Explorer that matched the long, brown hair purposely left at the murder scene, the entire focus of the investigation would shift. Rush hoped that she *had* put a transmitter on her ex's car. Because if she could track him, so could he.

There were other questions of course, if this mysterious Leigh was the woman who'd gone into the McElroy house. First, what could possibly drive a woman to take the risk of not only being seen by the man she was following, but of being arrested if caught? And why sit in the passenger seat in an old car in a nice neighborhood and risk being noticed by a passerby? And finally, if her ex had killed McElroy, why not call the police and have him arrested?

Shaking his head, he felt overwhelmed, as if three feet of questions had been crammed into six inches of space.

After arriving at the station, he stopped and asked Paula, one of the CID secretaries, if she'd seen Chinbroski. She hadn't, and Chinbroski wasn't checked out on the mark-out board. Pulling off his scarf, he was about to shrug out of his coat when he heard Hanisch shout from inside his office. "Rush, come in here."

Several other detectives stopped and looked as he made his way across CID. With a frown of annoyance he said nothing as he stopped at Hanisch's door.

Hanisch sat behind his desk, fingers interlocked, knuckles white, his face a picture of distress. Opposite him sat a petite woman with small wire frame glasses and dark hair. She sat poised on the edge of her chair, fingers tapping the surface of the desk glaring at Hanisch. As Rush stepped into the office, she glanced toward him. Her hair, matted from the hood of her coat, had wind blown strands sticking up over her forehead. A heavy winter coat was draped across her lap. Rush guessed her not more than five-two and one hundred and ten pounds. She had the look of a scrapper, of someone eager for confrontations.

"This is Nanci Brookfield," Hanisch said. "She wants to speak to a detective. Got some story about being stalked." His sentence died and he flipped his hands toward the woman.

Rush was about to remind him that he was too busy, when it suddenly occurred to him that complaining was exactly what Hanisch would want.

His grin made Rush's ears turn hot.

Rush stuck out his hand. "Nice to meet you."

She didn't take it. Instead, she looked back at Hanisch. "Some kind of *story*? Someone stalking me is some kind of *story*? I spent twenty minutes explaining everything to you, and you just dump me off? I'll have you know that I spent thirty minutes sitting out in that lobby before I spoke to you. And now I have to repeat it all to someone else? My, my, aren't I lucky to be provided with such personal attention?"

Rush dropped his hand, resisting the temptation to grin at Hanisch's discomfort.

Hanisch scooted his chair back and stood. "I supervise the detectives, Ms. Brookfield. My subordinates do the legwork." He had emphasized the word subordinates. Then he sniffed, pulled at his pants, and turned to Rush, "You can sit in here. Or use your desk. Whatever." With another vague gesture, he stepped around Rush and disappeared.

Wishing he'd disappear for good, Rush closed the door and sat down behind Hanisch's desk.

Before he could even form a question, Nanci Brookfield demanded, "I want to talk about the report I filed. I was told you have my case."

Rush could feel his blank expression. "When were you told that?"

"Just before that rude man shouted out your name."

"And what case is it exactly?"

She spouted off the numbers. "98-4459302."

"Which is?"

"I'm being stalked. I made a police report yesterday and I wanted to find out which detective is assigned."

It was a new law, stalking, one hard to prove. He didn't even know if anyone in Plano had been charged with it yet. "Why don't you tell me about it."

As she gathered her thoughts, her hard, determined face softened. "I'm not always like this. I mean, I don't usually come on so strong. It's just that ... I'm scared again."

A lot of meaning in that last word. "Again?" he asked.

She twisted her fingers. "I knew ... have known ... since I filed the police report yesterday, that I would have to talk about the attack. A year ago, in Kansas City, I was attacked. Raped. I've recovered. After a year of counseling I can finally admit that my mind is what cracked, not my body." She dug in her purse and pulled out a tissue. "I lived alone in Kansas City. Ran a business out of my house."

Nanci hugged herself and looked at the floor, silent for several moments. "I'm scared," she said finally. "I'm as scared now as I was right after the attack. I didn't sleep last night, I'm frightened of shadows, I've been jumping at small sounds all night." Her voice sounded unsure, so different from the sharp tone she'd used only minutes before.

Rush saw Mallory when he looked at Nanci Brookfield. Mallory had gone through a similar stage, of totally transforming when she spoke aloud of her ex husband. Even two years after the beating, Mallory visibly shook when the name Roger Hamilton was mentioned.

"I worked out of my house, writing computer software. I've always lived alone. I mean, since college. I was really involved with my work, and the phone rang. I let the machine get it."

"Ten minutes later a man kicked in my back door. He, um, assaulted me. He... never mind."

Rush stared at the desk, reliving the sessions he'd had with Mallory, who still couldn't discuss her many attacks. "I wouldn't ask you to go into that," he said gently. He hated to put her through telling her story a second time only to pass her on to someone else, but he still didn't have time to work her case. "Did they catch him?" he asked.

"They did. Later that night. We finished the trial last month. Anyway, my report describes the phone calls I received yesterday. I got four more today." She dug into her purse again and pulled out a slip of paper. She wiped her eyes with the back of her hand and placed the paper on the desk. "This is the number of the person who's been calling. From my Caller ID."

Rush took the paper.

"The first call came while I was absorbed in my work. I thought about letting the machine get it until I had a flash of last year's attack. I grabbed it on the third ring, heard heavy breathing ... then a deep, kind of guttural laugh." She shivered.

He jotted some notes on a small pad he'd dug from his pocket. Nodding, he encouraged her to continue.

She had stopped crying, the hardness returning. Anger, he figured. "I slammed the phone down and ran to my Caller ID box."

Rush looked at the paper. SBMS 972-555-1009. A cell phone. Southwestern Bell Mobile Systems, the same company as Mallory's cell. "Then what?"

"I paced around. Not sure what to do. I thought it might've been a wrong number. My mother," Nanci laughed through her drying tears, "in the dramatic tone that is so uniquely her, said 'my fear was an open, oozing wound. But a thin scab of courage now protects me'." She looked at Rush and smiled. "Pretty dramatic, huh? Poetic?"

"And the 'scab of courage' was intact until yesterday?"

She nodded weakly and smiled. "My mother would be proud of you. After the first call I looked out the window. I remember thinking how arctic the weather was. How the front had moved in and paralyzed the city. And how that one call had paralyzed *me*." Her head dropped and she wiped her eyes again.

She was gathering herself to go on, he could tell, so he waited.

"Just as I convinced myself that the call was a wrong number, the phone rang again. I jumped and knocked over an end table. Broke a lamp. Instead of snatching the phone, like the first time, I stared at the Caller ID box. It was the same number. I peeked out the window to check for cars that might be sitting down the street. You know, thinking that if someone wanted to break into my house like last time, I'd want to see him coming. I had my gun out by then.

"I thought if I answered I might discover it was just some guy playing a joke on his wife or girlfriend, dialing the wrong number by mistake. Or maybe a friend of mine playing a trick, although I don't have many friends in Texas."

She wiped her hands across the front of her jeans. "I picked up the phone. The breathing was there, so was the laugh. Then he said my name."

Rush was torn between compassion and impatience. After a moment she said, "I called the police. Two other calls came while I waited for the officer to arrive. That was yesterday. I'm convinced this case can be solved because the calls came in on my private, unlisted number, a number only a few people know. And most of those people are the contractors I've recently hired to remodel my house."

She looked at Rush and waited, finished with her story.

He jotted a couple more thoughts. "So you've only received phone calls? Has he actually stalked you? Followed you anywhere? Called you at any other location?"

"I couldn't wait for…"

He waved her off. "I wasn't suggesting you not report it. But the report still has to reflect the true offense."

"Would you have taken an obscene phone call report seriously?" The hardness was all the way back.

"I am taking it seriously."

She crossed her arms and glared at him the way she'd glared at Hanisch. "What should I do?"

"I'll get with the phone company and get a trace put on your line. I'll get them to speed it up. It's Wednesday now, maybe by Friday. You can hook up a recorder, tape the guy. Got an alarm?"

"Yes."

"Use it. Are you trained with the gun you mentioned earlier?"

"I shoot every Friday. I'm good."

Her face told him she believed it. "Lock your doors," he said. "Watch your back, call people ahead of time and tell them you're on your way. Invite people over, spend time with friends, put your lights on timers, put call forwarding on your home phone and send the calls to your cellular."

"In other words, I'm on my own."

He sighed. "I'll have someone investigate this. The guy was stupid to use his cellular. We'll have his name by tomorrow noon."

She glared at him. "We? Not I. You're dumping the case to someone else?"

"Trust me. Okay?"

She reached into her purse and pulled out a cassette tape. "I want you to listen to this."

"What is it?"

"It's proof. I wanted to tell you about the phone calls to gauge your interest. Now I'll tell you the rest."

Rush stood and leaned over her. "To gauge my interest? Lady, I don't play games. I'm in the middle of a murder investigation. I don't have time to listen to a tape of some guy breathing into your phone. I believe your story and I'll make sure someone gets working on it." He reached down and grabbed his coat.

"Wait." She jumped from her chair and touched his sleeve. "It's not a tape of somebody breathing. It's of two men talking, plotting to break into my house."

That stopped him. He stared at her hard. "Explain."

"Last night, just before dark, a woman stopped by my house. A woman I'd never met before. Talked her way inside and told me I'd been chosen as a target. Then she gave me this tape. Told me to take it to a detective."

A thought tickled him, but the odds were astronomical. "Did this woman have a name?"

"She refused. Said it didn't matter."

"Describe her."

"A little taller than me, dark hair chopped short, slim. She had on a heavy coat and gloves and she didn't stay long." She thrust the tape toward Rush. "Listen to it."

He hesitated, then took it and turned toward the mini stereo system Hanisch had on a shelf behind his desk. Nanci Brookfield leaned against the door and watched. He pushed the play button. Static came from the stereo speakers and then, "*... got a job for you. Oughta see her, man, tiny. Short, dark brown hair, olive skin, little wire glasses. Money, too.*" Rush knew immediately that the voice was a black male's.

"*She's got money, huh*?" A white male asked.

"*Brotha, she gotta be loaded. Boss-man tell me she payin' cash money for her remodel. Eighteen large. That's some serious bread, man.*"

"*She's home all the time*?"

"*Yep. Got some computer business she runnin' out her house. Wicked bitch, tell you that. Don't trust nobody. Looking at us all the time. Watchin'. Won't let us in the house at all. Don't matter how cold, neither.*"

The white male paused and static filled the room again. "*What kind of stuff does she have*?" he asked finally.

"*Buncha computers. Could bring cash. Ain't never been wrong, have I*?"

Static again, but no voice for a moment. Finally, "*Never have. Any guns in there*?"

"*How I know that? Ain't never been in. Seen her computers through a window. Easy pickins'.*"

"*Plano, you say?*"

"*Sixteenth Street.*"

An even longer silence. "*I'm busy right now. Can't get to her for a few weeks. Do it yourself if you want.*"

The black man laughed. "*Man, I on the construction crew. Whatcha think I callin' you fo? First place cops'll look is the construction crew. My record, they lock me up by sundown.*"

"*I'm pretty busy with Christmas.*"

"*Come on, I needin' me some Christmas cash my own self. Work's bad with this cold weather. Simple break-in, how long would that take*?"

The white voice paused again. "*Sorry. Can't get...*"

The voices cut off.

Rush looked at Nanci. "That it?"

She nodded. "It's me they're talking about. My house." Her face was still hard, her eyes boring into his.

Turning away, he rewound the tape and listened again. Then, a third time.

Nanci remained silent. When he turned back to her, her arms were folded across her chest, but the hard look was gone. He took the tape out. "Can I keep this?"

"Does that mean you're working my case?"

"It means your case will be put in front of all the others. If not me, then somebody just as concerned. And I am concerned, Nanci."

He stepped toward her and reached for the doorknob. "I want you to look at something."

He opened the door and pointed to his desk across the room. "See that desk over there, the one with the Dallas Cowboys calendar behind the chair? Go have a seat and I'll be there in a minute."

Slowly, she grabbed her purse and coat and walked out of the office. He closed the door behind her, now alone in the Hanisch's lair. He unplugged the mini stereo and set it on the floor behind the door. He turned Hanisch's clock upside down, turned off the ringer on his phone, put the trash can on his chair, opened all of his file cabinet drawers, and unplugged his computer, hiding the keyboard between the desk and wall.

At his desk Nanci had recovered some, down to sniffing every few seconds. "Would you follow me?" he asked.

He grabbed the videotape Willard Jackson had given him and led her to the CID equipment room, popped it into a VCR. "Take a look and tell me if you recognize the woman."

The tape played for almost a minute before Leigh drove up. Nanci leaned in and put her face to within six inches of the screen.

The tape played on. When Leigh jumped from the car, Nanci's eyes widened. As soon as Leigh started climbing into Jackson's Explorer, the video zoomed in. When Leigh glanced up, toward the surveillance van, Rush pressed the pause button.

"That's her!" Nanci said. "Her hair is shorter now, but that's her! My God… how did you… who? Is she a criminal? Is she dangerous? Was I…"

A theft suspect, Rush told her. Low-level street criminal. A nobody.

Before she could ask anything else, he led her back to his desk. He picked up the phone and beeped Chinbroski.

Waiting for his call back, he told Nanci what he wanted to do. "We'll do some surveillance at your place. Around the clock. We'll find out which construction worker is on that tape. I'll get the state police to wire your phone, run a tap, record all of your incoming calls."

She nodded at these things, dazed, Rush thought, at his sudden change of attitude. Dazed, but not stupid. Her eyes seemed to clear and then her face turned hard again. "All of this for a thief? A nobody?"

"We're not trying to catch *her*. We're trying to catch … maybe someone she knows. I'm hoping she can lead us to him."

That seemed to satisfy her.

His phone rang. Chinbroski. Rush told him to meet him in the north parking lot in ten minutes.

Replacing the receiver, "Go home," he told Nanci. "My partner and I will be out to your house in a few minutes. I wanna look around, scope out a surveillance spot, get a feel for everything."

She grabbed her coat and purse and stood. "Okay." She stuck out her hand. "Thank you."

"Don't mention it."

He walked her out of CID, passed Hanisch's office. Hanisch was rounding the corner heading that way. Rush smiled as he passed. Hanisch ignored him. A few seconds later Rush heard him curse.

Life was good.

EIGHT

Leigh's listening post was also her watching post, a sturdily built, rugged deer stand enclosed on all four sides. It had a rusty tin roof, doubled-layered particle board walls separated by two-by-fours, and a thick plywood floor solid enough to hold several two-hundred pound men. Each of the walls, with twelve-inch squares cut into the center, allowed Leigh concealed visibility. Twenty feet off the ground, the five-by-five wooden box sat squarely in the center of a century old oak three-hundred yards from Enoch's hideout, a small, rough-looking house far enough away for her to watch without worrying about being seen.

The house – a wooden framed rat hole that appeared abandoned – and the seventy acres surrounding it, belonged to a retired trapper named Gilbert McGraw, according to the tax roll search Leigh had conducted after following Enoch here a week ago. She hadn't seen any evidence of the old man, who, according to records, had never married.

Probably dead. That was Enoch: find a remote location and kill his way into the house.

Then again, maybe he'd found it abandoned. She didn't care. She knew only that Enoch was here now. The police could worry about Gilbert McGraw later.

Bundled up like an Eskimo, fighting to stay awake, she thought about tonight's mission; entering the house to wire up the cameras and microphones. She'd made one trip to tap the phone, but she'd done that from outside. She'd rigged a wireless transmitter into the phone tap, and hidden that transmitter underneath a pile of firewood sitting against an outside wall. She could receive and record all calls up to a distance of a half-mile, well within the distance to the deer stand.

She had transformed the deer stand into her electronic control center. Audio receivers, laptop computer, VCR, TV monitors, scanners, tape recorders, she had everything she needed to monitor Enoch's phone tap and cell phone calls, watch his movements inside the house once the cameras were installed, and record it all. With the hole in the floor as the only access into the stand, the equipment covered nearly every inch of wall space.

She powered the center with inverted AC from two deep-cell marine batteries she rotated daily because of the power-zapping cold weather. A third battery was dedicated to powering the ten electric blankets keeping the equipment from freezing. Hauling the equipment in under the cover of darkness had only been possible wearing the night vision goggles she'd gotten from the stolen surveillance van. Enoch had taught her well. Too well for his own good.

The van from B&A Enterprises had provided her with most of the equipment; although two of the cameras she'd be installing in the house came from the open dock of a trucking company foolish enough to leave their business unguarded on the weekend midnight shift.

She had the cameras ready to go. Packed in a case with her installation tools, pinhole lenses, mounting brackets, video transmitter and power cords configured to tap into existing electrical lines, the installation would be quick. The only problem might be finding adequate attic space in which to maneuver around. The pitch of the house's roof appeared steep enough to give her the room, but she wouldn't know until she got in.

It was noon by the time she pulled the plywood over the hole in the floor, settled into her canvas lawn chair, and aimed her binoculars toward the house. Enoch's Land Cruiser was parked beneath a large cedar tree at the end of the front porch. And in the three hours since her arrival, he hadn't used a phone, either landline or cell, and hadn't set foot outside.

Leigh didn't especially expect him to move tonight, but she wouldn't be surprised if he did. She couldn't push his conversation with the black construction worker from her mind. Nanci Brookfield was an easy target, one Enoch would be hard pressed to blow off without a cursory inspection. She only hoped that she hadn't waited too long before paying Brookfield a visit. She'd debated with herself a full 48 hours before finally finding the house on Sixteenth Street, and approaching the woman.

It'd been a risk warning her, for the same reason she hadn't been able to call the police while Enoch was in Jane's house. She couldn't allow him to be caught yet. Maybe in a few days, after the cameras were in place and his house was wired for sound. Certainly as soon as she had the information she needed. As for Brookfield, if she went to the cops, and the cops took her seriously, decided to watch her house, and if Enoch decided to make a move...

Leigh shook her head, pushed the thought of his being caught from her mind. As big of a risk as she'd taken contacting Brookfield, in the end she just couldn't allow another woman to come eye to eye with that monster.

The rest of the afternoon passed slowly. An hour before sundown, just as the shadows began hiding details of the house, Leigh noticed movement near the front porch. She raised her binoculars in time to see Enoch open the driver's door of his car and climb in. A few seconds later she heard the distant roar of an engine and saw the tail lights come on.

Leigh felt her binoculars quivering. She set them down and closed her fists tightly. Then she blew out a nervous breath and steeled herself. This was it. This was what the last ten months were all about. Of all the other things she'd done to this point, none measured up to what faced her now, stepping inside the lair of the person she hated most on this planet.

* * *

So they had a Leigh-sighting trifecta, Rush thought as he stood just inside the north door of the police station, waiting for Chinbroski to arrive. And from what he'd just heard, Leigh was a woman with a conscience, not the murderous tag-a-long he'd first suspected, assuming she was involved at all. He couldn't shake the feeling he was being led down a path to nowhere. That his killer was someone totally unrelated to what he'd been given by Willard Jackson and now, by Nanci Brookfield. If that were true, he was wasting time, hours he'd never be able to have back.

When he looked at Nanci Brookfield, when he had watched her transformation from fear to anger, and recognized the memory of her attack lurking just behind her eyes, he couldn't help but see Mallory. Brookfield's mention of her seeing a doctor for a year was no doubt to battle Post Traumatic Stress Syndrome. And though he was certain that Brookfield's rape wasn't nearly as life threatening as the incredibly brutal beating that had left Mallory within an inch of her life, he didn't discount the resulting mental damage she would have suffered.

This morning, just before he had left the house, he checked the entry hall floor and looked for the stain that Mallory insisted still marred her beautiful tile. If she hadn't been complaining about it up until the point she nodded off to sleep, he might not have taken the time for such a close inspection. But she had. At one point she'd been near tears in frustration as she explored the possibilities of conquering the stain. So before leaving the house, Rush flooded the entry hall with as much light as possible, squatted, and searched every inch. The floor was perfect. Clean enough for a surgical procedure. It was time for a phone call to her doctor.

To the north, across the parking lot, Rush saw Chinbroski's car skidding sideways, almost on two wheels as it whipped into the lot. Rush stepped outside and waved, the frigid wind biting him.

After Chinbroski screeched to a stop, Rush climbed in. "When I said hurry, Chin, I didn't mean run people off the road."

"Hey, for all I knew you was buying dinner. You ain't buying dinner?" Chinbroski punched the car forward and turned west on Fifteenth Street. "What's up? Where we going?"

"The other direction," Rush said, jerking a thumb over his shoulder. "If you'd stopped to breathe, I could've told you before you pulled out."

"That ain't a problem." Chinbroski ripped a U-turn in front of an oncoming pickup, slamming Rush's head against the passenger's door window. He looked over and grinned as Rush righted himself in his seat. "This the right way?"

"One of these days, Chin. One of these days." But looking over at his partner, at his massive chest, his ham-sized forearms, Rush knew that day would never come.

Chinbroski laughed. "So what's the deal? Dragging me away from the first good dinner I had in two days. Oughta charge you. Six bucks down the drain."

"Six bucks?"

"Yeah. Pisses me off."

"What's your idea of a good dinner for six bucks?"

"That new roast-beef smoky-cheddar thing from Arby's," Chinbroski said. "Big order of fries and a beer."

"Arby's sells beer?"

"Seven-Eleven sells the beer, wise ass. Where we headed?"

"Address on Sixteenth." Rush gave him the house number. "You're drinking a beer in the middle of your workday? Hanisch know?"

Chinbroski's face flashed red. "It's almost six o'clock, Rush. My workday's over. Besides, dumped it out as soon as I thought about what I was doing. Didn't even get a sip."

"Oh. I see."

"Thought you might. You still ain't told me what's up."

Rush spent the next several minutes updating him about everything he'd learned last night and so far that day. The other murder with an earless victim

Zeke had discovered in California, the Boontling, the strange visit he'd had with Willard Jackson and his group, the videotape, the theft of B&A's electronic equipment, and finally the strange story Nanci Brookfield had told and the audiotape she'd played for him.

Chinbroski listened with rapt attention. "You found out all this out since last night?"

"The Boontling was last night, the rest was this morning and afternoon. But I've got this feeling I'm going the wrong way. That I'm letting myself be pulled away from what I should be doing. Know what I mean? Going down the wrong road?"

Chinbroski snorted. "What road's that? Ain't like we got a hell of a whole lot. Just so you'll know what all I got since I seen you last, let me fill you in.

"Nobody else saw the woman in the old car. Rhonda Neibrook didn't add anything new. Bill McElroy is solid - his alibi - I mean. And he couldn't give me anything that might lead to somebody with a grudge against the family. McBride didn't find nothing on the note, so there ain't a print to be found." He threw up his hands and then grabbed the wheel when the car drifted into the oncoming lane. "So the road we're on ain't got a name."

Rush shrugged. "I just can't get out of my mind how astronomical the odds are that this thing would fall into place like it has. Three people see a woman, all of a sudden, and this woman might be able to lead us to the killer?" He shook his head. "If it were a movie, nobody'd believe it."

Chinbroski pulled to a stop down the street from Nanci Brookfield's house, threw the car into park. "It don't sound so strange to me," he said. "The first sighting of the mystery woman was a fluke, right? Total luck. Who could've known the realtor would drive by that late on a Friday night? The second sighting happened two weeks before the killing. Only reason Jackson called you at all was the killing, after it pricked his brain about what she said about him hunting in Plano. Then this third thing, this Brookfield woman, I don't know, maybe that one does stretch things. But it ain't that big a deal. Gives us a chance, I know that."

"Actually," Rush said, "the first contact, the one with Jackson, gives us the best chance."

"Why's that?"

"The tracking system. If Leigh found her ex's car, found his house, then somehow got that transmitter on his car, we'll find him in a couple days."

"That's pretty bold, Rush. If she put that transmitter on two weeks ago, what makes you think the battery ain't dead?"

Rush shook his head. "If she's that desperate, that brave, has enough balls to install a transmitter, don't you think she'd hard wire it? Like direct to the car battery?"

Chinbroski shrugged.

"And if she did, we got him."

"How?"

"From the air. Airplane or helicopter. Tracking units only transmit on a few frequencies. I forgot to ask Jackson about what freek his unit transmits on, but I'll correct that problem soon enough."

They sat in silence for several moments, the windows of the car slowly fogging. "So, you ready?" Chinbroski asked.

Rush gazed out the window before finally turning to his partner. "Do you remember where they found Mallory?"

"What? When?" Chinbroski turned full in his seat and faced Rush. "You mean when she came back from the dead?"

She hadn't officially died, Rush knew, but Chinbroski had always taken the emergency doctor literally. "Right. You remember where the attack occurred?"

"Who could forget? Why?"

"Something's happening with her. She spent over an hour last night trying to scrub a stain off the floor. But there's no stain there, Chin."

Chinbroski stared at him, his face scrunched in concentration. "Just inside the front door?" he asked finally.

Rush nodded.

"Oh, man." Chinbroski turned and looked out the window, tapped the steering wheel with his thumbs. "Eight weeks?" he asked, turning back to Rush.

Until the anniversary of her beating, he meant. "Six," Rush said. "It's not like she's delusional all the time. It just comes in little spurts. Know what I mean?"

"Yeah. So you're wondering when to call the doc."

"Or if."

"I'd call. She didn't almost die in your house, Rush. If she's seeing blood stains someplace else because of what happened to her ... I ain't no doctor, but ... "

"I know. You're right." Rush married Mallory knowing the possibility existed that something like this could happen. He just didn't think it would. "Okay. You ready to do this?"

Chinbroski dropped the car into gear. "Sure." He pulled away from the curb, drove down the block, and stopped in front of a small classical Victorian located in Plano's five-block historical district. Mature trees, narrow streets, large front yards. Most of the houses had been restored. And the ones that hadn't dotted the neighborhood like pimples on a teenage girl's milky skin.

Located two streets from the First Baptist Church, Nanci's backyard was enclosed with a new six-foot wooden privacy fence. A new garage, facing the street, was half finished and looked odd next to the small but immaculate Victorian. The old garage was in piles in the front yard. The cold front, almost a week old now, appeared to have severely suspended her remodeling project.

Stepping around the pallets of shingles and other construction materials stacked in the driveway, Rush led Chinbroski to the front door. He couldn't feel his numb fist as he slapped it against the hard wooden door. He saw a curtain move in one of the windows and a few seconds later Nanci Brookfield swung the door open and motioned them inside.

Rush stepped in with Chinbroski on his heels. The entry hall had bright yellow floral paper from floor to ceiling. A doorway to the right opened into a formal area, a door to the left to a small study. Straight ahead was a swinging door, propped open, leading to the kitchen.

Chinbroski introduced himself to Nanci before Rush had a chance. Something in his partner's voice caused Rush to do a double take. He sounded sweet, gentle. Chinbroski had taken his stocking cap off and shoved it under his left armpit; he'd ripped the glove off his right hand, and actually did a little bow while he allowed the introductory handshake to linger longer than necessary. Then he zipped his coat all the way to his chin, glanced at his shoes, ran a hand over his polyester pants. He stepped behind Rush as though hiding from her.

Nanci turned from Chinbroski to Rush. "So, would you care to come in?" She pointed to the right. "Excuse the mess outside. I'm hoping the house will be finished in another month. It would sure help if the cold would break."

Chinbroski stepped around Rush and followed her into the formal living room. He'd taken his other glove off, but kept his coat zipped tight and it strained to contain his massive chest, arms, and back. His neck, if one could call it that, disappeared into his shoulders, seemingly just under his hairline. Even with thighs as large as tree trunks he moved with a certain cat-like grace. He followed Nanci with quiet intensity, studying her, watching.

Nanci sat in a formal antique loveseat and gestured both detectives to sit opposite her on a sofa. Chinbroski sat without taking his eyes off her. Rush could hardly take his eyes off Chinbroski.

Finally, Rush was about to speak when his partner cut him off. "Ms. Brookfield. Detective Rush here told me a little about what's been going on with you. About the visit from that strange woman." He paused, cleared his throat, and looked at his hands. "He also told me some about what happened in Kansas City last year." Chinbroski's face flashed red and he wiped his brow. "Now, I'm gonna tell you one thing, Ms. Brookfield, that ain't gonna happen here. No, sir! Not in Plano. I want you to rest easy on that point.

"Even if I have to pull my car into your driveway and live out of it. I'm saying right here and right now that you ain't got nothing to worry about." He pounded his finger against his leg for emphasis.

It was all Rush could do not to laugh out loud.

"Well, thank you," she said. "That makes me feel ... well, it makes me feel good. Thank you." Nanci crossed her legs and folded her hands on top of her knees.

When the silence reached a ridiculous point, Rush decided to drag them back to reality. "Listen, Nanci, we need to take a look around, check out how secure your house is. While we're doing that, why don't you get the information about the construction firm you hired for the remodel? We'll need it." Rush looked at his partner.

Chinbroski jumped up and looked at Rush. "How about this, I'll stay with Nanci here, while you look the house over. I'll work on getting a good description on all of the guys on the construction crew."

Looking from his partner to Nanci, Rush nodded and stood. He started in the room across the entry hall, Nanci's office. Beaded oak, flowered wallpaper, matching border paper trimmed with oak crown molding. In one corner two desks were positioned in an L shape, with more computer equipment than Rush had ever seen in one place, an answering machine, and a cordless phone.

The windows in the room were protected two ways: magnetic contact and glass break tape. Looking up, Rush noticed a glass break sensor as well as a motion detector. Knowing what Nanci had gone through in Kansas City, knowing the state of mind she'd been in only an hour ago, Rush slid into her desk chair and ran his fingers under the bottom of the desk. There, on the right, was the small button he fully expected to find. He climbed out of the chair and dropped on his hands and knees, looking up under the desk. A small wire ran from the button straight to the back of the desk, down to the floor, disappearing under the carpet. Panic alarm.

Looking out the window just to the left of the desk, he could see the construction project, the building of the garage that the black man on the tape said cost eighteen thousand dollars. Rush could see how the construction worker could scan Nanci's office and think the lady was loaded.

Moving on, he stepped back into the entry and turned left into the kitchen. Spotless. Modern appliances, wood floor, ceramic tile countertops, pots and pans dangling from the ceiling over an island sink. A door led to the back yard. Rush noticed the alarm contact, the motion detector, the glass break sensor, the control pad just to the right of the door. Searching the room carefully, he looked for the panic button. It wasn't until he stood at the sink that he saw it hiding just under the electrical switch that turned on the garbage disposal.

The woman was obsessed.

From the kitchen, Rush moved into a hallway that led to the back of the house. He passed a bathroom on the left, a bedroom filled with boxes on the right, another bedroom on the right with exercise equipment. He was about to pass the exercise room when he noted the door. Standing half open, it looked heavy, solid.

Into the master bedroom. Decorated in early American, the room was full of antiques, had a queen-sized, canopy bed, and an oak-framed, full-length mirror. Another solid door protected the room from the rest of the house. He saw another alarm control pad, and found another panic button, motion detector, and glass break sensor. The phone sat on the nightstand to the left of the bed. One of the speed dial buttons had 9-1-1 programmed. Another had his office number written next to it. Rush thought about that. Nanci had been home from the police station for no more than thirty minutes before he and Chinbroski had arrived. So she must have gone straight to the phone and programmed it as soon as she hit the door. More evidence of her mental state.

He'd seen enough to be satisfied that she could alert the police of an intruder from anywhere in the house. That wasn't a problem. The question was where could she hide while she awaited the cops?

She needed a safe room. She also needed a back-up cellular call-in transmitter for her alarm system in case someone cut her phone line. Walking back toward the living room, he thought of the best place for the safe room, a room with a door you couldn't breech, walls you couldn't penetrate, and a ceiling you couldn't kick your way into from the attic. A room from which you could make a telephone call, one where you could spend a great deal of time if necessary. One centrally located, with no windows.

The hall bathroom fit the bill.

Rush walked into the den and found Chinbroski sitting next to Nanci on the loveseat. She had a notepad on her lap, but wasn't doing any writing. They were laughing about something Chinbroski was telling her. Rush caught the tale end of the story and recognized it as the time Chinbroski, playing the part of a homosexual, had been grabbed and fondled in Bob Woodruff Park on the east side of Plano. He'd allowed the unsuspecting queer to work himself up to a lather before slamming him to the ground, breaking his nose.

They both looked up when Rush stepped into the room.

"Can I show you something," Rush said to Nanci.

Both of them stood too fast, as if children caught necking behind the school building. The notebook slid off Nanci's lap and both of them scrambled to pick it up. When one of Chinbroski's arms bumped against Nanci's shoulder, he practically dived at her to keep her from falling into a lamp. After uprighting her, he held her a moment longer than necessary. She didn't seem to mind.

Rush left the room and glanced back to confirm they were following. Stopping outside the hall bath, Rush turned to Nanci. "Your house looks great. Solid doors, good alarm system, panic buttons all over the place. And from what you told me earlier, you have a gun somewhere. The only thing that concerns me is where you would go if an intruder made it through all of your perimeter defenses. You need a room that's safe, almost impossible to penetrate. One from which you can call the police and sit tight without worrying." He pointed to the bathroom. "This is the best place. No windows, small, easy to secure, water."

Nanci looked puzzled.

"Get a solid door, a dead bolt, a strike plate with five-inch screws. Put plywood under the sheetrock. Seal the area in the attic above the bathroom with more plywood. Since the house sits on a concrete slab you won't have to do anything to the floor. Oh, and a phone."

She stared at the bathroom, then nodded, seemed to tense as her brow wrinkled in thought. "So does this mean I'm in more danger than I first thought?"

"No," Chinbroski jumped in. "He doesn't mean that. Every house should have a place like the one Greg just described. Especially pretty, single women." He grinned sheepishly. "I can say one thing." He turned to Rush. "I don't want that construction crew in here doing the work. Huh?"

Rush nodded.

"How about me?" Chinbroski asked Nanci. "I'm gonna be busy with this murder investigation, and I ain't no professional or nothing, but I can drive a nail. If you can paint and wallpaper, we can do a great job. I don't wanna be forward or nothing. I'm just thinking about your safety, and all. You know, until we get this mess all straightened out."

Rush felt like the third person on a high school date. When Nanci nodded, a little sound escaped Chinbroski that reminded Rush of a rag getting sucked down a vacuum hose.

"Well, now that that's settled," Rush said. "I want to tell you about a change to your alarm system." He told her about cellular calling backup. "And I want you to have the alarm company put a panic button in the bathroom. That way you won't have to have a phone in here. Unless you want one, of course."

He paused. "Well, that's about it." Rush stepped past the couple and walked back into the den. They followed.

"We'll be doing some surveillance on your place starting tonight," Rush said. "At least for a few days. We'll find the construction worker who made the telephone call and talk to him. I want you to start a log and write down exactly what's said if the guy calls back. If you can record it, great. In fact, Chinbroski will swing by here tomorrow and drop a recorder off. Maybe set it up if you ask real nice." Rush winked at his partner. "It's a system that will record as soon as you lift the receiver. You'll have to remember to pause it if you want to make a call to someone." Rush slapped his hands together. "Chin, is that all? Did I forget anything?"

"Uh, nope, I don't think so. Do you have any questions, Nanci?"

"I can't think of any."

Rush headed for the door. Chinbroski was hanging back. "Hey, partner," Rush said. "See you in the car. Toss me the keys."

Pulling his coat on, Rush stepped to the door and stopped. "Oh, Nanci, I forgot. Stay off the portable phone. Don't use it at all."

She was about to protest when Rush held up a hand. "Chin, will you explain how someone could scan her calls?"

Rush stepped through the door and into the frigid night air. Lights shone from every house except an abandoned house across the street, two doors down. Shivering, he turned and headed toward the car. As he hurried along he thought about what a nice surveillance spot the old house would be. Maybe they'd use that instead of sitting in their car.

After cranking the engine, he pulled directly in front of Nanci's house to wait on Chinbroski. He punched a button on the AM radio and found a sports talk station. It was football season and the Cowboys were still stuck in the basement of their division.

Rush leaned his head back as the heater fought its battle against the bitter cold. Through the darkness and shadows he could tell that the bushes at the abandoned house were badly overgrown, the grass in the front yard was long and scraggly.

He glanced at Nanci's front door. No Chinbroski.

Was the guy proposing?

The dark house *would* be the perfect place to do their surveillance, but with no heat it'd be a torture assignment.

Nanci Brookfeild's front door opened. They were laughing and carrying on as if they'd been friends for years. Rush cracked his window a half-inch to try and catch a few words. No luck.

Finally, Chinbroski pulled himself away and jogged down the sidewalk. When he rounded the front of the car, Rush caught another glimpse of the old place across the street. By the time Chinbroski jerked open the passenger's door, Rush couldn't take his eyes off the red glow of a cigarette staring out one of the darkened windows.

NINE

It wasn't static that filled Leigh's headphones as she gently pried open the back door to Enoch's cabin. It was the sound of the frigid wind blowing out of the north and into the phone lying in the weeds near the edge of Enoch's driveway a quarter-mile away. Her early warning system. The phone on her hip, and the headphones, would allow her to hear the crunch of tires on gravel, the rumble of a car engine, if Enoch returned before she finished the camera installation.

Leigh stepped into a small, enclosed porch not much bigger than a closet. A couple of old brooms leaned in the corner, next to three overflowing trashcans. Spider webs hung in all four corners and dead roaches showed their bellies among stacks of yellowed newspaper.

She closed the door quietly, then pocketed her lock picks. With a Polaroid camera hanging around her neck, she'd be snapping pictures before moving anything to insure she put everything back correctly. Although Enoch wasn't a neat freak, he was just paranoid enough to notice even small items out of place.

In the ten months she'd been hunting him, she'd used unscented soap, shampoo, and laundry detergent. Perfume was a thing of the past, as was mouthwash, chewing gum, or anything else that might leave her scent hanging in the air.

Enoch's scent was everywhere, and it nearly stopped her when she stepped into the enclosed porch.

Another door led into the house. Unlocked. Carrying her case of equipment, Leigh eased the door open and stepped through to the kitchen. Knotty pine everywhere: the floor, the walls, the ceiling, the table. The kitchen counter, varnished pine, wore decades' worth of nicks and cuts.

Rugged, wood-hewn furniture filled the living room. Rusted farm implements adorned the walls; dusty, heavy curtains partially covered dirty windows.

Down a short hallway on the opposite side of the den she discovered Enoch's high-tech room: computers, VCRs, several cell phones, scanners, cameras and camcorders, and a stack of credit cards two inches thick. The room had been stripped of furniture and then outfitted with metal shelving and a rugged wooden desk.

Pulling out her camera, she snapped several shots, including close-ups of some of the names on the credit cards. She powered up the four cellular phones, punched a few of the buttons, and copied down all of the phone numbers.

She stared at the computer for several moments and considered looking around inside, but knew she was out of her league. Enoch would notice immediately if she didn't leave it exactly as she found it. She turned off the phones, restacked the credit cards, and left the room.

A quick search through the rest of the cabin produced nothing of interest. Other than the high tech equipment, she didn't see anything new, anything modern. But compared to what Enoch grew up in, this was paradise.

In the short hallway outside the equipment room hung a thin rope attached to foldaway attic stairs. The springs popped as she pulled the stairs down.

Swiping at the building sweat on her forehead, she pulled a small flashlight from her back pocket, and started up. At the edge of the darkness, just out of the range of her beam, she saw the board with the blue felt. She refused to look. Didn't have to look to know what monstrosities hung displayed. A flash of Jane McElroy's missing ear caused bile to rise in her throat. She swallowed hard and turned the flashlight to inspect the rest of the attic.

There would be enough room to work, and plenty of places to hide the video transmitter. Now she just needed to decide which rooms to do. She had four cameras, but wanted one for outside, in front.

She clicked off the light and climbed down into the hall. Time to get to work. She didn't know what Enoch was up to or how long he'd be gone. She only knew that she couldn't get trapped inside this house. She'd go mad if she were forced to live in the attic for a day while Satan wandered around just below her.

* * *

Rush sat as still as road kill waiting for Chinbroski to stuff his wide body into the passenger's seat. The red glow had disappeared under the bottom frame of the window by the time his partner slammed the door. Rush didn't dare take his eyes from the spot for fear he'd lose its location.

Chinbroski was rubbing his hands together for warmth and cursing about the cold. He must have finally sensed that something was wrong. He started to speak, then choked off the words, slowly following Rush's stare into the blackness of the night.

When a full minute passed without the red glow returning, Rush started doubting himself. Slowly, he dropped the car into gear and pulled away from the curb.

"The old house across the street," he told Chinbroski. "I think I saw a cigarette glow in the far right window. Only there a second. Don't look when we pass. Don't want to spook the guy. If there's a guy. We'll circle around."

As they passed the house, Rush caught the corner of the window in a sideways glance. Nothing.

"You sure it wasn't a reflection or something?"

Rush stopped at the end of the street. Hung a left. "It was there. I saw the red first, then it glowed like somebody took a drag."

Left again. East on Fifteenth Street. He slowed the car, searched each side of the street. "Whoever's in there wouldn't have parked too close. We'll check north next."

Chinbroski picked up the police radio microphone. Rush grabbed his arm. "Don't call it in."

"Why?"

"Remember what we have. If this is the guy, Leigh said he's a Listener. He may be scanning. I want him to think we've left."

Chinbroski replaced the mike and pulled the cell phone from his coat pocket. Rush took it from him and slipped it between his own legs. "Think, man. McElroy had her cell phone duct taped to the side of her head. The only option is to use a landline."

"Damn it," Chinbroski snapped.

"Okay. We cruise to Williams High School. There's a pay phone outside the cafeteria. You call it in. Get dispatch to send some squads, dispatch the call over the MDT'S. Have them come in blacked out. All of them park around the corner, three on one end of the street, three on the other. Go in on foot."

"And wake up every damn dog in East Plano," Chinbroski said. "Dude'll be gone in a flash."

Rush hadn't considered that. They were on Ave. R now. He hung a left on Seventeenth Street. "How about a diversion?"

Chinbroski looked at him through the darkness and said nothing.

"I'm thinking we call Nanci, tell her we're sneaking in her back door.

Then we send her out, away from the house. Then…"

"Whoa, Rush. Whoa right there. Ain't sending her out by herself. She goes out, I go with her." Chinbroski's voice was hard, unforgiving. There'd be no arguing the point.

"Okay, fine. You go with her. Lay down in her back seat. She'll cut all the lights in her house. I'll stay at a window, see if I can catch the glow again."

They cruised west on Seventeenth and stopped at Ave. P. "Once I'm in the house, I'll have a landline. I can direct the troops in slowly, one at a time. We'll get a team staged close enough to rush the house. What do you think?"

Chinbroski was silent, mulling over it. "Sounds like a plan," he said finally.

Rush whipped a right, raced into the Williams High School parking lot, and pulled up at the pay phone. Chinbroski climbed from the car. "Call Nanci first, then dispatch?"

"Just Nanci," Rush said. "We'll do dispatch from her house."

Not even a minute later Chinbroski climbed back into the car. Rush took off before he'd closed his door. "She's scared," Chinbroski said. "But glad we're coming."

"Glad you're coming, you mean."

They parked at a glass company on Fourteenth Street, a few blocks south of Nanci's house, and approached from the rear. Nanci was waiting for them at the door. Her hands trembled as she closed and locked the door behind them. She seemed to gravitate toward Chinbroski's large frame, almost wife-like, Rush thought. Chinbroski told her the plan.

"But how can you get in my car?" she asked. "It's parked at the end of my driveway by the street."

Rush slapped his own forehead. "I'm losing it. I forgot about your old garage being all over your front yard." He turned to Chinbroski. "You go out the back, head to our car. Nanci, you leave out the front, drive over to the glass place on Fourteenth at Ave. P. Chin will be waiting."

"Hold it, Rush. I gotta see that she gets in her car all right. After she drives off, I'll slip out the back." His 'no questions asked' tone again.

"Fine. Nanci, grab your coat. Bundle up tight. Cut the lights, and head out. And do not, I repeat, *do not* look at the abandoned house across the street. You've gotta be cool. This may be our only chance."

She nodded and looked at Chinbroski, who put a hand on her shoulder. "We'll be just inside the house here," he said gently. "Twenty yards. He's two doors down and across the street. A lot farther than us. He'd never make it to you. Okay?"

She nodded again, and then turned away, heading out of the kitchen.

Rush looked at Chinbroski. "She'll be fine."

The big man stuffed his hands in his pockets and didn't answer.

Rush called dispatch and briefly told the dispatcher on duty what was going on, how many officers he needed. He told her to have a supervisor call him back. Gave her Nanci's number.

A couple minutes later, Nanci was back in the kitchen dressed warmly enough to battle a blizzard. Her right coat pocket bulged unnaturally. When she caught Rush staring, she wasted little time confirming his suspicions. "My gun. And I'll use it."

Rush shrugged. "Just don't miss." He turned to his partner. "Chin, you ready?"

"Let's do it."

Nanci started turning off house lights. Just before she exited the front door, Rush took up a position at the corner of one of the windows in the den.

Chinbroski stood behind the front door. "You be careful, Nanci," he said. "I'll see you in a minute. Just wait for me."

She nodded and went out, locking the door behind her.

Rush focused on the front corner window of the abandoned house across the street.

"We need some night vision, Rush," Chinbroski said, as he peeked out one of the small windows in the front door. "Can't see anything."

Rush stared at the dark house. No red glow. Nanci's car started, lights came on. Once she was moving, Rush immediately felt better. "Take off, Chin. Go to the station with her. Sit at your desk until I call."

"Got it." Chinbroski started toward the back door but stopped suddenly. "Hey, Rush, you've got our phone. Give it to me just in case."

After handing it over and hearing the back door click shut, Rush relaxed even more. The house was warm, comfortable. Whoever was across the street couldn't say that. *If* someone was across the street.

The minutes dragged and his muscles slowly stiffened. He had to stand to keep himself from becoming cemented in one position. He should exercise more. Cupping his hand over the face of his watch, he hit the small light to check the time. Chinbroski had been gone for only six minutes. Seemed like thirty. Dispatch still hadn't called.

How long since he'd seen the glow? Fifteen minutes? Twenty? If the guy was a smoker, how often would he need one? No way to know. Maybe he'd smoked several already. Maybe he'd left already. Maybe there'd been no cigarette glow.

He suddenly felt stupid.

And then he saw another glow. Different window. Rush sucked in a breath and watched. The glow brightened, then dimmed. Then it moved from the center of the window down and over about eighteen inches, as if the smoker was resting his hand on the windowsill. The window was partially obscured by overgrown bushes so he didn't have a perfect view. But when the glow went back to the center of the window and brightened again, the view was good enough.

Nanci's house was so silent Rush could hear his own choppy breathing. He could hear the leather in his shoes squeaking against the wood floor.

And then the phone rang. He jumped and bumped the back of his head against the window when he spun around. Cursing quietly, he stepped back and suddenly realized there wasn't a phone in the room. Nanci's office. He was halfway there when he remembered the phone in the office was a portable.

No good. A Listener.

Racing to the kitchen, he picked up on the fifth ring.

"It's Kramer in dispatch. What do you have and where do you want the guys?"

Noel Kramer was the night shift dispatch supervisor, ex-cop, retired. He'd do things right. "All right," Rush said. "It's cold, but the guys are gonna have to walk. Have three squads park at the First Baptist Church. All three go north on Ave. N. Stage at Ave. N and Sixteenth. Three squads stage along Fifteenth at Ave P. They go north to Sixteenth and wait." Rush paused a moment as he suddenly thought of something new. "Listen, when the patrol guys are in position I want someone to drive Chinbroski's Mustang down Sixteenth in front of the house. They make one pass. That way I'll know everybody's about to move in. Chinbroski is at his desk. Call him and see if he'll donate his car for this. See if he'll drive it, in fact. Tell him to bring his date. We might need her out here for an ID. Got it so far?"

"You want SWAT?"

"Not for this part of it. No time. It's cold and I don't know how long the guy's gonna stay. Listen, I've gotta get back to the window. After the pass is made, I want the men to move in on foot. If dogs start barking I want them to bust ass until they have the house contained. The guys to the west will get there first so those to the east better be on the ball for someone being flushed their way. Got it all?"

"Got it. You want them to make entry or contain it for SWAT?"

"Contain, but don't call SWAT until we know we have him. One other thing, I want both canine cars in the area. We might need them."

"Okay. That it?"

"Squad car computer transmissions only. No radios, no cell phones. Got the address?"

"Ten-four. Call me if something changes."

Rush hung up the phone and scrambled back to the window just in time to see a darkly clad figure walk out of the abandoned house. Black stocking cap, long dark coat covering dark pants, black shoes and gloves, and a cigarette glow in the middle of his face.

Cigarette Man stopped at the end of the sidewalk, looked both ways, and turned right, away from Rush.

So much for well laid plans.

Swearing under his breath, Rush buttoned his coat, pulled on his hat and gloves, made sure his gun was snapped securely in its holster, and wished he had his cellular phone because he didn't have time to call Kramer in dispatch.

He opened the front door and stepped into the bitter cold. Looking left, he could barely make out the figure as it disappeared into the darkness five houses away.

Speed. Rush wished he had more. He pushed out into the yard and picked his way through the piles of construction debris.

Cigarette Man was gone.

Couldn't be far. Rush ran across the street and skirted the front of the houses to stay in the shadows. He saw the shape turn right at the corner of Sixteenth and Ave. N, the exact spot where three uniforms would be gathering in another five or ten minutes. Rush jogged fast enough to close ground but not enough to get seriously winded. He reached the corner of Sixteenth and Ave. N forty-five seconds later.

Cigarette Man was sixty yards north, moving fast, head down, hands shoved deeply into his pockets. Rush kept to the shadows as the wind, ripping out of the north, watered his eyes and affected his ability to track movement. He couldn't believe he'd allowed Chinbroski to drive off with the phone.

With no other choice than to follow at a distance, Rush worked on trying to close the gap without attracting attention. Making ground. Cigarette Man was forty yards ahead when he suddenly stopped. Turned.

Rush jumped behind a row of hedges.

The dark figure stood at the corner of Ave. N and Seventeenth Street scanning the darkness, searching all directions. Rush wiped the back of his gloves across his watery eyes and waited for Cigarette Man to move again.

A set of headlights pierced the darkness from the north. Cigarette Man jumped to the left and flattened himself on the street between the curb and a Ford pickup.

And that cinched it for Rush. This guy was up to no good. It was not yet seven PM and no one would consider it unusual for a man to take an evening walk. Even in this cold and even though the streets were deserted. Rush took the chance to close the gap and snaked his way north along the hedgerow, stopping behind a telephone pole a half block south.

The beam from the headlights sparkled off the frost on the grass, twinkled through the windshields of frozen cars and flickered against the windows of the neighborhood houses. The wind continued to moan. Cigarette Man had flattened himself enough to roll under the truck and was completely hidden in the shadows. Rush, figuring the man would be focused on the approaching car, crawled toward the truck and stopped fifteen yards away, hiding behind an oak tree with a trunk as wide as a phone booth.

The approaching car stopped at the four-way stop one block north and sat there, idling, blinding Rush, who would be lit up like a Christmas tree if he stepped out from behind the tree. The sound of the engine echoed through the deserted streets. Several seconds turned into a full minute. Rush still couldn't see Cigarette Man because the idling car continued to blind him. His plan was to take Cigarette Man as he was crawling out from under the truck after the car passed.

But the car wasn't passing. It just sat there, a block away, under the streetlights of the intersection, exhaust billowing from the tailpipe. Rush turned his full attention to the car. All white, it was a late model Chevrolet, similar to the unmarked cars patrol lieutenants drove. And CID commanders.

Rush felt frozen in place. Flexing his fingers, he squatted, stood, then squatted again to keep blood flowing into his legs. The car at the intersection revved and rocked, exhaust filling the cold night air. There was nothing between Rush and the truck fifteen yards in front of him. He considered approaching it immediately, while the man underneath was distracted. But he didn't trust himself physically. On a warm night he might go for it. But with the cold he didn't know if he'd be able to slap handcuffs on the guy. And what if he resisted? Or ran? He sure wasn't capable of running a foot race. No, the best plan was to wait until he crawled out from under the truck, tackle him then.

But as he slowly slid his frozen handcuffs from his belt, gripping them in his left hand, being careful to position them correctly, Rush saw that plan go awry, too. There was movement under the truck. Cigarette Man was sliding to the right, toward the curb, out from under his hiding place.

Rush tensed and prepared to charge.

TEN

The car in the intersection inched forward toward them, slowly, as though searching. Cigarette Man pushed himself up onto his knees, moved around to the back of the truck. Rush took a step to the right, crouching, still mostly hidden by the tree.

The car approached slowly. One occupant. Male. Smoking a cigarette himself. Cigarette Man moved to the side of the truck, crouched as the white Chevrolet passed. Rush watched him, but glanced at the driver of the car as it passed under the nearest streetlight.

Gerald Hanisch.

Rush cursed under his breath.

Hanisch, his head swiveling and bobbing, was obviously looking for something.

Cigarette Man followed the car with a hard stare until it turned left on Sixteenth, toward Nanci Brookfield's house, and disappeared.

Cigarette Man bolted from behind the truck and ran straight north, glancing back every few steps. Rush had to decide quickly. Chase him or not? To go after him now, in the cold with no back up, no radio, and no cell phone was a lost cause. With Cigarette Man looking back every few seconds he'd know he was being chased. He'd never come back to finish whatever job he had planned at Nanci Brookfield's house. Might even flee the state, leaving Rush with nothing. Not that he had much now.

Rush clenched his jaw as Cigarette Man continued north, cut west through the intersection, and disappeared behind a church on the corner. He cursed under his breath again as he stuffed his handcuffs back into his belt and turned away, heading south. Through the darkness he saw three patrolmen walking north.

"It's over," Rush shouted at them. "Over." He grabbed an officer's portable radio and canceled the operation, told dispatch to have Chinbroski meet him at Nanci's house.

Then he walked back, alone, his face hot with anger.

Hanisch's car was parked in front of Nanci's house. As badly as Rush wanted to look inside the abandoned house, he wanted Hanisch more.

The lieutenant stood at Nanci's front door smoking a cigarette, pounding on the door. "Open up, Rush," he shouted loud enough for the entire neighborhood to hear.

Rush stopped at the curb next to Hanisch's car, breathing through his nose, controlling his rage.

"Hey, it's cold out here," Hanisch shouted as he pounded on the door again.

"Trying to catch pneumonia? Maybe do us all a favor?" Rush asked. He had impressed himself with how completely he had controlled his tone of voice.

Hanisch spun around. "What are you doing out here?" He stepped off the porch. "What's going on out here, Rush? Why you calling out half the patrol division?" His big strides down the sidewalk put him in front of the car in a few seconds. "Who gave you the authority to tie up every unit on the east side?"

Rush waited a beat before speaking, not trusting himself to remain calm. "Trying to make some headway on a case." He'd have to tell his lieutenant everything eventually, but he wouldn't do it tonight standing out in the cold. "Why are you here?"

"I'm a lieutenant, I go where I'm needed."

His words were so slurred from the cold they reminded Rush of the time several years before when he'd seen Hanisch drunk at a police party. Hanisch had drained a Jim Beam bottle and was hitting on another officer's girlfriend. Hanisch woke up the next day with a busted nose, two black eyes, and a fat lip. He'd been too drunk to remember that it was Rush's girlfriend. Too drunk to remember Rush's fists doing the damage.

"Who said you were needed?" Rush asked. "In fact, you're the last thing I needed."

Hanisch took a step forward. "*I* said I was needed. When Chinbroski wouldn't tell me anything, I came out to see for myself."

A sudden gust of wind watered Rush's eyes. "You talk with Kramer in dispatch?"

"That's how I knew you had the entire east side tied up." Hanisch's steamed breath shot out in little spurts.

"What else did he tell you?"

"That's all I needed to hear."

"He tell you about me wanting the officers to stage up around the corner?"

Hanisch shifted slightly, turned away to look at the abandoned house across the street.

"He tell you how we had a guy watching Nanci's house from over there? He tell you that once the officers were in position Chinbroski was gonna drive his Mustang by the house? That we had radio and phone silence?"

Hanisch leaned against the side of his car. "What are you driving at, Rush?"

"Did you even think *not* to drive up the street? That maybe you'd spook the guy in the house over there? That he'd split before we were ready to take him?" Rush locked on to his lieutenant's eyes, and shook his head.

"I wanted to see what was going on. You got a problem with that?"

"I've got a big problem with it." Rush took a step forward. Only a couple of feet separated them. "And what were you doing back at the intersection around the corner?"

A moment of confusion crossed his face. "What are you talking about?"

"Back there at P and Eighteenth. I had the guy within fifteen yards before you showed up."

"I was on the MDT with Kramer. I was told the suspect was in the house."

"If that's what you thought, why'd you drive up and park in front? You screwed everything up. That's the point here."

Hanisch wiped his runny nose with a closed fist.

But Rush wasn't through. "Just because you have a bar on your shoulder doesn't give you the right to stomp all over everything. That's what's wrong with you, Hanisch. You think you own the market on investigative police work, when in fact you can hardly find your way around town unless you're chasing a skirt." Rush stuck a finger in Hanisch's face. "I don't want you in my investigations. I don't want your advice or input. I don't need you hovering around looking over my shoulder. If the guy across the street," Rush jerked a thumb over his shoulder, "hadn't sneaked out before the troops arrived, you'd have screwed things up worse than you already have.

"You know what's scary about that, Hanisch? That you didn't think about any of that. All you wanted was to chew my ass for tying up six patrol units." Rush snorted and shook his head, walking past his lieutenant toward Nanci's house. "You beat everything."

"Don't you walk away from me."

Rush didn't respond. He knew Nanci's front door was unlocked because he hadn't locked it on his way out.

"Come back here, Rush! I'm talking to you!"

A low rumble at the end of the street, then the flicker of headlights, announced the arrival of Chinbroski's Mustang a few seconds later. Nanci Brookfield's car followed closely behind.

Chinbroski skidded to a stop behind Hanisch's Chevrolet and jumped out. He glanced at Hanisch, then took a long look at Rush. Nanci pulled her car into the driveway.

Rush felt frozen in place by the time Nanci climbed from her car and walked to the door. Hanisch turned and climbed into his car. He cranked it and stomped on the gas. The rear tires bit the cold pavement and squealed as the car shot away from the curb.

Rush blew out a breath as he and Chinbroski followed Nanci into the house.

"What happened, Rush?" Chinbroski said once the door closed them inside. "What was he doing out there?"

"Exercising his dictatorial visions. Or trying to." Rush pulled off his gloves and stocking cap.

"Would you like some coffee?" Nanci asked, her face full of questions. "You look like you're about to freeze to death."

"That'd be great," Rush said.

After Nanci brought the coffee and sat down, Rush told them both the story. Afterwards, they all sat looking at one another. Sunk down in her seat, Nanci hugged the arm of the loveseat, her face void of color, her coffee untouched. "So we don't know who the guy was," she said. "Or if he'll come back. Or if he was going to kill me."

"Or if he had anything at all to do with this," Chinbroski said in a soothing tone. He looked over to Rush. "Think it'll do any good to get McBride over to the house tonight? You know, in the dark?"

"I was just thinking about that. I'm tempted to put a patrol guy in front and seal it until morning. As much as I'd like to look around tonight, I'm not sure it'd be the wise thing. I'd hate to step on something that might help us."

"I say seal it," Chinbroski said. "No sense fighting the cold either." He turned to Nanci. "Want me to camp out in the den here? It ain't a problem."

"No. No. That's not necessary. This place is pretty safe." She looked at Rush. "Do you think he knows cops were here?"

Rush was silent for a moment. "He probably does. He had to see us come out. We were driving our CID car. Any criminal can spot those a mile off." He rubbed his eyes. "But that doesn't necessarily mean anything. He can't know about the tape, right? He couldn't know you know anything. So even though we were here, he's gotta be wondering why."

"Which may be enough," Chinbroski said. "Think about this, Nanci. If the guy's wired in, pretty street savvy, if he thinks you're close to the heat, maybe even dating a cop," he paused and blushed. "I ain't meaning nothing by that, by the way. But if he don't know that much about you yet, then hey, he might think you *are* dating a cop. That'd be enough to drive the guy off." He shrugged. "If I'm making sense."

She smiled and looked up at him. "You're making sense." She sighed. "I'm still nervous."

Chinbroski slapped his leg. "I got it! Here's how we'll play it tonight. I'll leave my car outside until tomorrow. I'll call a squad and have them pick up Rush and me a couple blocks over. We'll slip out the back. If the guy's done any surveillance before tonight he already knows you live alone. With my car outside there ain't no way he comes in." He appeared proud of his suggestion. "What do you think?"

"I really hate for you to go to that much trouble."

Chinbroski jumped up. "No trouble. Be right back." He went to the kitchen to make the call.

Nanci sat with folded hands and stared at the floor. After a few beats she said, "He's a good man, isn't he?"

Rush smiled at her. "The best. And I have to say I've never seen him act this way. You've made quite an impression."

Before she could respond, Chinbroski bounded back into the room. "All set. Rush, let's hit the back door. We'll hitch a ride to the station and I'll take a CID car home."

By the time Rush stood, Chinbroski was all bundled up.

"You lock up behind us," Chinbroski told Nanci. "Sleep with that gun. Lock yourself in your bedroom." He grinned at her. "Though really, I don't think the guy will ever come back."

She walked them to the door. "When you come to get your car tomorrow," she asked Chinbroski, "are you going to bring your hammer so we can start on that bathroom?"

His face colored. "I sure can. Have to be the evening, though. I'll call in the morning. Check on you a couple of times tomorrow, then be over after dinner. How about that?"

"How about before dinner?"

"Before dinner, then."

"I have an idea, Chin," Rush said. "You can stop at Arby's and get that smoked cheddar sandwich thing. Buy some beer. Huh?"

"What?" Nanci said.

"Forget it," Chinbroski said. "He's being a wise guy."

Outside, Rush turned to Chinbroski and whistled. "You are one smooth operator. Less than three hours and you're practically moving in."

Chinbroski ignored him.

Rush stopped, looked at his partner. "No mood for jokes? You have it bad."

Chinbroski shuffled his large frame and glanced back toward Nanci's house. "Need a 24-7 on her house, Rush. Maybe someone inside." He cut his eyes and grinned.

"I bet I know who you have in mind."

"I'd grow on her."

"Like a fungus," Rush said. "Like some kind of black mold."

"Yeah, well, the lady looks lonely to me." Chinbroski looked back again.

"There's a problem with the 24-7."

Chinbroski snorted. "Hanisch."

"Right. That's a lot of manpower."

"Lot of overtime pay."

"And I'd have to tell him everything."

"He'd want to run herd on your case."

"Our case, Chin. Our case."

"Whatever. Hanisch'd be everywhere. Information leaking so fast the killer'd be in Canada by tomorrow sundown."

Several beats of silence passed. The cold wind cut against them as they crossed the street one block south of Nanci's house. Rush could see the Big Dipper hanging off to his left. It was almost obscured by the brightness of the moon.

"So maybe the mystery woman found her ex's house, huh?" Chinbroski said. "If that was him you chased. I know this, we've gotta contact the Sheriff about that Oldsmobile. And the highway patrol. Gotta find her."

"And McKinney PD," Rush said. "In fact, I'm sending out a regional teletype when I get back to the station. Might as well get everybody looking."

* * *

Over her headphones during the last two hours, Leigh had heard the sound of three cars pass Enoch's driveway, two at a high rate of speed, one much slower. The sound was distinctive, and caused her little concern. What did cause her concern was the battery life on the phone in the weeds. Exposed to the cold, she didn't expect it to last much longer.

She'd worked quickly and efficiently, cleaning up her mess as she went, careful to arrange things just as they had been. She put the first camera in the master bedroom, in the corner, over the head of the bed. For that install she'd simply drilled a small hole into an existing crack that spider webbed diagonally from the top corner all the way to the floor. The pinhole lens stuck flush against the crack and would give her a panoramic view of the entire bedroom.

The second camera was in the living room, where the wall met the ceiling, in the center, just above a rusted wagon wheel. The wagon wheel would cast a shadow directly onto the small hole she'd drilled for the lens if Enoch ever turned on the only lamp in the room.

The third camera looked in on Enoch's high-tech room. It was the trickiest installation, but the one that most satisfied her. She drilled the hole directly over his desk chair, slightly angled toward the computer keyboard and screen. Since she had the names from the stack of credit cards, the phone numbers from his cell phones, his land line tapped, the transmitting frequency of the cell phone he was currently using, the only intelligence-gathering blank spot was his computer. She didn't have the software or the computer knowledge to slave his computer into hers, although she knew it could be done. But by capturing his computer transactions on videotape, she could, at the least, record some of his illegal activities, and at the most recreate his comings and goings. Her business was collecting evidence against him. And although she had indisputable verification of felonies in three different states, none of those would interest a Plano detective looking to lock her up for not preventing Jane McElroy's murder.

She had just closed the attic when the unmistakable sound of tires crunching gravel filled her headphones. Then the low rumble of an engine, and more crunching. She cut off her flashlight, grabbed her case from the floor, and ran through the house. Had she left a mess? Some sign that she'd been in the house? She didn't think so. She'd been so careful to clean after every hole drilled. But with no time to worry, she closed the door to the kitchen and made it out the back door just as flickers from headlights danced in the branches above her head.

The tree line formed a short thirty feet from the back door and she had totally concealed herself by the time Enoch's car stopped near the front porch. She took several more steps into the shadows before squatting and listening, holding her breath, hearing nothing now except her heart pounding in her ears and Enoch slamming his car door.

It wasn't until his footsteps thumped across the front porch, the front door slammed, and light began glowing from behind the heavy curtains in the living room that she relaxed and exhaled. Then the shakes came. Wrapping herself tightly, she shivered more from the adrenalin dump than from the cold. But she allowed herself that because she'd done it. She had totally turned the tables on the bastard. One mistake. One misspeak. One errant comment on his part and she'd be home free. Two thousand miles, ten months, and twenty-six felonies later, she had finally hemmed him in.

Her video recorders would do most of the work for her now. She was finally ready to start contacting cops. Ready to start building Enoch's legal coffin. She'd use Rush's son, convince him she was serious by having him contact out-of-state police agencies to match the evidence she'd send him. Then when ready, she'd start piecing together the crimes Enoch had committed in Plano.

It was almost over, her journey, her odyssey. Enoch just needed to make one more mistake, utter just a few harmless words. But would he?

ELEVEN

It was before the crack of dawn when Rush's phone rang. Having just pulled on his suit pants, he grabbed the portable off the nightstand and headed toward the kitchen to avoid waking Mallory.

He recognized the Caller ID number and punched up the call.

"Danny," he said, pulling open the fridge for OJ. "I typically don't like your morning calls. Is today going to be any different?"

"Depends on your perspective," Daniel said. "And good morning to you, too."

"Since you understand my perspective better than I do, you can answer the question." Rush pried open the juice container and drank.

"I can see it swinging either direction. Depends upon my level of cooperation."

Rush sat down and looked at the ceiling. Was this really his kid? "I might as well start cussing now, then."

Daniel laughed. "And you wonder why I won't marry Sally. Why do that when I have you to sass me?"

The coffeemaker dripped the last few drops into the pot and Rush hurriedly poured a cup.

"You've got a problem," Daniel said.

"I've got a lot of problems, and a smart-ass lawyer son is the biggest. Are you going to make me late for work?"

"You're looking for a woman. On the McElroy murder."

That stopped Rush in mid-sip. He set his cup down and frowned. "Okay. You have a source at the PD. I'm impressed, but not surprised. If you expect a comment, you didn't pay attention in lawyer school."

Daniel laughed again. "Come on, Pop, give me *some* credit. I'm serious. I didn't call to jerk your chain."

"Then why did you call?"

"I think your mystery woman called me yesterday."

Rush had to be careful here. If it *was* Leigh who had called, Daniel could make a case that he represents her now, even if no money had changed hands.

He also knew that Daniel needed to be careful. Lawyer or not, he could easily find himself withholding evidence in a criminal investigation.

Rush sipped his coffee to keep his mouth occupied.

"Did you choke on your bagel?" Daniel asked. "I expected more of a reaction."

"We're both standing at the edge of legal quicksand here, Danny. If I make a mistake, I could screw up a case and piss off a lot of people. If that happens, you win. And we both know you wouldn't want that to happen."

"That puts *you* at the edge of the quicksand. You said both of us."

"A bar ethics violation, for starters. You can't recruit clients, especially just to go head-to-head with your old man."

Daniel chuckled. "First of all, it happens all the time. Not that you could prove that I've ever done that. But regardless, in this case I was sitting in my office minding my own business."

Rush sliced a bagel in half and started spreading cream cheese. "Okay. Then let me ask what you expect me to ask. What's her full name and date of birth?"

"I don't even know her first name."

"Then you know less than I do." Rush took a bite of the bagel and laughed when Daniel asked her name. "You called me, remember? Let's stop playing games. Why do you think she's who I'm looking for?"

"Because she mentioned your name, alluded to the McElroy murder, and said she had a box of evidence against the guy who did it."

"And?"

"And what?"

"Come on, Danny. She called for protection. She knows we're looking for her, knows we'll find her, and wants to deal. What'd she authorize you to offer?"

"Don't flatter yourself, Pop. I talk offers with the DA's office, not a homicide dick."

"Homicide dick? You pick that up in a crime novel?"

"Well, I just can't come out and call my father Dick, can I?"

"Your mother would give you permission."

"I'm sure. Hold on."

Rush heard paper rustling in the background. He chewed on the bagel and waited.

"Okay. The mystery woman was vague. More of a 'feeling-me-out' phone call. I got the impression she was making contact in case she needed a lawyer later."

The wall clock in the kitchen read five after six. Rush needed to get to the station. "You record it?"

"I'm opposed to one-party knowledge phone recordings, despite the fact that the law allows it in Texas."

"Can I listen to it?"

"No."

"And I can't subpoena it later, either."

"Right. Attorney-client. There's nothing that would help you, anyway."

"Sure there is."

"What?"

"You have Caller ID. And you keep a log because you're anal."

"That'd be akin to me telling you her location."

"She's a material witness ... No. She's a suspect in a murder investigation. And by noon I'll have a warrant for her arrest. Now you know that. Are you going to obstruct justice?"

"It was a Caller-ID blocked call. Besides, I'm her lawyer now, I can't obstruct justice."

"Is she going to call back?"

"I guess that depends on how close you get to finding her."

Rush threw the rest of his bagel in the trash, suddenly not hungry anymore. "Can I assume you'll call me if she does?"

"No."

"I didn't think so. Pay attention to this one, Danny. This one's a loser. You recognize a loser?"

"Plenty of experience, Pop. But this mystery woman sounds pretty sharp. I'd bet money that neither of us gets a sniff of her."

"You might be right," Rush said. "But I'm sure going to do my best bloodhound act. Talk to you later."

He punched off the phone, drained his OJ, chased it with his coffee, and headed for the door.

At six-thirty he pulled into the north lot of the police station. One of the first things he wanted to do was inspect the abandoned house across from Nanci Brookfield's. Knowing the way Cigarette Man had been dressed the night before, he didn't expect to find much physical evidence. So he'd inspect the house himself before calling Randy McBride.

He also wanted the frequency of the tracking transmitter stolen from B &

A Enterprises. After which, he could arrange for the manufacturer to overnight a receiver and set of antennas.

But those two things could wait until later in the morning. The first thing on his agenda was to write an arrest warrant affidavit for "Leigh LNU's" arrest. It took an hour. That done, he wrote a subpoena for the phone records of the cellular number Nanci Brookfield had copied from her Caller ID box. The number was from Southwestern Bell Mobile Systems.

Rush stared at it. To think it would be that easy almost made him laugh out loud.

The odds were astronomical. On the other hand, he'd seen some pretty stupid criminals in his day. Like the time a murder suspect left his engraved watch beside the kitchen sink where he'd cleaned up after stabbing his boss to death. And the time a teenager robbed his uncle's pawnshop while wearing the unique ski mask his uncle had given him for Christmas a month before. And the time a forty-year-old rape suspect assaulted a woman he hadn't recognized but once dated in high school.

Could it be, if Nanci Brookfield's stalker was Jane McElroy's murderer, that something as simple as a poorly thought out phone call was the key to unlock the mystery?

He had the subpoena finished an hour later. Since a judge wouldn't show for another thirty minutes, he called Chinbroski at home.

"Yeah." Chin's voice was thick with sleep.

"You gonna sleep all day?"

A yawn. "Hey, Rush."

"I have the subpoena for the cell phone records. Waiting for a judge. I thought I'd serve it later this morning, after I look at the old house across from Nanci's. Wanna go?"

"To serve the subpoena or out to Nanci's?"

"Either. Both." Rush waved at a forgery detective walking by with a cup of coffee.

"Wait a minute," Chinbroski said after a moment. "Remind me. What cell phone records?"

"From the guy who's been calling Nanci."

"Oh." A pause. "Yeah. What are you doing first?"

"Check the house. Won't take long to look around. I'm heading out as soon as I see the judge. Then I'm off to Dallas."

The silence on the phone made Rush wonder if Chinbroski had dozed off.

"I can't get out there that fast," he said finally, his voice clearing. "I think I'll hang around Plano. Gotta check on Nanci. Want me to get hold of Jackson? Get the frequency of that tracking system?"

"I'll handle that. Probably need some help when I visit the owner of the cell phone, though."

"No problem," Chinbroski said. "Hey, I still got our cell phone from last night. Wanna swing by and get it on your way to Dallas?"

"There's a couple burglary teams on vacation. I'll talk to their Sarge and borrow one."

"Okay, then. Talk with you later."

By nine-thirty Rush had the subpoena and Leigh's warrant signed and stood shivering in the eighteen degree weather outside the abandoned house. Calling it a house was being generous. Only an old string of Christmas lights strung along the roofline reminded him that people had actually lived there at one time.

Broken windows, missing shingles, peeling paint, a roofline like a swayback horse; the house had a front porch with one support beam so bowed, it seemed to give a curtsy to the beam across the steps.

Rush told the patrolman sitting guard in the squad car to shove off, then climbed the crumbling stairs onto the porch. The front door stood open several inches. Fallen leaves from the oak in the front yard had blown against the door. With the door partially open, Rush had to step over the little wall of icy leaves to enter. Just before doing so, he noticed a scuff mark on the wooden floor just inside the door, a few of the frozen leaves kicked loose from the others. Searching the door itself, he found nothing like threads or small scraps of cloth.

The front room was small, with a high ceiling, peeling wallpaper, and faded-wood floors. Leaves, old newspapers, candy wrappers, and cat turds. Broken doorjambs, holes in the walls, missing light fixtures, and a dead bird. But no evidence of Cigarette Man.

Through the kitchen, a small formal dining, two bathrooms with broken toilets and smashed bathtubs, then through one back bedroom, Rush searched for evidence but found nothing. He saved the two front bedrooms for last. In the room where he first saw the cigarette glow, he found an old, broken dresser that had been dragged over to the window, turned on its side, and used by Cigarette Man as a perch to watch Nanci's house. Footprints and scuffmarks in the dust under the window were barely recognizable under all the cigarette ash. On the windowsill he found a burn mark, as though someone had let a cigarette burn down it to its nub. On the floor, near the dresser, was an empty and crumpled package of Winston cigarettes. No butts anywhere, which meant no saliva, no chance for a DNA sample.

In the next room his luck changed. He smelled it before he found it. In the corner opposite the window, Cigarette Man had urinated on a rug. With the cold the smell of urine was faint, but the yellow ice was unmistakable. He'd peed away part of his identity, his blood type. Or had if he was a secretor. Again, Rush found footprints, ash, a perch, another burn mark on the windowsill, and no cigarette butts.

He touched nothing. Pulling the borrowed cellular from his pocket, he called Randy McBride and told him the address. Then he walked to his car to wait.

McBride arrived twenty minutes later, stopping the crime scene van with a jolt behind Rush's car. He wore brown coveralls with Plano PD Crime Scene stamped on the back and an embroidered badge on the left side of his chest. He wasted no time jumping from the van and grabbing his collection kit.

Rush climbed from his car and met him on the sidewalk.

"Hey, Rush, what's up? Another frozen lady?"

"Naw, Randy, just need you to collect some urine. That your kind of job?"

"No different than collecting somebody's guts." McBride looked around. "Where's Chinbroski?"

"In bed, the last I knew."

McBride started toward the house. "What is it with him, Rush? The guy hates me."

Rush chuckled. "He's never forgotten the Neanderthal comment."

McBride shook his head. "Which proves my point. The guy's even got a primitive sense of humor. It was only a joke."

Rush stopped at the front door. "Take some pictures here, where the door was left standing open. And here, where these leaves have been displaced."

"Yeah, sure. I mean, you have to admit that Chinbroski looks like a hairless ape. He's got a forehead that looks like some Steven Spielberg creation. You ever see the cantina scene in Star Wars?"

"Wasn't that a George Lucas film?"

McBride waved him off. "Don't be so technical, you know what I mean.

His arms are too long, he doesn't have a neck, his legs are so thick they rub together. How does the guy relieve himself?"

"Just get your camera out, huh? That's my partner you're talking about. What do you want me to say?"

"I'm just saying that my comment did have a thread of truth."

"Tell that to Chin."

"And have him pinch my head off?"

"Then drop it. And follow me around the house so I can show you what I want. I need to hit the road."

Rush led him into the first bedroom. "Photos of the dresser, ashes, burn on the windowsill and most importantly, the view out the window toward the house across the street."

McBride stepped up next to him. "Which one?"

"Two doors down. The remodel job. The one with the pile of trash in the yard."

"Got it."

Rush stepped away from the window, leading McBride into the other bedroom. "Collect part of the urine soaked rug and take the same photos as the other room."

"No problem. That it? Dust for prints?"

"The guy was wearing gloves."

McBride frowned. "You saw him?"

"Not good enough. But it was eight degrees." Rush started toward the front door.

"Hey, Rush, one other question."

He stopped and turned.

"Think Chinbroski will ever come around? You know, change his mind about me?" McBride's face looked pained, yet hopeful. And if it hadn't been so cold, Rush would have sworn the water in the man's eyes were tears.

"He might," Rush said. "He might."

McBride wiped his nose and lifted his shoulders. "It was just a joke."

Rush nodded. "How about I remind him of that?"

"Sure. Wouldn't hurt." McBride wiped his eyes and turned away. "Better start moving around, before I freeze to death."

Rush walked out silently, leaving him alone.

TWELVE

Rush stood at a podium in the front of the conference room, ready to start the briefing. He had assembled a group of five detectives, including Chinbroski and himself, to serve the warrant on Martin Grant, the owner of the cell phone used to call Nanci Brookfield.

It was three in the afternoon and Rush wanted to get to Grant's house before dark. Martin Grant had a criminal history as long as a four-year-old rattlesnake. Robbery twice, burglary a half dozen times, weapon's charges, drugs, resisting arrest. Plano PD had popped him on three different occasions, the last time being nine months earlier on a minor dope charge. He stood six-feet-two, weighed 195 pounds, and last wore his red hair short on the sides with a ponytail to the middle of his back.

His last arrest report mentioned his membership in a motorcycle gang, The Roughnecks. Rush recognized the gang as one that operated a couple of hot pillow joints in northern Collin County. Along with the prostitutes, they also peddled heroin and marijuana, fenced stolen property, and were believed to finance a small gun-running operation. Rush didn't know how involved Grant was with all of the gang's activities, but with his history he was probably knee deep.

They'd have to tread carefully once they stepped onto Grant's property with the warrant. Harassing phone calls was only a misdemeanor, and Grant wasn't likely to rattle by having that waved under his nose.

The cops Rush had assembled were the best he could find on short notice. Steve Waverly was a thick-boned forgery detective with a nose that had been broken a dozen times during his ten-year kickboxing career. Danny Wilson was an out-of-shape former power lifter who worked juvenile. And Lance Swearingen was a black sprinter in the Police Olympics every year, the fastest man at Plano PD. He worked auto theft and served on SWAT.

Rush was about to start the briefing when Gerald Hanisch slipped in the door and sat on the edge of a table at the back of the room. Every detective present knew Rush's relationship with the lieutenant and every one of them suppressed a smile once they'd turned, looked at him, then turned back to

Rush.

Ignoring Hanisch, Rush began.

"Each of you has a copy of Grant's jacket. Inside you'll find his history, his mug shot, and a copy of the warrant. If he's not armed, he probably has a gun within reach. He's resisted every time he's been popped, so be aware. I drove by the house about two hours ago and there was a pickup and old Caddy parked there. I want to approach from…"

"What's the warrant for?" Hanisch interrupted.

Rush said nothing for a moment. *Just hold your tongue.* "Harassing phone calls."

Hanisch nodded quietly and began tapping his fingers on the top of the table.

"Now I want to approach from the south," Rush continued. "We'll take three cars. Swearingen, you're the rabbit. I want you in the woods out back. Waverly and Wilson…"

"What's this have to do with your murder investigation?" Hanisch interrupted again.

Rush rubbed the back of his neck and let a beat pass. "He's a suspect."

Hanisch nodded, tapped louder.

"I want Waverly and Wilson in the lead car. Chinbroski will…"

"Why's he a suspect?" Hanisch pressed.

Rush dropped his folder on the podium and looked at his lieutenant, then silently counted to three. "Remember the woman you dumped off on me yesterday? You did me a favor. I thank you." He hadn't succeeded in hiding the sarcasm.

"What about her?"

"She's received several calls from Grant's cell phone. He fits some of the evidence we found at the murder site. Primarily his criminal history, size, and hair color."

Hanisch nodded yet again. His mouth hung partially open, his tongue was visible against the back of his lower lip, and his lazy eyes stared off into space. His retard look, was how Chinbroski had always described it.

When Hanisch didn't say anything for a moment, Rush continued. "Chinbroski will drive my car. We'll go in second. But I want Swearingen in place before…"

"How'd you connect Martin to the murder site?" Hanisch's eyes were brighter now, like someone had turned up the dimmer switch in his brain.

Rush could feel the tension in the room. Chinbroski had shrunk in his chair, Wilson and Swearingen had scooted theirs in opposite directions creating a divide in the center of the room. There was suddenly nothing between Hanisch and Rush except empty tables and chairs. "Can we do this later?" Rush asked.

"Let's do it now. You're supposed to be working a murder. I wanna know how this *piss-ant* warrant fits in."

Was Hanisch's finger tapping louder, Rush wondered, or was the room so dead still, so saturated with tension that each tap echoed like a gunshot?

The other detectives in the room wouldn't step into the middle of this, especially Chinbroski, who had hidden in a closet as recently as two days before. If Rush were alone he'd tell Hanisch to take a nosedive into the toilet, then deny it later. But with witnesses? Since he'd have to update him at some point anyway, he decided to do it in front of a crowd.

"My warrant fits because of a video tape I received from Willard Jackson. On the video is a woman who wanted to hire someone to find her ex common-law. The ex is from California where another earless murder victim was found a year ago. This same woman showed up at Nanci Brookfield's house with an audiotape. The tape has a conversation between a black man and a white man plotting to break into Nanci's house. The white man's voice matches the one calling Nanci the last couple of days. She got the phone number of the caller's phone from her Caller ID. The owner of that phone, a cell phone, is Martin Grant."

The heads of the four other detectives turned to gauge Hanisch's reaction. He wore his retard look again. The tapping against the tabletop continued. There were a lot of holes in the hypothesis Rush had just thrown out, a lot of assumptions. But with light in his brain turned down most of the time, the odds of Hanisch finding those holes were slim.

"Grant's not from California," Hanisch said after a brief pause.

And that proved an old saying true, Rush thought. *That even a blind squirrel finds an occasional acorn.*

Before Rush could respond, Hanisch spoke again. "And you're taking a video from a felon? Do I need to send you back to a basic investigators' school?"

"Jackson isn't a felon."

"He takes a Mexican by the neck, slams him against the wall, crushing his throat, then Jap slaps another one in the head so hard that it kills him, too, and that's not a felon?"

"With a knife sticking out of his side!" Rush shouted with a sudden flash of rage. He stepped around the podium, his face burning as if the temperature in the room had instantly shot up ten degrees. "You'd have shot those two Mexicans. Every one in this room would have. But they'd still be dead. Tell me the difference."

Hanisch stopped drumming. He slid off the table and strolled back to the door he'd entered through. "You never told me how this warrant for Martin Grant ties in with your murder. He's not from California."

The silence hung in the air like a rancid odor. The other detectives sat so motionless it seemed time had stopped. "We're serving this warrant," Rush said. "Only the judge can rescind it. And I'll tell you another thing. Chinbroski and I have the McElroy investigation well under control. We don't need you following us around trying to match a random fact here and a random fact there. When it comes together it'll be from doing the things like serving this warrant."

Hanisch stood at attention at the door, frozen it seemed, like Jane McElroy in her tub.

"After you run the warrant I want you in my office." Hanisch's voice fluttered as if rage had seized his throat and pinched his windpipe shut. "You hear me, Rush? *In my office*!" He opened the door, then stopped, looking back at the other detectives. "The rest of you will find that I always get the last word. Always." Then he slammed the door.

No one said anything for a moment. Rush hoped they wouldn't.

"Well, he can lick my Hershey highway," Chinbroski said, standing, cracking his knuckles like a street fighter about to brawl. "He can kiss my silky white, pimple-free, baby oil scented butt. Know what I'm saying, partner?"

Rush gave him a look and shook his head. "Spoke up just in time, Chin. And can you imagine, I was beginning to think I was on my own?"

Chinbroski's face turned red so fast Rush thought his ears might bleed.

"Let's get on with this." Rush walked back behind the podium. "You'll each find a map in the folder. Swearingen, you head out. Get in position and let us know when to drive up. Radios on Ops Two. Questions?"

Everyone shook their heads.

"Good. Let's hit it."

Martin Grant's house had no easy approach. A doublewide mobile home, it sat a hundred yards from the road with no trees to block an approach. A creek with thick trees ran along the back of the property. Swearingen would have to park his car on a narrow county road to the north and hike a half mile to get in position.

Rush and Chinbroski sat in their car a quarter mile from Grant's house waiting for Swearingen to radio them. The wind had calmed. Now almost five in the afternoon, the temperature was at a weeklong high of thirty-four degrees.

Chinbroski had the radio tuned to Christmas carols. He quietly hummed along with Perry Como's *White Christmas*, actually staying on tune.

"You know," Rush said, "it's two weeks from Christmas and I haven't even thought about buying Mallory anything."

"Hard to get in the spirit, thinking about a dead woman all the time," Chinbroski said. He hummed a few more bars. "But I'm in the mood. Thinking about buying Nanci something. What do you think? What should I get her?"

Rush shrugged. "A computer?"

Chinbroski laughed. "Yeah. That's what I was thinking. One for the bathroom."

"A bigger gun?"

"Be serious."

"I can't even buy Mallory anything without her giving me a list. Don't think I'd be much help."

Chinbroski nodded. "I was thinking maybe a gift certificate. You know? Maybe to Home Depot."

Rush almost spit up the Dr Pepper he was sipping. "Now that's probably what she's always wanted."

"You don't think so?"

"Just cut to the chase and buy her a new toilet."

Chinbroski didn't say anything for a few beats. "You're just a real funny guy, Rush. I'm trying to have a serious conversation here."

"A gift certificate wouldn't be a bad idea, I mean since you've just met her. But not to Home Depot."

Chinbroski stroked his chin, mulling it over. "Yeah, maybe you're right. You think a jewelry store?"

"Well ... it may be a little soon for that."

"Victoria's Secret?"

"Chinbroski, do you have anything between your ears?"

Chinbroski shrugged.

"How about Laura Ashley's?" Rush said. "She seems the type."

"What type is that?"

"The Laura Ashley type. Her house is Victorian. Or haven't you noticed?"

"What's that got to do with it?"

Rush looked up as an old pickup passed in the direction of Martin Grant's house. Two large, scraggly-bearded biker types glanced back. Rush radioed to Waverly and Wilson, who were assigned to watch Grant's driveway. "Let me know if a ragged blue Ford pickup pulls in. I think they made us."

They both watched as the truck disappeared around the bend.

"So answer my question, Rush. What's her house got to do with her being a Laurie Ashby type?"

"Laura Ashley. There's a store in Collin Creek Mall. They sell country dresses. Homey stuff. You know, frumpy."

"Frumpy? You saying Nanci's frumpy?"

Rush threw up his hands. "I don't even know her. I'm just saying her house looks like she might like those kinds of clothes."

"Oh."

They sat without speaking, the radio playing *Silent Night*.

Then Swearingen announced it was time to move. A second later Waverly told them the old blue truck had turned into Grant's driveway.

"Waverly," Rush said into the radio. "Get close enough to that truck to stop those guys from going inside. We'll be a couple minutes."

Chinbroski stomped on the gas, throwing Rush back against the headrest. By the time he stopped their car in front of the mobile home, Waverly and Wilson were surrounded by five bikers. Chinbroski skidded to a stop several yards from the crowd.

Waverly and Wilson stood back to back, Waverly addressing Martin Grant, who stood too close for conversational purposes. Rush radioed for Swearingen to join them, then he and Chinbroski jumped from the car.

Grant turned and took a step away from Waverly. His red hair was pulled back into a tight ponytail, and despite the cold, he wore a sleeveless Harley-Davidson T-shirt without a jacket. His blue jeans were tight enough to reveal powerful legs. His arms, knotted with muscle, each appeared to be one continuous tattoo.

"I'm Greg Rush, Plano PD," he said, stopping within kicking distance, but no closer. "You Martin Grant?"

The other bikers, each leathered out in heavy jackets, slowly closed in behind Grant. Waverly and Wilson circled around and flanked Rush on each side. Chinbroski stood rigid, just to Grant's left. Which proved to Rush yet again that Chinbroski had done his homework. Grant had a scar from his left ear to the middle of his nose. The knife that left that scar had blinded his left eye, leaving the eyeball foggy and drifting to one side. Rush had forgotten to mention it in the briefing.

"And you want to know for *what* reason?" Grant said.

"I need to know which of you to arrest."

Grant chuckled. "That's what this other cop said. 'Cept there's a problem. I ain't done nothing."

The front door of the trailer squeaked and then slammed shut. Two biker girls had come out to watch the show.

"Just to make sure I'm all nice and legal, listen up." Rush read Grant his Miranda warnings. "You own a cell phone?" he asked when finished.

"Like everybody else in America. So what?"

"There's a lady in Plano who doesn't like the way you're using it."

The freckled skin on Grant's nose, red from the cold, twitched when a spastic nerve in his cheek decided to dance. Acne dotted each temple and around the edges of his nose. His teeth were West Texas, hard-water green.

"What the hell you talking about? What lady?"

"You ever let anyone use your phone?"

"Don't nobody use my phone 'cept me."

"Where is it?"

"Ain't none of your damn business." Grant glanced at his troops. His crooked grin looked drug induced with the nerve in his cheek still dancing.

Swearingen coughed. All five bikers turned and looked. Swearingen leaned against the end of the trailer with an MP-5 machine gun strapped across his chest. The biker girls retreated closer to the front door of the trailer.

"What is this?" Grant said. "How many more cops you got hid back there?"

"More than enough. So, are you sure you have the phone? Sure that no one is using it without your knowledge?"

Grant shifted his stance, moving slightly to the left, toward Chinbroski. "I told you. Nobody uses my phone."

"Where is it? Before I put the cuffs on you I want to make sure it's not stolen."

Grant's face went slack as something started processing under his freckled forehead. "So what if it *is* stolen?"

Rush smiled. "It won't keep you out of jail tonight, if that's what you're thinking."

The women on the porch turned and went inside, mumbling about the cold.

"Why don't you tell Marty what's going on," the tallest biker said.

"Who are you?" Chinbroski asked him.

"Mr. Nobody." The tall biker inched closer to Chinbroski. "Maybe all you peckerheads wouldn't be so brave if you didn't have guns strapped to your hips." He towered at least eight inches above any of his leather-clad friends and almost a foot above Chinbroski. His hair looked as though he'd mixed in an entire tube of grease. Strands were plastered against his forehead, hung over both eyes, and disappeared under his leather jacket. A scar ran across his right cheek, dropping just under his lower lip. The other bikers were nodding, shifting, each picking a detective to try and intimidate.

"Is that what you think?" Chinbroski said. "How about this, Mr. Nobody, after we cart your buddy off, I can stay and we can go three rounds." He grinned. "I ain't kicked a tall, skinny guy's ass in a long time."

"Put you hands on top of your head, Martin," Rush said, pulling out a pair of handcuffs.

"I ain't done nothing wrong. I ain't going to jail for something I ain't did."

"Hard or easy?" Rush asked.

"I ain't called no woman." Grant maneuvered his feet, sliding his left foot back a few inches and digging his right toe into the gravel. He looked away, rambling, his voice dropping an octave. "Just cause somebody said something about me don't mean nothing." Dropping his right shoulder, he stuck his right hand into the back pocket of his jeans. "You boys think this is legit?"

As if sensing Grant's slight movement shifts, the other four bikers began moving, too, shuffling feet, cracking knuckles, flexing necks.

"This warrant a felony?" Grant asked.

"No," Rush said.

Grant smiled, then dealt his play. He stepped forward as he launched a right-handed roundhouse that came from downtown.

Rush dropped his handcuffs as he pivoted on his left foot, cocked his right, and drove a perfect sidekick into Grant's ribcage.

Then everything happened fast.

Chinbroski grabbed Nobody and drove him into Grant's falling body. A short, muscular biker jumped on Chinbroski's back and was attempting a choke-hold when Waverly, the kick boxer, crushed his nose.

Rush bent to retrieve his handcuffs as Chinbroski drove his knee into Nobody's face. Grant was trapped underneath both of them. Wilson, the former power lifter, grabbed a fourth biker, spun him around, kicked the back of his knee, and clamped on a choke-hold.

The fifth biker pulled a knife, a six-inch Bowie, and sliced the air just over Rush's head. Rush pulled his .45 and shoved it against the man's forehead. Before he could scream to drop the knife, Swearingen slammed the butt of the MP-5 into the side of the biker's head.

The knife wielder was the first handcuffed. Wilson's sleeper victim was next. The one with the crushed nose was cuffed just as Chinbroski was bending Nobody in three different directions.

That left Grant. He scrambled out and stood in the center of the mess, clutching his ribs and sucking air like he'd just run a mile.

Chinbroski was laughing. He sat straddled across Nobody, lightly slapping him across the face like a kid in a school-yard fight. The biker's face was crimson as he strained to move, the veins in his neck as big as pencils.

"Look at this boy blow snot," Chinbroski said. He looked at Grant. "This skinny guy your enforcer?" He laughed again.

"Put your hands on top of your head," Rush told Grant.

Grant slowly lifted his hands and interlocked his fingers. "I'm suing," he said. "You hear me? I am suing your ass."

Waverly cuffed him.

"Hey, Chinbroski," Rush said. "Enough already."

Chinbroski laughed again and climbed off his prisoner. Then flipped him over and cuffed him.

"Hey, Swearingen," Rush said. "Go call the Sheriff's office. Tell them we have four pieces of trash to haul off. Wilson, put Grant in Chinbroski's car."

Rush noticed the biker girls staring out a window. One drinking a beer, the other eating a cookie.

Chinbroski dragged each of the bikers into a straight line. Face down on the cold gravel, two of the four were spitting blood, the other two screaming obscenities.

Rush climbed onto the porch and knocked on the door. The taller of the two answered. Not more than twenty-five, she wore tight jeans and no bra under her Harley tee shirt. Her brown hair hung limp and she smelled of cigarettes and beer.

She stared at Rush with glazed eyes and said nothing.

"I need Martin's phone," Rush said.

"Martin?" she slurred. "You mean Marty?"

"Yeah, his phone."

She leaned backward into the trailer and looked over her shoulder. "Hey,

Suzy. Get Marty's phone. Next to our bed." She turned back to Rush. "How come you need it?"

Rush turned away from her and looked back to the driveway. Chinbroski was hunched over Nobody, laughing at him again. Martin Grant sat in the back of Chinbroski's car with Wilson standing guard just outside the door. Swearingen was on the phone with the Sheriff's department, and Waverly was walking back and forth along the row of prisoners.

"Here it is," the girl at the door said, holding it out.

Rush turned and took the phone from her. It was an Oki, model 1335, the same model as Chinbroski and his department-issued phone.

"Hey, Rush," Swearingen said. "Couple deputies are on the way. Ten minutes."

He nodded, heading for the car.

Chinbroski joined him. "Know what I think, Rush?"

"What?"

"I think these Roughnecks fight like a bunch of girls. Great side kick on Grant, by the way. First time in a year I got to see any of that black belt stuff."

"I'm surprised I even got my leg up."

"Instincts, my man. You're just a born killer. A fighting machine."

"Yeah, that's it."

"Let's hit it, *podna*," Chinbroski said. "Waverly and the other guys can wait for the sheriff."

They walked to the car and climbed in. Rush sat in the back seat next to Grant.

Grant opened his mouth to complain.

"Shut your hole," Chinbroski said, firing up the car. "I ain't in the mood."

Rush powered up the phone and pressed a button, pulling up the numbers Grant had programmed.

"You got a warrant for that?" Grant asked.

"For what?" Rush asked, punching through each number, looking for Nanci Brookfield's.

"You can't read the numbers on my phone without a warrant."

"This comes from your jailhouse-lawyer course?" Chinbroski asked from the front seat. "He's got a warrant. And I said shut your hole."

Grant had twenty-two phone numbers programmed. A wealth of information, Rush was sure, for law enforcement everywhere, but none of the numbers meant anything to him. He checked the call log of numbers dialed. Nothing.

They rode to the jail in silence. Grant's head slumped against the window. He stared out the glass, his face hard, his lips moving quietly as though rehearsing words he would speak later.

After Chinbroski pulled the car into the sally port at the jail, Rush opened Grant's door and watched him climb out. A jailer escorted Grant into the lockdown.

"Hey, Rush," Chinbroski said. "Start the arrest report, Nanci just beeped me."

"She has your beeper number?"

"Gave it to her last night." He grinned.

Rush shook his head. "Sure, go on."

Within ten minutes Rush was at a book-in computer, typing. He wasn't through a third of the first page when Chinbroski walked up and stared at him.

"What?" Rush asked.

"Nanci got another call ten minutes ago."

Rush stopped typing and looked at him.

"From the guy who's been calling. Same number on her Caller ID box. Same voice. She recorded him. Played the tape for me so I could hear."

Rush felt his stomach churn, felt the blood drain from his face. "The guy on the tape says to her, 'I seen the cops out there last night, and let's just say you're lucky. For now.' Then he hangs up."

THIRTEEN

Rush sat in a chair outside the CID captain's office. Lieutenant Hanisch was in the captain's office griping about what had transpired two hours before. Rush was alone, except for the captain's secretary, who kept stealing little glances his way, smiling when she got caught.

He could hear Hanisch ranting…faintly, could see him through the glass waving his arms as he sat on the edge of his chair, the back of his neck as red as a sunburn. Captain Williams didn't seem impressed by his tirade. A totally bald man, Williams gazed at the ceiling, his glasses high on his nose, his thick fingers folded across his immense stomach.

Rush hadn't yet digested the information about Nanci Brookfield receiving another phone call when he'd been ordered to the captain's office. He wasn't too concerned about what might happen to him, as the history between him and Hanisch was well known. What concerned him was the possibility that Hanisch could convince the captain to authorize a tighter rein over the investigation. The Rush/Chinbroski team was the only one in the Capers Unit not to have a sergeant checking the daily progress of a major case.

After another five minutes, Rush saw the captain wave at him through the glass.

"Have a seat, Greg," the captain said after Rush came in and closed the door.

Hanisch was to Rush's right. He scooted his chair around to face Rush.

Williams began. "Gerald tells me the two of you had words a couple of hours ago."

Rush slowly released his breath. First names. The captain was keeping it informal. A good sign. "You could say that."

"He also tells me you served a warrant that has no apparent link to the McElroy investigation. And that your suspect is being released as we speak."

"Released? I wasn't aware of that. And since I'm charging him with assault on a police officer ... How is that possible?"

Williams glanced at Hanisch, who answered the question. "I don't see how we can charge him with resisting arrest when he was arrested for something he didn't do."

"News travels fast," Rush said. "Who told you that?" One of the female jailers, Rush suspected. Hanisch had a couple down there he'd spent some personal time with.

"That's not the point," Hanisch snapped. "I questioned the connection of the warrant before you served it. Our officers were put in unnecessary danger. And now we have a situation where we risk a lawsuit for roughing up members of a biker gang on a bad warrant."

Somebody from the arrest team must have called him, Rush thought. But there was nothing he could do about it now. He took a deep breath, silently counted to three. "It wasn't a bad warrant. And Grant didn't resist, he assaulted me."

"Were you hurt?" Hanisch asked.

"Does it matter?"

Hanisch scooted to the edge of his chair. "It's something his attorney will ask."

Rush could feel the heat in his face. "Is that your function, to question the integrity of your detectives while acting as an advance scout for defense attorneys?"

Williams held up his hands. "I think that's enough."

Hanisch pulled his lips into a crooked grin and slid back in his chair.

"I have no doubt the warrant was based on facts you suspected were correct at the time," Williams said. "That's not an issue with me. Nor am I concerned with the how many Roughnecks were slapped around. I do agree with Gerald about charging Grant with assault when you suffered no injury. That decision was mine and it stands." He took his glasses off, which shrunk his eyes. "The real reason you're in here has to do with the insubordination during your briefing."

Rush wouldn't give Hanisch the honor of seeing him beg for mercy. "Guilty," he said. "I'll take what you give me, but I won't apologize. Hanisch needs to stay out of my investigation. The fact that we have someone out there with the capability to clone a cellular phone only substantiates that I'm on the right track."

"How can you say that?" Hanisch blurted. "You have a dead woman and a totally unrelated case of harassing phone calls. How can you possibly link the two?"

Williams rubbed the bridge of his nose and folded his hands across his stomach again, waiting for Rush's answer.

"I'm not prepared to discuss what evidence I may or may not have," Rush said finally.

"How dare you!" Hanisch shouted, jumping from his chair.

"Sit down!" Williams boomed.

But Hanisch didn't. He took a step toward Rush, shoved a finger within a foot of his face. "I'm your supervisor! And you'll damn well tell me anything I want to hear."

"I said to sit your ass down!" Williams shouted again.

"Now you see what I have to put up with," Hanisch said, turning toward Williams. "He's a smart ass. He's arrogant. And he's damn sure insubordinate."

"And if you don't sit your ass down, Hanisch, you'll be taking vacation. And it won't be paid."

Hanisch sat, eyes flaring.

Williams looked at Rush. "Why the secrecy?"

"That's not it. I just don't want Hanisch involved. I don't trust him." Rush could almost feel the heat being generated by Hanisch. But Rush wouldn't look at him. "Captain, you know our history. It's not like it's a big surprise. If this were your run-of-the-mill dead body I wouldn't feel as strongly as I do. But there are aspects of this case that trouble me. And the last thing I need is a leak."

"Why you son of a bitch!" Hanisch shouted, jumping from his chair again.

Rush stood and pivoted on his feet. He wasn't sure what Hanisch would do, but he wasn't taking chances.

"Hanisch, go to your office," Williams said quietly, snapping off each word. "Now."

Hanisch glared at Rush several moments before moving. His lips quivered, his hands shook, the red in his face invaded the roots of his enhanced blonde hair. Keeping his eyes locked on Rush's, he slowly moved to the door and pulled it open.

"Not a word, Hanisch," Williams said. "That's an order."

Hanisch slammed the door behind him.

Rush rubbed his face and sat down. Williams scooted his chair back and reached behind him, grabbed a can of Diet Coke from his credenza. He took a drink before saying anything.

"I hope you have something unusual, Greg, because otherwise I'm not going to stand for a detective speaking that way to a lieutenant, even considering the history."

Rush knew this was his chance. If he could convince the captain to order Hanisch off his back, he wouldn't have to go through hell when he made his request to make a trip to California, which he strongly suspected would happen sooner than later.

So Rush told him. Everything. The strange condition of Jane McElroy; the odd note written in Boontling, a language only spoken in a remote valley in northern California; the hair left by the woman; and the witness who saw the Oldsmobile the night of the murder. He told of the Jackson video; of the mysterious Leigh, who drove an Oldsmobile; of her ex common-law who made a living by electronic eavesdropping; of her comment about someone else being gutted and him looking in Plano; of her calling Daniel, preparing for legal protection. Of the strange calls to Nanci Brookfield and the delivery of the audiotape, of Nanci being sure that Leigh was the deliverer of the tape. He told of the theft of Reese Morgan's electronic equipment, of his plan to try and track the signal of the stolen transmitter, of Cigarette Man the night before, of how Hanisch had ruined the capture attempt.

"So the last thing I need," Rush finished, "is for any of this to be talked about over police radios, cell phones, cordless phones, or anything else wireless. And now, knowing this guy has the ability to clone cells, I'm even more sure of just how easily everything could get screwed up. There can't be any leaks. I can't have this case talked up in the hallways or at drinking fountains."

Rush let all of it sink in. Williams had listened intently, jotting notes every few seconds, nodding occasionally.

Then Rush made his final plea. "You know Hanisch, Captain. He can't *not* talk about big cases. He uses information on high profile cases to impress women out of their panties. I think I'll eventually need to take a trip to California, I mean if nothing else develops here. If I have to go through Hanisch, he'll order me to tell him everything. I'd like you to allow me to update you directly. To bypass him."

And that was enough.

Williams picked up a pencil and tapped it against his cheek. He took another drink of Diet Coke while he thought it through. "We don't know why this woman is after her ex?" he asked, staring at the ceiling.

"Not yet. And I really don't care. We just have to find her. Without it getting out."

"I can't let the insubordination go. You'll have to face it."

Rush nodded.

"Unfortunately you're right about Hanisch impressing women with cop talk. Although this case isn't on the front page anymore, if we have another one, God forbid, the front page is where it'll live until the guy is caught." He paused, thinking it out. "I have to agree, I guess. If this guy is an electronics expert there's no telling what he can do. We have to keep it low key." He stood. "Hanisch is out on this one. But I'm telling you, Greg, don't get in the habit of withholding information from him. He's still in your chain of command."

"Yes, sir."

"You'll be getting paper on the insubordination. Expect a few days off when the investigation is over."

"Yes, sir."

"That's all. I'll deal with Hanisch."

"Yes, sir. Thank you, sir." Rush stood and walked out. He smiled at everyone he passed on the way to his desk.

Three hours later he was still at his desk, relaxed, chin in hand, feet propped on the edge of his filing cabinet. Chinbroski sat in a chair opposite him, his feet tipping a trashcan back and forth.

"We have to find Leigh," Rush said. "Whatever it takes."

Chinbroski rolled his eyes. "Damn, Rush, you sent a teletype out to the surrounding departments. You had dispatch send every patrol unit a computer message. You sent a department wide e-mail. You got Crime Prevention notifying all the Neighborhood Watch leaders. You put it on the City of Plano web page. You got the paper doing an article. Crime Stoppers has the information. You got the local-access channel at the cable-TV place running a spot. You got the Narc boys running the word through their snitches. What else? Stand on your head and address the crowd at the next balloon festival?"

"Until we get her in custody, we're at a standstill." Rush suddenly swung his feet off the desk. "I just remembered something! I can't believe I forgot." He stood and pulled out his wallet.

"You finally remember you owe me twenty bucks?"

Rush gave him a look. "I think you got that backwards. I just remembered Jackson and the stolen transmitter. I can't believe I let the entire day pass. I even mentioned it to Williams earlier."

"You've been so happy you got Hanisch out of your life, I'm surprised you remembered anything."

Rush dug through his wallet until he found the paper with Jackson's beeper number. He dialed it.

Chinbroski rolled his head in a slow circle, stretching his neck. "Waste of time."

"What?"

"Trying to track the guy. Waste of time."

"Hell, Chin, it's worth a try."

"Look, we're dealing with a guy smart enough to clone a cell phone and send us chasing after another guy who not only has red hair but a criminal history longer than my schlong. You think he ain't gonna know if some broad puts a transmitter on his car?"

"Stranger things have happened."

"That right?"

"That's right."

"Yeah, well," Chinbroski said, standing. "It's almost seven-thirty and I told Nanci I'd be over to help fix up her hall bathroom. You need me for anything?"

"I'm heading out myself as soon as Jackson calls."

"See you tomorrow."

Once alone, Rush kicked his shoes off, pulled off his socks, rubbed his feet.

"Hey, Rush."

He looked up and saw Randy McBride staring at him.

"Something wrong with your feet?" he asked.

Rush grabbed his socks and started pulling them on. "Just a little rub down. Been on them most of the day. What's up with you?"

McBride yanked at his customary baggy pants, then sat in the chair Chinbroski had just vacated. His white hair stuck straight out on back as if he'd gone to sleep with it wet. "Didn't find anything more out at the old house this morning."

"No?"

"Got a match out of Jackson's truck, though. You know, the brown hair from the woman. Just like you said. Same woman. Kind of late with my results, but I've been busy."

"So that confirms it," Rush said. "Leigh was in our crime scene."

"Confirmed. I searched the abandoned house this morning with a fine-tooth comb after you left. Didn't find a thing that would amount to a hill of beans."

"I really didn't expect you to," Rush said, as he pulled on his socks.

"So," McBride asked. "You see Chinbroski today?"

"Sure. You just missed him."

"Well ... yeah, I know. Saw him in the hall."

Rush nodded.

"Did ... well, did you tell him what I said, you know, this morning?"

He'd forgotten. But he didn't have the heart to tell McBride that. "It's no problem, Randy. Everything's fine. It may take a few weeks, but Chinbroski will come around." He smiled.

McBride smiled back. "I'm not losing any sleep over it, you understand."

"Of course not."

"It's just that ... well, a man don't like to leave this earth with people thinking bad thoughts about them."

"Leave this earth?" Rush said. "You know something the rest of us don't?"

"Just a figure of speech."

"I see."

"Well, listen," McBride said, slapping his knees and standing. "Got to get home to the missus. She gets madder than a hornet when I don't get to see her."

"Take it easy, Randy."

"You too." He hitched his pants again and walked away. Then stopped before he turned the corner. "Hey, Rush."

"Yeah?"

"Thanks a million." Then he was gone.

Rush was about to beep Jackson again when his phone rang. He grabbed it.

"It's Willard Jackson. What's up?"

"Got a minute?" Rush asked, hearing the light static of a cell phone and the car radio playing in the background.

"Almost home."

"I need the transmitting freek of your tracking system."

Jackson was silent for several seconds. "What did you have in mind?"

"If this Leigh woman stuck the transmitter where we both think she meant to stick it, we can find it from the air. Need the freek so the company can send me a duplicate system."

Several more seconds passed. "I'm turning around. Meet me in my office. It'll take me about twenty minutes. I don't want to say anything more on this cellular. Reese Morgan may still be there. Go over now and you'll probably catch him before he shoves off."

"I'll see you there." Rush replaced the receiver and rubbed the back of his neck. Tired. He wanted to get home to Mallory, then remembered her finals. She wouldn't be there, anyway. He wondered where Leigh was, wondered what in God's name was driving her.

FOURTEEN

She dialed the number from memory now. Parked in the courthouse parking lot across from Daniel Rush's office, Leigh could see him at his desk, hunched over, comparing a written document with whatever was on his computer screen.

He was definitely a chip off the old block. He'd been cursed with his father's receding blond hair, his narrow shoulders, and his rugged, no-nonsense jaw line.

Leigh couldn't see much of the office other than his desk and computer, but she'd been watching the front door for three hours. His secretary had left nearly an hour ago, and the paralegal ten minutes after that.

Daniel's office was a small but well positioned firm situated just a quarter-mile from the county jail in McKinney, the county seat of Collin county. Located in a stylishly restored Victorian on the edge of McKinney's historical section, the office competed with half a dozen other defense attorneys within a two-block radius.

Leigh was in the van tonight. Having splurged on a two-hundred dollar paint job - a small portion of the money she'd stolen from the dead guy rotting in his car on the other side of the county - the surveillance van, now green, wore magnetic signs advertising three-rooms-and-a-hall carpet cleaning for $49.95. The phone number on the signs was one of her cell phones mounted in a charger just over her right shoulder. She'd answered it three times today, explaining that they were booked for the next six weeks.

The mid-December sky was nearly dark a few minutes before six PM and the courthouse parking lot had thinned to the danger point. She couldn't afford to have Daniel notice anything odd outside his window once the courier service made its delivery. If he were a smart lawyer, he would assume he was being watched once she placed the phone call explaining the contents of the box. And although the van was fifty yards from his office window, the fewer the cars in the lot the bigger the chance he'd have of figuring out where she was.

She'd pretty much gutted the van of its high-tech equipment, but had left the video periscope; a mirror system encased in a tube, installed through the roof. With black & white and color cameras mounted side by side and pointed into the mirrors, with the video signal fed into the monitor in front of her, she watched the lawyer's office while reclining in a comfortable swivel chair.

The electronic zoom lens, pulled all the way in, gave her a close enough view of Daniel to read his lips as he pored over whatever held his attention.

Through a side porthole window she watched the front of the law firm. It was 6:15 when the courier service arrived. The enthusiastic driver jumped from his little truck, bounced onto the porch, and rang the bell. On the monitor, Daniel looked up, distracted, then peered out his window and saw the courier's truck. He got up and walked out of view.

At the front door, Daniel signed for the package, and closed the door. Back on the monitor, Daniel returned to his desk and sat down. Leigh hit *Record* on the VCR.

Daniel grabbed a letter opener and sliced the tape at the end of the box. Then he frowned and looked at the courier company's paperwork.

Leigh picked up another of her cell phones and made the call. As his phone rang in her ear, Daniel opened one end of the box and started to pull out the contents. Then he stopped, looked at his phone, and lifted the receiver.

"Daniel Rush."

"You should have received my package by now," Leigh said. "From Lone Star Couriers."

Daniel quickly reached over near the phone and made a jabbing motion with his finger recording her, although she couldn't see the recorder. She'd suspected it during their first conversation, hoped for it, but hadn't asked. Good. She would insist both tapes be played at her trial if there ever was one. Anything to prove her innocence in front of a jury.

"Can I assume this is the mystery woman from the other night?"

"You can assume. Now answer my question. Did you get my package?"

"Indeed. Quite intriguing."

"What? My package or my calling?"

Daniel looked into the box, then dumped the contents onto his desk. Large manila envelopes, a standard white envelope, audio and videotapes, and several typed pages stapled together. "The fact that you're calling me in such a timely fashion." He looked out his window, up one end of the darkened street, down the other. "You must be psychic."

"You'll find a one thousand dollar retainer in the white envelope. That officially makes you my attorney, right?"

"Assuming I take your case."

"I have to have a case for you to represent me?"

Daniel ripped open the white envelope and removed a sheaf of one hundred dollar bills. "Since I'm a defense attorney, that's usually the situation. Are you saying you don't have a case?"

"I won't have a case if they don't find me."

"Who's 'they'?"

"Let's not play games, Mr. Rush. As I told you the other night, I have things they want. In that box are small samples of what I can deliver. I'm handing them this sample as a show of good faith."

Daniel picked up a videotape and read the label. "'Maryville, Arizona – Pearl Street.' Might I ask what's on this tape?"

"An edited copy of Plano's most wanted man leaving a murder scene seven months ago. Full living color. I've scrambled his face on the tape, but you can see the blood on the front of his shirt. There's a piece of that shirt in the manila envelope marked Arizona One."

Daniel frowned and rubbed his forehead. "Anything else in 'Arizona One'?"

"A hair sample from both the victim and the suspect. A photograph of him going into the house, then coming out. And a copy of a pawn ticket showing one of the items he stole from the dead woman. With all traceable information blacked out, of course. I can't have him caught yet."

He sifted through the material on his desk, picked up the envelope by the corners and set it aside. "Well, haven't you been a busy lady?" He leaned over, out of sight, as though digging through a bottom drawer, and came up with a pair of latex gloves. He spoke as he pulled them on. "Can I assume this Arizona murder is unsolved?"

"I wouldn't be in Plano if they had caught him."

"Why?" Daniel asked, picking up a second manila envelope. "Why are you doing this? Why now?"

Leigh leaned forward and studied Daniel's face in the monitor. "What law school did you attend?"

"Cornell."

"Ivy League. So you're a smart man doing a simple-minded lawyer's work. Why?"

Daniel grinned. "Defense work is for the simple minded?"

"You cut deals. On the few occasions you actually go to trial, it's either because the state has a weak case anyone could beat or you have a dumb ass, three-time loser client desperate to stay out of prison."

"Got it all figured out, huh?"

"Cornell. You could have a top corporate job. Why defense work?"

Daniel picked up one of the audiotapes and inspected it. "Let's just say I have a penchant for justice. There aren't enough Ivy Leaguers doing what I do. Even dumb-ass, three-time losers, desperate to stay out of prison, need smart lawyers. You were pretty slick avoiding answering my question. Maybe you should have gone to law school."

"Maybe I will one day. If you really don't know why I'm doing this, maybe I've hired the wrong man."

He got up from his desk, reached out of Leigh's monitor's view, then came back with a small camera. Standing over his desk, he took aim and snapped a picture. "This is a preemptive move on your part, I suspect." He snapped another from a different angle. "A show of good faith. Solidifies future claims of cooperation." Daniel sat down, rearranged some of the items, and snapped close-ups. "My question about your timing does intrigue me."

"How so? What does it tell you?"

Daniel set his camera down and stared out the window, into the darkness beyond the glass. "It tells me that your motivation is about to change. That whatever reason has prevented you from turning him in is about to become a non-factor. Or..."

Leigh reclined in her chair, watching Daniel think it through. "Or..."

"Or you believe you're about to be caught. Is that insightful? Am I smart enough to defend you? Or do you have other qualifying questions?"

"Getting caught is not the issue here. It so happens that the police in Arizona have arrested an innocent man. I want you to contact them and call them off. I can't stomach that kind of mistake."

"As if I had a choice."

Leigh perked up. "What does that mean?"

"Simply, while I have no legal obligation to contact the police if a client professes involvement in a crime, I am not allowed to withhold physical evidence of a crime. Remember that if you decide to send me a box of stuff from the McElroy murder."

Leigh wasn't a lawyer, but that didn't sound right. She *hoped* it was right, it is what she'd been counting on. But something in his face, a slight shift in his eyes, sent up a red flag. A lawyer would have to turn over evidence? It just didn't sound right. But for now she had no choice but to take him at his word. "Fine," she said. "Then forward that evidence with a cover letter, preferably on your letterhead. And in the meantime let's hope you can keep Plano off my back until I'm ready to reveal his identity."

Daniel sighed and started repacking the box of evidence. "Keep them off your back? You're an enigma. I can't imagine what would possess me to represent you."

"Please don't insult me, Mr. Rush."

"I beg your pardon?"

Leigh pushed her chair away from the counter holding the monitor and stretched her legs. She quickly debated the pros and cons of making a speech. She knew he was recording her, and couldn't be sure with whom he might share it. Then she remembered attorney/client privilege and realized that making a speech wouldn't matter.

"What I'm doing right now is my life," she said. "It consumes every waking moment of every day. Every thing I do is carefully calculated, well researched, much considered. I didn't throw open a phone book, make a blind stab, and happen to land on your name. I've spent hours at the courthouse. You have defended an unusually high number of criminals arrested by your father. Especially considering you've only been out of law school for two years. I can only imagine the number of crimes Detective Rush would charge me with if he had the chance. A smorgasbord. Loser cases for the lawyer who defends me. Or are they?

"Maybe I'm smart. Maybe my reason is so compelling no jury would ever convict me. You've lost every case you've ever argued against him, Mr. Rush. Maybe you could beat him defending me. I think you could. If my reason for not having the killer arrested wasn't worth my going to prison, I wouldn't be doing this at all."

Leigh took a breath. Daniel had stopped repacking the box of evidence and was staring at the ceiling, the corners of his mouth upturned slightly.

"So there you are, Mr. Rush. I have evidence against Jane McElroy's killer, I will identify him when the time is right, then I will testify against him if the cops catch him. I will trade what I have, but it will be an even trade. Every criminal charge filed against me must come with a price tag for dropping it. The theory is simple, I'm trading absolute convictions of a monster who has committed felonies in five states, for my freedom."

Daniel was silent while he digested her speech. "You have reason to believe he's settled near here, taken up residence. You fully expect my father to catch him."

"Are you exercising your Cornell intellect?"

"Nothing else makes sense. If he were just passing through on his way to another state, why bother with all of this?"

"Bravo. I like a man who can think on his feet. You're definitely hired." Leigh watched as Daniel once again started repacking the box of evidence. "You won't be hearing much from me from this point forward, Mr. Rush. But you will be receiving similar packages in the future. All instructions will be included within. Please temper speculations as to my identity and my whereabouts in future conversations with your father. I wouldn't take kindly to betrayal."

And with that she hung up the phone. Daniel sat there for several moments, appearing somewhat amused, then reached over and turned off his tape recorder. He rubbed his face, looked at the box of evidence, and shook his head.

Leigh cut off her VCR, turned off the monitor, and prepared to leave. She had one other stop to make tonight before retrieving the videotapes of Enoch's house from her deer stand. And she needed to call her mother, give her updates. Leigh hoped the poor woman wasn't going crazy with worry.

* * *

B & A Enterprises looked even more like an abandoned building after sundown. With every window boarded over, the heavy metal door, and the gray concrete blocks, it appeared totally void of life. Some of the trash he'd noticed earlier had been hauled off, but the graffiti, the broken beer bottles, and low riding gangsta cars still gave the neighborhood that don't-come-in-after-dark look.

Parked in front were two vehicles he hadn't seen earlier. One was a green Dodge Ram pickup. The other a faded red, seventies model El Camino. The El Camino wore Virginia plates and car dealership chrome from Dale City, Virginia. *Interesting,* Rush thought. Dale City was a suburb of Washington DC, where many of the Washington DC FBI field agents lived. And the Langley crowd. So were the Masterson rumors more than just that?

Rush opened his car door and climbed out. The temperature had dropped with the darkness, the wind had picked up. He tied his overcoat and walked to the metal door. It opened before he got there.

Jacob Masterson held it open, searching both ends of the street as Jackson had done the previous morning. Rush stepped through and jumped when Masterson slammed the door behind him.

"You're allowed to follow me," Masterson said.

Allowed?

Rush kept back a few feet as Masterson led him into the same small conference room. Masterson's nervous tics, most noticeable in his face, also invaded his walk. His right foot snapped out farther than normal, his left foot pointed inward every other step. He jerked his shoulders back and forth, and cocked his head to the side every few seconds. Rush wondered if he suffered from Tourette Syndrome.

Reese Morgan sat just inside the office inspecting the December issue of *Playboy*. Powdered sugar still coated much of his desk, as well as what appeared to be yesterday's doughnut bag. "Find my equipment yet?" he asked, not looking up.

"Any day now," Rush quipped, sitting in the same chair as the previous morning.

"It's still in town. I can feel it." He glanced up from his *Playboy*. "I can feel it. She's using my stuff while we're sitting around doing nothing."

"We? You just blowing off steam?"

"Why would I blow off steam? I was a cop long enough to know the score. I know the case is sitting on somebody's desk being used as a coffee coaster. And I ain't complaining about it. But I listed this Leigh as a suspect and I ain't even got a call from a detective."

Rush shrugged. "Not much to go on."

"And that's why I ain't complaining. But I'm still pissed off." He dropped his eyes to the magazine. His cheeks were flushed, his ears red. His baggy tee shirt had food stains half way to his belly.

"And what brings you here this late, Detective Rush?" Jacob Masterson asked, sitting erect in his chair, his hands folded in front of him. The jerking in his right eye and the constant movement of his lower lip, drew one's attention away from his five foot, ninety-five pound frame. He looked bird-like in the large rolling chair.

Rush wondered if his feet touched the floor. "I need the freek to the tracking unit."

"Why?" Morgan asked, looking up.

"It's obvious, Reese," Masterson said. "He has suddenly deemed the Leigh woman a much more serious candidate than Willard thought possible. He proposes to track the signal. And, I must say, he is affording her a vast amount of ingenuity."

No one said anything for a moment. Rush certainly didn't have a comeback.

"Well, Prophet," Morgan said. "He may have a problem."

"Why?" Rush asked.

"Cause I might not have come across that unit legally."

Rush wasn't surprised. "What difference does that make?"

"Tracking systems aren't sold to private firms like ours. That's why I ain't done what you wanna do. I can't get another unit."

"But he can, Reese," Masterson said. The Prophet looked at his colleague and raised an eyebrow.

Morgan snapped his lips and looked back to his magazine. "Oh, yeah."

"Do you have the frequency?" Rush asked.

"Sure," Morgan mumbled. "In the safe along with some other stuff like that. Jackson will have to open it for you."

Rush nodded.

"So has something happened to ignite this sudden interest in the woman?" Masterson asked.

"I just need to cover every angle," Rush said, his voice sounding hollow.

"May I ask you a question?" Masterson's platinum hair stood straight up, his eyes appeared slightly swollen behind his thick glasses.

"Sure."

"Have you analyzed the tapes we gave you? Studied the words she spoke?"

Rush shrugged. "Not really. I mean, I understood what she said when I heard it the first time."

"But did you *listen* to her words?"

"What do you mean?"

Masterson leaned back in his chair. "On the tape, after Willard told her he had two full time investigators and several more at his disposal, do you remember what she said?"

"Something about it not being enough."

"Close. She said, 'Three is not enough. Not for *this* guy.'"

"Okay. And?"

"The word 'this' indicates distance. She then said 'my' ex-husband. 'Ex' being the confirmation of the distance she feels using the word 'this'."

Rush rubbed his head. "I don't see the signif…"

"It tells us that she is speaking the truth."

"And you get all of that from two words?"

"I do. Combine that with what she told us about his occupation." Masterson gripped his hands together even tighter. "She's told you more than you realize."

Rush looked at Reese Morgan, who was grinning like he'd just been caught peeking up a woman's dress.

"Have you checked with your burglary unit to determine if the number of residential burglaries have increased over the last four months?" Masterson asked.

"Not ... no. The burglary rate isn't something I spend much time tracking."

"Certainly. How about credit card abuse? Not stolen cards mind you, I speak of the unauthorized use of credit card numbers or new cards sent to legitimate cardholders who didn't order them. Stolen identity."

"I'm not sure how that would relate."

"I'd be particularly interested in the number of new P.O. boxes opened in the last three months and the amount of mail generated into those boxes. An impossible piece of intelligence information to gather, I'm quite sure."

Rush rubbed his forehead, somewhat bewildered.

"The type of mail to those new boxes would be entirely predictable," Masterson went on. "You'd find an amazing number of credit cards in a wide variety of names, all legally issued of course, ready to use as soon as the phone call is made to activate them. Given all of this, I don't suspect the man will be too terribly hard to catch."

That statement grabbed Rush by the ears. "Say again."

Masterson grinned. Morgan laughed behind Rush's back.

Rush turned and looked at him. "Am I missing something here?"

Reese Morgan kicked his feet onto his desk and laughed again. "The Prophet's been studying on this for over a month. See, ever since that Leigh woman showed up around here he's been predicting that the man she's chasing would do something to draw attention to himself."

Rush was about to ask a question when Morgan went on.

"And now, since the murder's happened, he's been studying on how to catch the guy. And his theory ain't a bad one."

Jacob Masterson went back to sitting as erect and proper as any rural school teacher.

"Easy to find?" Rush asked him.

"I didn't say easy," Masterson said. "I said not too terribly hard. Leigh gave us a very big clue. Clues, actually. First she told us his occupation, a 'Listener' I believe is how she put it. And she said she'd seen him at the mall."

Masterson's eyes grew wider as he paused, waiting for a response.

Rush felt like a dullard. "And...." he said finally.

"A person shops at a mall. Or steals. I doubt the man is careless enough to steal. Leigh obviously knows he spends a lot of time at malls because she knew where to find him. To shop, a person needs money. Or credit cards." Masterson leaned toward Rush and lowered his voice. "I suspect, if this Listener is the McElroy woman's killer, that he stole some cash from her. Am I right?"

"But not credit cards?" Rush asked, knowing that none of those kinds of details had been released.

"Not from her. He wouldn't be so foolish as to use the credit cards of a murder victim. No, I suspect he stole cash. And possibly some easily pawnable items such as silver or jewelry. If my theory is accurate, he probably heard her mention a sum of cash while scanning her."

Masterson raised his eyebrows for the conformation Rush wasn't about to give, though he was dead on. "I'm still waiting to hear how you'd catch this one-man crime wave," Rush said.

"Based solely on the first clue, I'd go shopping for Leigh. You know what she looks like. What her car looks like. A person can assume that if she knows her ex well enough to find him at a mall once, she'll find him again. Find her, you have him."

If Chinbroski had been there he'd have laughed in Masterson's face. "Is that it?" Rush said instead. "I feel so fortunate that I've started that process. I'd hate for you to think that I've been sitting on my hands these last few days."

"A little manpower intensive, I admit," Masterson said, ignoring the sarcasm. "Especially since you don't know in which city to start your search. But finding her beats the alternative."

"Which is?"

"Assuming your attempt to find him with the transmitter fails, and I think it will, your only option would be to network with other area law enforcement agencies and compare credit card abuse cases. There's not a database that I'm aware of, so the man hours, the task of creating enough interest for genuine cooperation, the amount of time reviewing surveillance videos would simply be overwhelming."

Rush's ears perked. "Surveillance videos?"

"Department store videos. I'm certain your killer is on any number of videotapes making purchases with the stolen identity credit cards. The problem is that you don't know what he looks like so I don't consider that a feasible investigative avenue. Nor do I consider checking fences for the property he's selling."

Rush nodded. He felt like a rookie in an academy class being drilled by an instructor. "And why do you think tracking the transmitter signal will fail?"

"No valid reason. Just a feeling. Maybe I'm affording him his own level of ingenuity."

"I see."

Masterson stood and walked to a small refrigerator in the corner of the room. "Would you care for a beer?"

"No thanks," Rush said.

"Throw me one," Morgan said.

Masterson took two and handed Morgan his. "So have you begun your search of California parolees?" he asked Rush.

"I'm sorry?"

"Recent California parolees. The biggest clue Leigh gave us."

Rush leaned back in his chair. "What are you talking about?"

"You do remember the California reference," Masterson said, as he twisted the cap off his beer bottle.

"Yes."

"She also said, and I quote, 'He's loose and looking in Plano.' Loose from where, Detective Rush?"

He'd missed it, the word *loose*. He'd only focused on the part about him being in Plano.

"I can't imagine from where he'd be loose unless it's prison." Masterson took a drink, then dabbed his lips with the edge of his sleeve.

"He's got you there, Rush," Morgan said right after a loud belch. "And that's why we call him the Prophet. He doesn't miss much."

"I hadn't considered it," Rush said. "But you can bet I will. Good work, Jacob."

The sound of the front door opening drew Rush's attention away from Masterson, who sat rigid again, staring, slowly running a finger around the bottom of his bottle.

Willard Jackson walked in. "Hey, guys." He threw his gloves onto a chair next to Morgan's desk. "Let me open the safe, Rush, and I'll get the frequency." He disappeared from the room.

"You making any headway on the case, Rush?" Morgan asked.

"I have a couple of things worth checking."

"Yeah?" Morgan said. "I've heard that before. Used to say it myself when I didn't have jack."

Jacob Masterson stood, leaving the beer opened but untouched. "I need to be going, Reese. I'll see you at noon tomorrow."

"Remember to go straight to the lawyer's office," Morgan told him.

"I won't forget." Masterson looked at Rush as he pulled on his coat. "I think you can find him, detective."

Rush nodded. "Thanks for your help."

"Glad to be of service."

Willard Jackson stepped into the room just as Masterson was leaving. He handed Rush a slip of paper. "The frequencies. There were two transmitters stolen. But the first one on the list is broken."

"Thanks. I'll give the company a call tomorrow, have them Fed-Ex one." Rush stood to go. "Thanks for making the trip all the way back here, Willard."

"No problem." Jackson still wore his coat and scarf. He grabbed his gloves and headed toward the front door.

Rush wasn't quite ready to leave. "Hey, Willard. I'm gonna stick around for a minute and talk to Reese. I don't want to keep you, though."

Jackson glanced from Rush to Morgan. "No problem. Wife's waiting on me, anyway."

Once the door clanged shut, Rush pulled a chair over to Morgan's desk.

"What's this all about?" Morgan said. He still sat with his feet propped on the edge of his desk, the *Playboy* opened on his lap.

"What's the deal with Masterson?"

Morgan frowned. "What's the deal? You mean his tics?"

"His tics? I don't care about that. I'm wondering about his history."

Morgan closed his magazine and tossed it on his desk. "You talking about his government stuff?"

Rush locked his fingers behind his head. "Does he have government stuff?"

"That's what I hear. The Prophet don't talk much about it." Morgan smiled and Rush saw a piece of food stuck between his front teeth.

"You saying you know nothing?"

"I'm saying I know little." He let that rest a moment. "Why the interest? He a suspect or something?"

"A suspect? That's a stupid question."

"Is that a yes or a no?"

"Hell no, he's not a suspect. The guy sounds like someone I can use in the future. I'm just curious if his background will allow it."

Morgan worked his tongue around in his mouth and laughed. The piece of food dislodged and sailed within two inches of Rush's head. "You thinking employee or snitch?"

"Consultant might be the most accurate."

"Consultant, snitch, whatever, I wouldn't count on that. The Prophet barely makes it to work every day."

"So what's the deal with him?"

"Military intelligence, I know that. Worked a few years as a spook, some overseas stuff. Russia, Afghanistan, Bosnia. He speaks a couple of those guttural languages. We were working a surveillance once and he made a comment about being captured. Don't think he meant for it to come out. May be where he picked up his tics."

Morgan slid open his lap drawer and pulled out a candy bar. He ripped the wrapper off. "Bite?" he asked, holding it out.

"No thanks."

"So anyway, he wouldn't talk about the prisoner thing. Willard told me he had a nervous breakdown and that's what killed his government career. Jackson also said the guy's house is so full of books there ain't no place to sit. Ain't never been in there myself, but with some of the stuff he comes up with, it wouldn't surprise me if he ain't reading every minute he ain't working."

Rush let him swallow a bite before going on. "So he's a loner?"

"Even more than me. And that's saying something." Morgan paused. "I'd listen to him. I think the prison thing is a possibility. And so is the credit card shopping thing. I think your perp can be caught. Good idea about the tracking, by the way. I think you've got a real shot there."

Rush nodded. "Thanks, Reese." He glanced at his watch. "It's almost eight-thirty. I've got to hit it."

Morgan stuffed the rest of the candy bar into his mouth and swung his feet off the desk. "I'm right behind you," he mumbled.

Rush's house was dark except for the front porch light; no light from inside, even the faint glow from the master bedroom signaling Mallory's studying. Asleep at quarter till nine? Parking, he knew she'd been hitting it hard these last couple of weeks. Probably exhausted.

As he pulled up the driveway he noticed a note on the front door, saw the note taped to the peephole.

He stopped his car and walked over. Written on a piece of paper the size of a 3 X 5 card, he recognized the jagged, slanted letters immediately. He fought the urge to touch the note, a dread gripping his stomach.

"*Hey High Heel,*" he read quietly aloud. "*Pike to Highroller's dusties. Do not walter levi. Yattin the somerset grabe george bee. The grizz in Bear Waller. Harp Beark the neef, the nonch neemer.*"

Rage rose in his throat, and then fear twisted his gut as he noticed that the front door was unlocked and standing open an inch.

Mallory!

FIFTEEN

With the front door cracked open an inch, Rush drew his gun and knelt. No pry marks around the locks, no apparent forced entry. His throat constricted as he stood and unscrewed the light bulb above his head. Darkness flooded the porch.

Tactics. He couldn't be backlighted when he opened the front door. Pushing himself into a corner on the hinged side of the door, he waited for his eyes to adjust to the darkness. Rage engulfed him as he thought of the killer invading his home. He gritted his teeth, desperately fighting the urge to barge through the door and run to Mallory.

Rush had met her after a neighbor found her lying in her driveway next to her car, passed out from loss of blood. She had two broken legs; both practically crushed from the blows of a baseball bat. A compound fracture in her left arm, a series of knife wounds across her chest and back. Defense wounds on her arms that had severed a major artery, and four broken ribs with shoe prints still plainly visible on her skin.

She'd been left for dead. Her ex had packed his clothes, emptied their bank account, and fled town. She should have died. Only God knows how she opened her front door and crawled outside. Only the quick actions by the neighbor, and then the paramedics, had saved her.

With her already slipping back into something he couldn't bear watching, something like this would plunge her into... He shook his head, refusing to finish the thought.

His eyes adjusted and he slowly pushed the door open with his left hand, keeping his .45 in a combat ready position tightly against his chest. After the door lightly bumped against the inside wall, after he scanned the darkness of the entry hall, he stepped through the door, gun gripped in both hands, and visually swept the den on the other side of the entry. Nothing. Through the den and into the kitchen, the muzzle of his .45 inspected every hiding place large enough for a human. Heart racing, he moved toward the hallway, the passageway to Mallory. Every other evening at this time she was propped up in bed, books spread out in front of her. Dear Lord, he silently prayed, let me find her asleep.

He needed no illumination to maneuver through the house, and his search was silent and swift. After clearing the first bedroom and the hall bath, his heart nearly jumped into his throat when he heard whimpering drifting from the master bedroom.

Human whimpering. Mallory's.

He dropped to one knee, careful to stay away from the wall, fearing he might bump against it. He had one more bedroom to check before the master. Instinct screamed for him to run to his wife, training demanded that he not. He couldn't pass an unchecked door, couldn't walk into an ambush.

The door to the guestroom was closed, as usual. And to open it quietly was next to impossible. Every summer, as the Texas heat dried the soil, their slab foundation began bending. And the guestroom door was the first to feel its effects. The shifting concrete slab always warped the doorframe, making the door impossibly hard to open. Now almost Christmas, the door was still stuck. Last week he'd almost dislocated a shoulder trying to enter. No reason to think now that someone could open it quietly and ambush him if he passed it unchecked.

So he ignored it and went to his wife.

The master bedroom door sat ajar, the whimpering was irregular and soft. Again staying on the hinged side, he inched the door wider, scanning the room as it opened up to him.

When the bed was visible, he saw a mound in the middle. The door creaked. The whimpering stopped. The mound sprang to life. Mallory jumped from the bed and spun toward the door.

"Who's there!" she screamed. "Who's there?"

Rush almost collapsed from relief.

"Who's there!" Mallory screamed again, backing away from the bed toward the closet where Rush kept a wide assortment of guns.

"Mallory, it's me." He stood and holstered his .45. "It's me."

She jumped and stifled a scream, throwing her hands to her face. "You scared me to death!" Shaking, she reached over and flipped on the bedside lamp.

Books were spread across the bed. The room appeared as it did any other night, save the used tissues littering the nightstand. "Mallory?" he said, stepping toward her. "Why were you crying? What's wrong?"

She wiped her red ringed eyes and sniffed. "Why were you sneaking around the house with your gun out?" She sat on the bed and pulled a blanket around her legs.

"Because the front door was open, the house was dark. It's not like you. I was worried." He wouldn't mention the note, would never confess that a possible murderer had been standing on their front porch. He walked over and sat on the edge of the bed. "What's wrong, honey? Why were you crying?"

She closed her eyes and shook her head. "Give me a minute." She reached to the nightstand, grabbed a tissue.

Rush placed a hand on her arm. "Did you hear someone outside? Why was the door open?"

After blowing her nose, she pushed herself up against the headboard and looked at him. "I must have left it open after I got the mail." She paused, looked away. "I don't know... I started crying because I don't know what's wrong with me."

Swallowing hard, he kept his eyes on hers. Mallory's lips were a hard line, though the lower one quivered slightly. Her nostrils flared in and out, her cheeks were flushed as though she'd just come in from the cold. More to the point, she looked like she had a year and a half before, broken and terrified. "What are you talking about?" he asked.

"I'm talking about me. I just feel... I don't know, different today. Like I've regressed or something. I can't concentrate." She picked up a book and drummed it with a finger. "I look at the stuff in here and it's all foreign to me. How can that be?" She blew out a breath.

Rush said nothing.

She stared at him and rubbed her forehead.

"Did something happen today?" he asked.

She looked away. Her fingers twisted the tissue into a tight wad. "I've never hidden anything from you." Fresh tears slid from her eyes.

He waited.

"Never played games." Her voice sounded hollow, as though all emotion had been absorbed into her tears and drained away.

He released her arm and hugged her. "What's going on?"

"Is there something wrong with me?" she whispered.

He held her tighter. Said nothing, afraid of his answer. His throat felt constricted, as if a small bone had lodged itself half way to his chest.

Mallory pushed away, the large book falling to the side. She threw the blankets back and climbed down from the bed. Grabbing a robe, she pulled it on and wiped her cheeks. "What did you do for dinner?"

"Mallory. What hap…"

"There's some lasagna in the fridge." She quickly headed out of the room, drying her eyes with the sleeve of her robe. "I'll heat it up," she said over her shoulder.

Rush stood in the middle of the room and looked at the walls, speechless.

Sighing, he walked into the kitchen where Mallory quickly put the lasagna on a plate. He grabbed a beer from the fridge and sat down. He wouldn't push her. Her doctor had always advised against pushing her. Easier said than done.

"How's the case going?" she asked after heating his dinner and placing the plate in front of him.

She sat in the chair next to him. Almost normal. Almost.

He wiped a line of foam from his upper lip and shrugged. "Making some progress, I guess." He felt uncomfortable talking details. She only asked to be polite, he knew, to show an interest in the part of his life she'd never be involved in.

He ate in silence for several minutes. She watched him, sitting quietly, her hands folded in front of her.

"Can I ask you something?" she said finally.

Here it comes. "Sure."

"Will you get angry?"

He laughed with a mouth full of food. "I guess I might. What is it?"

Her dark hair was pulled back into a tight ponytail. Her freshly scrubbed face had worry lines that added years to her looks. With trembling hands she stood and walked out of the kitchen, her big fluffy house shoes flapping against the tile floor, her flannel robe hanging like a sack over her small frame. She was back less than a minute later and set an envelope in front of him.

"From Roger," she said with a small voice. "Will you read it?" She locked her fingers together and pressed her knuckles against her lips.

"Roger?" He looked at the postmark: Palestine, Texas. "He wrote to you from prison?"

She nodded.

So that was it. "But you didn't open it."

"I couldn't."

Roger Hamilton, her ex-husband, had been locked up for the last eighteen months, twelve of them in the Caldwell Unit of the state prison system in Palestine. Rush had heard that he'd killed a man a month after his arrival, but the guards had been unable to prove it.

He pushed his plate away and stared at the envelope he hadn't yet touched. "You got this today?"

She nodded again.

That's why she hadn't locked the door after getting the mail. He reached across and took hold of her trembling hands.

He looked back at the envelope. Hamilton's right slanted scrawl was unmistakable: So fluid, so graceful, so unlike the man.

"How did he know our address?" she asked. "How did he know we were married?"

Rush thought about that. And it didn't take long to figure. "Eugene Wright, probably. His lawyer. The guy is just as much a criminal as Roger."

Mallory nodded as she stared off at a spot somewhere over Rush's left shoulder.

"I can burn it, Mal. Right here, right now. We don't have to read it."

He watched her. She wore a thousand-yard stare as vacant as Jane McElroy's.

"If we read it," he told her, "he'll have what he wants."

She said nothing.

"He still wants to control you, your emotions, your feelings. Can't you see that? He wants you to feel fear. He wants you to taste it." He paused, hoping his words would penetrate. "See, Mal, if we burn it now he only has history. And that's yesterday's news. It's nothing. He probably knows you're recovering from the history and it pisses him off."

When she said nothing after what seemed a lifetime, he picked the letter up by a corner and walked to the stove, turning a burner on high.

"No, Greg," she said, right before he stuck it into the flame. "Don't burn it. I want to know." She stood and held out her hand. "I want to know."

He stared at her, not believing she was serious. "Why? What purpose would it serve?"

"Maybe he's finally come to terms with what he is. Maybe ... maybe he's finally realized that what he did was wrong."

"Don't kid yourself, Mal. He knows what he did was wrong. And he knew what he was the first time he knocked out one of your teeth and decided he liked it."

Her eyes were dry now, but her cheeks still glistened. She rubbed them with the heels of her hands. "I want to see it."

Rush still held the corner of the envelope, unwilling to contaminate what fingerprints might be readable. "I'll tell you what. I'll read it first. Huh? And then I'll decide if you see it."

Her face hardened. "You'll decide?"

He walked to the table and placed the envelope next to his plate. "Look, Mal, I don't think it's emotionally healthy for you to see it at all. If this thing is full of threats, tell me what good it does for you to see that?"

She wrung her hands as she thought it out. When she said nothing, he went on.

"You've had enough problems just dealing with the memories of this guy, of what he did to you. We've both been through some hard times. I'm not about to let that bastard drag both of us into the past. I'm not putting up with any of his games."

She crossed her arms and hugged herself, then collapsed in her chair.

"Deal?" he asked. "I read it first, then I decide?"

She nodded weakly.

"Good." He scooted his chair out and sat down. "I'm going to finish eating. Roger Hamilton is *not* going to ruin what few good meals I get to have at home."

Mallory rubbed the back of her neck, then stood. "I'll be in the bedroom." She bent and pecked him on the cheek. "I've got some studying."

As the flopping of her house shoes faded, he studied the front of the envelope. It was addressed to Mallory Rush, certainly no mention of her first married name. Had there been, he doubted the letter would have made it out of the prison. The state was pretty good about not allowing prisoners to send letters to their victims.

He pushed his plate away, drained his beer, and wiped his upper lip. The bastard was not about to drag Mallory back into the hell she'd been free from for almost three years.

Scooting his chair back, he walked over and grabbed a knife from the silverware drawer. Then he sat back down and lifted the envelope by a corner and slowly slit it open.

Careful to preserve what might later be evidence, he unfolded a single sheet of paper and held it flat by laying the knife along the edge.

"*Dear, Cop Lover,*" it began. "*I heard you hitched up with the peckerwood that stuck his nose in our business. How's it feel sleeping with the enemy? You used to like it rough. Except when I got rough you filed charges against me. Does he like it rough too? Or did I give you all the rough you can stand? I'll get out one day. You better hope that cop gets tired of you before then. Better hope you lose yourself someplace where I can't find you. Cause as it is now, I'm planning on taking you back. And that faggot you married ain't gonna do nothing about it. See you, sweet thing. And I mean that. I'll be seeing you."*

The letter was unsigned. Rush could hear his own heartbeat, could feel the pressure inside his head. Sweat beaded his brow, his hands shook.

"That bastard," Rush whispered to himself. If the letter was meant to piss him off, mission accomplished.

He sat and stared at it, reading it twice more before finally slipping it back into the envelope. He put the envelope in his briefcase.

Mallory was back under the blankets with an economics book in front of her face. Rush sat on the edge of the bed and took hold of one of her hands.

"Well?" she said.

"I put it in my briefcase. I want McBride to dust it for prints to confirm that Roger wrote it. Then I'm going to call the warden at the Caldwell Unit and make sure they stop anything else he tries to send us."

Her eyes were wide, probing. "To me, you mean."

"To us. We're married, Mal. Your problems are mine. But he is *not* going to be a problem."

They sat and looked at each other for several seconds. "So you're not going to let me read it?"

"I don't think you'd gain anything from it. He certainly hasn't reinvented himself. He hasn't repented his past. The whole thing is just what I thought it'd be, an attempt to crawl inside your head." He paused. "You don't want him inside your head, do you?"

She shook her head and smiled. "The only man I want is you. And I do think it's best that I don't read it." She pushed her book aside and wrapped her arms around his neck. "You too tired for a full body work out?" she whispered.

"Never," he whispered back. "Never."

SIXTEEN

The next morning broke clear and cold, but not as cold as the past week. With Christmas less than three weeks off, Rush was more than ready for a more normal mid-fifties North Texas December. The temperature was already in the low thirties by the time he arrived at the station. Never had freezing temperatures felt so balmy.

At nine AM a package was delivered to his desk, postmarked from California. It was the book he'd ordered detailing the history of Boontling. Written as a Ph.D. dissertation by Charles C. Adams, *Boontling, An American Lingo*, detailed the entire history of Anderson Valley, California. Rush glanced at the glossary and smiled. It was exactly what he needed to decipher the message left last night on his door, as well as the note left at the crime scene.

But first he called Florida, to the manufacturer of the tracking system stolen from B & A's surveillance van. After explaining what he needed, a senior vice-president agreed to overnight a loaner unit tuned to the correct frequency.

Then he set to work with the Boontling book.

Chinbroski dropped into a chair next to Rush's desk seconds after he finished deciphering both notes. Rush looked up. "Where've you been all morn…?"

Chinbroski's clothes stopped Rush in mid sentence. A pair of new shoes, Dockers, and a nice wool sweater. "What's with the clothes?"

"What'd you mean?"

"It's Nanci," Rush said. "I can't believe it. You've started dressing nice for a woman."

Chinbroski smacked his lips and looked away. "What are you talking about? I just got tired of all the crap you've been giving me."

"I've been on you about your clothes since Jesus was in high school. Then you meet Nanci and you come to work wearing new hiking boots, new pants, and a new sweater. Well, I think it's sweet."

Chinbroski leaned forward and lowered his voice. "No reason to shout." He glanced around. "You're way off track, anyway," he said, lowering his voice even more. "I got a good deal on these clothes, that's all."

"Tight as you are, it must've been a great deal. Or love."

"Can we drop this?"

"It is sweet, though. Mallory would just cry."

Chinbroski shook his head.

Rush looked at the notes he'd made translating the Boontling. "Got a weird message on my door last night." He handed a copy to Chinbroski.

"Hey High Heel," Chinbroski read. *"Pike to Highroller's dusties. Do not walter levi. Yattin the somerset grabe george bee. The grizz in Bear Waller. Harp Beark the neef, the nonch neemer."* He looked at Rush.

"Wanna know what it means?"

Chinbroski glanced at the book lying on Rush's desk.

Rush translated. "First, the message left in McElroy's bedroom: '*Hey cop, this dull witted, fat woman talked continually on the telephone about how wealthy she was. He was broke so he had to kill her. The reporters are gonna gather quick so hurry and catch him. PS, Go to Yorkville.*'

"Our theory about someone scanning McElroy's phone is dead on. By the way, Yorkville is a small town about ten miles south of Boonville, California." He tapped the book. "It's in here."

Chinbroski said nothing.

"The one from last night. '*Hey, cop. Go to Yorkville's cemetery. Do not telephone. Talk to the upset old trapper. The old bachelor living in squalid conditions off Point Arena Road. Talk about the aggressive person, the one who lost a finger, the one who has sworn off liquor.*'"

Rush looked up again. "That's it. Tells us where to go."

"And that book gives you an exact translation?"

Rush picked up the book. "Not exact. In Boontling one word may mean an entire sentence. For example *grizz* means an old bachelor; one living in squalid conditions. So even though my translation is longer than the message, the meaning seems pretty clear."

Chinbroski rubbed his chin. "So the woman wants us to go to California?"

"That's how I'd take it."

"Maybe it's a team thing like we thought at first and now she's having second thoughts. How'd she get your address?"

Rush shrugged. "Could have followed me home. Wouldn't be that hard."

Chinbroski went silent again. "Sounds weird to me."

"What other explanation is there?"

"Don't know any other explanation," Chinbroski said. "But I'll say one thing, we ain't gonna need no trip to California."

"Why?"

"Cause this guy's gonna screw up. I can feel it. It's in my gut. And when he does we'll bury his ass under the prison."

The prison. Rush had forgotten to call the warden at the Caldwell Unit in Palestine. He grabbed the phone, dialed information, and asked for the number.

"What do you got going at Caldwell?"

"Roger sent Mallory a letter," he said, as he dialed the number. "I'm not putting up with it."

"What'd the letter say?"

Rush asked for the warden's office. "Said he's coming for her when he gets out."

"Yeah? Is that what he thinks? Maybe we ought to go pay that boy a visit. Slip a couple guards a little green so we can spend a few minutes alone with him. Make the bastard spend the rest of his life eating meals through a straw."

Rush spoke to the warden's secretary and was told the warden was out. He left his name and number.

Randy McBride walked up just as Rush hung up. "Hey, Rush. I was hoping I'd catch you." He threw a quick glance at Chinbroski. "I got something interesting in the mail today." He had two large manila envelopes clutched in his hand. His baggy pants hung crooked, the left side three inches lower than the right. "Very interesting."

"Can we just see it?" Chinbroski snapped.

Rush glared at his partner. "Enough, Chin." He turned to McBride. "What is it?"

"Crime-scene photos," he said. "Of the McElroy murder."

"You gave me a set."

"Not of these. These were mailed." McBride held up an envelope stained with fingerprint powder. "Got them this morning. Dusted it. No prints. Pretty good photography work, though. Better than some crime-scene shots I've seen."

Chinbroski leaned forward. "Would you stop rambling and tell us what you're talking…"

Rush held up his hand, cutting Chinbroski off. "I think I know what he's talking about. You're saying someone came in before us and took pictures."

"And right after the murder. Before the house turned into a freezer."

Rush took the envelope from McBride and pulled out the contents. There were five 8 X 10 photos and a note written in Boontling. Fingerprint dust stained the lined paper and was smeared all over the photographs.

"I wiped off as much of the lava dust as I could," McBride said. "Wasn't a print found on any of it."

Three of the photos showed Jane McElroy's body propped up in the tub. The pink water had overflowed onto the floor and looked fresh, more revolting, Rush thought, than after it had frozen.

"If you'll lay these pictures next to my crime scene shots," McBride said, pulling open the other envelope, "you'll see that whoever took these pre-ice shots stood almost exactly where I did. Very good work."

Rush compared them as Chinbroski crowded him, peering over his shoulder. They were identical except for the ice. The other two photos were taken inside the bedroom, one of the blood-soaked bed, the other of the overall room.

McBride pointed to the wide-angle shot, which appeared to have been taken from the doorway leading into the hall, and then pulled out an almost identical picture from his envelope.

"You'll find this comparison interesting," he said.

Chinbroski pushed in closer, actually bumping Rush out of the way. "I don't see nothing so great. This another one of your games, McBride?"

"It's no game," Rush said. "Don't you see it?"

Chinbroski looked closer. "All I see is the room."

"But what don't you see? It tells us volumes."

Chinbroski picked up both photos and stuck them under his nose. "What?"

Rush said, "What you don't see is the note on the dresser."

Chinbroski studied the photos. Then he snorted his response. "So. You think that's proof Leigh wrote the note? Is that what you're saying?"

"That's exactly what I'm saying."

"That's nothing. Could be our red-headed guy took the pictures, wrote the note, and then hit the road." Chinbroski looked at McBride. "What do you think?"

McBride flinched, unaccustomed to having Chinbroski ask his opinion of anything. "Uh, well, I agree with Rush. I think the woman sent the photos so we'd know she's trying to help. I mean, what other reason could there be?"

"To pull our schlong," Chinbroski snapped. "I just ain't convinced she ain't jerking us around. I'll tell you one thing, first time I see her I'm planting her directly into jail. She's obstructing justice big time. And tampering with evidence."

Rush took the new note written in Boontling and flattened it on top of his desk. Chinbroski read it aloud over his shoulder. *"Rush, the trashmover is over. You teebowed? Time to treek to Bear Waller. My final note, thrib enough. I'm tellick, tongue-cuppy from the stringings. Beark has my tweed, my weech. White oak, monty in this monster. He's fence jumpy. Otto to catch him. Kraisey Beark, a greeney grey-matter kimmie. I have eeble on Beark, the rubberneck. Neemer notes."*

Chinbroski stepped back from the desk and looked at Rush. "Why don't she just use English? What's the point of this shit? If she's gonna snitch him off, just do it. She don't think we're gonna find out who she is?"

"You may not," McBride said.

Chinbroski spun around and stuck a finger in his face. "Nobody asked you."

McBride, who had sat down in the chair Chinbroski had vacated, jumped up. "Well, look, I don't know anything about all this. I've got stuff to do." He shuffled off, yanking at his pants.

After he was out of earshot, Rush glared at Chinbroski. "What's the matter with you? McBride's trying to help."

Chinbroski set his jaw and flopped down into the chair. "She's making us jump through a bunch of damn hoops. What's the point?"

"If I knew where she was, I'd go ask her. But you need to lay off McBride. Man, you need to forget the Neanderthal comment. It's been almost two years."

Chinbroski said nothing. He stared at the new note, a vein pulsing on the side of his neck.

Rush had it translated fifteen minutes later. Chinbroski hadn't said a word during that time.

"Okay, listen up. I think this proves Leigh is involved in all this. With this note and the others, we've got a pretty good picture of what we're looking for. And now we know what's driving her."

"What's it say?"

"'*Rush, the heavy winter storm is over. You hard of hearing? Time to travel to a wooded area south of Boonville off Point Arena Road. My final note, three's enough. I'm exhausted, nauseated from the killings. Beark has my child, my small child. Work hard, concentrate on this monster. He's an adulterer. Work hard to catch him. False identity, that's Beark, a strange scholar. I have an eyeball on Beark, the eavesdropper. No more notes.*'"

Chinbroski folded his thick arms across his chest; his face set in a scowl. "So she's after her kid."

Rush glanced at the photo of Jane McElroy's body and shuttered. That monster had Leigh's child? A bead of sweat broke under his hairline.

Chinbroski looked at Rush. "And she says he's a scholar? What's that mean to some hick from the northern woods of California? That he finished the eighth grade?"

Rush referred to the translations of the first two messages. "We also know he has red hair, has a missing finger, cheated on Leigh, and may have lived off Point Arena Road. We know some old trapper who hangs around a cemetery may be able to tell us his name, Leigh calls him Beark, he kidnapped a small child, and he's sworn off drinking."

"So you're saying you gotta go out there. To California."

"We, Chin. I'm not going without you. But neither one of us are going until we get that receiver tomorrow and try and find Reese Morgan's tracking signal."

Chinbroski stood. "Playing this game with some goofy wench is about more than I can stand."

"Hold it, Chin," Rush said, standing. "Don't I remember us standing out at the McElroy house where you told me that this is what we live for? That they make movies about this kind of case? That we could get famous?"

"I didn't say we could get famous."

"No?"

"I was just saying it was a weird case."

"So what's the deal? You have something better to do?"

"I ain't saying that."

"Then let's just work this thing. If it weren't for Leigh, where would we be?"

Chinbroski stuck at finger in Rush's direction. "We still need to throw her ass in jail."

Rush looked at his partner. Chinbroski's face was flushed, his sweater stretching against his shoulders. "When we find her, if we find her, we'll see if she cooperates. If she doesn't..." Rush shrugged and let the unfinished sentence hang in the air.

Rush's cell phone rang on the afternoon drive home. He glanced at the number before answering. "Daniel, I haven't heard from you so often since you were begging for money in college."

"Good afternoon, Pop. I'm beyond begging now. Being Ivy League educated, I petition, beseech or entreat. Found your mystery woman yet?"

"All in good time."

"She called me again last night. And I must say, she could hold her own within the halls of Cornell."

Rush heard scratching over his cell and quickly pulled into the parking lot of a gas station so he wouldn't lose the call. "She's been in contact with me, also. Care to trade what we know?"

Daniel chuckled. "You're such a kidder."

"What's the harm? Has she confessed to anything?"

"Confessing can occur other than by words alone," Daniel said. "You know that."

"If she's called you twice on the phone, what else besides words would she use? Based on what she's sent me I could easily get convictions for tampering with a crime scene, obstruction, and interfering with a police officer as appetizers for the main meal murder. Since it's obvious now that she followed the killer while the killer followed Jane McElroy."

"If that's all you'd charge her with, and promise there'd be nothing else added, I might cut a deal right now."

Rush reached over and noted the date and time of this phone call on a notepad he kept handy in the car. "Now that's an interesting statement. Care to elaborate?"

"Let's just say that I seriously doubt we'll ever be facing each other in court over charges filed against her. She's an intriguing woman. Focused. Calculating."

"Do I hear a hint of hero worship? You always were a sucker for women smarter than you."

"That's because there are so few," Daniel said. "But no, while interesting, I have the feeling she's near the end of whatever quest is driving her, and once finished, she'll disappear into the night."

"I see. Was there a specific reason you called? It certainly wasn't to be helpful."

"Actually, it was. I believe she was outside my office last night when she called. Parked at the courthouse."

Rush's pulse quickened, but he held his breath against any real information. "At the courthouse. And why would you be telling me this?"

"Never let it be said that I stood in the way of justice. This woman knows where your killer is. She needs to be found. Certainly, if I knew where she was, I wouldn't tell you. But since I don't, I'm not violating any trust or confidence. The law allows for me to make an educated guess. And her being parked at the courthouse is just that."

"And the courthouse has video cameras covering every inch of their lot."

"My, you do catch on quick, Pop."

"You'd love for me to catch her, wouldn't you? Another chance to even the game?"

"She called me. And I don't know what you're talking about."

"Has she paid you a retainer?"

"We've signed no agreement."

"Evasive answer, which tells me everything. Listen, when I find her, I'll give you a call. Are you and Sally leaving town for Christmas?"

"Going to visit mom. Want to come?"

"Gee, I think I'll pass this year. Tell her girlfriend I said hello."

"You'll never let it go, will you?"

"What, getting beat out by a woman? I let it go years ago. Even if I had known I was in a race, I couldn't have competed with that. Take care, Daniel. I'm sure we'll be talking soon."

"Bye, Pop. Take copious notes."

"I will."

Then they both said in unison, "Because it didn't happen if you didn't write it down."

Rush punched off the call with a smile on his face. His boy made him proud.

SEVENTEEN

The tracking system arrived by ten the next morning. Rush arranged for the use of a Dallas PD helicopter and pilot for as long as needed. Reese Morgan agreed to install the receiver on the belly of the chopper and had finished the job by noon.

The temperature, almost forty degrees, was expected to top fifty by mid afternoon. The deep blue, cloudless sky, with the wind almost nonexistent, offered up perfect flying conditions.

Rush would ride in the chopper. Chinbroski and Morgan would be on the ground in Chinbroski's car.

Because Rush thought it possible that Beark might be out scouting, they would start in the air over Collin Creek Mall, the last place he knew Beark to victimize. According to an information sheet sent by the manufacturer of the tracking unit, the scanning range of the receiver from five thousand feet was almost sixty miles, enough to cover most of the northern half of the Dallas/ Ft. Worth Metroplex.

The pilot, Ray Vance, was a trim, silver haired Vietnam veteran. He seemed relaxed, confident, told small jokes that lightened the seriousness of the assignment. After Rush confirmed that everyone was ready, he told Vance to take off.

From the north parking lot of the police department the chopper rose, whipping the bare branches that seemed to grasp at the sky like a collection of bony fingers. They dipped forward and then headed west over Highway 75, slowly climbing higher.

"Your first ride?" Vance asked over the radio headset.

Rush felt his stomach rise into his throat as Vance shot them straight up. "No. Army. Vietnam. More recently I've ridden with a friend who owns an air crane service."

Vance nodded. "Air crane, huh? That's precision flying."

Slower, too, Rush thought. "Yeah. Most of his jobs are tall buildings, you know, lifting big air conditioning units, stuff like that."

"Right," Vance said. "I've seen a few of those guys work. Like I said, precision flying. Think about being up there with two tons hanging out of your butt like a turd that won't drop. Between buildings, fighting wind tunnels. Having to set it down into a space with two inches to spare on each side." He whistled.

They rose higher, the ground shrinking before them, and hovered just above Collin Creek Mall while Chinbroski and Reese Morgan got into position.

Rush's radio crackled a few seconds later. "Yo, Rush, Chinbroski here. We're ready to sniff this guy out."

"Ten-four." The tracking receiver was a simple metal box with a circle of small red lights. The top of the circle indicated north, the bottom south. Rush flipped the *On* switch and immediately got a signal northwest of their location.

"Got a bite," Rush said into the radio, fighting to control his voice. "We're heading north. Get on the freeway." He hadn't really expected to find a signal at all, though he'd been hopeful. But like finding the Boontling on the Internet, he felt led, directed.

"Ten-four, heading north," Chinbroski radioed.

Vance turned the chopper and rose to one thousand feet, followed the freeway north at eighty miles an hour. The farther north they went, the more the signal moved to the west. When it showed almost due west, Vance turned in that direction.

"Turn west on Highway 121 in McKinney," Rush told Chinbroski. "The signal is still northwest, but 121 looks like the road to take. We'll wait on you."

"Won't be long," Chinbroski answered. "We're running almost ninety."

"Let me know."

"Any way to know how far away the signal is?" Vance asked.

Rush looked at the receiver. "There's a signal strength indicator, and it's getting stronger. But how far, I don't know. Reese told me before we lifted off that once we have a signal, make three turns to confirm the direction, then drop closer to the ground and keep making turns until we zero in. He said the signal strength indication will lead us in."

A couple minutes later Chinbroski was with them. They headed west on 121 and the signal began moving back to the north.

"Highway 121 runs southwest," Rush said. "We're moving at an angle away from it. We need to forget about following roads. Let's just find the thing and we'll direct Chinbroski in."

"Ten-four." Vance turned the chopper and headed straight west, passing over barren farmland, new housing developments, and small ranches. They were still south of the signal, though Rush didn't suspect by much, and by the time the signal showed directly north again they were over the community of Little Elm in Denton County.

"Okay, Chin," Rush transmitted, checking his map. "Cut north on Highway 289 and go to Farm to Market Road 720. It runs through Frisco. We'll hover here at the intersection of 720 and F.M. 423."

"Ten-four."

It took them twenty minutes to catch up. The transmitter was just to the northwest and the signal strength indicator had peaked. Vance followed F.M. 423 directly north for five miles until the signal showed west. They were a couple of miles south of Highway 380, southeast of Navo, Texas, hardly a speck on the map. He dropped the chopper to five hundred feet and slowly followed a dirt road that snaked along Panther Creek, a trickle of a stream that dumped into Lewisville Lake.

"You see us heading west?" Rush asked Chinbroski.

"Ten-four. We're a half-mile back. There a road up there?"

"Dirt. You'll have to keep your eyes peeled."

Vance flew low enough to see everything. The dirt road worked its way through several groves of trees and past a number of small, poorly built shacks, each with its own collection of abandoned cars.

"We got the road," Chinbroski announced. "Turning now."

The signal showed southeast, the dirt road pointing the way. To confirm the bearing, Vance told Rush that he would fly directly west and drop to three hundred feet.

Several hundred yards ahead the houses ended, the road became narrower, almost a path, then the path died under a mountain of garbage that appeared to serve as the neighborhood dump.

"Fly out over the lake and see if our signal points back to the east."

"Okay," Vance said into the headset.

As the chopper swung west and then south, Rush saw a glimmer of chrome through bare branches of a grove of trees to his left.

"Got a car about a hundred yards off the road," Rush transmitted. "We're going to drop directly over it. It has to be the signal source. Nothing else with a power source within a half mile."

"Ten-four," Chinbroski said. "You see my car?"

"You're still a quarter mile off. We're trying to get a better look."

Vance maneuvered the chopper, but the trees were so thick even the bare branches hid most of the car. "Want to land this thing?" Vance asked. "I can drop it just to the lake side of the trees."

By the time Vance landed the helicopter Chinbroski transmitted that he was at the end of the road, about to walk around the trash dump. "I can see the car through the trees," he said. "No tire tracks. Must've been there a while. How far are you?"

"We're about fifty yards," Rush said. "Vance is gonna stay and power this thing down."

Rush climbed out and immediately sank a half-inch into the mud. Texas black gumbo stuck to his feet. He struggled through knee-high grass toward the car.

"We got a ripe one," Chinbroski transmitted just as Rush began to smell the familiar scent of rotting flesh. At the edge of the groves of trees, Rush saw Chinbroski on the other side, thirty yards from the car. Rush pulled his .45 and shoved his radio into a coat pocket. Chinbroski gave a hand signal indicating his move to the right. Reese Morgan stood off to the left, behind Chinbroski, one hand in his pocket, the other covering his nose.

The car was a rusted gold colored Crown Victoria, mid eighties. It had spider cracks in the windshield, a blue right front fender, no hubcaps. The raised hood exposed wires running out from the engine department, across the hood, and onto the roof of the car. A small black box with a six-inch whip antenna sat propped up by two small rocks in the center of the roof.

The transmitter.

The smell was almost too strong to breathe. Rush figured the body, wherever it was, was in the peak of decay. He moved carefully toward the car, watching the ground, making sure he didn't trample potential evidence. Chinbroski did the same. Reese Morgan wasn't approaching at all. He leaned against a tree still holding his nose.

They approached the car from different ends, Rush from the front, Chinbroski from the back. And toward different sides, Rush to the driver's, Chinbroski to the passenger's.

Chinbroski saw the body first. "Back seat. Face up. Head propped against the door on your side of the car."

Rush stepped forward and saw the top of the head, the short hair, the black skin that covered the face, the moustache. The victim's right hand, propped up to his ear with some kind of cord, had a cellular phone duct taped to his hand.

"Damn," Chinbroski said. "Another one."

The man's body had swollen to the point of skin splitting. Channels of raw, pink flesh ran down his upper left arm and across his suspended right forearm. The hair was a white man's, but his rotting skin made him look black. Maggots crawled in and out of his mouth and nose and tunneled through the exposed entrails from the cut that ran from his sternum to his crotch. Flies buzzed around inside the car and feasted on the blackened body fluids that had settled and then leaked out of the lowest parts of the body. Rush could see the left side of the victim's head and saw the empty space the left ear had once occupied.

"I say we back out and let the Denton County Sheriff handle this," Rush said.

"So how come Leigh didn't tell you this was gonna happen?" Chinbroski's face was flushed, his lips a tight line. "How come she didn't write it in one of her stupid notes?

Rush looked at him and cocked his head. "She didn't tell us about McElroy. She may not even know about this."

"She had the transmitter last."

A gentle breeze blew into Rush's face and momentarily deadened the stench that always made him think of evil and death. "We don't know that, Chin."

"And we don't know she ain't pulling our dick, either. For all we know, she's doing all this to try and send us half way across the country for nothing."

"And why would she do that?"

"The hell if I know!" he snapped. "All I know is we ain't got nothing but dead bodies and we're back to where we started." He set his jaw and spun around, storming off.

It was one of the few times Rush didn't get in the last word.

EIGHTEEN

"So," Captain Williams said. "Who was he?"

"Henry Blankenship," Rush said. "A four-time loser from Austin, last seen a few days before Jane McElroy was murdered. Austin PD took a missing person report from his brother who said he was in Dallas to interview for a job."

Rush and Chinbroski were in Williams's office the following afternoon laying it all out.

"He was a coke mule," Chinbroski said. "They found six kilos in a false compartment in his trunk."

"But this isn't drug related?" Williams asked, adjusting the tie that appeared to be choking him.

"I doubt it was a drug deal or a robbery," Rush said. "The car hadn't been searched at all as far as we could tell. Didn't look torn apart. And it should've been with that much dope. There was a gas receipt in the front floorboard from a station in McKinney dated two days before McElroy was killed. He had his ID and a wallet full of money. I think Blankenship just ran into the wrong guy."

"Yeah, ran into a bigger piece of shit than he was," Chinbroski chuckled.

Rush tried to throw a hard stare in Chinbroski's direction, but his partner wasn't making eye contact. He sat there with the corner of his mouth slightly cocked, his face turned away, his eyes focused on his shoes. One of his favorite activities, Rush knew, was being cute in a serious meeting.

"Any way to tell how long he'd been there?" Williams asked.

"Well," Rush said, "if he was killed before McElroy there would've been some decay before the freeze hit. Then after the thaw the decay would have started again. The decomposition was so advanced that…"

"Should've seen this guy," Chinbroski cut in. He scooted forward in his seat, his face flushed with the memory. "Looked like he was melting. Maggots so thick his black, rotting skin…"

"I think I get the picture," Williams said, cutting him off.

Chinbroski dropped his smile and folded his hands across his lap. "Well, it don't really matter how long this guy's been dead. It's gonna be our guy who did it."

"I'm a little confused about this whole transmitter thing," Williams said. "The guy who owns it, Reese Morgan, is convinced Leigh stole it. You think she put it on the suspect's car. And this would have happened before the McElroy murder?"

"Right," Rush said.

"But then the suspect finds it and snatches this Blankenship, kills him, and puts the transmitter on his car so the cops could find the body."

"Or so Leigh could find the body." Rush rubbed away a line of sweat on his forehead. "To send her a message."

"But then you say all that happened *before* McElroy. If so, how did Leigh know McElroy had been killed? If the transmitter was already gone how did she track him?"

That thought had occurred to Rush, though he hadn't spent much time on it.

"That's a good point," Chinbroski said, scooting forward in his chair again. "And it runs right into another point. If this Beark already found the transmitter, then he *had* to know something was up, that somebody was watching him. Knowing that, how would Leigh be able to follow him?"

The three of them said nothing as Rush shrugged.

"I'm telling you right now, she's up to her nose in all this." Chinbroski pounded a finger into his leg for emphasis, his face flush again. "And I'll tell you something else. Why would Beark – or whatever his name is – kill McElroy when he's probably thinking somebody's doing surveillance? Huh? And she drives an old beat up Oldsmobile with California plates? Not in my lifetime. I mean, if the guy's that clueless we'd have caught him by now."

Chinbroski's tirade over, Rush didn't have an answer.

"I'm interested in these notes, too," Williams said. "These messages. They're cryptic instructions to get you to California? To talk to some old trapper who hangs around a graveyard?"

"That's the way they translate," Rush said, knowing how it sounded.

"And what else we got?" Chinbroski asked. "The woman said she ain't sending no more notes. And it ain't like we got leads falling on top of our heads."

Rush waited a beat to make sure his partner had finished. "We need to go out there," he said, after catching Chinbroski with solid eye contact and giving him a little head shake.

Williams nodded. "I agree. Get with Kathy and she'll make whatever flight arrangements you need."

"Yes, sir."

"One more thing," Williams added. "I'm sending Gerald Hanisch with you."

Rush felt the blood drain from his face. He snapped a look at Chinbroski, who had also paled. "But ... I don't understand why…"

"Just kidding, Rush," Williams said, standing. "Lighten up, huh?"

Out in the hall Chinbroski slapped Rush on the back and laughed. "He really had you going there, partner. Should've seen your face. Looked like you took a big crap in your in-law's toilet that won't flush."

The American Airlines flight left Dallas at 6:05 PM that evening and landed in San Francisco at 8:15 west coast time. Rush, letting Chinbroski drive, wanted to get to Santa Rosa before calling it a night.

The ninety-minute drive was made with little talk. Rush dozed once Chinbroski had the rental car across the Golden Gate Bridge and heading north on Highway 101.

They checked into a Holiday Inn at 10:30 PM, and like every other time they'd ever traveled together, were forced by the department to share a room. Rush was barely conscious by the time Chinbroski slammed the motel-room door and threw the suitcases on the floor.

"I feel like a slave, Rush. What's wrong with you?"

"Tired." He felt like someone had hooked a siphon hose to the top of his head and sucked out every ounce of energy. "Don't let me oversleep," he barely heard himself say. "I want to be on the road by eight."

Chinbroski turned on the television and flopped onto the bed nearest the bathroom. "Want breakfast in bed, too? How about a cup of hot tea? Or a damn massage?"

"Massage sounds good," Rush mumbled through a fog of fatigue so thick he could hardly move his mouth.

"Well, I tell you, buddy," Chinbroski said. "I ain't that kind of partner."

Rush heard him flip through the channels, and finally stop on ESPN. Then he heard Chinbroski curse about the state of the Cowboys before everything faded to black.

Mid-December in Northern California was the early fringe of the rainy season. But the morning broke clear and cool, the sun burning brightly in the low southeastern sky. They ate breakfast at a McDonald's and were heading north on 101 by eight-fifteen.

With mountains on both sides of the highway and the sun filtering through the early morning mist, Rush suddenly understood *purple mountains majesty*. The trees were still green, the wild grass on the hillsides long and flowing. He was startled at how every inch of flat ground was devoted to vineyards. The vines were barren this time of year, but the lack of vegetation couldn't hide how incredibly straight the rows were. They seemed to fold into one another as the foothills rolled gently toward the mountains that were swallowed by the fog hanging just low enough to hide the peaks. Mile after mile of vineyards made Rush wonder who could own such large parcels of land.

"A lot different than Dallas, ain't it?" Chinbroski said, reading his mind.

"Makes me ask myself why I'm living there."

"Cause you got a great partner."

Rush grinned. "Oh, yeah. How could I forget?"

Highway 101 wound through the natural valley that seemed to rise steadily the farther north they drove, though Rush knew that was probably an illusion.

They exited onto California Highway 128 and took the road north toward Boonville. They immediately began to climb. The map indicated Yorkville was twenty-one miles ahead, Boonville eleven miles farther.

The narrow mountain road skated along bluffs on one side and cliffs on the other. Chinbroski drove slowly out of necessity, the shoulderless road almost daring someone to exceed its posted speed limit.

"Think anybody ever gets a ticket on this thing?" Chinbroski asked. "Damn good place to commit suicide."

Rush looked off to the right and saw the precipice that beckoned just beyond a beat up guardrail.

The automatic transmission downshifted in and out, up and down as it tried in vain to find the right gear.

After reading several chapters of Charles Adam's book on Boontling, Rush had a good feel for the history of Anderson Valley. "Did you know that Boonville was named after W. W. Boone, a relative of Daniel Boone?"

Chinbroski shook his head. "That one slipped by me. Does that mean all the people up here are a bunch of Tennessee hicks?"

"Wasn't Daniel Boone born in Kentucky?"

"Hell if I know. Tennessee, Kentucky, what's the difference?"

"Apples are the biggest crop," Rush went on. "They have an Apple Show at the fair grounds every September."

"And we missed it."

"Used to be a big sheep area."

"That explains what drew the folks from Kentucky."

Thirty minutes later they pulled into the parking lot of the Yorkville Mini-Market, a small deli that advertised groceries, beer, and ice. It sat on the right side of the road and was part store, part café.

"Hey, they take credit cards," Chinbroski said, pointing. "So we're still on planet earth?"

Rush climbed out and stretched his legs and back. "It's not that bad up here."

"No, I guess not. Not if you like inbreeding and real big families."

The store was also part antique shop and dime store, selling souvenirs, tee shirts, and locally produced wine. A little bell rattled when Rush walked through the door with Chinbroski on his heels. Two locals, old men wearing overalls, sat at one of five tables on the far right side of the store, near a small grill. They looked grizzled, rough, like they'd just come in from the field.

A clerk was stocking a shelf near the door. She looked up and smiled. "Hi there."

"Hi," Rush said.

"Help you folks?" She wiped her hands on a grease-splattered apron stained with mustard and ketchup. Her face was round, her brown eyes slightly magnified by glasses that covered half her face. She grabbed her lower back as she stood, and walked over to the counter by the front door.

"Could use a Diet Dr Pepper if you have some," Rush said.

She pointed to the other end of the store, away from the grill. "Row of coolers got anything you want."

Rush noticed her tee shirt as Chinbroski headed toward the coolers. "Yorkville, California, population 21." He read aloud. "The town really that small?"

She looked down and chuckled. "Just about. More of a standing joke round these parts."

"So is the number high or low?"

She thought a moment and cocked her head. "Well, the town itself probably doesn't have quite that many people. But the Yorkville metropolitan area has probably ... oh, I'd say a hundred and twenty-five. A local who got drunk right before he turned in the numbers did the census back at the turn of the century. Twenty-one was all he could think of. Been that way ever since."

Chinbroski walked up and handed him a plastic bottle of water. "No diet DP?" Rush asked.

"This is better for you."

Rush gave him a look. "You're my mother?"

"The water looks local, Rush." Chinbroski smiled and then changed his voice. "Probably dipped from a crick up in these hills here."

The clerk giggled. "Lots of liquid is bottled round here, but most of it'll give ya a buzz. Bottled water's brought in by truck."

Rush turned to Chinbroski. "Can you get me a Diet Doc, Mom?" Then he walked over to the counter. "So you were saying 125 people live in the Yorkville metropolitan area?"

She laughed. "Thereabouts. Barely enough to keep the post office open." She reached over the counter and pulled out a copy of *Highrollers*, more a homemade newsletter than newspaper. "Even get reminders for folks to buy stamps and mail stuff so the government don't shut it down."

Rush leaned against the counter, pulled his badge holder from his pocket, and showed her. "Town too small for a police department?"

She laughed again. "Good gosh, yes. Ain't never needed one, really. Least in the forty years I've lived here." She leaned forward and studied his police identification card. "Shirley's my name." She stuck out a hand. "Where about's Plano, Texas?"

Chinbroski walked up and handed Rush his soft drink. "Just north of Dallas," Rush said, twisting off the plastic cap and taking a sip. "We're here looking for a guy." He took another sip and glanced at Chinbroski, who had strolled over to the two locals.

"Well, I know 'bout everybody round these parts." Shirley smiled. "Must be serious to pull two of you all the way up here. Got his name?"

"Don't have a real name," Rush said. "Just a Boontling name."

She raised her eyebrows. "Boontling? This fella's got a Boont name, and he's from Texas?"

Rush grinned. "I doubt he's from Texas."

Chinbroski noisily scooted a chair over and joined the old men. He would keep them busy while Rush interviewed the clerk.

"The guy we're looking for goes by the name Beark," Rush said.

Shirley gasped and stepped back. Her hand made it halfway to her mouth before she caught herself and snapped a look toward the old men.

"I take it you've heard of him?"

She swallowed hard and rubbed her nose. "His name's Enoch," she whispered, her voice suddenly sounding dry. "Been gone from these parts for oh, 'bout three years." She reached under the counter and picked up a Sprite can. Her hand quivered as she raised it to her lips and took a drink.

Rush pulled a notebook from his pocket and wrote down the name. "Enoch have a last name?"

Shirley wiped the back of a hand across her lips and nodded. "Duke. Enoch Duke. Lived up in the hills with his grandfolks."

"What about his parents?"

"Dead. Enoch was just a boy, two or three. Killed in a car crash out on Highway 128, the road you took coming up here. Ran off a cliff."

One of the old men laughed out loud and slapped the top of the table. Rush heard Chinbroski say something about "calling Earl," then saw him hunch over the table, his hands out in front, his face and neck red from the telling of his favorite drunk story.

"His grandfather a trapper?" Rush asked, turning back to Shirley.

Her eyes opened wide. "Yeah. Old man Duke. How'd you know that?"

"His grandmother died a while back?"

She nodded and took another drink of Sprite.

"How about a girlfriend or wife? Leigh?"

Her brow wrinkled. "Don't know nobody by that name." She set her can down and leaned against the wall behind the counter. "Could be a Boonville girl, though. That's where Enoch spent a bunch a time. You know, all the Yorkville kids go to school up there."

Rush wrote it down. "What's Enoch look like?"

Shirley hesitated. Started to speak, but stopped. "Enoch's still gone ain't he? I mean, he ain't around here anymore?"

"A long way from here," Rush said. "I understand how you might be nervous talking about him. But no one will ever know we spoke." He smiled. "Promise."

She returned the smile, though it seemed forced. "Okay, then."

"So can you tell me what he looks like?"

"Like the devil possessed him. His eyes, I mean. Nothing in them. No life. Like he was born for just the kind of life he's had."

He nodded. "Think you could give me a description?"

She cocked her head and sucked on a tooth. "He's about six foot, I guess. Or was. Hair the color of sweet potato pie. Strong and muscular." She shrugged. "That sound like him?"

He nodded. "Could be. He has a finger missing?"

"By gosh, he does. I forgot all about that. Had an accident as a child, something to do with a hatchet. Cut off his pointer finger on his left hand."

"What about hobbies? Anything you know of?"

"Didn't know him that well. He's a smart boy. Never did no studying in school, least that's what I always heard."

As Rush slowly wrote it all, Shirley leaned forward again and lowered her voice. "Enoch kill somebody?"

He looked up and studied her for a moment. Her glasses had moved half way down her nose; her eyes were intense, shrouded by furrowed brows.

"Why do you ask?"

She glanced at the locals and then toward the front door. "There was rumors," she said. "That he killed somebody up in the hills 'fore he left town. Horrible murder is what I always heard."

Both of the old timers howled and leaned over the table. Chinbroski was half out of his chair now, his arms waving around like he was the lead part in a high school play.

"What kind of rumors have you heard? About the murder, I mean?"

"Well." She paused and gazed over Rush's shoulder. "I heard that he cut her up pretty good. I say he, but I ain't got no proof Enoch did it. Anyway, the lady was cut down the middle. And maybe her face. Had her nose missing. Or an ear or something." She lowered her voice even more. "Nobody found the body for a few weeks. Was all rotten according to what I heard."

"Who was the victim? You say a woman?"

"Lady named Edna Noring. Older. I'd say sixty-five. Widow who lived up north of Enoch's place. About two miles as a crow flies. Out off Point Arena Road."

Rush wrote it down. It could be the murder Zeke had heard about, the one mentioned by Nick Bass, the investigator who worked the other California killing.

"Did the sheriff work it?" he asked. "Why was Enoch suspected?"

She shrugged. "I know the sheriff went out there. Course I wasn't there or nothing." She threw her empty can in the trash. "Sheriff weren't the only one who suspected Enoch. The boy's been evil since he could walk. Gave old man Duke and Gracie hell. Killing small animals, hanging their hides all over Anderson County. Boy would go out of his way to kill something if he was mad at you. Then he'd do stuff like smear blood on your house, leave the innards on top of your car or in your mailbox." Shirley shook her head.

“Whole county’s better off since he left.”

“So he disappeared before the old woman’s body was found?”

"Ain't sure. About that time." She shrugged.

“You say his grandmother’s name was Gracie?”

She nodded.

“Was she buried at the Yorkville cemetery, by chance?”

“She was. Almost a year now. Old man Duke, Jacob, ain’t never recovered. Spends some part of every day up there.” She leaned forward again and whispered. “I think he might be going a little crazy.”

“Why is that?”

She snapped a look at the locals again. “Now I ain’t seen him myself, but I hear he sits next to Gracie’s grave and tells her stories. Reads things to her. Has the site all planted out with flowers and stuff?”

Rush glanced at his watch. “Think he’d be there now?”

“Not yet lunch? I’d say probably.”

Chinbroski was quieter now, telling a story in a much lower voice. “Where might I find this cemetery?” Rush asked.

She pointed north toward Boonville. “About two miles up the road. Gotta look hard. You’ll see a green farm gate up at the end of what looks like a private drive. On the right side of the road. Park down at the main road and walk up. The graveyard sits just to the right of the gate.” She lowered her voice again. “Can I talk about this?”

Rush could certainly imagine how local gossip was a major part of Shirley’s day and he hated to deprive it of her. “Make a deal with you. You give me until tomorrow noon. After that, tell whoever you want.”

A flash of disappointment crossed her face, but she smiled anyway.

“You understand don’t you? Investigations can be torpedoed by loose lips. I need a chance to talk with Jacob and find Leigh’s family.”

She nodded. “I can do that.”

Rush called to Chinbroski, then pulled out some money to pay for the drinks. “Just in case Mr. Duke isn’t at the cemetery, could you point me toward Point Arena Road?”

She gave him directions as Chinbroski walked up. He wrote it all down and thanked her again.

After he pushed out the door, Rush turned to his partner. “Let’s go find out who Enoch Duke is.”

NINETEEN

They headed north on Highway 128 with Chinbroski still driving. The two-lane road climbed through the fir and redwoods, the laurel and oak. They passed sloping grasslands that footed mountain ridges both to the east and west.

"Looks like you kept the old men from overhearing my conversation with the clerk," Rush said. "But the 'Calling Earl' story? How'd that come up?"

Chinbroski laughed. "I ain't had a chance to tell that one in years. With all that wine on the shelves I figured they'd appreciate a good drunk story." He glanced at the road and then back at Rush. "The clerk have anything to say?"

"Plenty." Rush filled him in.

"Sounds like our guy."

"Yeah. Stop here!" Rush said, throwing up his hands. "The green gate … at the end of that gravel driveway. Back up."

Chinbroski backed down the mountain road until Rush found the green gate. He pulled into the driveway behind a beat-up Ford pickup parked off in the weeds.

"Grandpa's truck?" Chinbroski asked.

"Hope so." The truck was a late-sixties model, faded so badly the green paint was turning white. Rust had penetrated the kick panels and lower driver's door with such vigor, Rush could see into the cab.

Climbing out of the rental, Rush wrote down the tag number and approached the driver's door. The cloth on the bench seat was threadbare on the driver's side and middle, as though a faithful wife had snuggled next to her husband every day for the last three decades. The cloth on the far side of the seat, next to the passenger's door, appeared unused.

"Let's check it out, Rush. See if this old man can tell us where his asshole grandson is hiding out." Chinbroski slammed his car door and slipped on a pair of dark sunglasses. His square body stretched the seams of his sports coat.

Thirty yards ahead was a green farm gate with a "Private Property, No

Trespassing" sign stuck in the center. Beyond the gate were perfectly aligned rows of grapevines. They bordered against both sides of the gravel driveway that wound around a couple of large trees and disappeared over a hill.

To the right of the green gate was another farm gate, closed, but unlocked. A saggy, pine wreath with little Santas hung from a wire in the center.

"Guess somebody decided to cheer up the dead people," Chinbroski said.

Rush caught his breath from the climb and looked at the cemetery beyond the gate. It was unlike any graveyard he'd ever seen. At first he saw no tombstones whatsoever, so thick were the trees that covered the small, hilly patch of ground. But he finally saw one, two feet tall, off to the right. Then, as he walked through the gate and approached that solitary monument, he began noticing the others. Most were small, unimpressive, made from granite carved by an inexperienced hand. One was a solid slab of wood, petrified by the pounding of weather, the inscription stamped by hammer and chisel.

They were old, the dates of deaths reaching back into the 1890s with one as early as 1877. Rush felt as he always did in cemeteries—like a trespasser unconcerned about treading on the surface of other people's sorrows.

He turned, expecting to find Chinbroski behind him. But his partner was still near the gate, pointing now, to a spot at the other end of the cemetery. Rush followed his aim and saw what they had come there to find, an old man, hunched over a grave, hoeing weeds.

Chinbroski met Rush in the center and followed him over to the tallest monument. And the newest. The tombstone read "*Grace Duke, Beloved Wife and Mother, the Lifeblood of my Soul*."

The old man didn't turn when they approached. He continued to work the soil, hands and knees across the grave, gently speaking to himself or to Grace, Rush wasn't sure. He looked as ancient as most of the grave markers, and as weathered.

"Mr. Duke?" Rush asked quietly.

When he didn't turn, Rush called out louder, "Mr. Duke?"

The old man jerked at the sound of his name and looked back. His dirty face was pinched and wrinkled. His chin sat so high on his face his lips appeared to rob his nose of space. He turned his bony frame and sat back on his heels, looking up, sizing up his visitors. "Help you fellas?" he asked, his voice screeching. His bushy, white brows almost hid his eyes, and sat so close together that his thick glasses looked miniature.

"You the Jacob Duke who has a grandson named Enoch?"

His face darkened as he studied Rush. "Might be," he said, his words clicking against the roof of his mouth. “Pendin’ on who’s askin’.” The skin on his bald head, so thin it reminded Rush of onion peel, was stretched tight and dotted with age spots.

Rush pulled out his badge case and flipped it open. “We’re from Texas.”

The old man leaned forward, wiped a dirty finger across the surface of his glasses. His hands, gnarled like claws, were caked with mud. “Texas, huh? Long way from here.” He turned back to the grave and picked at the dirt with his spade.

Rush looked at Chinbroski, who shrugged. “Are you Enoch’s grandfather?” Rush asked.

“Ain’t made that claim for more’n three years now.”

A gentle breeze rustled the branches of the trees overhead. Sunlight filtered through and highlighted the words written on the Duke headstone. Rush walked around Chinbroski to the other side of the grave, facing the old man. “Why? What happened three years ago?”

Jacob Duke swiped a bead of sweat off the end of his nose and gazed off into the distance. “God always said to turn from evil. Don’t matter who. Don’t matter why.” He looked up, his narrow-set eyes locking onto Rush’s. “Just turn away.”

“We need to find him, Mr. Duke.” Rush dropped onto his knees and sat on his heels. “Can I call you Jacob?”

“That’s my name. Jacob. Like Joseph’s father in the Good Book. Isaac’s second born.” He paused. “But I ain’t like the Jacob in the Bible. Ain’t a deceiver.” He cocked his head and looked at his knees.

“Well, nice to meet you, Jacob,” Rush said softly. “My name is Greg Rush. The man behind you is Rick Chinbroski. We’re both detectives from a town called Plano, just north of Dallas. Ever heard of it?”

Jacob’s expression was blank. He shook his head and looked over at Chinbroski. “You’re a big’un. A solid man.” He pulled his glasses off, rubbed them on the front of his shirt. “Be needin’ every bit of it, I suppose, once you hook up with Enoch.”

Chinbroski looked at Rush and raised his eyebrows. Then he licked his lips, rubbed his nose. Stress, Rush thought. Or fear. He’d seen Chinbroski truly terrified only once before and he’d licked his lips until they chapped. But Rush couldn’t blame him, standing in a graveyard with a man who spoke of his grandson as evil. Having seen that grandson’s handiwork, Rush felt chilled himself.

“We need to find him, Mr. Duke,” Rush said again.

After he inspected his glasses and slid them onto his nose, Jacob shoved the spade into the soil at the edge of the grave. Then he slowly pushed himself up and stood. "You ain't the only one," he said, his voice slicing into the stillness of the cemetery like a sickle. He dug into one of his overall pockets, pulled out a hand-rolled cigarette, and carefully struck a match against his thumbnail.

Rush watched Chinbroski rub the back of his neck, becoming impatient.

"Do you know where he is?" Rush asked.

Dragging so deeply his cheeks disappeared behind his jawbones, the old man kicked at a clod of dirt, then looked away. "Can't say as I do," he said finally, letting the smoke dribble out of his mouth with each word. "Can say one thing, though." He looked at Chinbroski and sniffed, then turned toward Rush. "If I was you, I wouldn't wanna hook up with him."

"Why's that?" Chinbroski said, eyeing Rush.

Jacob gave a little chuckle and took another drag from his cigarette. "Boy's the Devil, that's why. Ain't never smart hookin' up with the Devil." A film of sweat coated his skull and several drops started a slide down his forehead. "Know what I think?" he said.

"What?" Rush asked.

"He's the son of a demon."

A sudden gust of wind blew up leaves that swirled around Rush's feet. Chinbroski laughed and slapped the side of his leg, the sound echoing like a shot through the trees.

The old man turned on him. "It's happened 'fore round these parts. Ain't no laughin' matter, neither." He stuck a crooked finger in Chinbroski's direction. "I think he's one of them bein's what they talk about in Genesis."

Chinbroski stopped laughing. He turned to Rush, now leaning against the Duke tombstone.

"What are you talking about?" Rush asked.

"Genesis, chapter six, verses four and five. Enoch's one of those. Offspring of Satan. Smart. Pure evil. And it ain't no joke." He dropped to his knees again and picked up his spade. An assortment of flowers outlined the top of Grace Duke's grave. The old man began his digging again; turning soil that appeared to be tended daily.

"*'There were giants in the earth in those days,'*" the old man mumbled, quoting a verse Rush had heard before. He spoke slowly, his voice scratching like fingernails against a chalkboard. "*'And also after that, when the sons of God came in unto the daughters of men, and they bore children to them, the same became mighty men which were of old, men of renown. And God saw that the wickedness of man was great in the earth, and that every imagination of the thoughts of his heart was only evil continually.'"*

He looked up, first at Chinbroski, then at Rush. "Bible says it." He coughed and spit on the ground next to the grave. "Been studyin' on it, trying to figure what made that boy like that."

Chinbroski shook his head and shrugged.

Rush thought about what he'd said less than a minute before. "You said it's happened before around here. What's happened before?"

"Evil," Jacob said. "Other folks got the devil in them."

"Who?" Chinbroski blurted out. "What are you talking about?"

Jacob wiped his hand across his sweating scalp, smearing dirt down the center of his head like a Mohawk. "Jim Jones, that fella what poisoned all them folks down in Jonestown. In South America. Lived up in Boonville 'fore he ever got the Devil. Third-grade teacher he was, went over to the Methodist church. Nice fella, seemed to me. But that was before.

"Years 'fore that, fella named Manson lived just north of town, before he got the Devil and moved out to Los Angeles. Killed some movie actress." His gaze went from Rush to Chinbroski then back to Rush. "Enoch ain't like those boys, though." He wiped his head again and let the words hang in the silence. "No, sir. Enoch ain't like those boys at all. He'd chew 'em up and spit 'em out the side of his mouth."

Chinbroski turned away, rubbed the back of his neck again.

"I'm not doubting that Enoch is evil, Mr. Duke," Rush said, suddenly shaken. "But we need to find him. He's killed two people back in Texas and I doubt if he has any plans to quit."

The old man sat back on his heels again and closed his eyes, mumbling a quiet prayer. Rush saw a tear slide from under his glasses.

After he finished praying, Rush walked back around and knelt beside him. "We can't have anyone else hurt, sir. We need your help."

Jacob nodded and clutched his right fist around the handle of the spade, his knuckles distorted and twisted with arthritis.

"Do you have a picture of him?" Chinbroski asked, walking back to stand next to Rush.

He nodded again. "Up to the cabin." He stood and straightened himself. "You can follow me." Turning, he started to walk away from the grave, then stopped and looked back. "I'll be back, Gracie. Got to help these men."

Rush rode as Chinbroski followed the old pickup farther north toward Boonville. His partner was unusually silent, as though unable to shake the old man's words. Rush said nothing, either, his mind considering the possibility that they'd never catch Enoch Duke.

"What'd you think about all that Biblical crap?" Chinbroski finally asked. "About this asshole being evil?"

Rush shrugged. "Don't know for sure."

They slowed and turned left on a gravel road. The car rocked as it hit a chug hole. The road looked recently graded, loose rocks rattled underneath the car and left a thick trail of dust in their wake. Chinbroski slowed to let Jacob Duke gain some distance, allowing the dust in front of them to thin.

"And what was that Genesis stuff? Saying Enoch is one of them? One of who?"

Rush leaned his head back. "I remember some stuff from my Sunday school days as a teenager. Scary stuff. Some people think the Sons of God impregnated women on earth. The offspring was a mix, almost a supernatural being. They turned evil, so much so God sent the flood and destroyed them."

Chinbroski licked his lips and chuckled. "That's a hell of a Sunday school lesson. Nothing like I ever had." He drove, still avoiding chug holes, the car rocking back and forth. "These Sons of God. What, they angels or something? Demons?"

"Some people believe the old earth, the period before the flood, was a mixture of humans and whatever kind of being God is. And there wasn't supposed to be any mingling of the two."

Rush looked over. Chinbroski's face was hard in concentration. "What if some of these beings were the angels God kicked out of heaven?" Rush went on, "You know, demons, the ones who had to leave with Satan. If true, then it would only be logical the offspring would be more evil than anything we've ever seen."

The old pickup was a quarter mile ahead, still heading west. They passed nothing other than thick forest as the road climbed higher up the side of a mountain.

"You sound like some kid telling a ghost story," Chinbroski said. "I mean, even if all that was true back in Noah's day, what makes you think any of that would be now? How's some demon gonna impregnate Enoch's mother?" Chinbroski glanced over. "Know what I think? I think this Enoch is just some crazy son of a bitch who's got this whole valley spooked. Think about it. What kind of crime do these people see? Hell, let some guy steal something and they're gonna think he's Al Capone." He smiled, but weakly. "What do you think?"

"It's possible." Rush said without conviction.

Chinbroski must have heard it in his voice. "What? You believe what that old man was saying?"

"I believe the reaction I saw on the clerk's face when I mentioned Beark. I believe the fear I saw in Jacob. I don't know any more than that."

They rode without speaking as they followed Jacob Duke up the mountainside. After another mile he turned right onto a dirt path. They were near the top of a peak, the valley stretched out below. In another minute they were there. The tiny cabin sat underneath three towering pine trees. The small house, built with blackened logs tied together horizontally, looked hard and weathered. The roof, pitch black and sagging in the middle, was covered with old pine needles. A small window just left of the front door wore curtains blowing in the breeze. Several animal skins hung drying on a wooden rail next to a three-hole doghouse.

The dogs were sprawled out on the front porch. Jacob Duke climbed down from his truck and commanded the dogs to stay. Rush closed his door and glanced at Chinbroski, who had shed his coat and begun rolling up his sleeves. The old man shuffled to the cabin and disappeared through the door. Rush followed Chinbroski.

The cabin had been laid out without much thought. The front room led straight into the kitchen. Two bedroom doors sat to the left, a bathroom between those doors. Jacob knelt on the floor, his right arm buried inside a large chest behind a threadbare sofa. Pictures hung cluttered on all four walls of the front room. Most were of a much younger Jacob and a woman who must have been Grace. There were also photos of a young man in various stages of life, and an older one showing him with a young woman, and then even later, with a small child. Enoch's father, Rush suspected, Jacob's only child. There were several bare spots among this collection of family history. Someone had been omitted.

"Here," Jacob said, thrusting out an 8X10 picture of a young red-headed man wearing a cheap suit. "The last one we ever got took of Enoch. High school graduation." His voice cackled like it had in the cemetery, but was more pronounced in the confines of the cabin.

Enoch was a good-looking boy. Bright red hair, a square jaw, broad shoulders that stretched the seams of the coat. He wore no glasses and had a shadow of full whiskers. His eyes were piercing, as green as emerald, intelligent. No smile, lips straight across.

"So that's him," Chinbroski whispered in Rush's ear. "That's the devil boy."

"Is this the most recent?" Rush asked. "Do you have any snapshots of him taken around this time?"

Jacob slammed the lid of the trunk and sat on it. "Ain't no more. Wouldn't let us get near him with a camera. Had to go up to the school and stand over him to make sure we got that one." Jacob crossed his arms and set his jaw.

"So maybe he knew he'd be a wanted man someday," Chinbroski said quietly. "Maybe knew it for years."

"How old was he when he started getting camera shy?" Rush asked.

Jacob rubbed a dirty finger across his forehead while he thought it out. "I'd say maybe eleven, twelve. Ain't got but a couple of his face for all them years. Rest of 'em is the back of his head where he spun around every time he saw the camera." The old man shook his head as he stared at the floor.

Rush sat on a chair made from twisted tree branches and rested his arms on his knees. "I hear Enoch used to kill animals, spread their insides over people's cars, wipe the blood on their houses. That true?"

"True as the Good Book. True as the devil. Boy weren't never home half the night, sneakin' out all the time." He paused and shook a finger at Rush. "If you find him living near the woods, you best take him before he gets on foot. I been trappin' all my life and that boy passed me up by the time he was twelve. Huntin', fishin', trackin'. Best I ever saw."

"He a gun nut?" Chinbroski asked.

Jacob's face went blank, his eyes clouded over as though remembering some long ago event. "I wouldn't say that. He can shoot, mind you," he said, looking at Chinbroski. "Saw him hit a squirrel with a .22 pistol once from fifty paces." He rubbed a spot of dirt with his shoe. Then his face darkened. "The Bowie's his likin'."

"A knife?" Chinbroski asked.

"Never heard of Mr. Bowie makin' nothin' else." He sniffed and rubbed the end of his nose. "Saw Enoch take down a buck once. Biggest rack I ever saw. The boy jumped from up a tree. Cut its throat wider than a bass's mouth. He can sling a knife…" He cut himself off and stared off into space again.

"Is he smart, Jacob? Does he have any interests?"

"Cept spreadin' evil, you mean?" He paused and nodded. "Smart as a fox. Ain't never had to tell the boy nothin' more'n once. Grace used to say he had a picture memory. Look at something once, then it was up here." He tapped his temple.

Rush pulled out his notepad. "What about hobbies?"

Jacob nodded. "Anythin' had power runnin' through it. Ain't had much round this place, but he used to bring gadgets home. When he weren't off in the woods he was studyin' on how to take stuff apart."

"What kind of stuff?" Chinbroski asked.

"Oh, 'lectric stuff. Little radios, telephones. Even brought a TV box in here once. Said he'd power it up for me if I wanted. I didn't never have no need for it, so he watched it in his room. Stuck a wire on top of the roof so's he'd get a picture."

Jacob shifted and crossed one bony leg over the other.

"What about girls? A girl named Leigh? Ever heard of her?"

He grabbed his chin and squeezed it while he thought. "That's the girl he was goin' on about when he left. Ran off with her. Last name Adams. Boonville girl. Lost her daddy in a fire some years back. Enoch never brought her round here." He looked up and met Rush's stare. "Mamma's name's Betty. Heavy woman. Been wantin' a husband ever since hers burned up. Lives in town, right down from the county fair buildin'."

Rush wrote it down. "How old is Enoch? His birth date?"

"Born on Halloween. He's twenty-six."

Rush looked at Chinbroski, who'd paled.

"He must have lived at home several years after he graduated high school," Rush said.

"Bout four years. Didn't never see him much, though. Always out makin' trouble."

"How old is Leigh Adams?"

"Ain't knowin' much about her. Younger than Enoch, though. Her mamma could tell you that."

"So you've never met Leigh," Rush confirmed.

Jacob shook his head. "You're puttin' words in my mouth. Said Enoch never brought her around. But she came up later, told me some things."

"Came up later? What do you mean?"

"After Enoch stole her baby girl."

Rush noticed Chinbroski moving around the cabin, inspecting things. Jacob Duke didn't seem to notice.

"What did Leigh say about that?" Rush asked. "About Enoch stealing her child?"

The old man's shoulders slumped, his face pinched as he thought. "Said

Enoch killed a girl who Leigh made best friends with. Neighbor. He strung her up on her toilet, taped a telephone to her hand. Leigh found her while the blood was still runnin'. Said Enoch stole the girl right after. Swore if Leigh ever tried to find him, he'd mail the girl back to Boonville in pieces." He shook his head as he dug into a pocket for a cigarette.

"Was that in Santa Rosa?" Rush asked.

Jacob nodded.

"What's the little girl's name?"

After Jacob's match caught, Jacob shook his head. "Don't remember."

Chinbroski disappeared into the bedroom directly behind Jacob.

"Leigh's been leaving notes for us," Rush said. "She said Enoch swore off drinking. Know anything about that?"

"Sure do. Told me once he didn't like the way it made him feel. Said it made him feel like a woman."

"A woman?"

"Made him cry. Got sad all the time. Made him too nice, I reckon."

Chinbroski came out of the bedroom and shook his head. He disappeared into the other one.

Rush lowered his voice, almost a whisper. "Did Enoch kill a woman farther up the road? Edna Noring?"

The old man squeezed his hands together and spit on the floor, rubbed the wet spot with his shoe. "No proof says it. No lawman locked him up. But they come round askin' all the questions of him."

He stood and walked to the window, his old body bent with a weariness of a man who'd suffered years in a private hell. "Rumors said Edna had a bucket of antique coins buried in her back yard. Enoch always used to talk about it as a kid. Said one day he'd find out." The old man paused, still staring out the window. "The sheriff counted seventy-six holes in that little old yard. And no coins." He shrugged.

"Did Enoch do it?" Rush asked as Chinbroski walked up next to Rush and shook his head again.

Rush watched Jacob smear tears across his cheeks. Chinbroski was silent.

"I think he done it," Jacob finally said, turning. His close-set eyes, red ringed, burned with a fierce intensity. "And when I told him I think he done it, he just looked and laughed." The old man stuck a crooked finger at Rush. "The devil's in that boy, and I ain't envyin' nobody who's gotta hunt him down."

TWENTY

It was the tape Leigh had been waiting for. She caught her breath as she pushed *Pause* on the VCR and confirmed what she'd almost missed. With a shaky hand, she pressed the *Rewind* button and reversed the tape a few frames.

She'd put this tape into the machine a few minutes before midnight, then fallen asleep in the deer stand just before two AM, wrapped tightly in an electric blanket, while Enoch surfed the Internet. When she awoke at six AM, the chair in front of his computer sat pushed against the desk, empty, so she punched the video switcher to the camera in his bedroom. Asleep. Discouraged, she'd popped out the tape, put in a fresh one, and driven back to her apartment.

Enoch didn't spend much time in the cabin, evenings mostly, and she watched most of his activities real time. With the cameras installed, she didn't follow him as much. Eventually, she knew, he would bring Hannah to the cabin.

Now fatigue was a distant memory as she stared at Hannah's sweet face on her television screen. Leigh reached out with her hand to touch the screen, but quickly withdrew it, stifling the urge to cry.

The blurry picture was angled funny, and part of it was blocked by Enoch's left shoulder. The ceiling camera pointed more to capture Enoch's keyboard strokes than the image on the screen. She cursed herself now for not angling it more.

An E-mail, she knew for sure, with the picture as an attachment, and definitely Hannah, though her hair looked much longer than when Leigh had seen her last. In the photo, taken at a playground, her little girl sat at the top of a slide, the corners of her mouth turned up into a sweet smile.

Swallowing hard, Leigh fought a sudden flash of panic. What if she never got her back? What if Enoch...

She wiped her eyes again and stood, turned away from the television, and regained her composure. She hadn't come this far, done this much, to break down. Hannah needed her to be strong, to survive.

She turned back to the screen and stared at Hannah's face. Now, anger heated her cheeks. How dare that son-of-a-bitch steal her little girl.

She rewound the tape to the point where Enoch pulled up the E-mail. There was no way to read his screen and determine who had sent him the picture. The camera lens was too far away, the letters on the computer screen much too small. To get the E-mail address she'd have to sneak into the cabin and pull it up. Impossible. His biggest talent, besides killing people and getting away with it, was protecting his computer. She just didn't have the knowledge.

Staring at the screen, Leigh checked off every possible scenario to obtain the origin e-mail address, but came up with nothing that worked. She could break into the house and steal the computer. But that would scare Enoch into moving again. Enoch was no fool. And he didn't believe in coincidences. He would hit the road at the first sign of something strange.

She could turn herself in, give the police everything she had. The cops would arrest Enoch, find the E-mail address, and rescue Hannah. She only wished it were so easy. Enoch used the same foreign Internet providers used by pedophiles worldwide, businesses whose very existence depended upon insuring confidentiality. Any correspondence with whoever had Hannah would be cloaked in precautions — layers and layers of precautions. It was *possible* that the police could find Hannah by tracking the e-mail, but Leigh knew they'd have a better chance if Enoch didn't know they were trying.

The best option, though it pained her, was to wait. Hope he called Hannah, or called whoever had her, and insist they bring Hannah to him for Christmas. Leigh still believed that Enoch *would* spend Christmas with his daughter. Even though she saw no evidence that he was preparing for such a visit, the fact that he'd received the E-mail gave her hope.

The problem was timing. How quickly would Detective Rush and his partner find her full identity and visit her mother? Would her mother hold up during an interrogation? Her mom didn't know much, but she knew more than she was instructed to tell. And that was worrisome. The cops had a picture of Leigh, of that Leigh was convinced. But at the most it would be blurry, from a distance, probably a side view shot. Without a full facial photograph, would they plaster what they had all over the news, run it above the fold in area newspapers? They probably had at least one warrant for her arrest, and with her full name and date of birth, would undoubtedly get more.

She probably should not have sent them to California, but without the notes in Boontling, the California link, they would never find her diary, never understand what kind of monster Enoch was. Without that, she'd have no chance of cutting a deal if caught before she got Hannah back.

The real disaster would be if Enoch left the Dallas area before she had Hannah back. Always a possibility. But Enoch seemed settled, having been here a record three months. And Hannah felt close. Like a whisper of a familiar voice, Leigh sensed a peace that the end was near.

Now she needed Enoch to make one phone call, one mistake. She'd rescue Hannah, then bring Enoch's entire world crashing down around him.

* * *

They rode in silence down the mountain road heading for Highway 128. Once there, Chinbroski turned the car north toward Boonville. As the mid afternoon sun streamed through the windows, as Rush's eyes grew heavy with the heat and the gentle rocking of the car, he considered everything Jacob Duke had told them. He certainly didn't believe the Son-of-a-Demon theory, although the McElroy butchering would be a strong supportive argument.

He suspected Enoch Duke wasn't much different than Ted Bundy, John Gacy, or Jeffrey Dalhmer. From his high school graduation picture, he appeared as normal as anyone else, was probably just as smart, with enough social skills to blend when needed.

Before they left, Rush had asked Jacob Duke about Boontling, about whether Enoch knew the dialect. His response wasn't surprising. He said Enoch had been exposed to it like every other child born and raised in that part of Anderson Valley, but had never taken the time to learn it. Jacob said he hadn't spoken the old language himself in almost sixty years, since his own high school days.

"You gonna call back to Plano?" Chinbroski asked, breaking a silence that had lasted most of the way down the mountain road. "Get this asshole on all the lists?"

"Not until we talk with Leigh's mother. If she can tell us where Leigh is..." Rush let the sentence die as he looked out the window.

Boonville, California was a half-mile strip of tourist spots, populated by people dependent on visitors and their money. The few houses visible off Highway 128 were small, old, many poorly kept. The businesses, close to the road, advertised trinkets and souvenirs the locals would care nothing about.

On the right, just inside the city limits, stood the Anderson Valley Brewing

Company, a two-story building with a large metal tank shaped like an overgrown still, advertising the locally produced wine. The brewery was also a restaurant that appeared clean and inviting with flowering bushes, hanging ferns, and a trellis covered with climbing vines.

"Wanna grab a bite after we find a hotel?" Rush asked.

"Hotel? In this dumpy town?"

Rush shook his head. "You beat everything, you know that? This place isn't that bad." He pointed to the right, just beyond the brewery. "Look at that. A beauty salon and a real estate office operating out of two old train cars hooked together by a little covered walkway. Where you going to find a place like that in Plano?"

"Why would I wanna find a place like that in Plano? Look over there," Chinbroski said, pointing across the street. "The Mendocino County Fair building has a sign up advertising a damn fiber show. What the hell is a fiber show, Rush?" He shook his head. "I'm telling you, this place is for hicks."

Fifty yards ahead Rush saw a hotel on the left. "There, pull in there."

Chinbroski stopped in front of the Boonville Hotel, a two-story building with porches on both floors spanning the width in front, double French doors, wood-encased windows, and hand-carved wood railings.

"Looks nice," Rush said. "Homey."

Chinbroski grunted and stopped the car with a jolt.

Their room carried a turn-of-the-century theme: floral walls, antique furniture, hurricane lamps, hand-woven rugs. After a late lunch, Rush stopped at a gift shop and, posing as a long, lost friend, asked where he might find Betty Adams.

"Works mornings at the real estate office," he told Chinbroski, climbing back into the car.

"The one you thought was so damn precious?"

"The very one. Lives in the house next to the Methodist church. Has a Santa scene in front. That way." Rush pointed south.

A bungalow with window awnings, a spacious front porch, and a front door painted bright yellow, the house was small but clean. Santa glowed in the shaded yard, as did seven of his eight reindeer.

"Mountain people don't unplug these in the middle of the afternoon, do they?" Chinbroski asked, stopping the car in front.

Rush said nothing as he climbed from the car. He noticed curtain movement to the left of the front door. "She knows she has company," he said, stepping toward the house.

They hadn't made it half way up the sidewalk when the front door swung wide. Betty Adams was large, well-fed, just as Jacob Duke had told them. Big hair.

"Help you fellas?" she asked in a singsong voice, her chin hanging low enough to brush the collar of her dress. Her rosy cheeks sagged and folded in on her smile.

"Certainly," Rush said, stepping in front of Chinbroski and digging out his badge. "Detective Rush from Plano, Texas. This is Chinbroski. Came to talk about Leigh."

Betty's smile faded, her jaw slackened. The skin under her upper arms jiggled when she put her hands on her expansive hips and took a step back. The rest of her face suddenly colored, matching her cheeks. "Where's Plano?" she asked in a voice that cracked.

Rush stopped at the bottom of the steps in front of the porch. "I think you know the answer to that, Mrs. Adams. Mind if we come in and talk?"

The front door open, she stepped aside and held out her arm, allowing them passage.

Rush nodded as he passed, Chinbroski said nothing. The front room was done in earth tones, country style furniture, and oil paintings of mountain scenes. The room was spotless, antiseptic almost. Something about it bothered Rush, but he wouldn't have been able to verbalize it. Too clean maybe? He shook his head.

"I suspected I might hear from somebody like you one day," she said to Rush's back. "And I haven't been looking forward to it."

Rush stopped in front of the sofa. "We can make this fairly simple, Ms. Adams. Not take up much of your time. You agree?"

She closed the door. And with a grace that belied her size, moved across the room and sat in a chair opposite the sofa. "Please, have a seat."

Both detectives sat.

"I don't know much," she answered. "So it shouldn't take long, regardless." She looked from Rush, to Chinbroski, then back to Rush, hands folded on her knees, eyebrows raised, lips pursed.

"Why don't we start with a few easy yes or no questions," Rush said.

Betty nodded.

"Uh, excuse me," Chinbroski said. "While Detective Rush is doing this, I wonder if I might use the restroom?"

Betty frowned, then pointed down the hall past the kitchen door.

Chinbroski grinned and nodded, excusing himself.

"Does Leigh know where Enoch is?" Rush asked.

Without a flinch Betty surprised him. "Yes. She told me she found him."

Such honesty. "When? Where?"

She cracked a smile. "I guess yes or no wouldn't work here?"

Rush smiled and waited.

"She didn't tell me where," she said. "Only that she did. Been a couple of weeks now."

"Is she willing to meet with us?"

Her eyes wrinkled, smiled almost. "Wouldn't you ask her attorney that? You probably even know his number."

Rush ignored the comment, refusing to be baited. "Is that an 'I don't know?'"

"Yes." Betty gripped her hands together tightly enough to drain the blood from her knuckles. "But if I know Leigh like I think I do, she probably would agree to meet. On her terms, of course."

"Does Enoch have Leigh's daughter?"

"Hannah. Yes ... and no. He stole her. He beat Leigh up and stole her." She held up a hand. "Leigh hasn't actually seen Hannah, but she knows Enoch knows where she is."

And then she went silent. She folded her arms and stared at the ceiling. When the silence reached a full thirty seconds, Rush spoke.

"Are you going to tell me the background?"

She shifted in her chair, toward Rush. "Leigh's daddy died in a fire a few weeks after the start of her junior year in high school. She's an only child and part of her died with him. It just killed her. After several months of trying to make sense of it all, she rebelled. Went bad." She waved a hand in front of her face and swallowed hard. "No need in going into all that. The point is she started hanging around Enoch Duke, the most evil boy this valley's ever seen. They ... well, they made a name for themselves. It wasn't good."

Rush pretended to jot a couple of notes.

"They ran off less than a week after Leigh graduated high school. I didn't see her again until she came crawling home after Enoch stole Hannah. Now, she's trying to get her baby back." A tear slid down Betty's right cheek. She sniffed and looked away.

"And?" Rush asked.

"And nothing. That's all I know. Leigh's called a couple of times. Collect. Always from a pay phone. She won't tell me anything." Her voice cracked on that last word. "Well, much, anyway. And I'm scared to death." She spread her arms, the tears flowing freely. "My baby's out there following a monster. She won't say what she's doing, how she's surviving, if she's eating right. And... and she won't answer one question about how she plans on getting Hannah back."

Betty paused, swallowed, and wiped her eyes. "I'm alone," she went on, "I sit up here imagining all kinds of horrible things. Leigh said she followed Enoch to a murder. My God! A murder! And she refused to tell me anything else." She scooted close to the edge of her chair. "Can you tell me anything?"

After a brief silence, Chinbroski walked back into the room, clapping. "Bravo! Bravo! You should be in the movies." He walked over and sat next to Rush, leaned forward toward Betty.

Rush noticed a bulge under Chinbroski's shirt in the small of his back as he leaned forward. His sudden change in demeanor could only mean that he had found something important.

"What an acting job!" Chinbroski went on. "But before you leave for Hollywood, remember something. We can lock Leigh's ass up for all the laws she's broke. And this great performance, this bunch of slop you're feeding us won't help her."

"How dare you come…"

"Hold it!" Rush shouted, holding up his hands between them. "Just hold it! This won't get us anywhere." He stared at Betty, who wouldn't take her eyes off Chinbroski.

"Who are you kidding, Detective?" Betty snapped at Chinbroski. "Lock her up? You don't even know where she is. Nor will you until she decides the time is right. If ever."

Chinbroski's face flashed red. He looked at Rush.

"Why won't she just come forward?" Rush asked. "Work with us to catch him?"

"Because she doesn't know where Hannah is. And Enoch would spot a police surveillance a mile off."

"Oh, I get it," Chinbroski said. "She's a whole lot smarter than a bunch of dumb ass cops. Is that it?"

Betty nodded. "Yes. That's it."

Chinbroski slapped his leg again. "This is…we drag ourselves all the way out here…"

"Just hold it, Chin," Rush said.

Rush looked at Betty. The tears were dried now. She crossed her arms and began tapping her foot.

"You can sit there if you want and rant about throwing Leigh in jail," she said. "But you won't get close to her if she doesn't want you to. She knew you'd come out here. The reason she left all the Boont notes was to get you here. She told me that much. Told me I'd get a visit one day. But she's no criminal. She just wants her child back. She's desperate. And that's all."

"Did she steal a van full of equipment from a private investigator?" Rush asked.

Betty's face went blank. "I ... I don't know. She never mentioned it."

"Oh, come on!" Chinbroski shouted.

"I don't know!" Betty shouted louder. "I'm telling you she hasn't told me anything like that! The only thing I know about any equipment is something to do with Enoch's phone. She tapped it or something. And she thinks that's how she'll discover where Hannah is."

"Where'd she learn to tap phones?" Chinbroski asked.

"Enoch taught her. In their wild days. That's how he makes his living. Listening to other people's phone conversations." She shuddered.

Both detectives stared at her for several moments. Rush hoped the silence would start her talking again. It did.

"The last time I talked with her she said that after she has Hannah back she'll give the police all the evidence she has against Enoch. Said she would trade it for not going to jail." Betty looked at Rush with pleading eyes. "She's not a bad person. She just wants her baby back. She's not a bad…"

Rush held up a hand, cutting her off. "What kind of evidence? What are you talking about?"

"Leigh said she took some pictures of Enoch coming out of that murder house. Has some of his hair. A blood sample. Took the shoes he wore in that murder house. Stole them from where he's living." Betty sniffed, her lower lip unable to remain still. "She's been keeping notes of his activities, of some other crimes he's done. Break-ins, and I don't know what all. She said there's something in his attic that will put him *under* the prison. But she wouldn't tell me what."

"So she's been inside where he's living?"

"That's right."

"But she ain't giving us any of that evidence until she gets the kid," Chinbroski said.

"Hannah!" Betty snapped. "Her name's Hannah!"

"Yes, Hannah," Rush said softly. "But that's the deal? She gets her child, we get the evidence?"

Betty closed her eyes and pressed her cheeks with the palms of her hands. "I don't know if that's the deal. She only made a passing comment or two. That's what I assumed she meant." She blew out a breath. "Leigh is making me crazy! I haven't slept eight hours in a row in months. I just want it to end."

Chinbroski stood and walked to the front window, stuffed his hands in his pockets, and gazed out. Betty followed him with her eyes.

"How did Leigh track him all the way to Texas?" Rush asked.

Betty turned to Rush and rubbed her forehead. "She was watching the mail of a friend of Enoch's who lives just north of here. Enoch's only friend in this whole valley. Works until late every night. Leigh looked at his mail every day for months. Finally saw a letter from Arizona, a small town, I can't remember the name. She found him there, then followed him to Plano."

"What's this friend's name? His address?"

"I don't understand why you want it."

Rush just stared at her.

"This is exactly why Leigh hasn't called the cops. I give you his name, you'll go visit, he'll get a hold of Enoch, and Enoch disappears." She shook her head. "No."

Betty jumped up and went into the kitchen, came out with a glass of ice water for herself. She offered nothing to either detective.

The room. Something about the room. Rush still couldn't put a finger on it.

Betty slumped back into her chair and sipped her water.

"We need a picture of Leigh," Chinbroski said, turning from the window. "A recent one."

And that was it, Rush realized. The room had no photographs.

"No," Betty said. "You can't have a picture."

Chinbroski's chin dropped and he took a giant step toward her. Rush felt his own ears heat up with the refusal.

"Say that one more time," Chinbroski shouted. "I don't remember asking."

She violently shook her head. "No. She's not a criminal. I took everything of hers out of the house weeks ago. If you come back with a warrant you can search all you want, but you won't find one."

"Now damn it! We need…"

Rush cut Chinbroski off. "Betty. We just want to help. Can't you see that?"

The glass quivered as she raised it to her lips. Her eyes were locked on the floor. "It's not my nature to disobey a law officer," she said, after taking a sip. "Never has been. But I'm not giving you a picture. I watched enough detective shows to know you'll have every law man in Dallas looking for her." She shook her head again. "No. I won't have it. She ain't a criminal."

She was right, of course. They couldn't force her to cooperate at all. Rush knew that. But it sure pissed him off.

"Well, Miss High and Mighty," Chinbroski said, crowding her. "Tell me something. If your brilliant daughter slips up and Enoch guts her, leaves her for wild animals to chew apart, how are you gonna know? And how will we identify her?"

Betty winced at the question. Tears slid from both eyes and she smeared them with the palms of her hands. "She won't slip up. I know her. She's smarter than him." Her lips clamped shut and then opened again, as though about to say something else. But she hesitated, exhaled, and shook her head.

"What?" Rush asked. "You were about to say something."

She paused. "Only that Enoch doesn't expect her. And she looks different than when he saw her last. That's all. She won't slip up."

Chinbroski went back to the window.

Betty suddenly jumped from the chair and left the room again. This time she came back clutching a photograph. She pushed it at Rush. "You can have this."

The picture, torn in half, showed a small child, grinning crazily. Hannah, no doubt. Blond hair with a slight strawberry tint, pudgy arms, and small hands, she wore a jumpsuit and tennis shoes, her hair pulled back into a French braid. A beautiful child. An adult, female arm was wrapped around her waist, a hand tickled her belly. The adult arm was severed at the shoulder where the photo had been torn.

"My granddaughter is more important to me than anything," Betty said. "Leigh has her past. She knows it, and I know it. But Hannah is innocent. I want her back." She wiped her eyes as Chinbroski walked away from the window to peer over Rush's shoulder.

"Thank you both for coming. That's about all I can tell you. I'm sorry there's not more."

Rush remained seated. "Tell me about the Boontling," he said, looking up from the photo. "Why leave notes in Boontling?"

She looked him square in the eyes. "Which would have been more effective? Coming out here like you have, seeing things for yourself, or having some woman walk into your office and tell you a crazy story?" She raised an eyebrow, waited for an answer.

When she got none, she continued. "And because it's unique to this area. It added an intrigue that wouldn't have been there otherwise."

Rush had no response.

"Let me tell you a little story," Betty said. "About Enoch Duke's mindset." She stood and hurried from the room again. Returned seconds later with a small stack of photographs. She looked away as she handed them to Rush.

The photographs were of two dogs, boxers it seemed, though Rush couldn't tell for sure. The pictures were numbered on the back from one to six. The first showed the dogs, evidently beaten, inside a small room. The rest were of worsening stages of starvation.

He felt his stomach tighten.

"They were living in Santa Rosa," Betty said, still looking away. "Renting a house. She was four months pregnant. Their neighbor had a pair of champion Boxers.

"Enoch worked nights at a trucking company. The only real job he ever had. He slept during the day. On two different occasions the dogs woke him up. The first time he walked next door and asked the neighbor to keep them quiet." She paused and swallowed hard.

"The next time he stormed out of the bedroom and looked at the dogs through a window. Stood there like a statue, just ... *staring*. Finally, he turned and went back to bed without saying anything. Leigh didn't think anything of it. The next day the dogs disappeared. The owner was frantic. Called the police, put posters up around the neighborhood, ran an ad in the paper with a reward. Enoch didn't say a word. No bragging, no comments about how sorry he was for the man, nothing.

"Six weeks went by and nothing ever turned up with the dogs. Then one day Enoch showed up with them in the back of his car. He parked in his driveway, walked next door, and told the neighbor he'd found them in a ditch about a mile from the house."

She paused again, took a sip of water. The silence in the room grew thick. Chinbroski was back at the window, staring out. Rush watched Betty Adams.

"Enoch starved them. For six weeks he kept them alive with water and crumbs. They were so weak they couldn't stand, could barely breathe. They shook and whimpered, their eyes oozed, they had cuts and welts that hadn't healed. The most horrible torture Leigh had ever seen. They died at the vet's."

Rush let his eyes slide back to the photographs. Anger, like steam inside a boiler, slowly pressurized inside him. "And Leigh's sure Enoch did this?"

"Not at the time. She suspected it, but didn't know for sure. Several months later she found those pictures. Tuesday was her laundry day. Lying right on top of Enoch's socks in his socks drawer. He left them there for her to find." Betty swiped away a tear. "Their relationship was beginning to crumble. She was about to give birth to Hannah and I think he planted those pictures as a warning for her not to leave. He was obsessed she might leave him."

Chinbroski walked away from the window and took the photos from Rush. His face tightened.

"And when he told Leigh he'd send Hannah back to her in little pieces if she tried to find him ..." She let the unfinished sentence hang in the air.

Rush said nothing as Chinbroski walked to the door, opened it, ready to leave.

"She just wants her baby back," Betty cried. "She just wants her baby back."

TWENTY-ONE

Chinbroski climbed behind the wheel. Rush eased into the passenger's seat, watching him. After he pulled a U-turn heading back toward the hotel, Rush stuck his hand out. "Let's have it."

"What are you talking about?"

Rush said nothing, his hand still out.

"You accusing me of something?"

"Your bathroom trip. What'd you find?"

"What do you think? It's long and kind of looks like a snake."

Rush let him have his fun. He dropped his hand and looked out the window. Just before pulling into the hotel parking lot, Chinbroski chuckled. "Okay, partner. Don't sulk. Here." He reached behind him and pulled out a small book. "Insight," he said. "We need to get a copy of this to Santa Rosa PD."

"A diary?" Rush said, taking the book.

"From Leigh's bedroom. Found it right on top of the dresser. Right in the center."

"So now we're stealing evidence?" Rush said. "Is that the deal?"

Chinbroski stopped the car with a jolt in front of the hotel, and threw it into park. "Intelligence, Rush, intelligence. No evidence in that book that applies to us. It might help Santa Rosa, but not us."

Rush shook his head. "You're kidding, right?"

"Okay, look. That lard ass wasn't gonna help us. So I helped myself."

"What if she notices?"

He shook his head. "No way. It won't be gone that long."

Rush laughed. "Oh, I see. We're just gonna walk in and put it back."

Chinbroski opened his car door and stepped out. "Know what your problem is?" He slammed the door and spoke through the glass. "You don't give me any credit."

The worn five-by-seven book was dated at the top of each page. Rush turned to the middle of the book and quickly read the fluid handwriting at the top of one of the pages. "*Enoch so far away. So distant. Out most nights. No friends in this ratty neighborhood. Don't know what Enoch's up to. Constantly accuses me of cheating on him. When somebody accuses you of doing something, they're usually doing it themselves.*"

Chinbroski had walked around to the passenger's side of the car and opened the door. "You coming?"

Rush closed the book and got out. "How you going to get this back?"

"I unlocked the window, which is right next to the dresser. Easy." He raised his eyebrows. "Almost as smart as you, huh?"

Rush shoved the book at Chinbroski. "You make copies. Read it. Let me know if there's anything important. And I'm not going when you take it back. Just don't get caught." He left Chinbroski standing by himself.

Two hours later Chinbroski handed several pages to Rush after throwing their last suitcase into the trunk. "The diary is under the bed. I got a copy of the whole thing for Santa Rosa, and I kept an interesting story for you to read."

Sighing, Rush opened the passenger's door. He was tired, ready to get back home. "Okay. I'll read while you drive. But we're not giving anything to Santa Rosa PD."

"Why?"

"Because, Chin. If they come up here sniffing around with a copy of Leigh's diary, who do you think Betty Adams will suspect of stealing it?"

Chinbroski snorted. "Who cares?"

"I care! We don't steal evidence!" Rush shook his head. "I don't want other cops ... forget it."

"Okay." Chinbroski held up his hands in surrender. "I read you loud and clear." He threw Santa Rosa's copy in the back seat and pointed to the papers in Rush's lap. "You're gonna like that story, but there's something weird about it."

"What?"

"Just read it. See if you get the same impression."

Rush studied his partner for a moment. Chinbroski shrugged and raised an eyebrow.

Rush read: *Two weeks ago Enoch asked about Melissa. Asked why her husband had to travel so much. Later I found him sitting on the curb smoking a cigarette, staring at her house two doors down. He's started staying home some nights, came home a few times after only being gone for a few minutes. I think he's after Melissa. That scares the hell out of me.*

Rush knew where this was going. He felt a sudden chill, his thoughts slipping to Mallory.

February 3. I'm gonna call the cops on Enoch. Then I'm going home to Mom. I packed our clothes. And the stuff to give to the cops. Evidence. Called Melissa for a ride. She was running late. Said her mother hadn't shown yet to watch her kid. Thirty minutes went by. Forty-five. An hour. Tried calling several more times. Got the answering machine. Didn't know what happened. Finally wrapped Hannah in a blanket and looked down the street. Melissa's car was in her driveway. Walked down and noticed her front door open a few inches.

Rush looked up from the page. Chinbroski glanced at him, but said nothing.

When I put Hannah down I thought I saw Enoch's car parked down the street. Not for sure. Maybe not. But I suddenly felt something bad had happened. The car started. Did a U-turn. Saw a red front fender, black exhaust fumes. Still couldn't tell. Too far. But my whole body started shaking. Saw Hannah climb Melissa's steps, run to the front door. I ran over and grabbed her. I didn't want to go into the house.

Rush could hear his own heartbeat, could feel Leigh's emotion through the paper. He thought of Mallory again and closed his eyes to drive her from his mind.

I nudged the door open. Melissa didn't answer. Hannah kicked and swung her arms, wanted down. But I held on. I searched the living room, the kitchen, down the hall. Everything looked okay. Then I smelled something in the back bedroom. Maybe blood, maybe sweat, I didn't know. What does horror smell like?

The car swerved and Rush looked up. A deer jumped into the forest to the right. He wiped sweat off his hairline and turned the air conditioner on high. Chinbroski looked over.

"Finished?"

Rush shook his head, only a couple of pages left. "I don't like reading this, Chin."

"Why?"

"Because if we ever find Enoch, I won't be objective. I'll do something I'll regret." He tapped the pages. "This is pissing me off."

He nodded. "It's why I gave them to you. We gotta get this guy and I want you as pissed as me."

Rush read on:

The bathroom door was closed. Hannah was screaming to get down. I carried her back to the living room, turned on the Cartoon Channel. Back in the bathroom I found Melissa split open, propped up on the toilet. A phone taped to her ear. I grabbed Hannah and raced home. Found Enoch there. He'd parked in back. His hands and shirt were bloody. Said I was a Judas. Said Melissa shouldn't have talked on a cordless phone.

He snatched Hannah and she screamed. He backed away. I went after him. He warned me off. Said a traitor doesn't deserve to raise a child. I begged him to give Hannah back and he laughed.

I lunged at him, grabbed his throat, clawed at his eyes. Hannah was screaming. He punched me in the face and ran to the car. I charged him again, trying to grab Hannah. He punched my nose, broke it. I couldn't see, everything was dizzy. He said I'd never see Hannah again. That if I ever tried to find him he'd mail her back to me in little pieces. He held Hannah down in the seat and drove away. I have to find her!

Rush laid the copies on the seat and stared out the window. The sky was a blue sapphire. Pine trees on the mountains stood straight, a light haze obscuring the very tops.

"What do you think?" Chinbroski asked.

Several seconds passed before Rush knew how to answer. "I think," he said finally, "that we're gonna get that kid away from that bastard."

Chinbroski nodded and smiled. "Notice anything about it? The writing? Anything funny?"

Rush shrugged. "About the style? Is that what you mean?"

"Yeah."

"No. What?"

"Canned. Can't really tell by those few pages, but when you read the rest of it, it looks canned."

"Made up?" Rush asked. "Fake? Like none of it really happened?"

"Yeah. Doesn't really read like any diary I ever seen."

"And you're a diary expert? There's a certain formula every woman follows?"

"See, I try and make an observation and you mock me."

Rush watched Chinbroski as he slowly drove the winding road. "Okay. So you say it's canned. Why?"

"Grab Santa Rosa's copy. It's in the back seat."

Rush reached around. "Alright, what am I looking for?"

"It's like she's writing it for us to read. There's not any real rambling going on, no blabbering that women always do."

Rush frowned and flipped through the pages. All of it looked like the pages he'd already read. "So she's neat, concise. So what? Maybe she doesn't ramble."

"You seen many diaries?"

"No."

"My niece kept one. Looked like she puked the words. Looked like scribble. I asked her one time how come she wasn't neater. She said diaries ain't suppose to be neat. Schoolwork is neat. A diary is a place you can let yourself go. Then she said hers was neater than any of her friends'."

"So Leigh isn't your niece. Maybe she's a neat person. I just don't get it."

Chinbroski waved Rush off. "Fine. I'm just saying that she don't write about nothing else except stuff that would hurt Duke if he ever got arrested. Almost looks like a log written just for us. About all of the stuff he stole, the places he broke into, the mail he took out of people's boxes. That kind of crap. What kind of diary is that?"

Rush said nothing.

"And if she's such a big diary writer, how come she didn't take it with her? She had a quarter of the book left to fill in. And I found it right out in the open." He shook his head.

Rush flipped through the pages, scanned them. Chinbroski was right. The text did seem scripted. "Maybe you're right. So what do we do about it?"

"Just watch her real close when we find her. That's all we can do. There's something about this whole thing that makes me wanna call a fortune teller to read my tea leaves."

"That's a sound plan. How about we just go back to Texas and find Leigh before she gets herself killed."

Early Monday morning back in Plano, six days had passed since the discovery of Jane McElroy's frozen body. The morning broke warmer over North Texas than any since late November.

Rush had mixed emotions about their trip to California. They had the photo of Enoch Duke, which alone made the trip worthwhile. But they were no closer to finding him. Not that it would help their case a whole lot if they did. He couldn't arrest Duke without a warrant, and couldn't get a warrant without probable cause.

All Rush had were a few strands of red hair without roots, which meant no billion-to-one DNA matches. They had nothing to establish that Enoch had ever been inside the McElroy house. Nor was a series of cryptic notes from a woman he couldn't find likely to pique the interest of a judge. In short, they just *had* to find Leigh Adams, get what evidence she possessed, get her statement, her cooperation.

Investigations are often fueled by a series of little things that, when taken separately, amount to hardly anything at all. A scrap of paint, a single phone call, a strand of hair – little things, that, without any glue to hold them together, would blow away from only the slightest argument from a defense attorney.

The glue, Rush knew, was placing the suspect at the scene. Through an eyewitness, evidence, or a confidential informant who possessed personal knowledge.

Leigh Adams wasn't just glue. She was a special adhesive, a super epoxy, almost cement. She could place Enoch Duke at the McElroy murder, not only with eyewitness testimony, assuming she would agree to that, but also with photographs. She could provide a log of his activities, a list of other crimes that could probably be proved once they arrested him and searched wherever he lived. And with all of that, Rush was sure Enoch Duke would never get a chance to hurt anyone again.

They needed to find him. For reasons of pride, Rush wanted to find him without Leigh's help. But he wanted Hannah safe first. Her safety was foremost. All he had to do was to convince his superiors.

In his gut, Rush suspected that maybe it *would* be best to wait until Leigh discovered the girl's location before they made any move to find Enoch. He was convinced that as soon as Leigh had Hannah back, she'd call and reveal Duke's location. As much as he hated to admit it, there was a strong possibility the police *would* screw up a twenty-four hour surveillance. And if that happened? If Hannah was never found or hurt in anyway, he'd regret meddling in Leigh's business for the rest of his life.

Meddling. Now he was starting to think like Leigh. He shook his head.

When he arrived at the station at 7:30, the CID area was completely empty. He grabbed a cup of coffee, his file on the McElroy case, and headed to the conference room. Chinbroski showed a few minutes later. They were thirty minutes early for a briefing with Captain Williams, a briefing to examine the status of the case.

"So tell me about your weekend," Rush said.

Chinbroski wore a white shirt, blue slacks, and a fishing tie. *Quite dashing for him,* Rush thought, *even though a fishing tie on someone else would be considered ridiculous*. Rush smelled a hint of women's perfume.

Chinbroski smiled a little, rolled his head, stretching his neck.

Rush chuckled. "You're not about to start bragging, are you?"

"Me? A class guy like me kiss and tell?" He smiled. "All I'll say is that Nanci has found her paradise." Chinbroski laughed. "This may be love, podna, love."

"In less than a week?"

"You got it." He stuck his pen behind an ear, leaned back in his chair, and gazed at the ceiling. "What do you call what we got? The word is on the tip of my tongue."

"Debauchery?"

Chinbroski made a face. "De what?"

"Conjugation? Cuckoldry?" Rush grinned and slapped his forehead. "What am I saying? You're much simpler than that. Maybe rut would work. Or heat. How about plain old lust?"

"That's a word I know." Chinbroski set his chair back on all fours. "But it's more than that. We got something special. It's like, oh, I don't know, like we knew as soon as we saw each other. Is that weird?"

Rush smiled. "It's not weird. And I'm happy for you. Both of you. Maybe Mallory and I can get together with you two. I think they'd like each other."

"I know they would. I already told Nanci all about Mal." He paused. "I mean, not about, you know, her ex or nothing. Not about her past."

Rush waved it off. "I don't think it'd matter to her. And if anyone would understand, it'd be Nanci with her attack just a year ago."

"How is Mal?" Chinbroski asked him. "She letting that letter get to her?"

"Perfect," Rush said. "And that's what makes me crazy. Just when I think it's time to call her doctor, all of her symptoms disappear. She sat down last night and talked about everything like it was a case in a textbook. I'm at a loss."

"Just let it be. Nanci told me last night that she was having to work through some stuff she thought she was over. Said the phone calls opened a door in her brain. Or something. Maybe Mallory is working through it, like she said." Chinbroski paused, seemed to consider what he'd just said. "It's weird how we both ended up with crime victims, ain't it?"

Rush was silent.

"I wonder what it says about us, though? I ain't trying to over analyze or nothing, I'm just saying it must mean we're pretty good guys."

"Or so insecure that we need our women to beg us to protect them."

Chinbroski locked his fingers behind his head. "You know what she said to me last night?"

"What?"

"She said, 'Rick, I feel like a princess who's been locked away in a dungeon.'"

"What?"

"Right after that she rattled something about being a prisoner of fear or something." He shrugged.

"You're one sensitive guy, Chin. Nanci has a lifetime of laughs ahead of her."

"Lifetime? It ain't like we're getting married."

At 8:00 AM, with Rush at the head of the table, his chain of command filed into the room. Chinbroski sat at the corner of the table and nudged Rush as Gerald Hanisch ambled into the room behind Captain Williams. "What's he doing here?" he whispered.

Rush shrugged. As usual, Hanisch looked like an ad for a fashion magazine. He wore a tailored suit, highly polished shoes, and a crisp white shirt. He sat directly across the table from Rush.

The captain spoke first. "So you have it all, Greg? Is that what I hear?"

Rush started to stand, but stopped. The meeting was informal. "Just a matter of finding the guy now." He pulled out his first page of notes and began.

He spoke for what seemed an hour reviewing every aspect of the case, leaving out his conversations with Danny, his lawyer son. From the first minute he entered the McElroy house until he left Betty Adams' living room. He filled in blanks, gave background information, and explained how a child's life rested in Leigh Adams' hands. Then he explained the deal Rush expected Leigh to offer if they found her before she got Hannah back.

"On one hand, she plans on giving us enough to have him strapped to a gurney on death row. On the other, we have nothing unless we find her. What I'd like…"

"So she's guilty of criminal conspiracy," Hanisch interrupted, "and needs her ass thrown in jail."

"There's no evidence that she conspired with Duke in this," Rush said, keeping the irritation out of his words. "She's trying to help us. In her own way."

"That sounds like B.S. to me," Hanisch countered. "She wants to help? She needs to pick up the phone." A trace of a smirk creased the corners of his mouth.

Calmly, Rush said, "Without her we'd have nothing."

Hanisch drummed the top of the table. "You *have* something?" He stuck a finger in his ear, wiggled it. "My hearing must be bad. I thought I just heard an hour's worth of you admitting you had nothing."

"His identity," Rush snapped. "Without her leading us to California we'd have…"

"You seem to be missing the point," Hanisch interrupted again. "She's made it clear she'll let Duke kill again. Already has. She's as much of a monster as he is."

Rush glanced at Williams, who showed nothing. "I'm not condoning her method. I'm simply saying that without her information we'd still be scratching our collective asses. I said a minute ago how Enoch Duke left very little physical evidence at the scene. Hair. That's it. And if she'll provide a sample of that ..."

Hanisch stopped drumming and pointed at Rush. "So you're saying that until she gets her daughter back we just need to sit on all of this? Because even though you haven't said it in those words, I get the distinct feeling that's where all of this is heading."

Hanisch was right and it made Rush's face hot to admit that to himself. He hadn't talked this out with Chinbroski. Maybe he should have.

"That is what I'm saying. I don't think we have a choice." Rush heard Chinbroski suck in a little breath, saw Williams rub his forehead. Both bad signs.

"Well, I think that's just about as irresponsible a thing as I've ever heard," Hanisch said. "So we sit on our hands. We don't put him on NCIC, we don't enter his fingerprint information into AFIS, and we don't search for him ourselves. We just sit around scratching our collective asses? Your words. All the while waiting for this poor little woman to call us so we can resume doing our jobs."

Rush sighed. "I'm not saying we don't look for him. We look hard. But if he's picked up, interviewed, charged with capital murder, he might never get out of jail. And Leigh might never see her child again."

Hanisch chuckled. Like a patient father trying to explain the facts of life. "Have you even considered the fact that Duke may have already killed the child? That we may be waiting forever for this woman to call? That she may follow him to five other murders before she finally figures that out for herself?" He rolled his eyes and blew out a long sigh. "And have you considered what will happen if someone else dies and it's discovered we didn't make every attempt to bury this bastard? What if after he kills somebody else, we find the girl and she's been dead for months? Has any of this occurred to you?"

Rush could feel his stomach churn. He swiped sweat from his forehead, tried to keep his voice steady. "Of course. But I'm more concerned for the child. We *have* to find her. Leigh is convinced that Enoch will go see her for Christmas. That's twelve days. I'm not asking for a permanent injunction here. I'm saying it's worth the wait. We'll look, but let's not pull out all the stops for twelve more days. Leigh's done a damn good job so far and she may be within a day or two of getting the girl back." He paused for a moment. "For Hannah's sake," he said finally.

The room was silent. Rush knew that Williams would make the decision. He also knew that Hanisch had made valid points. He wasn't making this argument to disagree with Hanisch, he was keeping the little girl out in front.

"Look," Rush said, breaking the silence, "let's keep Duke's picture out of the papers, off of the television. At least until Christmas. And since I don't have a warrant anyway, and won't have until Leigh gives us what she has, we can at least agree on that. Meanwhile, Chinbroski and I will be looking for him. Quietly. If Leigh doesn't call by Christmas morning we'll pull out all the stops."

"And if you find him before then?" Williams asked.

A glimmer of hope. "Then we set up a surveillance like none we've ever had," he said quickly. "Use every available officer. The FBI would help us if need be." Rush paused and looked at the captain. "It comes down to this: if we tip him off, if he sees his picture plastered all over the news, he'll run and we'd lose Leigh because she'll follow him. Or even worse, he'll panic and hurt that child."

"If he still has that child," Hanisch reminded them all. "If she's still okay."

"True. But the bottom line is I want to give Leigh Adams every chance to get her kid back." Rush paused. "And you have to admit that she's done a great job so far."

Williams stared at the tabletop, his brows knitted in concentration. Rush reached into his pocket and slid out the torn photo of Hannah. Standing, he slid the picture to the captain. "To make sure that everyone understands. Hannah is a little girl being held by a cretin who gutted one of our citizens for kicks. Look at her."

And then he shut up, his argument over.

Williams glanced at the photo, his face hard. The room fell silent as he made his decision. It didn't take long. Shoving the photo back at Rush, he stood and glared. "That was cheap." He leaned over the table, closing the distance between the two. "The child would never have been just a name. I have two daughters myself. I understand. Don't you dare try a guilt trip on me." He breathed deeply. "Start your warrant. See if you can convince a judge with what you have. Send teletypes out to all area departments. I want fliers up everywhere, and I mean everywhere, Rush. Newspapers, TV. We have to make every effort. If we drag him in before Christmas we'll tear his place apart. He'll have *something* written down about the kid. A phone number or something. If not, we'll trade something for the location." He raised his hands, relaxed, his voice softer. "I understand your concern, but we can't hang ourselves out like that."

Rush nodded. He refused to look at Hanisch even though he heard a soft snort of victory. The room fell silent as everyone but he and Chinbroski filed out like convicts on a work farm.

TWENTY-TWO

"I don't much give a shit about what kind of plans you have. Either you're meeting me and handing her over or I'll hunt you down and drop your body parts all over the county."

Enoch's voice sounded strong, alert, focused. Leigh recognized the intensity. Something major was up with him. The scratchy silence over Leigh's headphones allowed her to hear her heartbeat pounding in her ears. She was in the tree stand monitoring Enoch's phone tap, running tape on the call, fighting to control her breathing.

This was it. The beginning of the end.

"Well, I paid a load of money for her and I ain't gonna give her up on our first Christmas. Dena would kill me."

The second voice, although deep and commanding, had a thread of uncertainty.

"Dena will kill you?" Enoch laughed. *"Partner, Dena won't get the chance if you don't give her over. Tomorrow. Got it? I'll meet you at the same place where we met before."*

"Two weeks? You want her for two weeks? How do I know I'll get her back?"

"Cause I ain't got time to keep her in my line of work. We talked about this. Remember? I'm an uncle. You agreed. You bitch about it, you lose. Tomorrow. Noon."

The phone went dead. A wash of chills enveloped Leigh. She stared at the tape recorder in front of her, too shocked to move her hand and shut if off.

He'd sold Hannah. The bastard sold his own daughter! She closed her eyes to imagine the scene, but couldn't come up with anything, so foreign was the possibility. But it meant Hannah was alive, and with that thought the chills turned to shakes and Leigh slumped to the floor in relief.

Tomorrow. Noon. But where? Enoch had been as careful as ever, having not used his name, Hannah's name, or any locations. The other man wasn't so careful. Dena – his wife, girlfriend, mother, sister? No way to be sure, but Leigh suspected wife. It didn't help her now, but it was something. And she had it on tape. With his voice. Good for court later.

Leigh picked up the binoculars and studied the house through the trees. Smoke drifted from the chimney and Jane McElroy's cat pawed at the front door. She was surprised the cat was still alive after a week. She hadn't noticed a litter box when she installed the cameras, but it hadn't been foremost on her mind.

Leigh's monitor showed Enoch in the living room, sprawled across the sofa, drinking a Dr. Pepper. She wished he'd get drunk, although that would never happen. He talked non-stop when drunk, answering any question asked of him.

It was nearly noon now and she needed to run to her apartment and prepare for her departure. If Enoch did get Hannah tomorrow, there would be no time to waste. When she made the snatch, it'd be time to go. And although she hated to leave the deer stand, afraid of missing some crucial piece of information, she figured she had everything she needed to know.

* * *

Three hours later Rush sat alone inside a Whataburger nibbling on his fries. Chinbroski was at the station trying his hand at writing an affidavit for Enoch Duke's Capital Murder arrest warrant. Rush had promised to bring him three chicken sandwiches, two orders of fries, and a giant chocolate shake.

For the moment Rush pushed Enoch Duke and the entire McElroy case from his mind. He was tired of it, needed a vacation, wanted to spend some time with his wife. He had hated leaving her alone during the California trip, so soon after the letter from her ex. The day he first realized there was a future between them, he told her she would never have to worry again, that she could lock her past away like a crazy aunt. And she had, for the most part. She was healing, almost strong enough to bear her horrid past as she pushed forward with her life.

Then his beeper went off, pulling him from his thoughts. He almost dropped his Coke as he read the message. "*Found Leigh. Call me. Masterson.*"

Rush grabbed his cell and ran out of the restaurant as he dialed Willard Jackson's P.I. firm. Jackson answered.

"Just got Masterson's message," Rush said, unlocking his car door. "What's going on?"

"Masterson found the Leigh woman at a McDonalds in McKinney. He's watching her now. They're still there."

"The one on Highway 75? At Louisiana?"

"Right."

Rush cranked the engine and gunned the car north on the Highway 75 service road. "Anyone with him?"

"Reese Morgan's on the way. You gonna roll some of your people?"

"Absolutely." Rush hit his brakes and skidded to a stop at the red light at Spring Creek. "Get Masterson on the phone and tell him I'm running hot, heading his way. I'll be there in ten. And give him my cell number. Have him call if anything changes." Rush gave him the number.

The light changed. Rush squealed through the intersection. "And Willard?"

"Yeah?"

"Tell Morgan to stay away from her. I know he's pissed about her stealing his stuff, but if he screws this up I'm gonna put him in jail."

There was a short silence. "Already told him," Jackson said. "Cause I knew you'd say that."

Rush broke the connection and called Chinbroski's desk. It took the secretary a minute to hunt him down.

When he came on the line, Rush spoke fast. "Get to McKinney. Now. One of Jackson's men has Leigh Adams under surveillance."

"Where?"

"McDonalds on the highway. Hurry!"

"Fifteen minutes. I'll be on the tact channel."

Rush hung up and pushed the car even harder. He was coming into McKinney when his phone rang.

"She's moving." It was Masterson. His voice sounded as small as his ninety-eight pound frame. "We're going north on the service road toward Highway 380."

"Morgan with you?"

"Not yet. I just talked to him. He's only a minute out."

"What's she driving?"

"Old Blazer. Mid-eighties. Brown. Dark windows."

Rush swerved around a slow-moving semi. "Tag?"

"Not yet."

"By herself?"

"Yes. Wearing a red jacket and blue jeans. Her hair's all cut off. Remember in the video, it was down past her shoulders?"

"Right. Where are you now?"

"Just passed White Street. Still north bound."

Rush flew by the Eldorado Parkway exit. He was only a couple of miles back. "You have any cover?"

"Got two cars between us. I'm about fifty yards back."

"Good. I'm coming up on Louisiana. Couple minutes out."

"Okay. I think I see Reese behind me."

"Don't hang up, Jacob. Stay with me."

The seconds dragged by. Rush weaved in and out of traffic and hit the Highway 380 exit at over seventy. The traffic was light. "Where?" he said into the phone.

"East on 380. Pulling into the Wal-Mart on the left."

"Got you. I'm seconds away." Rush hit the brakes and cut through a gas station to avoid the traffic at the red light. "Hang back, Jacob. Let her go in."

"Affirmative."

"Where you at?" Chinbroski's voice crackled over the police radio.

Rush gave him the update. "How long for you?"

"I'm in Allen. Still five minutes. Just sit on the car."

"If we can." Rush grabbed his phone. "She parked?"

"Affirmative," Masterson said. "Getting out now. On the west side of the lot."

Rush told Chinbroski.

"Walking into the store," Masterson said. "Morgan is out near the exit, by Target. I'm in my El Camino, two rows over from her Blazer."

"I'm pulling into the lot, now," Rush said. He scanned the cars and found the Blazer facing east, three rows from the western edge of the parking lot. He gave Chinbroski the exact location. Pulling in behind Masterson, he threw his car in park and tapped his horn.

Masterson looked. Rush motioned for him to join him. After Masterson was inside the car, Rush shook his hand. "Hell of a job! How'd you find her?"

The Prophet looked fragile sitting there in his large windbreaker, and almost embarrassed by the praise. "I figured she had to eat," he said. "On the tape she told Willard she thought her ex might live near McKinney. She didn't look as though she had much money. Thus, McDonalds." He raised an eyebrow. "I've been watching it on and off for nearly two weeks. I hesitated to mention it to you just in case my theory was in error."

"You make me feel like a dullard."

"Not to worry, you have her now. That's the important thing." Masterson rolled down his window. "Have you identified them yet? Leigh and her ex?"

"Yeah. Name is Leigh Adams. He's Enoch Duke. He's hidden their two-year-old daughter, Hannah."

Masterson nodded. Stared at his hands. "And you think she will tell you where Enoch lives? Before she has her child back?"

Rush rolled down his window. A breeze blew in across his face as he looked away. "No," he said. "I don't think she will."

"And yet you are going to attempt to convince her?"

"What else?" Rush said, turning to face him. "I can't just let her drive off."

"Why? Have you obtained a warrant that commands you to arrest her?"

Masterson wore an amused look, his eyes as wide as quarters, a smile dipped one corner of his mouth.

"Is this another one of your riddles?" Rush asked.

He shrugged. "A woman who would allow people to die for the mere *hope* of discovering the location of her child is not a candidate for unqualified cooperation. She would be faced with a choice, I suspect, of saving herself or her daughter. I don't need to tell you the probable outcome of *that* decision."

"Jacob, are you saying she'd sit in jail rather than tell us where Enoch is?"

He shrugged again. "Not knowing the woman personally, I can't give you a definite answer. And since you have identified her, I assume you know much more about her than I. However, if she wanted the help of the police, I can clearly speculate that she would have sought that assistance by now." He paused. "To answer your question, yes, I believe she would face charges if it meant revealing Enoch's location."

Rush nodded. "So, humor me, Jacob. What would you do?"

Masterson looked at him. A nerve in his cheek made his left eye twitch. "May I ask you something first?"

Rush said nothing.

"Do *you* believe that she will talk if you snatch her now?"

No, he didn't. But he also knew what his superiors, namely Hanisch, would say if he let her drive away. "I'm not sure," he said. "I have my doubts."

"Do you know why she hasn't sought help from law enforcement?"

"She doesn't trust us. She believes that Enoch would spot a full-scale police surveillance. That if Enoch is arrested before he leads her to Hannah, she'll never find her."

Masterson nodded. "It's as I suspected." He rubbed his hands across his legs. "I would follow her," he said. "I would move back and tail her from here. She will lead you to Enoch. Maybe not today, but soon. At that point she will *have* to assist you."

Rush mulled over that. It made sense. And he didn't have to tell anyone at the department that he knew Enoch's location until Leigh had Hannah back. "I could live with that."

"I'm in the game," Chinbroski announced over the radio.

Rush picked up the microphone. "Meet me in the Target parking lot." He turned to Masterson. "You're right when you said that she may not lead us to Enoch today. Can you commit to as long as it takes?"

"Certainly. And I'll call Willard. We could use another car."

Rush shook his head. "I'd rather you not. She's seen him."

"Ahh, that is true. How silly to forget such a simple point."

"But call him and tell him I'm asking for your and Morgan's help. In the meantime, let's pull back and give her some room. Call Reese and tell him."

"Right." Masterson opened the door and climbed out. He looked down at Rush before going back to his car. "This is a good thing you're doing ... for the girl. The right thing."

"I just hope everybody else will see it like that, Jacob. Especially if I screw it up."

Rush met Chinbroski in front of Target and told him what he wanted to do.

"So you're not gonna grab her?"

"I think it'd be more profitable not to. At least for right now." Rush was about to elaborate further when his cell phone rang.

"Masterson here. She's out. At her truck."

"Tell Morgan to take point. Since you've been on her longer. And Jacob, let's not use her or her ex's name. Or exact locations. Remember, she might be listening. Pass that on to Morgan."

"Affirmative."

Rush dropped his car in gear and looked at Chinbroski. "She's out. Keep it loose."

"You got it."

Rush circled around to the east side of Target just as the old Blazer backed out of its parking space. He could see the silhouette of the petite driver, the short, dark hair, and the sunglasses. She looked both directions when she stopped at the end of her row. Masterson was behind her, one row over, slumped in his seat. Reese Morgan was to her left, in his Dodge Ram pickup, sitting in the passenger's seat. Chinbroski had pulled out onto Highway 380, west, back toward the freeway to cover that direction. Rush was to her right. He would take her if she turned east on 380.

She did. "East," Rush told his partner. "And I'm on the point."

"I'll flip." Chinbroski said.

Rush grabbed his cellular and called Masterson. "Can you and Morgan keep up, or do you want to keep this line open?"

"We can keep up," Masterson said. "Had I thought it through I would have instructed Reese to grab two extra radios prior to leaving the office."

Leigh sped up and changed lanes. "If you fall back give me a call," Rush told Chinbroski. Then to Masterson on the phone, "I want us all rotating the point every few minutes, unless we get trapped in a procession. Try and keep a couple of cars between you for cover."

"Affirmative," Masterson said. "I'll relay to Reese."

Highway 380 was older businesses, a light industrial area. The traffic was just enough to blend in without worry of being spotted. Rush ended the call and fell in behind the Blazer.

Highway 380 east of the freeway was five-lane, two each way with a center turn lane. Leigh had just moved to the far right. She increased her speed and caught a green.

"I've flipped," Chinbroski said. "But I'm the last tick on this dog's ass. I'll catch up in a minute."

"Hey, don't make it obvious. We've got her blanketed."

"Rush, you're talking to Houdini. The last time I looked, I could watch a whore in the White House without being seen."

"We're at a red at Highway 5. She's moved back into the left lane." Rush was still at the point. He allowed a pickup to pass before he made the lane change. He had three cover vehicles. Masterson was directly behind him, Morgan two cars back.

"I'm a hundred yards back," Chinbroski said.

The light turned. The Blazer shot forward and whipped a U-turn.

Rush grabbed his radio. "She flipped, Chin, coming at you."

"I got an eyeball. Turning around now."

Rush clicked his microphone to signal he'd received the transmission. He was looking for a place to turn around when Chinbroski transmitted again.

"She's doing heat runs. She flipped right after I made a U-turn. Heading back your way. And I'm going the wrong way again."

Rush pulled off onto the shoulder and waited.

"You hear me, Rush? Coming back at you. Moving fast, headed your way."

"I got you." He pulled into a small market and waited.

"I flipped again," Chinbroski said. "But I'm about out of the game."

The Blazer hit a green light and flew by Rush. She *was* moving fast. He pulled out and fell in behind her. Masterson and Morgan had pulled off somewhere behind him.

The road squeezed from five lanes to two. Sixteen miles east was Farmersville, a town that matched its name. Masterson was two cars back; Morgan, one behind him.

"Hey, I need some help back here," Chinbroski said. "I'm choking from eating all your exhaust fumes."

"You made the light yet?" They were at least a half-mile past the intersection.

"Quarter mile back. I see the Dodge that fat guy is driving."

"His name's Reese Morgan," Rush said.

"Yeah, that guy."

The frost-covered grass made the landscape prettier than it really was, the sparkling moisture glistened like diamonds. The land became rolling pastures the closer they came to Lake Lavon. Straight ahead, eight miles before Farmersville, was Princeton, a town that looked nothing like its name. Rush was grateful for the small hills. He was able to drop back and pull off onto the shoulder as soon as the Blazer disappeared over the horizon. Masterson took point and Rush fell in behind Morgan. He saw Chinbroski in his rearview mirror still a hundred yards out.

They followed her for several minutes more. Just before they hit the Princeton city limits, the Blazer turned left – north – on a small, blacktop road. Masterson went by. Morgan slowed and let her disappear around the first bend in the road before he turned. Rush made the turn behind him, pulled onto the shoulder, and let Chinbroski pass. When he finally rounded the bend he caught a flash of Chinbroski's brake lights topping a small hill.

"What do you see up there?" Rush asked.

"The Blazer's a couple hundred yards up. On a long straight. The fat guy in the Dodge just turned up a driveway. It's only me now. How close are you?"

Rush topped the hill. "I got you. As soon as she makes it around the next bend, pull off. I'll hit it hard and close."

Masterson was on Rush's bumper. The Blazer made the bend and he floored it. He passed Chinbroski and hit the curve at almost fifty. The Blazer was a couple of hundred yards ahead and Rush slowed as it turned onto a gravel road.

"Turning left," Rush said into the radio. "I'm going past. Masterson should go with her. Give him a few beats, then you follow."

"Got it," Chinbroski said.

Rush looked as he passed the road. "She's riding her brake lights."

"Ten-four."

As Masterson made the turn, Rush whipped a 180. He pulled over to the shoulder and waited. He saw Morgan sitting on the other side of the gravel road, facing him. Probably waiting for Masterson to give him an update.

Chinbroski waited several beats and then turned onto the gravel road. "I don't see it," he said. "But Masterson's sitting in the middle of the road like he wants her to see him. What the hell is he doing? I'm stopping here until you find out."

Rush dialed Masterson's cellular. "What's going on?"

"She pulled off the road and drove through a field," Masterson said. "There's a heavy tree line on the right and I can see a narrow break where she drove through. I lost her after she went off road."

"How far away are you from the break in the trees?"

"Sixty yards, I'd say," Masterson said.

"Give her a couple of minutes, then drive past and tell me what you see."

"Affirmative."

Over the cellular Rush could hear Masterson's breathing.

"I can see where her tires beat a path through the weeds," Masterson said. "Looks well traveled. There's a small pond or something. The tracks go around that and disappear through more trees on the other side. Without driving in there…"

"No. I don't want that. Listen, you go straight and find some place to sit where you can watch that opening. Call Morgan and tell him to back up and watch the gravel road. Chinbroski and I are gonna park and go in on foot."

"Affirmative."

They parked just on the other side of a small hill two hundred yards from the gravel road. Rush pulled his coat on and shoved his cellular in a pocket. Chinbroski, who sweated in fifty-degree weather, threw his coat in his car over the police radio mounted in front of the bench seat.

"Let's take it slow," Rush said. He looked down at his slacks and loafers. "I mean, it's not like I'm dressed for hiking."

"Just lead the way, Rush. And if you start whining like a girl, I'll carry you."

"I don't want your John Wayne act today."

Chinbroski flipped him the bird.

They cut through a thick wooded area and walked at an angle along the gravel road. The winter sun had melted the frost and their shoes were soaked by the time they'd gone fifty yards. Rush felt his toes begin to stiffen. After several minutes he stopped at the edge of a clearing and pointed to the small pond Masterson had mentioned.

"You can see the tracks from here," Rush said, moving his toes, trying to generate some heat. The sun was to their back, as was the wind. "I hope Leigh doesn't have a dog."

"What?" Chinbroski asked, "You see her with a dog?"

Rush shook his head. "How do you want to do this? Get on the tire tracks or follow them from the side?"

Chinbroski rubbed his chin. "Well, when I was hunting grizzlies as a ten-year-old with my bow and arrow set, I always tried to stay off a heavily traveled path."

Rush sighed.

"So I think we should cut across the other side of that pond and duck behind the biggest tree we can find until we know where to go from there."

"Fine, Mr. Boone, lead the way. And don't walk very fast. My feet are killing me."

Chinbroski set off to his right, skirting along the tree line. Rush followed, keeping his eyes toward the spot where the tracks disappeared into the trees. The only sounds he heard were his breathing and both of their feet slapping against the wet grass. When they turned left toward the backside of the pond, Chinbroski stopped and held up his hand.

"Smell that?"

Rush sniffed the air. "What?"

"A mixture of Dial soap and baby powder." Chinbroski sniffed and pointed toward the trees. "It must be her."

"All I smell is cow dung and pond scum."

Chinbroski winked. "Oh, is that what that is?" He laughed quietly and walked on.

Just inside the tree line, fifteen feet from the car tracks, Rush could see the corner of the Blazer under a tarp.

"Look at that," Chinbroski whispered. "She parks under a clump of trees, then covers it with a damn camouflage tarp. Who's she hiding from, the military?"

Rush considered her angle of entry, from where she had driven in, how she had approached this spot. "I think we're safe if we approach from where we are," he said. "I mean, whatever she's doing has to be on the other side of the car."

"Enoch Duke's house, you're thinking."

"Right."

"Because she wouldn't pass by his place to get to her surveillance spot," Chinbroski said.

"I wouldn't think so. And since she's covered her car already, she has to be on foot by now. And probably close. I say let's stay in the trees and try and find her footprints leading away from the car."

Chinbroski nodded and started to move.

Rush grabbed his arm. "No noise."

His partner made a zipping motion across his lips and quietly stepped around a low-hanging branch. They walked, stopped, looked, and listened, kept to the shadows, moved like soldiers on enemy grounds. Rush felt silly.

He tried to step in Chinbroski's tracks, tried to see around his wide shoulders, tried to keep his breathing under control. When they made it to the Blazer, sweat was running down his scalp and onto his neck. He'd wiped his forehead a half dozen times, and cursed himself for wearing his coat. But his feet still ached from the wet and cold.

Chinbroski lifted the tarp and looked in through the driver's door window.

"Nothing. Some trash on the seat, a McDonald's bag. Bunch of luggage in back."

Rush found footprints in the wet grass and leaves around the car where she'd thrown the tarp over.

"Here," he whispered, pointing down to tracks heading north through the woods.

Chinbroski knelt down and felt a footprint. "Fresh tracks, Kemo-sabe. Me think she only minutes ahead. You ride to town, get help. I stay, watch for girl."

Rush sighed again. The stress was killing his partner.

"You want both of us to follow these tracks or one of us to stay by the car?" Chinbroski asked.

Rush was just thinking about that. "I'd rather have you with me. You think you can disable the car? Maybe pull the distributor wire? Maybe we'll hear if she slips by us and tries to leave."

"Lucky this thing is old," Chinbroski said, flopping down onto his back and sliding underneath. "Lucky it still has a distributor. It'll just take a sec."

Rush pulled out his phone, called Masterson, and updated him.

"Okay. Ready." Chinbroski slid out and brushed himself off. "Let's go," he said, and started to go, but then stopped. "What are we gonna do if we see Duke?"

He'd thought about that, too. "We'll play it by ear."

Chinbroski looked at him and shook his head. "What a plan."

The tracks went on endlessly. They moved slowly, taking care to stay off Leigh's tracks in case she headed back. The ground was flat and rocky – the trail easily seen among the damp leaves that covered most of their noise. They had little cover, just a few bushes and some waist-high weeds. Chinbroski held up his hand again once they'd gone what seemed like a mile. He squatted next to a small cedar tree and pointed straight ahead. Off in the distance, more than a quarter mile ahead in the middle of a small clearing, sat a house that appeared ready to collapse. Half way between them and the house was a deer stand, twenty feet off the ground, nailed to a hundred-foot oak. The underbrush was thick under the tree, enough so that if Leigh squatted as she walked, her approach would never be seen from the house.

"I think we've got her," Chinbroski whispered. "That's gotta be her surveillance post."

"I can't see well enough to know if she's up there."

"She's gotta be. Look at the tracks. They lead right to it."

Rush sat on the ground to rest. A cluster of shoulder-high bushes hid them both. "Could be."

Chinbroski sat next to him. "So, what'd you wanna do? Wait here until she comes down?"

"Let me think."

"The captain said arrest her."

Rush wiped his sweaty forehead and looked toward the deer stand. "I say we wait. Sit right here until she comes down. We could camp out here until we see the little girl."

"Rush, that kid's probably dead."

"Don't you dare say such a thing!" a voice said from behind them.

TWENTY-THREE

Leigh Adams stood in a fighting stance ten feet behind them. She wore a camouflage ball cap pulled low over her forehead; little fluffs of raven hair stuck out over both ears and around her neck. Her brown eyes were slits as she stared hard at both detectives. Army fatigues, pant legs tucked into hiking boots, matching shirt hanging out, partly covering a black fanny pack around her waist.

"Don't ever say that Hannah is dead! Because she's not!" She kept her voice low, but her intensity would give pause to a man twice her size.

Rush heard a low rumble in Chinbroski's throat and knew he was about to make a move. As the big man started to get up, Rush placed a hand on his arm.

"How do you know she's alive?" Rush asked quietly, taking the lead as he slowly climbed to his feet.

"I have recordings of Enoch on the phone talking about her. She's not dead."

Chinbroski was up before Rush and took a half step to his left. He remained silent, his face hard. Pencil-sized veins in his forearms pulsed as he flexed his fists. Leigh turned toward him and set her feet as though ready for battle.

"How recently?" Rush asked softly, trying to keep things calm.

Leigh glanced at Rush and then peered over his shoulder toward the house. "This morning. She'll be here tomorrow at noon. And I'm taking her back." She glared at Chinbroski. "Mom told me you were the asshole of this partnership. Told me how you want to lock me up." She moved another half step toward him. "Well let me tell you something. *Nobody* is going to stop me from getting my little girl back."

Rush glanced at Chinbroski, whose face had relaxed and transformed to something between a smile and a smirk.

Chinbroski stuck an arm out and leaned against a tree. "First, let's get one thing straight. I'm gonna lock you up. We got a warrant. But if I wasn't, what makes you think you can get the kid back all by yourself?"

Her eyes were locked on Chinbroski, her breathing even, controlled. "The kid? Is that what Hannah is to you?"

"You didn't answer my question."

"How?" Leigh paused, a flash of indecision. "I want her more than he does. I'll do what it takes." She looked at Rush. "I'll kill him if I have to."

"And that would help you?" Rush asked. "That would help Hannah?"

She glanced over Rush's shoulder again. "Don't preach to me. You've got no idea what I've seen him do. No idea the hell I've lived through. I don't plan on killing him. But, by God, I will."

And then what, Rush wondered. *Go back to Boonville*? She wouldn't do that unless she was sure Enoch would never get out of prison. She didn't seem worried about it, so maybe she *did* have enough evidence to lock him away for life.

"Seems to me you got a little problem," Chinbroski said.

"Yeah?"

"Us." Chinbroski looked at Rush.

"Just what I thought. Look, I don't need you. All I need is one more day. One." She pointed toward the house. "And then you can have him. One more day would… "

Chinbroski sprang while she was talking and looking toward the house. She saw him too late, tried to jump back, but landed flat on her back after a hard shove. Chinbroski flung her onto her belly, jerked both hands behind her back, and cuffed her.

"A warrant is a command by the court," Chinbroski said. "Relax and it'll go easy."

"You bastard. You'll kill Hannah!"

"Not so loud," Rush said.

Leigh struggled for a second longer, but gave up after Chinbroski put a foot in the middle of her back.

"We'll try to help you," Rush said. "But we have a job to do. Don't forget that you could have come to us on your own terms."

She remained silent, stared at nothing, her face tight with anger.

Chinbroski knelt beside her and spoke softly. "Rush told me before we started our little hike in the woods today that if we had a chance to get the kid back... then, well, that's what we're gonna do. But we ain't gonna let you run off and do everything by yourself."

Rush hadn't said that, but he'd wanted to. And once again his partner had read his mind.

Chinbroski smiled. "See, this is how we figure it. Since you've come this far, and now we're here with you, there's no reason we can't work together. No reason for you to get into more trouble than you're in now." He glanced at Rush, raised his eyebrows.

Rush nodded. "He's right. We have a warrant. But we don't have to arrest you today."

"I'm already arrested."

"Handcuffed ain't arrested," Chinbroski said. "Look around, I don't see nobody who knows we caught you. Cooperation is still on our offer board."

"We told your mother we'd help you get Hannah back if we could," Rush said. "Your problems come once we have Hannah back. You've got a truckload of criminal charges facing you."

"Can you get my face out of the dirt?"

Chinbroski sat her up and leaned her against a tree. "See, I ain't the asshole you think I am."

"So who has Hannah?" Rush asked, working to get her past the distrust. "You said she'd be here tomorrow noon?"

Leigh glanced at the house again. "The woman's name is Dena. There's a man. Don't know his name. No last names. Enoch called him this morning. It's the only phone call I've heard between them. I have it on tape."

"So this man is bringing Hannah to Enoch?" Rush confirmed.

She nodded.

A sharp breeze rustled the branches over Rush's head and he suddenly felt cold. He needed to move around. "Let's head back to the car. Or is there some reason you need to stay out here?"

"Like I have a choice? I want my lawyer."

Rush nodded at Chinbroski, who pulled Leigh to her feet. Rush stepped close to her. "Listen, we'll help you, but you start answering questions right now. I won't ask you anything you'll need a lawyer for. Think about it. I won't beg." Rush turned and headed off, leading the way back to the car.

"Are you refusing me my lawyer?"

Rush stopped and turned back. "To the contrary. I want you to call your lawyer. But we'll do it when we get to the station."

Leigh looked at him, then wiped the side of her dirty face against her shoulder. "Let me say clearly. I want my lawyer before you question me about anything."

Rush considered her request, nodded, and looked at Chinbroski.

"How did you follow that bastard?" Chinbroski asked her, totally ignoring what she'd just said. "That's a hell of an accomplishment."

She sighed and shook her head. "You want me to answer that? Before I talk to my lawyer?"

"Just making conversation, babe," Chinbroski said. "Answer it if you want."

Leigh started walking, Chinbroski following closely behind. After several moments of silence she glanced at Rush, caught him watching her, and gave him a defiant smile. "Enoch thinks I'm dead."

Rush cocked his head. "Then why is he hiding Hannah? I don't understand."

Her face grew hard again. "He's not hiding her. He just doesn't want to raise her. He only wants her at his convenience." She paused and took a breath. "He sold her."

"Your mother never mentioned..."

"I didn't know until the phone call this morning."

Rush's mind raced as he considered how to capture Enoch Duke while keeping Hannah safe. He thought about Leigh, about what she had gone through, about how nervous she must be to suddenly have to trust two people she didn't know. He thought about the unknown couple that had bought a child. And the thought of that made his blood boil.

"So how come Duke thinks you're dead?" Chinbroski asked after they'd walked a while longer in silence.

Leigh looked straight ahead, shoulders back, as though wearing her handcuffs with pride. "Remember the guy in Boonville my mother told you about, the guy whose mail I was watching? His name's Yancy. Mom followed him into town, struck up a conversation, got around to talking about me. Mom cried, told him I was dead, killed in a wreck in Baja, Mexico, had me cremated. I can't prove Yancy ever told Enoch, but I think so."

"Why?" Rush asked.

"Because he's been sloppy. Enoch knows I'm smarter than him, knows I'd want Hannah back, that I'd never stop looking. If he thought I was hunting him, he'd be a whole lot better than he's been."

"So you ain't the wonder woman we thought you was," Chinbroski said.

"Sent you both to California, didn't I?"

Chinbroski shrugged.

"And I found Enoch, didn't I? And I've gathered enough evidence to bury his ass under the prison, haven't I?"

"That remains to be seen," Chinbroski said. "We got to talk about that evidence, by the way. Agree to a little trade before tomorrow."

She snorted.

"You ain't calling the shots anymore," Chinbroski said. "We ain't gotta be friendly. We can make it easier on you."

"Yeah? How do you figure that?" she asked. "Let me remind you of something. You *have* to have the evidence I've collected against Enoch. You can't do anything without it. You can't even put him at the scene of the crime without my help."

"We gotta have details, gotta know everything about Duke before we pop him. We got less than a day, if you ain't lying about noon tomorrow. Get my drift?" Chinbroski gritted his teeth.

They walked in silence the rest of the way to Leigh's car. Rush pulled his phone out, called Masterson, and thanked him for all of his help, told him they wouldn't need anything else from them.

Leigh leaned against her Blazer facing the road and leaned her head back.

Chinbroski leaned against a tree.

"How did you find Enoch once you got to Texas?" Rush asked her.

"Still full of questions?" she said, closing her eyes.

"Listen, we haven't asked you anything Daniel will be worried about," Chinbroski said. He had pulled out a pad and was now jotting notes.

"Just trying to follow the rules. I've asked for an attorney three times now."

Chinbroski looked up. "Chill, we know when we're crossing the line. And we can't even see it yet."

She opened her eyes and stared at the woods leading to the road where Rush and Chinbroski's cars were parked, then said without emotion, "Collin Creek Mall has a Sears store. A big one. He's queer about Craftsman tools." She looked at Rush. "I'd lost Enoch in Arizona, for a month I searched for him there when Mom saw a letter in Yancy's mailbox with a Plano postmark. The first thing I did when I hit town was find the Sears store. I watched the tool department for eight days before he finally came in."

"That is sloppy," Chinbroski said. "He's stupider than I thought."

Leigh frowned at him, but said nothing.

"How come he didn't recognize your car?" Chinbroski asked.

"Because I didn't buy it until right before I left Boonville. Do you think *I'm* stupid?"

"So you found him at the Sears store before you stole all the stuff from Willard Jackson, the P.I.?" Chinbroski asked.

She squirmed, looked off into space, rubbed her nose against her shoulder.

"Did I mention I have a lawyer?"

"But you needed equipment," Rush said.

"If I stumble across anything that looks like the stolen stuff you're talking about, I'll let you know."

"I'm not going to file any theft charges," Rush said. "Relax. I'm sure Daniel would allow you to talk to me if he were here."

She thought that over, then sighed. "Okay. In that case, yes, I stole all the stuff."

"Where is it now?"

"Some of it is in Enoch's house. I tapped his phone, as you know already. Installed cameras and microphones everywhere. The deer stand is full of stolen stuff. I left the tracking system with a dead guy. Blankenship, I think his name was. I watched Enoch kill him. Videotaped it. Living color. I did nothing to stop it because I have to save Hannah. I did steal a bunch of cash out of Blankenship's trunk that Enoch didn't find. The money's been a lifesaver, but I left a bunch of money, too. The rest of the equipment is still in the van, parked somewhere easy to find. Any more questions, since my lawyer won't mind me confessing to everything?" She looked hard at Rush, then stared once again toward the woods leading to the road behind him.

A faint alarm bell went off in Rush's head.

"So you didn't put the transmitter on Enoch's car?" Chinbroski asked.

"Since I knew where he lived I saw no need. I saved it for exactly what happened because I'm a decent person."

"How'd you know we was following you today?" Chinbroski asked.

Rush looked at him and frowned. "What difference does that make?"

"I just wanna know."

"I saw Detective Rush when I pulled out of Wal-Mart."

The alarm bell got louder, but Rush couldn't figure what was wrong.

"Why'd you give that tape to Nanci?" Chinbroski asked.

"Who?"

"Nanci Brookfield, the woman with the house under construction. Enoch got a call from a black guy about breaking in."

"Oh, yes." Leigh paused. "So she *did* go to the police. I've been wondering about that."

"You didn't know?" Chinbroski asked.

"I knew she was pretty upset when I left her house, so I suspected she might, but no, I wasn't sure. I'm glad she did, even though it was risky for me."

"What do you mean *risky*," Chinbroski snapped. "Trying to save a woman's life is *risky*?"

"Don't yell at me! It was risky because if you had caught Enoch I'd never have gotten Hannah back. So I'm not the monster you make me out to be." She looked at Rush. "I'm ready to talk about a deal."

Rush studied her for a moment, the alarm bell clanging now. "Without your lawyer present?"

"Look around, do you see him here? I've told you everything you wanted to know." She glanced at Chinbroski, then looked at Rush. "Okay, I do want my lawyer present. Just tell me what you'll need from me."

"We'll need your testimony." Rush said. "That's the first thing. And the evidence you have against Enoch."

She shook her head. "I need Hannah first."

"You'll get Hannah. Chinbroski and I agree on that. But I want a solid warrant on Enoch when we grab her. Then we're covered legally if we have to use deadly force to arrest him."

The wind rustled the branches overhead while Leigh stood in silence. Finally, she responded. "What is the minimum you need for your warrant? I'm not giving up everything I've got. No way, not yet."

"A statement," Rush said. "With your name on it. No confidential informant stuff. And you'll write how you followed him to Jane McElroy's house, saw him go in, waited outside until he came out. That's what happened?"

"That's what happened. I did nothing to stop it because I want Hannah back."

"I have the photos you mailed to us from the crime scene," Rush said. "The hair you left behind, the Boontling note. So you write that you went in and did all of that."

"That I altered your crime scene. Yes. And then what?"

Rush stared at her, processing what she'd just said. *That I altered your crime scene.* The alarm in his head sounded like the Old North Church from Paul Revere's ride.

"And then what?" she repeated.

He suddenly knew. "Hold it." Rush turned to Chinbroski. "Don't ask her anything else. Interview's over."

"And then what?" Leigh asked for a third time.

"Then we get our warrant," Chinbroski answered her. "And tomorrow we help you get Hannah. After that, you give us the rest of it. All of it. And a videotaped statement telling us the entire story."

"Enough, Chin," Rush said. "Don't ask her anything."

"I didn't ask anything. I answered her question."

"So you'll use what I've told you today to get your warrant against Enoch?" Leigh asked Chinbroski. "To get the warrant to search the house?"

"That's right," Chinbroski confirmed.

"No more!" Rush shouted. He knew what she'd done, and she knew he knew. He stared at her, searched her face for a hint of victory.

It came slowly, to her eyes first, then the corners of her mouth, and finally to the way she held her head.

She looked past him, to the woods, and smiled fully. Then Rush heard what she obviously saw; footsteps, the crunching of leaves, the rustling of branches.

Rush turned and saw his son, desk jockey turned mountain man, striding toward them in a double-breasted suit with a notebook under his arm and a camera around his neck.

"Hello, Pop," Daniel said, smiling as though he'd won the lottery. He raised his camera and snapped a picture of the handcuffed Leigh.

Rush turned and looked at Leigh, who locked eyes with him and nodded.

"In each pocket, Daniel," Leigh told him while looking at Rush. "The cargo pocket of each leg. My whole conversation with these two fine detectives. I used two recorders just in case one failed." She smiled at Rush, then looked at his son. "You might be the best thousand dollars I've ever spent."

Daniel stopped in front of her and smiled. Then he looked at Rush. "You didn't do anything stupid, did you Pop? You didn't question her after she informed you she wanted an attorney, did you? After all, I don't want softball pitches right over the plate. I want to win fair and square."

Chinbroski looked at Rush and frowned. But Rush knew what they had done. They had just given Leigh every ace in their deck.

TWENTY-FOUR

The meeting took place in Daniel's law office in spite of Chinbroski's objections. He'd cussed a blue streak when Daniel strutted out of the woods, watched in stunned silence when Daniel pulled the two tape recorders from Leigh's pants pockets, and nearly attacked Daniel when he bragged about instructing Leigh to bait them.

In Chinbroski's view Leigh was their prisoner regardless of what had happened and should have gone straight to jail, where she would sit while they got warrants for every single criminal violation possible.

But his partner's ranting hadn't swayed Rush. There was a bigger picture than getting even with Leigh and Daniel. Rush knew where they stood, was fully aware of the long-term legal problems they would encounter if they proceeded with Chinbroski's plan. So they'd come to Daniel's office, given Daniel time to instruct Leigh of the possibilities for her continued freedom, and calmed Chinbroski enough to allow him to sit in on the meeting that was about to start.

Daniel's conference room was the former master bedroom in the old Victorian. He'd placed a small refrigerator in the corner, just outside the bathroom door, and stocked it with soft drinks. Rush and Chinbroski had drained two Dr Peppers each and were nursing a third when Daniel finally entered with Leigh trailing behind him.

He smiled and closed the door, pointed Leigh to the chair farthest from Chinbroski, and sat himself directly across from his father.

"Well," Daniel said. "I think we're ready to proceed. Would you like this meeting taped?"

Chinbroski grunted and Rush shot him a look. "I think we've generated enough tape recordings for one day," Rush said. "Just cut to the chase."

Daniel placed a pad in front of him and looked at the first item. "The Supreme Court has ruled, and reaffirmed, that when an arrested subject asks for an attorney, all questioning must cease immediately. I've listened to one of Leigh's tapes. Both of you clearly violated that ruling. As a result, anything she told you from that point forward would not be admissible to use against her. In addition, any information gained during that illegal interrogation would spoil any warrant you obtained for arresting Enoch or searching his cabin."

Daniel took a breath, made some check marks on his pad, and looked at Rush.

Rush glanced at Chinbroski, who appeared tongue-tied with rage.

"Would you like me to continue?" Daniel asked. "Or would you like to debate the point?"

"Please continue," Rush said. "I'd hate to break your rhythm."

"Of course you could find a magistrate to sign any such warrants for Enoch ..." Daniel waved his hand. "Well, you're both experienced in these things. Let's talk about Leigh."

Rush glanced at her. Her defiant look was gone, replaced with calm confidence. She looked younger than her twenty-four years, yet older at the same time. Battle worn around the eyes.

"Leigh has finished talking to you," Daniel said. "Under advice of counsel, she has said everything she will ever say under the current conditions. Nor will she be providing evidence of Enoch's past activities."

Daniel paused again and looked at Rush.

"Negotiable, I assume?" Rush asked.

"Everything has its price." Daniel smiled, then glanced at Chinbroski. Rush looked over.

Chinbroski sat stiffly, hands folded in front of him, veins showing in his neck, jaws clamped shut, staring at Daniel.

"I understand your frustration," Daniel told him. "But if we'll keep our eye on the prize, we'll all sleep better once Hannah is safely returned to her mother."

Chinbroski made no sound or movement that indicated he even heard Daniel. Rush had only seen him like this one other time, and he broke both arms on a suspect he'd caught burglarizing his apartment one afternoon when they'd stopped by for lunch.

"Can we cut to the chase?" Rush asked him. "We don't have all afternoon."

"Leigh remains free. No criminal charges. Not a single one. In return she'll tell you everything, give you a video deposition, sworn statement, everything she's collected against Enoch. She gives you what you need right now to get warrants for Enoch. You can name her in your warrant affidavits and case reports. She'll testify. Not only during the initial trial, but also during any subsequent appeals. Comment?"

Rush shook his head. Chinbroski stared at Daniel. "No," Rush said. "Go on."

"In return for her uninhibited cooperation, you two will assist her in getting Hannah back. You'll use whatever resources you see fit, including additional manpower."

"What about the warrant we already have?" Rush asked.

"Recall it. You're the affiant. Tell the judge new information came to light that casts doubt on the probable cause as stated in the original affidavit. Happens all the time. You knew the answer to that. Why ask?"

"I'm not the affiant," Rush said. "Chin is." Rush looked at his partner. Chinbroski hadn't changed position.

"Then the ball's in your court, Detective." Daniel scooted his chair back and glanced at Leigh, who couldn't take her eyes off Chinbroski.

Chinbroski sat there, stared for a while, his fists closed, his forearms knotted with muscle. Finally, he scooted his chair back and looked at Rush. "This whole thing pisses me off. This pencil-necked kid of yours may think he's holding all the cards, but he ain't."

Chinbroski turned and glared at Daniel again. "As of right now, she's still under arrest. And I ain't inclined to un-arrest her. You can talk all you want about how we screwed everything up today." He pointed a finger at Leigh. "But we control her freedom. Yeah, you may beat us, but that'll be a long time from now. Yeah, Enoch might get some fancy-pants lawyer and beat us, but like your old man says, 'You can beat the rap but you can't beat the ride.'"

Rush cut his eyes at Leigh. She'd been the perfect client thus far; sitting quietly, her face a mask of indifference, confident her hired gun would arrange everything. But Chinbroski had just shaken her up. Face red, eyes tight, hands clenched together, Leigh looked ready to leap across the table and grab Chinbroski by the throat. But she remained quiet, sneaked a glance at Daniel, who tapped a pencil against his chin while he waited for Chinbroski to continue.

Chinbroski smiled at Daniel. "I think we can get all the warrants we want. I'll be the affiant again, use everything wonder woman told us, list her as a confidential informant, to hell with a statement. We'll lock Enoch up, if he don't resist, that is. If he does resist, we'll kill him. Either way, he's out of our hair. If we do arrest him it'll be a hell of a long time before the courts throw anything out. Meanwhile, this arrogant bitch does some time herself, we put her kid in foster care and let somebody decent raise her."

"You son-of-a-bitch!" Leigh said, coming out of her chair.

Daniel grabbed her arm and held on for the ride.

"You're not the judge and jury!" Leigh shouted.

"And you're not the legal magician you think you are!" Chinbroski shouted back. "You and Perry Mason here think you can dictate every damn thing. Well, I got some news: this meeting is about to be over and you're still under arrest." Chinbroski turned to Daniel. "You file all the damn motions and writs you want, but you can't stop the one thing that sits sideways in your ass, me exercising the power of arrest." Chinbroski climbed from his chair, strutted over to Daniel's fridge, and grabbed his fourth Dr Pepper.

Daniel looked at Rush and raised an eyebrow. Rush smiled at him, then glanced at Leigh. She stared at the table in front of her, tears gathering at the edges of her eyes, her bottom lip trembling.

"So we're at an impasse here?" Daniel said.

"Impasse my ass," Chinbroski said.

Leigh looked at Daniel for several moments before finally turning away. Daniel looked at Rush. "Maybe I should re-state our case once again," he said.

Chinbroski laughed as he sat down.

"Can we remember Hannah!" Leigh snapped, glaring at Chinbroski. "What's so damn funny?"

To his credit, Chinbroski wiped the smile from his face. "I ain't forgot her. We're gonna get her back. But I damn sure ain't letting a renegade mother and a snot nose lawyer call the shots. And as soon as the two of you get that through your thick brain plates, the better off you'll be." Chinbroski drained half the can of soda and belched.

"I have an idea," Rush said to Daniel. "How about you and Leigh go to your office and leave me and Chinbroski alone for a few minutes?" Rush gave Daniel his most sincere *Father Knows Best* look, and glanced at Chinbroski.

Daniel nodded and slapped the table. "Good idea. Leigh, let's take a breather."

Once gone, Rush leaned back in his chair and studied his partner. "You're all about center stage, aren't you? I give your performance an A-plus. Now what do you think we should do?"

Chinbroski drained his Dr Pepper and crushed the can against the table. "I ain't heartless."

"I know."

"But your kid ain't leading me around by the nose."

"He does come off a tad arrogant."

"We gotta get the kid," Chinbroski said. "Even if she thinks I don't care nothing about that."

Rush sighed and spoke to the ceiling. "Let's pretend you and Nanci have been married for five years. You have a three year-old daughter. Some prick steals her, sells her to the highest bidder. Exactly what has Leigh done that you wouldn't do?" Rush leveled his gaze at Chinbroski.

"She did a bunch of stuff I wouldn't have to do."

"Yeah?"

"I mean once I found him. I'd have strapped him to a table and he woulda told me what I wanted to know."

"But it's obvious she couldn't have done that." Rush got up and grabbed a Pepsi from the fridge, wondering if he and Chinbroski had already overdosed on caffeine. "You get my point? Leigh's crimes weren't motivated by the same impetus that drives street thugs."

"She let a woman die, Rush. Come on."

"I know. And that'll be the sticking point." Rush popped the top and stared at the can for a moment. "This could be a media circus. And with that comes scrutiny. All the way up the chain of command." He took a sip and looked at Chinbroski. "Know what I think?"

"What?"

"I think Daniel's hoping we haul Leigh away in handcuffs. She'd be his ticket to stardom. Imagine playing up her story in the press and in front of a jury. And he'd get to beat me in open court. Yeah, that's exactly what he wants."

Chinbroski studied him for a long time. "Am I being played here?"

"Absolutely not. It's your warrant. The big picture is Hannah and Enoch. Leigh helped us get to where we are. You say you would've found him and strapped him to a table. If it had been me, I'd have found him, tapped his phone, waited until he had Hannah at the cabin and shot him with a high-powered rifle. Either way he's dead and we get our daughter back. The thing we would *not* have done is left clues behind for the cops. But Leigh did that. She's willing to step forward and testify. I think the DA would give her immunity for her testimony. Yes, you can give her hell by filing a bunch of charges, but in the end she'll get immunity."

Chinbroski looked away and thought it out.

"In the meantime," Rush continued, "Hannah is passed off to someone else."

"Out with it," Chinbroski said. "What's your bottom line?"

"I say we get enough for search and arrest warrants, get a team of guys out to the cabin, wait for the girl to arrive, and take him down. Once we have him, take it from there."

"Drop everything against Leigh except the McElroy thing?"

"We do a Grand Jury referral," Rush said. "They'll indict, Daniel gets his trial, Leigh keeps her kid while everything is adjudicated. We're good to go letting her walk today. Nobody knows we have her, and she's not going anywhere until she has Hannah back. What do you think?"

"I think you played me. Hanisch would go ballistic if he knew we let her walk today."

"What Hanisch doesn't know only makes our life easier. I'll go talk to Daniel." Rush got up from the table and tossed the half-full Pepsi can into the trashcan.

Rush met Chinbroski at the station at 8:00 the next morning. They were to meet Leigh Adams at 9:00 at the McDonald's in McKinney and be in position near Enoch's house by 9:30 - two and a half hours before Hannah's expected arrival. Daniel would stay in his office, waiting for Rush to call once Hannah was safe. He would then collect all of the evidence Leigh had assembled against Enoch, and turn it over at Rush's convenience.

Very quietly, Chinbroski was attempting to round up the same three detectives that assisted in the arrest of Martin Grant, the biker with the cloned phone. Rush waited in the small conference room just off Crime Analysis.

Rush doubted if any of the three would agree to come and meet with Chinbroski. They had taken pressure after Grant's arrest. Hanisch was still pissed they'd jumped so blindly to help Rush. This morning, Chinbroski would stress that Hanisch wouldn't know anything until the arrest of the *real* suspect was over, and that this warrant *was* for the real suspect.

Danny Wilson, the power lifter, was the first to show. He was as big as Chinbroski, and as strong. His ruddy, pockmarked face matched his physique. Like Chinbroski, he spoke his mind. Well suited for felony warrants, he was fearless, quick, and relentless. It was his tendency to go by the book that worried Rush. He sulked into the room and slumped in a chair, quietly, without eye contact.

Steve Waverly, the thick-boned forgery detective who kick-boxed for ten years just for an opportunity to hurt somebody, showed next. The women in the department swooned over his olive skin, dark hair, and perfectly trimmed moustache. Waverly winked, grinned, and belted a loud good morning. He wouldn't have a problem with the game plan.

Following on his heels Lance Swearingen, the SWAT team speedster who worked auto theft, was probably the fairest black man Rush knew; baby faced, smooth, blemish-free skin that shone when he got excited. Rush wanted Swearingen because he was the best pistol shot in the department.

Behind Swearingen came Chinbroski, wearing blue jeans, a turtleneck sweater, and a serious expression. He clicked the door shut, and then locked them in.

Rush sat on a table in the front of the room, leaning against a portable podium beside him. "Guys," he said, "it's time to do it right. Chinbroski and I found Jane McElroy's killer. No doubt, without question."

Chinbroski cracked his knuckles.

Swearingen glanced at Wilson and Waverly and nodded. Waverly smiled, Wilson didn't.

"Chinbroski wrote a Capital Murder warrant. Got it signed last night. Killer's name is Enoch Duke. From California." He paused and tried to make eye contact with each of them. Wilson wasn't taking. "And he is one bad ass S.O.B. It's why we called you three again." He turned to Chinbroski and nodded.

Chinbroski joined Rush at the front. "Guys, you know me. I ain't one to B.S. around. I speak my mind. If I see something and it looks dangerous, I'm gonna tell you. And this dick-head is dangerous." He stopped and looked at Rush. "You wanna give them the history?"

"You tell it." Rush slid off the table and walked to the edge of the room while Chinbroski told them the history of the case. He told it without fluff or sugar coating. They sat silently. Chinbroski focused on the emotion of the story, Enoch's personal history, his criminal activity, Hannah's kidnapping.

Meanwhile, Rush tried to gauge which of the men would help. Waverly eventually slipped out a pen and pad and jotted notes. Swearingen stared at the floor, winced during the part of the story when Leigh's nose was broken and Hannah was kidnapped, and then looked up, his eyes narrow and hard.

Then Rush studied Wilson. He sat statue still, eyes down as though reading a message written on the top of Chinbroski's shoes. His breathing was easy, relaxed, as though he'd already made his decision.

Chinbroski finished in less than ten minutes. Rush walked back to the front of the room. "So knowing everything now," he said, "this is why we wanted you to come in today. We're going to get that little girl back. Today.

One way or another."

Rush nodded at Chinbroski, who grabbed three folders from the top of the podium and passed them out.

"In the file," Rush said, "you'll find a map of the area surrounding Enoch Duke's house. The road to the driveway is a mile long. One driveway, Duke's. The most direct way from town is off County Road 3839. Duke's driveway is long, between a quarter and half-mile. Has a couple of blind curves, thick woods on each side almost all the way to the house. No way to see the road from the house, so we should be able to stop any cars that turn into the driveway. We can get in on foot and sit almost anywhere. The first contact spot will be thirty feet in from the road."

He paused and looked at them. "We put a car on each end of the road. Leigh will be in one of those cars. One of you will be in the other. When we see a car turn onto the gravel road heading toward Duke's place, two of us at the first contact point will get ready. If a car pulls into the driveway, we jump out and take it down."

"On foot?" Swearingen asked.

"Yeah," Rush said. "I know what you're thinking: what if the car doesn't stop? If that happens, we've got a portable tire shredder we can throw across the driveway at the second contact point. If the car blows by the second point, he'll be running on four flats."

"But even on four flats the car can get to the house faster than we can on foot." Swearingen shook his head. "Then we'd have a hostage situation."

"Good point," Chinbroski said. "That's why there's only gonna be two of us at each contact point. The guys at the second point will throw out the tire shredder and then come out with guns drawn."

"And then what?" Wilson asked. "Shoot at the car? With a kid in there?" He paused and glared at Rush, his ruddy complexion darker than normal. "Why not have the sheriff's office stop every car that turns onto the road? Hell, we see the kid, that's it. We got her. Then we serve the warrant."

Rush glanced at Chinbroski and blew out a breath. "That's why we chose you guys to help. We're taking the kid back and giving her to Leigh. Not exactly standard operating procedure."

Wilson rolled his eyes. "Not exactly legal. The way Chinbroski tells the story, this kid is just as much Duke's as she is the woman's. And I haven't heard anything about a California court order giving her immediate custody."

Rush nodded in agreement.

"And even if she had one," Wilson went on, "police officers don't have jurisdiction. That's the sheriff's turf. In fact, except for serving your warrant, we shouldn't even be out there."

Rush nodded again.

"What I don't get," Chinbroski said, "is how come you're the legal expert all the sudden."

Wilson turned red and pointed a finger at him. "Don't talk to me like I'm some damn rookie, Chinbroski. This is starting to sound like a personal crusade. I don't want the kid spending time with a murderer, either. But you sure ain't gonna browbeat me into doing something that's stupid as hell."

"No one's trying to browbeat you, Danny," Rush said. "We're just trying to tell you what we're thinking."

"Can I say something?" Swearingen asked. "The couple who bought the kid, they're not going to complain about losing her. And Duke won't have any recourse to get her back from prison. So with all that in mind, I don't have a problem with snatching her and handing her over to the mother. But what I don't understand is, why not just arrest Duke, haul him off, and sit in his house until the people show up with the kid." He shrugged. "I mean, wouldn't that make more sense?"

"We thought about that," Rush said. "Gave it some real thought. But Leigh didn't think it'd be a very good idea."

"Leigh?" Wilson snorted. "You're letting a housewife dictate tactics?"

Chinbroski took a step forward. "You know, you're starting to sound a lot like Hanisch. And since you ain't a lieutenant, you're liable to get your ass kicked."

Wilson jumped up and squared his shoulders. "Bring it on!"

"Okay! Come on! Stop it!" Rush put a hand on Chinbroski's arm and pulled.

Chinbroski glared at Wilson as he stepped back and leaned against the table.

"I don't mean to suggest she's calling the shots," Rush told Wilson. "But she said something last night that made a lot of sense. If Duke has a signal set up with the people who have Hannah, we're up a creek."

"What do you mean, signal?" Swearingen asked.

"For example: what if Duke told them he would call at exactly 11:18 AM to give them directions to the house? Or what if he's already made arrangements to meet them in town? Keep in mind, we don't know who these people are. We only have the first name of the woman. We don't know what they look like or what they drive. We need Hannah before we take

Duke."

"What if he drives out?" Swearingen said. "You know, comes right down the driveway while we're hiding in the trees? And we don't have the kid yet?"

"Then we wait," Rush said. "We can't risk a moving surveillance before we know he has Hannah. He has to come back to the cabin eventually."

"And if that happens," Chinbroski said. "We hit the house at three in the morning."

"Us?" Swearingen said. "Without SWAT?"

"Ain't no rule says we gotta use SWAT," Chinbroski said.

Wilson chuckled. A 'what-a-couple-of-dumb-asses' kind of chuckle. "So you'll hit the place at three in the morning for a Capital Murder warrant and not use SWAT? You're gonna let him go in the house with the kid where he might have more guns than us? And you don't want to call the sheriff because they might want some paperwork before you release the kid to the mother? Great, so let me ask you this. At three in the morning, when you're sitting your ass out in the cold, exhausted from being up all day, are you gonna make a courtesy call to the sheriff and tell them you're serving a warrant in their jurisdiction?"

"And that's just what it would be, Wilson. A courtesy call." Chinbroski cracked his knuckles again and stared at him.

"Why not use SWAT?" Wilson asked, throwing up his hands. "I gotta know why. The suspense is killing me."

"You afraid, Wilson?" Chinbroski asked.

"Go to hell!" Wilson snapped. "I'm just trying to follow the same rules every other department in the state follows."

"The last thing I want to do, especially with a child inside, is hit the house with a SWAT team," Rush said.

"Why?" Swearingen asked. "That doesn't make sense."

"Because SWAT has one way of doing things; hard. Smash the door, percussion grenades, screaming everywhere. You know it, and I know it. And once they're called, there's no making suggestions on trying it some other way. No offense, Lance, but we wouldn't know which room she's in. Wouldn't know if she might be in the same room as Duke. Hell, small as she is, even in the same bed." He shook his head. "No. A SWAT hit is out."

"Don't you get it, Swearingen?" Wilson said. "If they have to follow any rules, they don't like it. I'll tell you the real reason they won't use SWAT. Cause they'd have to explain how they got to that point."

Rush could hear Chinbroski breathing. Sharp little intakes of air like shots from an air compressor.

"First of all, you're not giving SWAT enough credit," Swearingen said. "We're pretty good, in my opinion. But that's your decision. So using the sheriff to block off traffic is a bad idea? Cause that's what you said. Did you ever say why? I just want to understand."

"A few reasons, Lance," Rush said. "First, they're going to want some paperwork, just like Wilson said. And Leigh doesn't have any. I admit that. The people who have the kid might put up a legal battle to keep her. Not that they'd win, but it'd be a court battle, they'd keep Hannah in Texas, put her in foster care. You know, the whole nine yards. And finally, if Duke does drive out to get Hannah, I don't want marked squads anywhere near."

The room fell silent. Chinbroski stared at Wilson.

"So, Waverly," Rush said. "What are your thoughts? You haven't said a word."

He shrugged. "Just waiting for you to tell me when it's time to go."

"What if all this goes to hell?" Wilson said.

"Bad things happen, Wilson," Chinbroski said. "Either accept that or go work for the gas company."

Wilson threw back his chair and waved Chinbroski off. "I'm out." He looked at Rush. "I'm not doing anything with him." He'd made it to the door by the time Rush spoke.

"Danny."

Wilson turned and looked back.

Rush chose his words carefully. "Because everything *might* go to hell, it'd probably be best if you denied any knowledge. And if you'll agree to that, it'll never be mentioned that you knew."

He stared at Rush and then glanced at Chinbroski. "Fine. Deal. I know nothing." He slammed the door behind him.

Rush looked at the others. "You two can also opt out. And if you do..." He shrugged. "I'll understand."

"I'm in," Waverly said.

Swearingen stared at the floor. Finally, he shook his head. "I can't. I can't do it because if it ends up that SWAT should have been called but wasn't, I'd be off the team in a heartbeat."

Rush slapped his legs. "Fine. I understand." He walked over and shook his hand. "If you could keep this to yourself..."

"Yeah. No problem." Swearingen started to leave, but stopped and looked at Rush. "Why are you doing it this way? Why take the risk?"

"Because," Rush said, "sometimes the system is screwed up. Sometimes to do what's right isn't the same thing as doing what's legal. Leigh led us to Duke. She's risked everything. She deserves her kid back. And me and Chin are going to help her." He shrugged. "If we get in trouble over this, hey, we did something that made us feel good. And we'll have Duke. At least we'll have Duke."

Swearingen nodded. "Good luck. I wish I had your balls." He hadn't even closed the door when Waverly was paged over the intercom by his sergeant.

Rush held his breath while Waverly made the call.

It didn't last long. Waverly slammed the phone down. "Can't go. We have a unit meeting and then our own warrant to serve."

"Damn," Chinbroski said. He looked at Rush, his face crimson.

And then they were alone. "Well," Rush said, looking at his partner, "we swung the bat on Plan B. It's back to Plan A. Just me, you, and a woman who doesn't care if we kill Duke or not. Your life insurance paid up?"

TWENTY-FIVE

Leigh gaped long enough to expose the fear she probably felt. Then she caught herself and looked away, her face hard. "So it's just us three? Against that monster?"

They were in the parking lot of the McDonalds in McKinney, leaning against Leigh's Blazer. She spoke in low, harsh tones, shooting looks at other patrons as they tramped out to their cars. She wore running shoes, blue jeans, and a light jacket over a multicolored sweater. Boxes and suitcases were stuffed inside the back of the Blazer because she planned to leave the Dallas area as soon as she had Hannah.

"I don't know what you're worried about," Chinbroski said. "Before yesterday afternoon you was planning on getting her back yourself."

She looked both ways and lowered her voice even more. "Because I was going to *kill* him! I doubt you'll let me do that."

"Look, we can still get her back." Chinbroski looked around, too. Then he paused while a young gangbanger type climbed into a car a few parking spaces away. "We got the most important thing. Surprise. We lose that?" He shrugged. "Then you start to worry."

"Well, I'm worried now." She looked at Rush. "What's the plan? You have to have a plan."

"Yeah, I've got something that might work. Let's sit in Chinbroski's car and talk about it."

Rush sat in back and suddenly found himself shivering. "Crank it, Chin, it's cold back here."

With the heater humming, Rush rubbed his hands and looked at Leigh. "I want you in the deer stand with binoculars and a radio. Monitor his phone from there. Once you're in position, Chin and I will make our move. Our radios are encrypted. If he leaves to go get Hannah, we'll get inside and wait for him to come back, take him down when he steps through the door."

Leigh wore the same hard look and said nothing as she listened.

"And if he doesn't leave," Rush continued, "if the couple delivers Hannah, we figure he'll come outside to greet them. When he does, we should be in position to take him down."

"Yeah, see, it's like this," Chinbroski said. "Since he ain't seen Hannah in a while, and he don't know we're coming, he probably won't carry a weapon outside. Besides that, he'll probably be carrying her into the house. He can't move as fast and his hands will be occupied. Both good things for us."

"And what will I be doing?" she asked.

"Sitting your ass up in that deer stand," Chinbroski said. "We don't want him to know you were involved in any of this. After we get him in custody, we'll bring a car around, haul him off. Then let you have Hannah. Simple."

Her face relaxed as she thought it through. "I'm just concerned about my baby. I don't want her hurt."

"Leigh," Rush sighed. "We know that."

Exhaling slowly, she looked at Rush, then Chinbroski. "Okay, I'm ready."

"Then let's hit it," Rush said.

Once in the wooded area, Leigh didn't bother covering her Blazer with the camouflage tarp. After she grabbed her binoculars, Rush handed her a portable police radio, and she took off through the woods at a frenzied pace. Rush and Chinbroski followed at a distance, knowing she needed to get in position before they began their approach.

"You ready to get this son of a bitch?" Chinbroski asked, as they headed off into the trees, both pulling on a pair of leather gloves.

"Ready to get it over with." Rush thought about Mallory and realized how hopeful he was with her normalcy over the last couple of days. "Ready for a Christmas break."

"After this is done, let's grab a beer. It's been awhile."

"We can do that," Rush agreed.

They walked for several minutes in silence, or tried to. Neither was a woodsman. They sounded like a herd. Finally, Rush's radio crackled with Leigh's voice. "His car's in front of the house. I'm in position."

"Ten-four," Rush transmitted. He looked at Chinbroski. "Let's go."

They planned to come in behind the deer stand and then circle around to the east, approaching the rear. The back yard was so small, so thick with trees they'd get within twenty yards of the cabin.

With the deer stand in sight, they moved east, carefully threading through underbrush. They had made it behind the house, albeit still three hundred yards out, when Leigh's voice crackled again. "Still nothing on the phone."

Rush stopped and squatted. He lowered the volume on his radio and held it to his ear. Chinbroski did the same. The cool breeze out of the north chilled Rush, rustled the bare tree branches overhead. He glanced at his watch. Almost eleven. Chinbroski turned away and Rush heard him unzipping his pants. He hadn't said a word in the last few minutes. Nor did Rush expect him to.

"We need to move closer," Rush whispered after Chinbroski finished with his business. "So we'll be ready when he leaves."

"Let's go."

They didn't belly-crawl, but they came close. Chinbroski led the way, pushing underbrush, tall grass, and bushes out of the way. Rush kept his radio turned low, listening for any news from Leigh.

By 11:45 they reached the tree line, less than twenty yards away. Time to wait.

The seconds ticked slowly. At straight up noon Rush whispered into his radio. "Still no phones?"

A pause followed. "Nothing. No movement. If he leaves, don't take too long looking around inside. He might only be gone a few minutes."

Chinbroski doubled clicked. "Bitch," he said under his breath. "Always wants to order us around."

At five after twelve Rush's radio crackled. "Got him!" Leigh said. "On the phone!"

Rush waited for more.

"He's talking to Dena. Stand by!" Leigh's voice strained with tension. "He's going to get her. Meeting them. Holiday Inn in Princeton. Said he'd be leaving in a few minutes."

At length Rush heard the front door of the house slam, then a car engine roar to life. Leigh told them to move.

Chinbroski whispered into his radio. "You sure there ain't nobody else in there?"

There was a pause before she answered. "There are cameras everywhere. Of course I'm sure."

Rush took the lead. When they got to the back door he could see faint pry marks around the cheap doorknob. He had it open within seconds. They stepped into a small porch not much bigger than a closet.

Another door led into the house. Unlocked. Chinbroski eased the door open and stepped into the kitchen. Careful to keep everything as they found it, Chinbroski swung the door open wide and stepped aside so Rush could enter.

Chinbroski went ahead, gun drawn, clearing the house, while Rush inspected the area just inside the front door. Plenty of room to take him, he thought, though the den was small.

"In here," Chinbroski called from around a corner.

Rush followed the voice to an open door down a short hallway on the opposite side of the den. Enoch's high tech room.

"It'll be fun going through all this stuff," Chinbroski said.

"Can't wait." Rush deadpanned. He turned from the room, strolled back into the den, and visually inspected the rest of the house.

Chinbroski walked up beside him and read his mind. "What a hole."

Rush shrugged. "Not when you compare it to what he was raised in. You see any evidence of Leigh's cameras?"

"Nope. Did a good job. Gotta give her that."

In the short hallway Rush saw a thin rope attached to the foldaway attic stairs. The springs popped as Rush pulled the stairs down. At the edge of the darkness above, he saw the board with the blue felt. He climbed up and pulled the string hanging over his head. The attic light illuminated a four-by-four board covered in blue felt. Four humans ears were mounted with long straight pins like a bug exhibit at a high school science fair. The ears appeared smaller - almost freeze-dried – and had a leathery texture. One obviously belonged to Jane McElroy. The large diamond studded loop still dangled from the lobe. Rush remembered the matching earring being stuck against her frozen, horror-stricken face.

Chills snaked up the back of Rush's neck.

Below him, Chinbroski edged closer. "Is it up there?"

"Yes."

"Let me see." After Rush stepped down, Chinbroski climbed up for a look. He stared for a long while. Then he climbed down and said nothing. No words were needed.

They waited just inside the front door for nearly thirty minutes.

And then, "He's coming!" Leigh finally shouted over the radio. "He's coming up the driveway right now!"

TWENTY-SIX

Rush peeked out a window. Still fifty yards away, but coming fast, was a dark blue Land Cruiser. Chinbroski took up a position just inside the front door.

"Tell me if he's got the kid in his hands when he gets to the door," Chinbroski whispered.

Rush nodded. The Land Cruiser drove straight toward the cabin. Forty yards…thirty…twenty. Through the glare of the windshield he could see the driver. Male, short hair, square jaw line. He wore sunglasses, had the pale skin of a redhead, and broad, thick shoulders. He circled around and stopped fifteen feet from the front door. Even through the Toyota's tinted windows, Rush could see a snatch of blond hair just above the panel of the front passenger's door.

"He has the kid," Rush told Chinbroski. "Front seat. He just cut the engine. Climbing out."

Chinbroski shifted, said nothing. He was crouched like a linebacker about to take on a running back.

Duke stepped from the driver's seat and walked around the front of the car. His freckled face looked pure, just off the farm. His hair was short, parted on the side with a little wave in the front. A grown up Opie Taylor, Howdy Doody. He walked with a slight limp, favoring his left leg. But even with the limp Rush could see the power, the thick muscle, the grace of an athlete. And his upper body was no different. Thick through the shoulders and arms, his stomach was as flat as a drain board.

When Duke reached the front passenger's door, he opened it and unbuckled Hannah's seatbelt. She looked like the photograph Leigh had shown them; blond hair with a slight strawberry tint, pudgy arms, small hands. She wore a jumpsuit and tennis shoes, her hair was pulled back into a French braid. She was healthy, Rush saw immediately, well cared for.

"Come to Uncle Eno," Rush heard Duke say as he hoisted her into his arms.

Duke walked around to the back of the car, opened the rear hatch, and grabbed a small suitcase.

"Get ready," Rush said. "Another fifteen seconds. As soon as he cracks the door open, take him. I'll grab the kid."

Chinbroski nodded, his breath coming in little spurts through his nose.

Duke slammed the hatch and headed toward the front door. When he stepped up onto the porch he dropped the suitcase and put Hannah down. She laughed and jumped up and down. Duke pulled his keys from a pants pocket and laughed at Hannah while he separated the front door key from the others.

As he stepped toward the front door, Rush turned away from the window and nodded at Chinbroski, who looked as tight as a coiled spring.

Hannah laughed again. Rush could hear her small footsteps as she ran the length of the wooden porch.

"Don't go out in the yard," Duke told her. "Come on inside."

Could things have worked more perfectly? Rush wondered as he heard Duke slip a key into the deadbolt. With Hannah several feet away.

Duke threw the lock and the doorknob turned. "Come back on the porch, Hannah," he said. "Let's go in the house."

The door opened an inch. Chinbroski took a half step forward.

Then Leigh's voice blasted out of Rush's radio. "Go get Hannah, she's running into the woods!"

Chinbroski froze.

Rush froze.

The door slammed shut.

Chinbroski jumped forward and yanked the door so hard Rush thought it might rip from its hinges. Duke was half way off the porch by the time Chinbroski made it through the door. Nearly on his partner's back, Rush moved as fast as he could.

"You're under arrest!" Chinbroski screamed as he lunged, slapping Duke in the lower back, pushing him forward.

Digging into a back pocket of his jeans, Duke stumbled forward from the blow. He regained his balance and ran across the front of the Land Cruiser.

Chinbroski cursed and stumbled, losing ground. Rush couldn't make it around him and fell.

Suddenly, Hannah screamed. Rush looked over. She stood at the edge of the woods, fist clutched to her mouth, eyes as wide as quarters.

"Get Hannah!" Rush heard Leigh scream over the radio. "Please get Hannah! Don't let her see this!"

Chinbroski threatened to shoot Duke in the back if he didn't stop.

Across a small clearing on the other side of the Land Cruiser, Duke suddenly stopped and spun around, waving a switchblade he'd dug from his back pocket.

Chinbroski skidded to a stop several feet away, red faced, blowing air from his mouth in huge gasps. He pulled his .45 from its holster and aimed it at Duke's chest. "Stupid to bring a knife to a gun fight, asshole. Now drop it!"

Duke's eyes darted from Chinbroski to Rush to Hannah.

"You gonna drop it?" Chinbroski snapped, "or do I drop you?"

Duke did nothing, his face tight, constricted, as though every muscle had climbed on top of each other. The small circling motions with his knife seemed less sure.

Hannah continued screaming. Rush snapped a look in her direction, not sure if he should go to her or help Chinbroski. Hannah's eyes were riveted on the gun pointed at her father.

Rush hadn't drawn his weapon yet. It was the way they worked things, he and Chinbroski. One of them needed free hands to handcuff the prisoner. And since Duke hadn't pulled a gun, Chinbroski could keep him under control.

"Get the kid, Rush!" Chinbroski shouted. "Take her around back. I don't want her to see what's fixing to happen because this asshole won't drop the knife."

"Where's Leigh?" Duke asked, snatching glances with quick head jerks. "She's here, I heard her voice."

"If you don't drop that knife that's the last thing you're gonna hear." Chinbroski took a step closer and rolled his head, stretching his neck.

"Hannah!" Leigh screamed from a distance, from Rush's left. He glanced over and saw her at a full run across the field.

Duke glanced, too. He swallowed hard, tightened the grip on his knife, looked back at Chinbroski. "Who are you? What do you want?"

"The police, you dickhead," Chinbroski said. "And one more time: drop that knife before I splatter your brains all over this yard."

"If you're cops like you say, you won't shoot. Not in front of the kid." His eyes had a glimmer, his mouth a slight smirk.

"Hannah!" Leigh screamed again. She was close, just a few yards. Hannah quieted as she turned to look at Leigh running toward her.

Chinbroski took another half step toward Duke. "Put it down," he said quietly.

Duke stepped back, glanced at Rush, then at Leigh, who had climbed the barbed wire fence.

"Hannah, oh, baby!" Leigh swept her child into her arms and cried into her neck. Hannah whimpered, no longer focused on Chinbroski or his gun.

"Get the kid in the house," Rush told her. "Now!"

Chinbroski took another half step toward Duke.

Since he didn't have the child to watch after, Rush also approached. He moved to his left, Duke's right, and slowly flanked him, cutting off any escape attempt down the driveway.

Leigh hadn't moved. She was still crying, stroking Hannah's hair, rocking her back and forth.

"How'd you find me, bitch?" Duke shouted. "I heard you were dead."

"Shut up!" Chinbroski said.

"Answer me, whore? How'd you find me?"

"Go in the house, Leigh" Rush said, still moving into position. "Don't say a word. Just go in the house."

Leigh slowly started toward the front door, still hugging Hannah tightly, stroking her hair. She hadn't acknowledged Duke.

"How'd you find me?" Duke shouted again.

Rush stopped. Duke was between them now. Rush was almost in Chinbroski's crossfire. He had taken his handcuffs out and would pounce on Duke as soon as he dropped the knife.

"You ain't leaving here with my little girl!"

Leigh spun on him. "She's not yours!" she screamed. "You sold her! And you'll never touch her again, you bastard!"

"In the house, Leigh," Rush ordered a third time.

She made it to the porch before she spun around a second time. "I got you! You hear me? I want you to know that before they haul you away. *I* got you! Nobody else. Everything. You hear me? I got you for everything."

And then she was gone. Through the front door of the house.

Duke said nothing as his face went blank. "What's she talking about?" he said finally. He looked at Chinbroski, who said nothing, and then turned toward Rush. "What's she talking about?"

"You're under arrest for the murder of Jane McElroy," Rush said. "And within a day or two will be charged with the murder of the man in McKinney. The guy you left laid out in the back seat of his car. Then Melissa Stanton in California. Then Edna Noring."

"In other words," Chinbroski said. "You're gonna be somebody's punk down in Huntsville."

Duke tightened his grip on the knife, waved it in small circles again. He glared at Rush. "What'd she mean that *she* got me?"

"She followed you from California," Chinbroski said. "She's been watching you from a deer stand. She bugged your phone, installed cameras." Chinbroski laughed and shook his head.

"She turned the tables on you," Rush said. "She studied your craft and then shoved it straight up your ass."

Duke's face darkened. Sweat beaded his forehead. He slowly knelt, crouched like a catcher in baseball, stared at the ground in front of him. A vacant stare, a thousand-yard gaze. Letting the knife go limp in his hand, his head sagged forward, his jaws went slack.

"Drop the knife," Rush said, taking a step closer.

"Watch it, Rush," Chinbroski said. "Don't get much closer until he puts that knife down."

In the edge of his vision Rush saw that Leigh had come to the open front door. She still held Hannah.

Chinbroski moved to his right, lowered his gun slightly, and looked at Rush.

Duke's arms were between his knees. When his hands suddenly went limp, the knife dropped onto the ground in front of him.

Chinbroski jerked his head toward Duke. Rush knew his partner wanted him to approach, to kick the knife away. So he stepped to the left and took a step forward. He was less than ten feet away. Sweat gathered under his arms, around his neck, on his forehead.

The knife lay in the dirt only inches from Duke's fingers. Rush knew he'd have to kick it away before he knocked Duke to the ground, but he had to be careful. He took a step forward. Almost directly behind Enoch now, he glanced at Chinbroski who had shifted even more, keeping Rush out of his line of fire.

Duke squatted, his head slumped forward, chin on his chest, hands resting on the dirt.

"Back away from the knife," Rush told him. "Now."

But Duke didn't move as he said, "I give up."

"Then back away from the knife."

Duke slowly edged away, still squatting, arms limp. He backed several feet from the knife before stopping.

Rush moved closer. Closer.

And then Leigh stormed through the front door. "My God, no! Greg, get back!"

Rush was about to kick the knife away when he saw it coming. Saw Enoch Duke cock his head, shift his weight, reach his hands forward. Rush heard him suck in a breath, and grunt.

And he knew. From all his years in police work, Rush knew exactly what was coming. And just as surely he knew, he also knew that his body wouldn't react in time.

Enoch Duke sprang like a mongoose. He grabbed the knife, thrust one leg forward and pivoted, using that leg to sweep Rush off his feet.

Rush landed on his right side, used his handcuff hand to break his fall, felt something snap. Pain shot through his wrist. Like a hot spear had been shoved into his skin, pain spread up his arm, into his shoulder. He ended up on his back, Enoch Duke attacking him like a rabid animal.

He felt the first slice hit him on the side of the face, across his cheek, the second ripped down his right shoulder.

And then everything slowed. Through the dust, through his blurring eyes, Rush saw everything. Chinbroski was screaming, shifting, trying to find a good shot. Leigh, clutching Hannah to her chest, jumped off the porch, ran forward, stopped, turned toward Chinbroski, screamed for him to shoot. Duke spun around, disappeared somewhere behind Rush.

And then he felt everything. Felt Enoch Duke grab him, tug, pull, force him into a sitting position. Felt himself being pulled sideways, felt his head slam into Duke's chest, felt it being twisted, pulled back, wrenched upward. Felt the cold blade of the knife against the skin of his neck.

Rush's right hand hung useless, the handcuffs in the dirt in front of him. Warm blood ran down his face, down his neck, oozed from the burning slashes in his leg, side, and arm. He couldn't tell how many times he'd been cut, couldn't move his head to look. He just knew that Duke had been quick, lighting fast, slashing back and forth, up and down, the knife held blade up, palm out.

Duke was behind him now, holding him still, hiding; using Rush's body as a shield. Rush had been stupid. Now he might die because of it.

"Shoot him," Rush choked out. The blade of the knife pressed against his neck. "Shoot him."

"Let him go, Enoch!" Leigh screamed, crying from across the yard.

Chinbroski was still moving, searching for a spot, his face hard, jaws clamped, left eye closed, his right eye looking straight through the sights of his pistol.

As Chinbroski moved, Duke twisted Rush's head, forcing him to spin, keeping Duke hidden.

His gun, Rush thought, *in his holster, on his right side, under a snap*. Rush felt Duke's hot breath on the back of his neck, could smell the sour stench. *Maybe I can get my gun with my left hand.*

"Enoch!" Leigh screamed, crying, clutching Hannah. "My God, Enoch, let him go!"

Duke can't take my gun, Rush suddenly realized. He couldn't risk moving the knife away. Chinbroski would shoot at the smallest opening. Duke had to know that.

Chinbroski stopped moving. Squatted. His right knee dropped down, his left elbow anchored on top of his left knee, his left palm supporting his gun hand.

A head shot. Chinbroski would only take a head shot. Nothing else would stop Duke.

"I'll kill him," Duke warned, pressing the blade deeper against Rush's neck. "Put the gun down or you lose your partner."

Chinbroski said nothing.

Leigh screamed, covered Hannah's eyes, and ran back into the cabin.

"Shoot him, Chin!" Rush choked out. "Damn you, don't worry about me!"

"Drop the gun," Duke warned again.

Chinbroski still said nothing, but the muzzle of his .45 wavered. His features softened as though he were actually considering it. Rush snapped his eyes shut, opened them, tried to blink away the tears that clouded his vision.

Duke tightened his grip, dug his knife even deeper into Rush's neck. Rush screamed. His voice caught and he tasted blood.

He screamed again to distract Duke, sliding his useless right hand over to his holster. The pain in his wrist made him nauseated, but he could move his fingers. Digging his heels into the dirt, he pushed backward against Duke's knees.

Duke didn't move. "I'll gut him," Duke said, his voice frighteningly calm. "I'll rip his throat out. Then you'll kill me and I'll be dead, but so will your partner. But if you throw your gun away, throw it far away, I'll let him go and run off. Then I'll be in the woods. I'll be gone."

Through his fog Rush remembered when Jacob Duke said that Enoch was the best trapper and hunter he'd ever seen. That if he got in the woods they'd never find him.

"Don't do it," Rush choked out. "You hear me? Training. Damn it, don't put your gun down!"

Duke twisted Rush's head. Pulled it up and over. Then he slid his hand up under his jaw, clamping his mouth shut.

"I figure I'm dead anyway," Duke said. "Either here or prison. You can save your buddy. Ain't no skin off your nose."

Chinbroski blew out a breath, opened the eye he'd had closed, and lowered his gun hand.

Rush tried to scream, to tell Chinbroski he was giving up their only chance of survival. But he couldn't. Duke was too strong, Rush hurt too badly. He slid his right hand closer to his holster, felt the wood grips of his .45 with the palm of his hand.

"I'm counting to ten," Duke shouted. "I don't have time to wait. One, two..."

Chinbroski tossed his Colt toward the house. His eyes locked on Duke's.

Through watery eyes, Rush saw his partner's gun lying useless in the dirt.

Duke shifted, pulled Rush back, started lifting him.

Rush unsnapped his holster.

"Take your handcuffs out," Duke shouted to Chinbroski. "Lock yourself to the door handle of my car."

Chinbroski hadn't moved. Still in a kneeling position, he slowly shook his head.

Good boy! Rush wanted to scream. *He'll kill us both if you do!*

"Do it now!" Duke screamed as he rose higher.

Rush had no air; his neck was pulled so tight that he couldn't breathe. Almost a hangman's noose.

Chinbroski slowly stood.

Duke slowly rotated as Chinbroski made his way over to the Land Cruiser.

"You lock yourself to that door handle and I swear I won't hurt your partner anymore," Duke said, his words hot against the back of Rush's ear. "And I won't hurt you. I'm not looking to kill a couple of cops. All I want is to get away."

Rush couldn't reach his gun. Not suspended between sitting and standing. Chinbroski faded as large white spots danced in Rush's vision. With a sudden urge to sleep, Rush jolted awake when he remembered that Chinbroski carried a small .32 in his back pocket. *He'll wait until I'm free, then kill this bastard!*

Chinbroski slid his handcuffs out and cuffed his left wrist, leaving his right hand free.

"The door handle," Duke said, "put the other cuff on the door handle. And throw the key to me."

Just as Chinbroski clicked the other cuff closed, just as the key left his hand and landed in the dirt, Leigh burst out of the cabin with a bolt-action rifle in her hand, head high, shoulders back.

"Stay back!" Duke screamed, spinning toward her. The grip on Rush's neck loosened as Duke shifted to the left.

Leigh continued to come. Veering to her right, she started to flank Duke.

"Stop or I'll kill him!"

But she didn't. She went wide. When she was directly to Duke's side she dropped to one knee and wrapped the rifle sling around her left forearm.

"Damn you!" Enoch screamed. "I'll kill him, I swear I will!"

Leigh propped an elbow on her knee, positioned the rifle against her shoulder, and aimed.

"Son-of-a-bitch!" Chinbroski suddenly screamed. "Son-of-a-bitch!"

Rush cut his eyes at his partner, who was digging in his back pocket for the .32. It wasn't there.

As Duke pivoted, Rush realized Leigh didn't have a shot. Duke was directly behind him again. Her rifle looked old, rusted. And she sure as hell didn't have a shot!

But she took one.

Rush jerked as he heard the firing pin snap against the primer of the casing. Then he heard Leigh curse, saw her look at the gun, watched her work the bolt, feed another round into the chamber, and pull the trigger again. Another click.

And Duke started laughing. With a sudden thrust, he pushed Rush forward and slashed upward. Rush felt the tip of the knife catch his jawbone and travel north under his left ear.

Gasping for breath, Rush collapsed face down in the gravel and grabbed his throat. Leigh screamed and ran toward the house.

Duke laughed louder. "Nowhere to hide," he said, stepping over Rush.

Rush rolled over, saw Duke head toward the house as Leigh raced for the door. With his left hand, Rush found his .45. Still gasping, he wiped his eyes and laid the butt of the gun on the ground in front of him.

Leigh stumbled on the steps of the porch and fell headfirst into the front door. Scrambling to reach the knob, she slipped again before finally rolling onto her back.

Rush could barely see the front sight of his pistol. He took a deep breath. Not much time. Duke was to the porch.

The gun almost fell out of Rush's hand from the jerk of the recoil. But Duke screamed, reached for the back of his left leg, fell to his knees.

Leigh scrambled to her feet directly into Rush's line of fire.

"Move!" Rush screamed.

She jumped to the right and Rush fired again.

Duke lurched forward and grabbed at the back of his right shoulder.

Rush struggled to his knees, his right wrist burning. Wiping his mouth, he climbed to his feet.

"No more!" Duke screamed, rolling over, facing Rush. "No more!" His knife lay off to the side, out of his reach.

Leigh stood frozen, eyes wide, hand clutched to her mouth.

"Finish it, Rush!" Chinbroski screamed, pulling hard at his handcuffed wrist. "Finish it!"

"I give up," Duke said. "No more."

"Finish it, Rush!" Chinbroski shouted again.

Rush slumped to the ground, squatting, his hands quivering.

"Finish it, damn it!" Chinbroski ordered a third time.

Enoch Duke glared at Chinbroski, his face twisted in confusion. "I...I said I give up. You can't just…"

Even remembering Jane McElroy and Melissa Stanton, and the ears mounted in the attic, Rush slowly lowered the .45.

Duke sighed. "I just want to give up."

Leigh turned toward Rush. "What are you doing? You're letting him live?"

"I can't just…"

"Get me the handcuff key, Leigh," Chinbroski said. "It's over there."

"He's a murderer!" Leigh shouted at Rush.

"I guess that'll have to be proved in court," Rush said.

Duke laughed.

"Get the handcuff key," Chinbroski said again.

"Then let me do it!" Leigh said, taking a step toward Rush.

White spots still danced in front of Rush's eyes. "Cops don't murder people," he said. "And you're not the judge and jury."

"Leigh, damn it! The handcuff key!"

Leigh straightened; her rigid face a blotchy red.

Duke laughed at her, his cackle echoing off the front of the house.

Leigh stepped toward Duke, then spun toward Rush, and jerked the gun from his hand. Rush lurched at her, but she kicked him in the chest, knocking him onto his back.

"I'm the only judge you'll ever face." Leigh said to Enoch. Then she shot him in the forehead.

Rush tried sitting up. "Leigh."

Leigh stared at Enoch's lifeless body, then turned toward Rush, her face a mask of indifference. "You'll never find me. So don't bother." She shoved Rush's pistol into the waistband of her jeans and dashed into the house.

"Rush!" Chinbroski whispered. "The handcuff key is behind you!"

Rush fell back, tried to sit up, but didn't make it.

Leigh burst from the house holding Hannah. She covered Hannah's eyes as she passed Enoch's body. Then she stopped in front of Rush, who had finally made it into a sitting position.

"I'll leave your gun in the deer stand." She made a wide arc around Rush, picked up the handcuff key, and looked at Chinbroski. "He's losing blood fast. So you can either help him or try and catch me. Your choice." She tossed him the key and ran off toward the woods.

Rush coughed against the back of his hand, spraying himself with blood. "Fading fast, partner."

Chinbroski unlocked himself and knelt down beside Rush. "Just hang on. I'm making the call." He started punching numbers on his cell phone.

"Chin, can you do me a favor?"

"Sure, partner."

"We're in a hell of a mess. Just get my pistol out of the tree stand before Hanisch gets here."

"No problem, dude. No problem."

TWENTY-SEVEN

Rush held the phone tightly against his ear, fingering the pink but fading scars on his face as he considered Daniel's question. *Is there a chance they'll fire you?* It was the primary question Rush had asked himself a couple of hundred times over the last six weeks, the time the chief had given him to "clean up the mess."

"I'll represent you *pro bono*," Daniel said, a hint of humor in his voice.

"Now that's a loser's creed if I ever heard one."

"What do you mean?"

"If you can't beat 'em, join 'em? I've got you pegged, son." Rush stood, grabbed his coffee cup from the table, and placed it in the sink.

"Then I withdraw my offer. And you still haven't answered my question."

"They can't fire me. Transfer me to Patrol? Sure. Suspend me? Yep. Make me investigate knocked over mailbox cases? No doubt. But we're a civil service department and Chin and I didn't do anything that would stand up in front of an arbitrator as a firing offense." Rush wiped the toast crumbs on the counter into his hand and dropped them down the drain. "But this one's gonna bug me for a while."

Daniel was quiet on the other end of the phone.

"I lost sight of Jane McElroy's family."

"How so?"

"Although I've come to grips with it now, Leigh traded Jane for Hannah. And as smart as she is, as calculating, she should have had a contingency for what happened to Jane. She should have been able to stop it." Rush leaned against the counter and stared at the floor.

"Can I make a confession?"

"Sure."

"That's the point I wouldn't have solved in court," Daniel said. "Had you locked her up, you would have strangled me with Jane's innocence."

"Chin never forgot," Rush said. "I should listen to him more."

"So she's in the wind?"

"She is." Rush walked over to the table and sat down.

"Was it a fair trade?" Daniel asked. "A trade you would have made?"

"The bigger question is whether it was a necessary trade. But... remembering back to when you were two years old, if I truly believed it would have led to never seeing you again, I would have made the trade." Rush waited for a comment he suspected wasn't coming. "You know, I've always wondered if I'd ever come across someone like Leigh. People like her are a double-edged sword."

"You used to tell me that when I was a kid," Daniel said. "You called them the 'Sword People.' You said you always worried about having to deal with one, but never explained what you meant."

"You've just seen for yourself what I meant. They're the smart ones, the people who commit crimes and never get caught. They calculate, set contingency plans, think four moves ahead, and never let themselves get backed into a corner. They can make a cop look bad." Rush drew a deep breath and sighed slowly. "You know as well as I do that we only catch the stupid ones. Sometimes the unlucky ones. You just hope that people like Leigh stay on our side of the penal code."

"So she's a double-edged sword because no matter what you would have done, you would have lost."

"Had Hannah died, I would have lost. Had we never gotten Hannah back, I would have lost."

"But," Daniel said. "Had Leigh not killed Enoch, she would have lost."

"How?"

"She couldn't have disappeared, and would have never lived in peace."

"Enoch's trial, you mean."

Daniel paused, as though considering his response. "Yes. The publicity, the criminal charges against her, and the shadow of all of that falling across Hannah's entire life. She's only two years old. If Leigh's never found, I can guarantee that Hannah will *not* know any of what happened. Which leads me to the most important question of the day."

"What?"

"You *had* to have considered all of that. How hard have you looked for her?"

Rush glanced at his watch, mindful of his eight AM meeting with the chief. "The truth?"

"It will set you free."

"She sends her regards." Rush heard a snicker, then an outright chuckle. "Gotta run, Daniel. The chief is anal about tardiness." Rush disconnected the call and grinned.

The meeting was formal, held in the chief's law library behind closed doors. Rush and Chinbroski, both in suits; Lieutenant Hanisch, Captain Williams, and Chief Damon Powell dressed likewise.

He had always been a fair chief, one Rush had gotten along with. Slightly built with thinning brown hair, Powell was a reader, a cop on top of all the latest trends in law enforcement. Rush expected the meeting to remain on an even keel, calm. And since it was his and Chinbroski's asses on the line, he hoped his expectation was met.

He wasn't sure which of his chain of command would conduct this inquest, this examination of his fading career, but he wouldn't have long to wait. Chief Powell had just come in, closed the door, and was making his way to the chair at the end of the table.

Chinbroski looked solemn. He sat statue still, hands folded on the table. Rush had instructed his partner to remain silent. Made him promise. Rush told him that this meeting might be the most important of their police lives.

Chief Powell began. He wore glasses, a crisp black suit, and a grim expression. A funereal look. "I've read all of the reports, Detective Rush."

No first names. Bad sign. Rush shifted in his chair, maintained eye contact.

"I'm more than disturbed," he continued. "And quite honestly, not sure what action I should take." He slipped his glasses off and held them while he spoke. "I've had several meetings with the others present here today, and although your reports are quite clear, we thought it best to clarify several points of concern. Give you a chance to add anything new."

Rush nodded. "Yes, sir."

"Lieutenant Hanisch will conduct the questioning today." Powell nodded at Hanisch.

Rush turned his chair to face the man he hated most on this earth. He'd told Chinbroski the night before that Powell would let Hanisch act as interrogator. Chinbroski hadn't believed it.

Hanisch opened a folder in front of him and pulled out a single sheet of paper. He wore no expression of humor. Not in front of the chief.

"I'd like to begin by reviewing what we know. Feel free to interrupt if you catch me adrift in errant facts." He smiled.

His shining moment.

"After the attempt to arrest Enoch Duke ended in failure, I asked you about the location of his common-law wife, Leigh Adams. Do you recall?"

"Yes."

"And your response wasn't immediate. It was hours later before I received your answer." He raised his eyebrows.

Rush remained quiet. Since a clown was running this circus court, he'd remain silent until asked a question.

"You told me she was probably en route to California. When confronted with the fact that you had just released a murderer, you denied it. True?"

"Yes."

Hanisch breathed deeply, his eyes now laughing. "Do you still deny that?"

Rush sensed Chinbroski stiffen. He cut his eyes toward his partner, who was staring holes into Hanisch. "She escaped." Rush said. "It's in the reports."

"She murdered Enoch Duke?"

"Yes."

"Then escaped?"

"Yes."

Hanisch nodded, seemed to consider the answer. "She was only able to commit that murder and escape because she had been released by you the night before?"

That was the whole point of this meeting. Rush opted not to answer the obvious.

"She admitted several felonies to you," Hanisch said. "Besides killing Enoch Duke and allowing at least two others to die, she confessed to the unauthorized use of a van, the theft of equipment from that van, the burglary of Duke's house, and wiretapping his phone. Correct?"

"The owner of the house," Rush said, "was found cut up and stuffed down the well. He'd been that way for at least a couple of months. So Duke would have had no legal basis to complain of a burglary, but yes, she admitted all of that."

"I stand corrected on that point. But you didn't know that at the time?"

The answer was obvious. Rush remained silent.

"She tampered with the McElroy crime scene, for which Chinbroski obtained a warrant. You haven't adequately explained why she wasn't placed under arrest when you took her statement, with which you used to get warrants for Enoch Duke. As a result of that negligence, you allowed her to commit first degree murder."

No question, no response. Rush wouldn't budge on that point.

Hanisch leaned forward. "Did she ever lie to you, Detective Rush?"

After a moment's hesitation, "It appears so."

"How many times?"

He didn't offer a number.

"Let me help you. She said she would hand over boxes of evidence to her lawyer. Did she?"

"No. I guess she felt no need since Enoch was dead."

"She said she would head home to California if she got her daughter back. Did she go there?"

Rush had to force the words out. He hated to lie in front of the chief. "Not that I could determine."

"When you and Detective Chinbroski traveled back to Boonville, you found her mother's house empty. Correct?"

A trickle of sweat slid down Rush's back. "Yes, that's correct."

"You discovered that her mother had fled Boonville without leaving a forwarding address. That her financial situation was secure from an insurance policy paid to her from her husband's death. That she could afford to move anywhere she pleased. All true?" Hanisch's eyes were intense.

"Yes, Lieutenant."

"Leigh Adams allowed you to see her old Blazer. Was that the car she fled in?"

All of this was clearly detailed in the reports. Every one of these men knew the answers to every one of these questions. Yet they continued to allow this bloodletting. "No, it was not."

"In fact, you found that Blazer abandoned at her apartment complex in McKinney. So you don't know what she was driving."

No question, no response.

"Were you able to lift any fingerprints from Leigh's apartment in McKinney?"

"The sheriff's office was unable to."

"From her Blazer?"

"Again, the sheriff couldn't."

"From Betty Adams's house in Boonville?"

Rush shook his head. "We matched one of Duke's prints to the dead doper's car. Blankenship. McBride went over the car again once he had a set of Duke's prints."

Hanisch looked confused for a moment. "What's that got to do with…"

"Duke killed him. Evidently met him somewhere, and killed him. Just wanted you to remember that while you're building your case against Leigh."

Hanisch glared at him, his face tight. He leaned closer, ignoring any discussion about Enoch Duke's guilt. "Everything Leigh and her mother touched was wiped clean, wasn't it? Even the surveillance van found next to the Blazer." He paused and leaned back. His eyes were as dark as marbles as he pulled another sheet from his file. "She played you both like the amateurs you are."

Rush glanced at Chinbroski again. His partner was as tight as a spring. Knuckles white, jaw clamped, eyes wide. He looked ready to vault the table and grab Hanisch by the throat.

"Did you search for weapons at any point during the hours you spent with this woman, this admitted felon?"

"No, sir, I did not."

"During the planning stage of the arrest, were you counseled by Detective Wilson in Juvenile about the legalities of allowing a woman from another state to leave Texas during a custody dispute?"

Rush wished he could argue that point, wished he could argue many of these points. "Wilson expressed his reservations. Though I had no evidence of any custody dispute."

Hanisch paused while he mentally rearmed. "So to sum it all up, you don't have a single clue as to the whereabouts of Leigh Adams or her mother or their eventual destination, do you?"

Rush took a deep breath, relaxed slowly. "No, sir, I do not."

"Isn't it a fact, Detective, that you got so caught up in helping a woman recover her child, you disregarded all manner of basic investigative police work? That you were so intrigued by a strange woman guiding you down a primrose path, you cast aside departmental regulations and state laws?"

No one in the room expected Rush to answer that. At least he hoped no one did.

Hanisch stared at him a moment and then winked. It was slight, but definitely a wink. "Those are all the questions I have, Chief." He closed his folder and leaned back.

Rush felt throbbing veins against his shirt collar. He stared straight ahead, fighting the urge to erupt against Hanisch's ridicule.

Chief Powell broke the silence. "Detective Rush, you've made no attempt to defend your actions. I was hoping you would use this opportunity to do so." The chief tapped his fingers lightly against the tabletop. "You'll receive no chance for a one-on-one meeting with me later. If you wish to state your defense, do so now."

My defense? Rush folded his hands and placed them in his lap. Then he chose his words carefully. "Enoch Duke killed Jane McElroy. That case is solved. I don't..."

"You don't know that at all!" Hanisch interrupted. "You *think* he was in the house because of his hair. But that's all you know. Leigh could have planted it. Hell, we don't even know for sure if that was her child you gave her."

Rush addressed the chief. "I don't remember interrupting the lieutenant."

Chief Powell nodded. "It won't happen again."

"Thank you. Enoch Duke killed Jane McElroy. He matched the forensics. He was left handed – proved in the autopsy - the correct height for the blood splatter stains, had the right hair color, was strong enough, and, as you read in the report, had McElroy's diamond necklace in his Land Cruiser and her ear in his attic. He did it. And he killed Blankenship, as I mentioned earlier."

Rush glanced at Chinbroski. His partner was staring at the table, breathing easily, nodding ever so slightly.

"As for Leigh's involvement, there are questions. And right now I don't have the answers. But she helped us. We would *not* have found Duke without her. To believe that she plotted all of this as some elaborate hoax is akin to believing in the Tooth Fairy." He shook his head. "Why leave notes directing us to California where we discovered her identity? Why send us pictures of the McElroy crime scene? Why warn Nanci Brookfield of impending danger? Why tap Duke's phone and watch him from a distance?" He took a breath and locked eyes with the chief. "Every single thing she did points to her trying to help the police, something she told me she had to do in order to sleep at night, while she waited for Duke to lead her to Hannah."

Rush swallowed and waited for the chief to respond. When he didn't, Rush gambled. "But you know what? His murder isn't our problem. It's the sheriff's problem."

Chief Powell's face tightened, turned crimson. "I can't believe..."

"Please, Chief," Rush said, holding up his hands, "I don't mean that I don't care about a homicide. But I don't care about Enoch Duke's homicide. He got what he deserved. I made mistakes. I recognize that. And I'm glad this investigation is over. At least for me." He nodded at Chinbroski. "I mean for us."

Rush reached into his jacket and pulled out a folded sheet of paper. "I'd like to read something, if you would allow it."

The chief nodded.

"Chinbroski found this note on the front seat of Leigh's Blazer. Since it was addressed to me, he did not consider it evidence. You are welcome to a copy, or if you insist the original be placed into the case file, I would have no objection."

The chief said nothing. Hanisch cocked his head slightly, his lips tight around the edges.

Detective Rush, please accept my gift to your police department with a clear conscience, that gift being the removal of a murderer from your community. I expect no return favors. Though I acted for Hannah's gain, and mine, I could have done nothing, and you would still be knocking on doors in Jane's neighborhood. Consider Enoch's death a mercy killing. Mercy for future women like Jane, mercy for the court system, for the prison system, for my sanity, and especially for Hannah's future. I grieve Jane's death, for her children and husband. But I rejoice in Hannah's future. One day, though it will be many years from now, you'll receive correspondence from me, and you'll see the results of Hannah's life free from Enoch's evil shadow. She will live a life that will give honor to Jane's tragic death. And if Jane is watching from heaven, she will know that she gave her life for a worthy cause.

As for you, do not second-guess yourself. You made a decision to help me and I betrayed you. For that I am sorry. Remember that your decision to help was a human decision, not one based on the writings from the cold pages of a law book. I am guilty. You are not. God bless you, and God help your partner.

Leigh

P.S. Just in case I'm wrong about you or you receive pressure from your superiors, I will begin every morning believing that you are still hunting for me. But know this: if you find me, and if you arrest me, you will curse Hannah with a past she will never know she had. And that will ruin her future.

Rush folded the paper and slipped it into his pocket. He heard Hanisch snort, but Rush ignored him and looked at the chief.

Chief Powell rubbed the top of his nose and put his glasses back on. He seemed to search for the right words, but finally just swallowed and folded his hands in front of him. "I'm suspending you both. Fifteen days for dereliction of duty. Starting tomorrow. No discussions." He adjusted his glasses. "You're excused."

Rush nodded and pushed away from the table. He glanced at Hanisch. The lieutenant stood and buttoned his jacket, sniffed, shrugged his shoulders. His relaxed face was turned away, his lips curled in victory.

Rush followed Chinbroski to the parking lot.

"So, did I do good?" Chinbroski asked, stopping at his Mustang. "Sitting in there as mute as a damn dummy?"

"Perfect," Rush said.

"And you think this was best, quietly taking a fifteen day suspension when we know where Leigh is?"

Rush opened Chinbroski's passenger door and shrugged out of his jacket, threw it in the back seat, took off his tie. "Fifteen days, Chin. Is that too much to give?"

"Still pisses me off."

Chinbroski climbed into the driver's seat and started the car. Rush settled in beside him and closed his door.

"One of these days, once you've had a two-year-old hug your neck, you'll understand."

They rolled out of the parking lot slowly, turned toward Rush's house.

"Think she'll be happy there? Santa Rosa?"

"I think so," Rush said. "And I think she'll be good for Melissa's kid."

Chinbroski shook his head. "And you think she knew we'd find her?"

Rush looked over at him and nodded. "She knew, Chin. And she wasn't worried."

"Why?"

"Because she read me right." Rush laughed. "And she knew you'd give in. After all, she gave you Nanci."

Chinbroski cursed under his breath. "I hate women who think they know every damn thing."

* * *

Leigh sat Indian style, her back against the park bench, watching Hannah run in circles, chasing Melissa Stanton's only child, Destiny. A longing for her dead friend tugged at the corners of Leigh's heart. And though Enoch had stolen Melissa's life the very afternoon he'd stolen Hannah, he had not managed to steal the one thing that would eventually drive him to his grave: the determination to risk everything for the one you love.

She had survived. And she would force Hannah to survive. Their lives began now. Anew.

Leigh glanced at her watch, then picked up her cell phone to call Destiny's father. She had punched half the numbers before she suddenly stopped, realizing what she was doing. No more cell phones. No more cordless phones. There were just too many ears. And she would never know who was listening.

THE END